# CAROLINA
# BUILT

# ALSO BY KIANNA ALEXANDER

## STAND-ALONE TITLES

*Drifting to You*
*A Radiant Soul*
*Working Overtime*
*A San Diego Romance*
*The Object of His Obsession*

## CLIMAX CREEK

*A Passion for Paulina* (Prequel)
*Seducing Sheri* (Book 1)
*Vying for Vivian* (Book 2)
*Adoring Ava* (Book 3)
*Persuading Patrice* (Book 4)
*Love and Life in Climax Creek* (The Complete Series)

## 404 SOUND

*After Hours Redemption*
*After Hours Attraction*

## THE SOUTHERN GENTLEMEN

*Back to Your Love*
*Couldn't Ask for More*
*Never Let Me Go*

THE GENTLEMEN OF QUEEN CITY
*This Tender Melody*
*Every Beat of My Heart*
*A Sultry Love Song*
*Tempo of Love*

SAPPHIRE SHORES
*A Love Like This*
*Love for All Time*
*Forever with You*
*Then Came You*

PHOENIX FILES
*Darkness Rising*
*Embrace the Night*
*Midnight's Serenade*
*Love's Holiday*

ROSES OF RIDGEWAY
*Kissing the Captain*
*The Preacher's Paramour*
*Loving the Lawman*
*A Ridgeway Christmas*
*Electing to Love*

PASSIONATE PROTECTORS
*Enticed*
*Enchanted*
*Enraptured*

# CAROLINA BUILT

*A Novel*

## KIANNA ALEXANDER

G

Gallery Books

*New York   London   Toronto   Sydney   New Delhi*

Gallery Books
An Imprint of Simon & Schuster, Inc.
1230 Avenue of the Americas
New York, NY 10020

First Gallery Books hardcover edition February 2022

GALLERY BOOKS and colophon are registered trademarks of Simon & Schuster, Inc.

For information about special discounts for bulk purchases, please contact Simon & Schuster Special Sales at 1-866-506-1949 or business@simonandschuster.com.

The Simon & Schuster Speakers Bureau can bring authors to your live event. For more information or to book an event, contact the Simon & Schuster Speakers Bureau at 1-866-248-3049 or visit our website at www.simonspeakers.com.

Interior design by Jaime Putorti

Manufactured in the United States of America

10  9  8  7  6  5  4  3  2  1

Library of Congress Cataloging-in-Publication Data

Names: Alexander, Kianna, author.
Title: Carolina built : a novel / Kianna Alexander.
Description: First Gallery Books hardcover edition. | New York : Gallery Books, 2022.
Identifiers: LCCN 2021028887 (print) | LCCN 2021028888 (ebook) | ISBN 9781982163686 (hardcover) | ISBN 9781982163693 (paperback) | ISBN 9781982163709 (ebook)
Classification: LCC PS3601.L35387 C47 2022 (print) | LCC PS3601.L35387 (ebook) | DDC 813/.6—dc23
LC record available at https://lccn.loc.gov/2021028887
LC ebook record available at https://lccn.loc.gov/2021028888

ISBN 978-1-9821-6368-6
ISBN 978-1-9821-6370-9 (ebook)

*For the women in my family line,*
*both known and unknown to me, whose love,*
*courage, and sacrifices allowed me to come into being.*

*And for my daughter, and the dream*
*of all she will one day become.*

# PREFACE

I first heard of Josephine Napoleon Leary's story from a tweet. A simple blip on my feed, a chance encounter with someone else's thoughts, led me to write this book. It's funny, because I was forced into using Twitter by a writer friend who insisted I'd need it for networking. I was already exhausted with Facebook, being a private person by nature. I fought tooth and nail but finally caved and got a Twitter account in 2011. Nowadays, I use it far more than any other social media site.

When I saw the tweet about Mrs. Leary, I was immediately intrigued. I was also upset that, as a native North Carolinian, I had never heard of her or her accomplishments. In eighth grade, I was required to take a state history class, one that was supposed to have given me an in-depth picture of North Carolina from its first colonies to the twentieth century. Where was the mention of Mrs. Leary, whose remarkable accomplishments should have more than secured her place in the annals of state history?

Years of independent research, to satisfy my own insatiable curiosity about my history, have shown me that this is often the case. The accomplishments of African Americans have so often been minimized, overlooked, or outright dismissed to serve a narrative that relegates us to the status of second-class citizenship. I decided to be a part of the solution, by putting my efforts into a project that would shine a light on someone who would otherwise be forgotten by history.

I began my research as most of us do in this age of technology: online. Using the Digital Archives of the Josephine Napoleon Leary Papers, housed at the David M. Rubenstein Rare Book & Manuscript Library on the campus of Duke University, I was able to establish a baseline of knowledge about Mrs. Leary's life and work, particularly as it pertains to her finances and her real estate transactions. The collection, acquired from Mrs. Leary's grandson Percy Almeria Reeves in 1991, has been an invaluable source of information. Most of the factually verifiable information known about Mrs. Leary's life is sourced from the materials in this collection.

My assistant and I first traveled to Duke University, to visit the reading room at the Rubenstein Library. As a registered researcher there, I'd requested the two boxes of items from the Josephine Leary Papers that had not been digitized to be brought up for my inspection. Holding the papers that Mrs. Leary herself handled only served to increase my level of passion and excitement for this project.

We then traveled to Edenton to get a firsthand look at Mrs. Leary's building, which is still standing today and in very good condition thanks to faithful exterior restoration. The building currently houses the local newspaper, the *Chowan Herald*. We spent several hours touring the town on foot, visiting the Historic Edenton State Historic Site, the site of Josephine's old barbershop at 317 South Broad Street, and Shepard-Pruden Memorial Library. We found valuable sources at all these locations, both in the form of documents and of helpful staff. Our walking tour also afforded us a view of many stately homes of the era, giving us a peek into life at that time.

At the library, I became the grateful recipient of a copy of the booklet *The Life and Legacy of Josephine Napoleon Leary, 1856–1923*, by Dorothy Spruill Redford. Mrs. Redford, a noted historian and former site manager of the Somerset Place State Historic Site in Creswell, North Carolina, compiled the booklet from primary source research during the 2010s. The forty-seven-page booklet is, thus far, the most in-depth writing that has ever been done on Mrs. Leary's life, and it has enhanced my research immensely.

I've spent the better part of the past two years combing through historical databases, newspaper clippings, and scholarly articles to form a solid basis of knowledge on the life Mrs. Leary lived. And now that the book is finally in the hands of you, the reader, I'm proud to share the fruits of my efforts. It is my hope that you will be just as inspired by Josephine Napoleon Leary's amazing life as I am.

# CAROLINA
# BUILT

# PROLOGUE

*July 1870*
*Williamston, North Carolina*

"Josephine? Josephine, don't you hear me calling you, child?"

Snapped back to reality by the sound of my grandmother's exasperated voice, I close my worn copy of Shakespeare's *Macbeth*. In the doorway of my family's small cabin is my grandmother Milly. She is dressed in her typical working uniform of tan blouse and earth-grazing brown skirt, her silver curls wrapped and tucked beneath a red scarf. Her brows are furrowed, her jaw tight.

"Heavens, Jo. It's good that you read like you do, but you get so wrapped up in those books, nobody can reach you." Grandma Milly shakes her head. "You liable to miss the Rapture, child."

I answer her with a crooked grin. "Sorry, Grandma. What do you need?"

"I need you to get out here in the yard and help me with Mr. Stutts's laundry." She props her fists on her hips, as she's apt to do when she's about to lecture me. "These linens ain't gonna wash themselves."

"Yes, ma'am." I tuck my beloved book beneath my low cot, climb to my feet, and follow Grandma Milly out into the front yard. The moment I step outside, the heat of early summer in North Carolina meets me, and I groan. "It's hot out, Grandma."

"You're telling me." Grandma Milly chuckles as we move across the crispy brown grass. "So hot out here it could fry the curls right out of your head." She reaches over, tousling my hair. I cringe, knowing that if she upsets my bun, it will be hard to wrestle my thick waves back into submission.

We stop walking as we approach Grandma Milly's washing station. Two large, galvanized tubs, each outfitted with a washboard, sit in the grass. One suds-filled tub stands ready for washing; the other is filled with clear water for rinsing. Each washtub boasts a crank-operated wringer, poised to squeeze every drop of water out of Mr. Stutts's bedspreads and pillow slips. Beyond that, we have six sturdy poles, from which Grandma Milly has strung the clothesline on which the freshly laundered items will dry, and a small basket containing wooden clothespins.

"All right. Time to call on the muscle of this operation." Cupping her hands around her mouth, Grandma yells, "Octavious! Come on and bring the laundry."

"Yes, ma'am," his small voice calls back. A few blinks later, here comes my little brother, pushing a wheelbarrow full of dirty laundry. His brown shorts and worn, once-white shirt are streaked with dirt as always. Parking the wheelbarrow near the washtubs, Octavious asks, "Can I go play now, Grandma?"

Grandma Milly smiles at him. "In a minute. First, get your mama. We gonna need some more help with this washing."

"Yes, ma'am." He runs off. Octavious is a ball of energy, most of which he uses to run around the farm, climbing trees and troubling the hens. Mama says he was born under the wandering star and that's why he can't keep still.

Octavious comes back with Mama, whose attire is similar to

Grandma Milly's. Mama isn't wearing the headscarf she normally wears; instead, she's wound her long wavy hair into a tight bun on top of her head, like me. Mama walks over with a smile and pinches my cheek. "Finished reading that play again, honey?"

I shake my head. "Not yet."

"This is, what, the fourth time you're reading it?"

"Sixth. I reckon I'll finish it in the next few days."

Grandma scoffs. "Honey child, how are you gonna find a husband if your nose is always buried in a book? You ought to look up once in a while; you never know who might be nearby."

I shrug. "I suppose it'll have to be a man who likes to read."

Mama sighs. "Anyhow, we just want to make sure there's some-body to look after you when we're gone."

"Gone? You two are gonna always be with me."

My mother and grandmother exchange a look, but neither of them speaks.

We womenfolk set about the task of the Stutts family laundry, while Octavious busies himself climbing trees. Mr. Stutts, a pretty well-known lawyer in town, hired Grandma Milly on as his personal wash-erwoman after Emancipation. I was a girl of nine at the time, and my brother was around seven. Ever since we left the plantation, we been working as free Blacks on a small corner of his land. The plot, and our one-room cabin built upon it, are considered part of Grandma's pay.

It isn't a fancy life by any means, but near as I can tell, it's far better than it used to be. The best part of being free is that I can read whenever I want and not get into trouble for it. That is, as long as I keep up with my chores. I took many a whipping from our old mistress for my desire to educate myself. Mrs. Stutts is nice enough to loan me books, since I always give them back in good condition. Reading is my favorite way to pass the time, and whenever I get the chance, I love to find a quiet corner and dive into a good story. I love to read about different times and different places, and all the lives that people can live.

Bent over the rinsing tub, Mama says, "My stars. It's mighty warm out here."

"Nothin's quite as hot as a North Carolina summer." Grandma Milly chuckles. "I mean, other than hell."

Mama shakes her head. "The hot weather always reminds me of summers gone by, you know, Mama? It's been five summers since we walked free from Master Williams. Twelve summers since I had Octavious. Fourteen since I had Jo. And fifteen since Colonel Lamb first visited the plantation."

Grandma Milly gives Mama a look. "Jeanette. Why you always talking about that white man? No good's gonna come of it."

Mama runs the bedsheet she's been rinsing through the wringer, then heads for the clothesline. She stoops, snatching up a few clothespins, then tosses the sheet over the line. "Mama, that man knows he fathered these children. Why else would he send me that portrait of him? And that lil' bit of money that we put toward outfitting the cabin?"

Grandma Milly just shakes her head. "That's neither here nor there. I'm not saying he didn't sire these children, just like a hundred other white men who tipped into the quarters when we had no other choice." She works a pillow slip over the washboard, stirring up a heap of suds in the hot, lye-laced water. "What I'm saying is, it don't make any difference to your life, or to my grandbabies. You and me, we the ones that's gon' make sure these children are all right."

I separate the pieces of laundry to hand to Grandma for washing, then carry them over to Mama for rinsing. Mama and Grandma don't talk about Colonel Lamb very often, especially when I'm around, so I follow with interest. I know the colonel is the stern-looking, dark-eyed man who sired me, then denied me. I suppose he's simply doing what other men of his status do, but I try not to think on him too much. All I know is, the folks with me right here, right now, are my family. My grandma, my mama, and my worrisome brother are my family. They love me, and I love them right back. Not knowing both of one's parents is a common predicament, so to me it makes no difference if my father comes around or not. The four of us have been doing just fine without him.

The sounds of wheels rolling over rutted earth and the clopping of horse's hooves make me turn my eyes toward the road. Seeing an approaching buggy, I point at the vehicle. "Somebody's coming."

As it stops in front of our yard, Grandma Milly drops the pillow slip into the rinse tub and wipes her hands on the front of her skirt. "I wonder who it is."

The laundry work stops as we watch a bespectacled white man, carrying a notebook, walk up the steps to the Stuttses' front porch. As the stranger carries on a conversation with Mr. Stutts, he jots something in his notebook.

"Who's that man talking to Mr. Stutts?" Octavious asks from his perch on a low-hanging poplar branch.

Mama shrugs. "I don't know. Looks like they doing some kinda business."

The man shakes Mr. Stutts's hand, then climbs back onto his buggy seat.

As the buggy moves away, I catch a glimpse of something. "Something's painted on the back of his buggy." I squint, shielding my eyes from the hot July sun as I try to make out the words. "U.S. Census Bureau."

Octavious calls out, "A census what?"

I roll my eyes. "Bureau, Tavious. Bureau." He's a bit younger than me, and he's not as inclined to read as me. I do read to him sometimes, though.

Mama chuckles and shakes her head. "It's a government thing. Every so often, somebody comes around and counts all the folks in every household."

I nod. "Right. So they can know how many folks there are, right?"

"Yep. Well, the show's over, folks. Back to work." Grandma Milly gestures to me. "Jo, give me the next thing to wash."

I hand off the next pillow slip while I watch the buggy rattle back down the road. That road leads away from Williamston to the whole wide world. I close my eyes and imagine what lies beyond the road in front of me. I picture myself in a fancy traveling costume, strolling up to the train ticket window, then boarding a train headed west. I picture my seat by the window, and the views of the rolling plains, the buffalo, the mountains, and the valleys. I've seen these places in drawings within the pages of my books, and in the paintings hanging on the wall in the Stuttses' big house. I can see it all so clearly in my mind, and one day, I will see it with my eyes.

When I'm full-grown, and my life is my own, there are so many things I can pursue. *Will I have a buggy of my own someday? Maybe a house, with a husband and a baby and a vegetable garden?*

I know freedom holds endless possibilities for me, but I can't see how any of those possibilities will come to pass until we leave Williamston. Yes, we are free now. But there are just too many memories here, lingering memories of the lash, the cold nights sleeping on hard dirt floors, and the long days tending the crops under the hot Carolina sun.

*My future isn't here. It's somewhere else . . . somewhere I can make a fresh start.*

# 1

*January 1873*
*Elizabeth City, North Carolina*

I take in the view, looking at the way the sun sparkles on the surface of the Pasquotank River. It looks like ribbons of light dancing over the water. Walking hand in hand with my Archer, I let out a happy sigh. We stroll toward the waterfront, and he gives my hand a squeeze.

"So what do you think, Mrs. Leary?" Archer smiles down at me. "Do you approve of your honeymoon so far?"

I melt, just as I do every time he looks at me this way. "As I said to you a few days ago, Archer . . . I do." I lean up, place a soft peck against his jaw. The two days' worth of stubble there make him look rugged, daring.

"I'm glad to hear it. Only the best for my bride." He cups my cheek, affection shining in his eyes.

His touch is familiar, soothing. I suck in my bottom lip and release it before speaking again. "Come now, Archer. We've been locked in the room for two days. If you really want to get this fresh air, keep your hands to yourself."

"You accusing me of tempting you?"

I give him a sidelong glance. "You know full well what you're doing, Archer Leary."

His answering grin is broad. "Heavens, Jo. What can I do to get you to call me Sweety, as everyone else does?"

I shrug. I never cared for that nickname. "Nothing. Besides, I'm not everyone else. I'm your wife." I circle my arms around his waist. "I love the way that word sounds. *Wife*." I never would have guessed I'd be fortunate enough to get married at a prime age to give my new husband all the babies he—and I—might desire. Mama and Grandma Milly were pleased when I met Archer on the Folly plantation, where I was sent to train in barbering.

We turn left toward the center of town, headed away from the water. An assortment of one- and two-story buildings line the road on either side of us. Some are fashioned of planks, while the older, more established ones are built from brick and stone. We pass a bakery, with its pink-and-white-painted exterior resembling a fancy wedding cake, a tailor shop with several fine suits on display in the glass-paned window, and a small general store advertising a sale on collards.

"Do you smell that?" Archer asks.

I sniff the air, and the scent of leather being worked sparks instant recognition. "There must be a tanner nearby." I inhale again, more deeply, and let the memory wash over me.

*I reported to the Folly barbershop at seven sharp, ferried there by Glasgow, Mr. Stutts's ornery older brother and right hand. "Get on in there and learn something, gal," Glasgow admonished as he pulled the buggy away from the walk.*

*Inside the shop, old man Folly stood by the door, wearing a fine black suit beneath a muslin apron. "You Josephine?"*

*I nodded shyly. "Yes, sir."*

*He foisted a heavy bucket into my hand.*

*The acrid scent of lye hit my nostrils immediately. But I detected something else in the water, something fruity. Lemon oil, maybe?*

*Before I could pinpoint the other scent, the old man started barking orders. "First thing you need to learn: how to clean your implements. There's four pair of shears and six combs in there. Take that bucket on the table over there and scrub 'em all clean. And be quick about it, gal."*

*"Yes, sir." I did as he instructed. Rolling up the sleeves of my worn shirt, I used the tattered cloth I dug out of the water to cleanse the tools.*

*I was still elbow-deep in the bucket of warm suds when he entered the shop. He was tall and well-built, his skin the color of Mama's coffee after she added a good dose of milk. His hair surrounded his handsome, angular face in a silken mass of dark curls.*

*I stopped, stared. For a moment, his golden eyes met mine, and my heart pounded in my chest like the sounds rising from a Sunday drumming circle.*

*Our gazes met, and time seemed to fall away.*

*Folly croaked, "State your name, boy, instead of standing there like a damn statue."*

*He snatched away his piercing eyes, leaving me both relieved and bereft.*

*"Sorry. I'm Archer, sir. From the Leary spread."*

*Archer. What a strong name for a sturdy young man. My tongue darted out to dampen my lower lip as I resumed my cleaning duties.*

*"Well, boy, go over there and get the clean shears from that gal, and I'll show you how to sharpen them on the strap."*

*He strode toward me, and I dropped the cloth into the bucket, trying to keep my composure. As he reached for the shears, I moved the clean pile closer to him.*

*For a moment, our fingertips touched.*

*Something shot through me, like a bolt of lightning firing across a storm-darkened sky. If his widening eyes were any indication, he felt something similar.*

*We stared at each other again, for another long moment, until Folly's angry shouts pulled him away from me. I moved across the shop to hastily grab a whisk broom, staying busy to avoid Folly's wrath. As I swept the floors, I watched Archer work a straight razor over the leather honing strap, the smell of warm leather permeating the air.*

Old man Folly wasn't pleased about us sparking, but nothing could stop what fate had already begun. In three months' time, when our training as barbers ended, our love story began in earnest. I was only thirteen, but old enough to know that he made my heart skip a beat. I was immediately smitten, but it wasn't until two years later, during my fifteenth summer, when Archer had shown up at our cabin at the Stutts place, intent on calling on me. I was so red in the face at his arrival, I must have resembled a large tomato. Still, I couldn't resist his charm, his sharp wit, and his wavy-haired handsomeness.

My mother and grandmother indulged my budding feelings for Archer. They listened with knowing smiles as I chattered on about him and encouraged us to spend time together under their watchful eyes. They were elated when Archer asked for my hand; he'd always been charming, considerate, and respectful during his visits, but their approval of the union went even deeper. Both older women were afraid I might be destined for spinsterhood. They say I've got a fierce independent streak.

*But Archer's different.* I can't count the number of afternoons we spent happily sitting in companionable silence, me lost in my books, him lost in his thoughts. When we daydream together about the places I've read about—striking out, traveling, and trying something new—he always has something to add that I'd never considered. Daydreaming together feels like more than just dreaming; it feels like planning a life.

Standing next to him, I admire his handsomeness. The tone of his skin allows him to pass for white, but no matter his race, no one with decent sight could deny his attractiveness. He has a head full of luxurious dark waves, framing a perfectly symmetrical face. His eyes are hazel, flecked with green, and easy to get lost in. And his mustache frames lips that are soft, smooth, and just full enough to cover mine when we kiss.

As easy as he is on the eyes, his looks alone wouldn't have been enough for me. After every indignity I suffered under the hand of old Master Williams, I could never have settled for less than true love. And I do love Archer. I love him as flowers love the sun, as fields love the rain.

"Let's go, Jo." He takes my hand again. "I don't want to be late for my appointment."

I chuckle. "I'm never going to let you forget what a reasonable wife I am, Archer. Not many wives would agree to allow a business meeting during a honeymoon trip."

"I know. And you have my endless gratitude." He bows with a flourish. "If I wait, though, this prime piece of land is going to sell . . . to someone else."

I sigh as we walk away from the water, not quite ready to leave the beautiful scenery behind. But Archer has his heart set on this property. He is more than handsome and affectionate; he's ambitious. He's been talking about this plot of land on Road Street for several weeks now. According to him, the location and size of the plot make it ideal for commercial development that has great potential to be leased for a good profit. And when the seller contacted him with a meeting date that happened to fall within three days of the date we were to be married, he'd agreed anyway.

I've got to admit, his excitement is a little bit contagious. I love the way his eyes light up when he talks about business, because I know the root of his ambition. To make something of himself, to prove to anyone that he can be successful in life. I want that too.

"You know this meeting is really about you, my dear. I'm looking at every opportunity to take care of you, to make sure you have a good life." Archer squeezes my hand again. "Remember that. My goal is for you, and our future babies, to enjoy all the fruits of freedom."

"I appreciate that, Archer." Easing closer to him as we walk, I rest my cheek against his strong upper arm.

Soon, we arrive at the intersection of Road and Main Streets. The intersection is busy with both foot and buggy traffic, and it takes some maneuvering to get around everyone else. Finally, we come to the lot, the only vacant land in the near vicinity.

"So where's this Mr. Charles?"

"He'll be here." Archer checks his pocket watch before tucking it back into the inner pocket of his coat. "There are lots of folks out today. Let's just give him a few minutes."

I stand with him on the edge of the lot, doing my best to stay out of the way of passersby. I shift my weight back and forth, growing somewhat impatient with the situation. *This business meeting is putting a damper on our romantic getaway.* Still, I know better than to try to persuade Archer to leave once he has his mind set on something.

Finally, a man in a fancy black wool suit appears a short distance away. He has a ruddy complexion, ice-blue eyes, and tufts of straight blond hair sticking out from beneath his bowler. As he walks toward us, he eyes us cautiously. "Are you Mr. Leary?"

He smiles. "I am. You must be Mr. Charles."

The man in the bowler nods, sticking out his hand. "A real pleasure to meet you." Charles's gaze swings toward me, and a slight frown creases his brow. "Is . . . this your, uh, wife?"

"Yes, this is my sweet Josephine." Archer beams. "We've not been married a full week yet."

After a few beats spent looking back and forth between our faces, Mr. Charles says, "Wonderful. Congratulations to you both." The compliment is strained; there's a tinge of disapproval, or maybe pity, in his voice.

I fight the urge to roll my eyes. Ever since Archer began courting me, I've seen that same look of disdain and disbelief from most of the white men we encounter. In a way, it tickles me. Archer and I are both of mixed race, but my husband possesses a fair enough complexion to pass; I do not. It's a mere coincidence, a trick of fate. Yet wherever we go, people assume he is white and that I'm Negro, and therefore unworthy of his love and his name.

"So let's talk business here." Archer claps his hands together. "What can you tell me about this property?"

Mr. Charles scratches his chin. "Yes, well, let's see. It's prime land, well-kept, as you can see. It's the only vacant lot for five or so miles, and this area is booming. We're seeing an influx of freed people; you know, like your ladylove here, looking to establish themselves by plying their trades to the locals. As more folks settle down in the area, more and more businesses will open to accommodate their needs." He gestures around at their surroundings. "Only a matter of time before somebody wants to build something here."

"I agree. Seems like a very sound investment." Archer smiles. "I'll take it."

"Wonderful. All I'll need is five hundred dollars, cash or bank draft." Mr. Charles sticks out his hand.

Archer's face crumples into a cringe. "Heavens. The whole purchase price, up front?"

Charles scoffs. "Why not?"

"Because that isn't what the advertisement said, Mr. Charles." Archer's jaw takes on a harder set. "The advertisement calls for one half of the purchase price up front. That's two hundred and fifty dollars."

"I see you're decent at math, Mr. Leary. But I had no intention of selling my land to anybody associating with coloreds."

I can feel the tension crackling between them. It makes the muscles in my neck and shoulders tighten.

"I'm willing to go as high as three hundred."

"You heard me. Five hundred dollars." Charles folds his arms over his chest.

"Three twenty-five is my absolute limit, Mr. Charles."

"You've seen the property, and we both know it stands to be very profitable for whoever can claim ownership of it. And no offense to you, but as I said, I don't normally have no parts of anything pertaining to colored folks, and I'm not going to leave such a valuable piece of business open-ended by letting you pay this off over time. So I'm gonna need the whole price up front, on account of your missus."

Archer's expression goes flat. "You ought to have been more up front in your advertisement if—"

"Pardon me." I stop him, as politely as I know how.

"What is it, my dear?" Archer shifts his gaze to me, appearing confused.

"I can buy it. I have five hundred dollars."

Mr. Charles looks as if he's swallowed a live trout.

"Come again?"

"I said, I have the money." I turn my head, looking around. "Is there a bank nearby where I can get the draft?"

Both men stare at me.

I smile, enjoying their surprise and confusion. "Is something the matter? I can absolutely see the potential of this lot." I point at the property. "Look there. Can't you see a bakery or a small eatery here?" I scan the surrounding area, searching for what might be lacking. There are certain goods and services a growing town needs, no matter the background of its citizens. "What about a seamstress? From what I can see, there isn't one nearby, and expert sewing is always in demand."

Archer's expression becomes thoughtful for a moment. "Yes, my dear. I can see exactly what you're saying."

"Good. Then you know it isn't going to remain vacant for long. We should purchase it now and enjoy the profits later."

Mr. Charles's mouth drops open.

"How far is the bank from here?"

Mr. Charles stumbles over his words. "Not . . . not far. It's right over there." He points toward a stately two-story building about a block away.

"Thank you, Mr. Charles." I take a step toward him. "Now, would you have any objection to selling me the property?" *Let's see if his greed outweighs his prejudice.*

"I, uh . . . no. As long as your husband gives his approval."

That's amusing. According to the law, I don't need anyone's approval. I suppose Mr. Charles is looking for a way out. "Archer?" I look toward my dear husband, already knowing his answer.

He meets my gaze, and I see the twinkle of mischief dancing in his eyes. "Absolutely. By all means, Mr. Charles. Sell her the property."

"I . . . er . . . Fine. I'll be happy to do that." Mr. Charles reaches into his inner coat pocket, removing a small leather-bound book. "So long as she actually has the five hundred dollars."

"My wife's word is irreproachable," Archer insists, still looking at me. "If she says she has it, then she has it."

"Let's walk down to the bank, Mr. Charles." My feet are already moving in the direction he'd indicated. "I'm eager to get this taken care of, so I can get back to enjoying my husband's company. We're on our honeymoon after all."

Archer walks alongside me, still clasping my hand. I can feel his pride through the warmth of his palm—comforting, solid, and sure. I love that he's not intimidated by me; it makes him a wonderful partner.

Looking utterly taken aback, Mr. Charles nevertheless falls in step behind us.

Within half an hour, I hand the freshly signed bank draft over to Mr. Charles. He exchanges it for the deed to the land. "Now you'll need to take that over to the registrar, so a copy can be saved in the town's record book."

"Not a problem." I fold the deed carefully, tucking it into my purse. "Thank you so much, Mr. Charles. It's been a pleasure doing business with you." Hand in hand with my husband, I walk with him out of the bank, leaving a still amazed Mr. Charles in my wake.

Outside on the walk, Archer stares at me for a quarter of a block as we walk. He's silent, but it's impossible not to notice his eyes on me.

Finally, I ask, "What is it, Archer?"

"You're amazing, Josephine."

"Really? How so?" I never pass up an opportunity to tease him.

"Pshaw. You just about shocked that poor fellow out of his shoes back there. Whatever possessed you to do that?"

"What, to buy the property?" I shrug. "It's just as I said. I had five hundred dollars."

"I know the colonel sent you a wedding gift, but you didn't have to spend it on this."

"That's true. But that money was for me to establish myself, so why not?"

"So then I'm right." He snaps his fingers. "There's some other mischief afoot here."

I can't help laughing. "You're very perceptive, Archer."

"I am when it comes to you." He strokes my jaw with his index finger.

"Fine, your perceptiveness will be rewarded," I say, smiling. "I bought the property because you wanted it. You've been talking about it for a long while now." I stop in front of the small building where the office of the town registrar is located. "I bought it because my mother and grandmother never had the right, or the funds, to make such a purchase, and I feel blessed to have the chance."

"That's really something, Jo."

"And do you know the most important reason I bought this property, Archer?"

He shakes his head. "Do tell."

"I bought it because I could. Old Mr. Charles would never have expected to sell that piece of land to a Negro, or to a woman." I prop my fists on my hips, looking at my reflection in the glass window of the registrar's office, feeling very pleased with myself. "I've shown him a thing or two."

"You most certainly have." Archer reaches for the door and swings it open. "Let's put the deed on record, shall we?"

"Absolutely."

As night falls, I extricate myself from Archer's embrace, careful not to wake him as I move across the room. I feel the chill in the air now that I've left the warm cocoon of blankets, and I pull my silk robe tight, tying the belt to close it over the thin nightgown beneath.

Our finely appointed suite in the Coastal View Hotel has many amenities, not the least of which is a polished mahogany writing desk and matching chair. A quill pen rests in a black ceramic inkwell, and a few sheaves of the hotel's linen stationery are stacked in a matching flat tray.

Opening the desk's small drawer, I remove the leather-bound book I placed there when we checked in.

Sitting down, I run my hand over the smooth surface of the cover. I've kept this journal since I was fourteen; it was a gift from my mother for my birthday that year. This small book holds the memories of every significant moment in my life, and a few mundane ones as well. I turn to the first blank page and pick up the quill.

*Things are finally starting to come together. My great-grandmother Amina was snatched from the shores of our ancestral home in Africa and never knew a day of freedom in this land. What would she think to know that her great-granddaughter now holds the deed to a piece of it, one that just a decade ago was likely worked by slaves?*

*I'm grateful to my grandmother Milly for the knowledge of my heritage she has passed on to me. She told me of her mother, Amina, and of her father, Dayo. My grandmother was still forming in Amina's belly when she was taken from the shores of Ghana. My great-grandfather Dayo fought valiantly to save his wife but was ultimately killed in the struggle.*

*On a plantation in South Carolina, my great-grandmother went on to birth three daughters: my grandmother Milly, Sarah, and Nan. Amina's master fathered the latter two girls, but that didn't stop him from selling them Deep South while my grandmother was sold to a slaveholder in North Carolina. She never saw her sisters or her mother again.*

*While the tale of our family has been tragic in many ways, it's given me a sense of purpose. All this strife led to my existence, and to my accomplishment today. It's a wonderful and triumphant feeling to own a piece of North Carolina, though knowing that those who came before me never had a chance to experience the same triumph makes the victory somewhat bittersweet. Their tears have watered the crops and their blood has stained the soil so that I can walk as a free woman, with my head held high.*

*And because of their sacrifice, because of the strength they imbued me with via the blood coursing in my veins, I'm determined to pursue a successful life. If not for myself, for the children I'll one day bear. And for Amina, Sarah, and Nan, and all those others who built this nation for free.*

*Their sacrifices, their pain, will not be in vain. I will amass more property, more land, than they could have ever imagined. And I will obtain the wealth they should have been afforded for their labors, and much more. My children will never lack food or shelter. And I will never, ever suffer the humiliation of surrendering my very existence to a white man, ever again.*

As I return the quill to the ink pot, Archer stirs.

His voice is muffled by sleep and blankets. "Jo? Come back to bed, darling."

Closing my journal, I tuck it away in the drawer once again and return to my husband's embrace.

On the last morning of our trip, I awaken Archer early. "Come, dearest. There is something I want to do before we return to Williamston."

We dress, check out of the hotel, and take our bags to our small buggy. As Archer grabs the reins, I stay his hand. "Honey, can we go to the general store?"

Archer directs Captain, his old gelding, as I've requested. He accompanies me into the store and watches in confusion as I purchase a small canning jar and a metal scoop. "Josephine, what are you about, exactly?"

I smile. "You'll see."

When we're back in the buggy, I say, "Take me to the land I just bought, please."

Shaking his head, my husband does as I ask. When we arrive at the plot of land, I climb down from my seat as soon as Archer brings the buggy to a stop. With the jar and scoop in hand, I go to a corner of the plot, near the sidewalk. Opening the lid, I set it aside and use the scoop to break the earth. Once I've got a nice little pile of the packed soil broken up, I add it to the jar and seal it.

Archer's perplexed expression awaits me as I climb back onto the buggy seat next to him.

I tuck the filled jar and the scoop into my carpetbag. "I wanted to take home a little piece of *my* land."

He chuckles. "You're so sentimental, Jo."

"I've been called worse." I peck him on the cheek. "Let's go home."

# JOSEPHINE

### *April 1873*
### *Edenton, North Carolina*

Tugging my wheeled trunk up the sidewalk, I pause to take a breath. Looking up at our new home, I feel a smile pulling at my lips.

The house is a simple two-story structure, occupying a modest lot on the south end of Broad Street. Both the house and the low picket fence surrounding it have recently been whitewashed, and the faint scent of paint still hangs in the air.

Our lot sits between a small dry-goods store and a cluster of other homes. Shaded by mature oaks and poplars, the house has a wide, covered front porch. I'm sure Sweety and I will enjoy sitting in rockers there, enjoying the warm air and the sounds of the neighborhood. My heart swells as I think of the years we will share here.

I've come to call him by the nickname that so many others call him. It tickles me now to think of how much I hated the moniker at first. Now I've found it fits his sweet and easygoing disposition quite nicely.

As if summoned by my thoughts, he appears at my side. "Dearest, let me take that." Grasping the leather strap, he pecks me on the cheek and strides past me, dragging the trunk with ease. I watch his muscles work as he lifts it over the two steps, onto the porch, and, ultimately, into the house.

Next comes my mother, grandmother, and younger brother, all carrying various items.

"Where shall we put these lamps and things?" My mama watches my face as she awaits a response.

Still caught up in the excitement of the moment, I say, "Just sit them on the floor in the parlor. I'll arrange things better later."

She nods, and the parade of relatives continues past me.

I return to the buggy, getting the two rolled-up throw rugs I plan to put in the parlor and the sitting room. Tucking one beneath each arm, I head up the walk into the house.

The interior bustles with activity as my family works to put things in place. I love the dainty pink rosebuds printed on the cream-colored paper that covers most of the downstairs walls, and I imagine it will look even better once I get to hang some paintings and family portraits.

Grandma Milly says, "Sweety, have you brought in my cooking pots?"

"Yes, ma'am," he calls from somewhere in the kitchen.

She claps her hands together. "Good. I'm going back there and put them away."

"Careful, Mama," my mother cautions. "Don't overdo it."

"Hush up." My grandmother, not one to be intimidated, breezes past my mother and disappears through the dining room opening.

I can only shake my head.

"You will certainly have your hands full with your grandmother," my mother remarks. "Are you sure you wish her to live with you, Jo?"

I nod. "Yes, I'm sure. She's getting older, and I don't know how many more years I will have with her." My grandmother has been a beacon of guidance and wisdom my whole life. Now that she's nearing seventy years old, giving her a comfortable place to live is the least I can do to repay her for all the love and care she's shown me over the years.

"All right, child. But I'll always have a room for her if she gives you too much trouble." My mother winks at me.

Octavious carefully lifts a plate from the wooden cart holding my wedding china, peeling back the newspaper wrapping. "I expect to be invited over for dinner often, sister dear. Since you have all these darn plates."

I walk over and bump my fist softly against his chin. "Don't fret, brother. You'll be here so often you'll tire of me." He and my mother reside together in a modest house on Queen Street, only a few blocks away.

A knock on the door draws my attention, and I swivel in time to see Hannibal Badham entering the front door. "Furniture delivery," he calls out, as he and Dorsey Stewart enter, each carrying two kitchen chairs.

Both men are attired in the Badham Builders uniform of brown shirt and trousers. Hannibal is tall and broad-shouldered, with a long beard shrouding the lower half of his face. His bushy curls are mostly contained beneath a tan bowler. Dorsey is a few inches shorter than his employer, with a wider frame. His close-trimmed hair has a touch of gray, and his thin mustache frames an easy smile.

"Morning, Hannibal, Dorsey." I go over to greet them. "Thanks for bringing it by."

"No problem, Jo." Hannibal is one of the best carpenters in the state, and Dorsey is his best apprentice. Beyond that, Dorsey and my mother have been courting for several weeks now, so I know both of them to be fine gentlemen.

I watch as Dorsey uses a length of rope to measure the width of the front door. "We'll have to bring the table around back. It just isn't going to fit through this doorway."

"Certainly, if you think that's best. Just go right through there and leave the chairs someplace out of your way." I point in the direction they should go, then step aside to allow them to pass.

I go to help Octavious arrange the china in the cabinet gifted to us by my mother; then we stack the empty crates in the pantry for later use.

I'm returning from the pantry when I notice someone standing on the porch. Going to the door, I smile at the young woman standing there with her back to me. From this position, I can only see a mass of shiny brown curls, barely brushing shoulders covered by a pink blouse. I notice that she's wearing denim trousers, something I don't usually see the women around here wearing. "Hello there, can I help you?"

She turns, revealing ice-blue eyes and a bright smile. "Goodness, where are my manners. I'm Rosa Jackson. My papa owns this house." She's gripping the handle of a wicker basket, containing a bundle of something covered with red-checked gingham cloth. "Are you Mrs. Leary?"

"I am." She looks about the same age as me, so I add, "You can call me Josephine, or Jo."

She grins. "Well, pleased to meet you, Jo. We brought this for you." She extends the basket.

I take the gift from her. "It's heavy, must be something good in here."

"Take a look," she encourages.

Lifting the cloth, I let my gaze sweep over several jars of pre-served fruits and vegetables. Smiling, I say, "Thank you so much, how thoughtful."

She shrugs. "We run a farm on the edge of town, and we always have plenty of food. Papa and I like to share it with folks." She turns again, looking back toward the road. "Where is he?"

"Here I am, sugar." Paul Jackson appears then, coming from the side of the house. "Just helping the boys get that table in the back door." He wears a red-and-black-plaid shirt with denim trousers and well-worn boots. A big straw hat shades most of his face, but I can still see his white beard and the single strand of hay hanging off his lip. Climbing up on the porch, he sticks out his hand. "Good to see you again, Miss Jo."

"Likewise, Paul." I shake his hand. "Thank you so much for the preserves."

"No problem at all. My Rosa cans better than anyone I know." He touches his daughter's shoulder. "She's a good egg, my little girl."

Rosa blushes. "Go on with you, Papa."

"Just stopping by to make sure you're getting moved in all right, and to let you know you can send for me if there's any problems around the house." Paul touches his hat brim. "I'm at your service, as much as this old body will allow."

"I appreciate that. Don't sell yourself short—you're still getting around pretty well as far as I can see."

He chuckles. "That may be so, but I'm no spring chicken anymore, either. I'll tell you now, I might be selling off this place in a few years' time. Getting a little long in the tooth to be maintaining property and all that."

I remember him mentioning that when we came to rent the place from him. Apparently, he was serious. "I see."

"Comes a time when a man wants to settle into his rocker and enjoy his land, you know?"

"I completely understand."

"Don't worry, though. I'll keep you informed on all that." He gestures to the basket. "Go on, take a look in there. We brought you some real good stuff."

I poke around the basket again and lift out a jar of something yellowish orange. "Look at this. . . . Are these peaches?"

Rosa nods. "Yeah. We had a bumper crop last season."

"In that case, I'm gonna have to have you over for peach cobbler and coffee."

"Sounds lovely," Rosa says.

"It'll just be you girls," Paul insists, patting his belly. "Watching my waistline, you know."

I swing my gaze back to Rosa. "I'll call on you in a couple of days."

"I look forward to it."

There's something about Rosa, be it her easy manner, ready smile, or unconventional dress, that makes me think we'll be fast friends.

Soon, the Jacksons depart, and I head back inside.

Sweety catches me as I enter. "Dearest, what do you want to do with this?"

He hands me the framed certificate of study I earned from the Williamston Unified Freedmen's School. I smile as I recall my three rigorous years there after emancipation. From the ages of nine to twelve, I expanded my mind by studying mathematics, literature, horticulture, and home economics. Taking it from him, I shake my head. "I'm not sure yet. Once we are better set up, I'll find a place to hang it." Tucking it under my arm, I carry it upstairs and set it on our bed.

When I return, Hannibal and Dorsey are moving the settee into place. Even though I ordered it, seeing it finished and sitting beneath the front window makes my breath catch in my throat. "Hannibal. It's beautiful."

He stands upright, smiles. "Why, thank you, Jo. You chose a real fine design, and if fits nicely with the style of the house."

I walk over and touch it, running my hands over the curved lines of the intricately carved backrest. It's made of rich mahogany, and glazed with a clear lacquer that gives it a glorious reflective shine. I press my fingertips into the cushion, finding it yielding yet firm. Amazingly, the rosebud-printed fabric is a close match to my wallpaper. "Where did you find this upholstery fabric?"

"Eunice Fitz, the seamstress, did the cushion for me." He adjusts the settee's position against the wall. "We were lucky, I snapped up her last couple of yards."

"I'll be sure to give her some business, then. It's fine work."

"Well, that's all the furniture," Hannibal says, dusting his hands on his trousers. "Heavens, let me collect my worker." He jerks his head, gesturing to the corner of the parlor.

Turning my gaze that way, I see my mother and Dorsey embracing. He whispers something in her ear, and she giggles like a delighted schoolgirl.

I laugh. "Those two are something."

Later, after everyone has left and my grandmother has retired to her room upstairs, Sweety and I sit on the new settee. His arm is stretched across the backrest, and my head rests comfortably on his shoulder.

"What a day," I remark. "I'm exhausted."

"Me too." He chuckles softly. "But to look around and see everything in place makes it all worth it."

I smile. "You're right."

"Just imagine it, honey. The smell of a roast coming from the kitchen. Little footsteps running through the house. Thanksgivings and Christmases and birthdays . . ."

"A stream of steady clients at the barbershop," I add. "A portfolio of property from here to the coast."

He touches my chin, tilts it up. "Now, Jo. Don't get carried away."

I shake my head. "I'm not. I am with you on the roast and the little feet and all of that; it sounds wonderful. We'll need some income to fill those little bellies, though."

He chuckles again. "Duly noted, Jo."

I snuggle closer to him. "I can't wait to do all those things with you."

"Patience, my love. We've a whole lifetime to do all those things, and more." He shifts, cupping my face in his hands, and presses his lips to mine.

And as I lean into his kiss, my heart is filled with the joy and wonder of what is to come.

# 2

JOSEPHINE

*June 1873*
*Edenton, North Carolina*

I feel as if I'm melting. Beneath my blue apron, I'm wearing my usual attire of skirt, blouse, shift, and drawers, and each layer holds in a little more of the sweltering Carolina heat. The old but sturdy brogans on my feet have grown heavy, each step feeling like a trek through a damp bog. My station is at the rear of our barbershop, the farthest away from the door, and that only makes matters worse. I pick up the folded copy of this morning's *Chowan Herald* and use it to fan myself, stirring the stale, tonic-scented air around my face. How can it be so warm this early in the day?

Unable to stand it any longer, I walk over to my husband, who's busy tidying his station between patrons. "Sweety, darling, I'm going to prop open the front door."

When he turns to face me, I can see the beads of perspiration that have formed around his hairline. "You've read my mind, Jo. I was just about to send Octavious to do that."

I walk through the shop to the front door, my eyes sweeping over the interior in search of things that might need my attention. I find myself doing this a lot, but it's my attention to detail that makes Central Barbershop run so smoothly. I glance at the walls, briefly inspecting the slate-gray paint for any stains. Seeing none, I shift to the copper-framed paintings of barbering implements to see if any of them are crooked. I commissioned the three images from a local artist and hung them myself. One depicts a pair of shears, another a comb with a few strands of black hair stuck in it, and the last painting is of a barber's chair. The paintings are large enough to take up most of the eastern wall, with our four barber stations lined up along the western wall. Had I left the choice to Sweety, we'd all be stuck staring at blank white walls all day.

Beneath the paintings, two knotty pine benches are placed, a comfortable spot for clients awaiting their turn in the chair. I sewed the gray cushions on the benches as well. A low table sits in front of the benches, and I straighten the copies of *Scientific American*, *The Freedman's Friend*, and the *Farmers' Almanac* that I've placed there as reading material.

As I pass the waiting area, I adjust the position of the two potted dwarf eucalyptus plants I keep on ironwork stands near the front windows. The plants, growing in large earthenware bowls, serve several purposes: decoration, adding a pleasant fragrance to the air, and providing the eucalyptus oil I use to make my scalp treatment tonic. Stopping for a moment, I get my watering can and add some water to the soil in each plant.

Beneath one of my plant stands, I keep a large rock I found by the creek. Grabbing it as I set the watering can down, I use the stone to prop the front door open. With that done, I step outside to enjoy the cooler air for a few moments.

Looking up and down Broad Street, I can see the town coming alive. Living here, among all the businesses and people and activity, is quite different from my life in rural Williamston. There are times when I miss the quiet, but I've also come to love the atmosphere of this thriving town. Traffic is already starting to pick up; folks are out on foot, on horseback, and in wagons, going about their daily business. And if they wish to look their best while doing so, they'll have to come to see us. We're the only barbershop in town, and aside from that, you'd have to go to Raleigh or farther to find a barber as skilled as my Sweety.

I see Eunice Fitz walking toward me and throw up my hand. "Morning!" She's fashionably dressed, as always. Her yellow summer-weight blouse is fashioned from fine cotton, and has a bright green vine filled with daisies stitched around the neckline. Her dark navy skirt has the same floral stitchwork around the hem. Her small yellow hat, perched at an angle atop her curls, has a small cluster of silk daisies as well. It's a well-coordinated look, and her appearance certainly fits her role as the best seamstress in town.

"Good morning, Josephine." She grins, stops. "How are those aprons working for you?"

I glance down at her handiwork. "They're a dream. We couldn't have asked for finer stitching." Eunice had whipped up nine aprons for us in a matter of days, turning several yards of fabric into enough for the three of us to always have a clean one available. She even embroidered some fancy gold bordering around them. "They're easily the finest I've ever seen. They stand up well to the washboard, too."

She waves me off in that modest way she does. "Oh, pshaw. I'm just glad they fit the bill."

"They sure do."

"Well, I'd better get on to the store. Good day, Josephine."

"See you later, Eunice." I watch her walk the short distance to her shop three doors down from ours. Turning around, I head back into the barbershop.

Octavious, seated behind the front desk, calls out to me as I pass him, "Thank you, dear sister. I was broiling!"

I can't help giggling at his exuberance. My little brother isn't so little anymore. He's fifteen now, not a boy, but not yet a full-grown man, either. His help around the shop is invaluable, as he keeps the floors swept and ensures that the clients mark their names down in our logbook. His presence leaves me free to attend to our clientele, which includes the wealthy whites and the well-heeled freedmen of our fair Edenton.

Sweety's fair complexion and dark, wavy hair have served this business well. Most assume him to be a particularly progressive white man who is married to a colored girl; that tends to work in our favor with the more tolerant whites of the town. I imagine they tell themselves that even patronizing a shop where colored people work makes them good people. There are also the occasional visits from whites who walk in, see my brother or me, and immediately walk out. Those are the ones who can't be bothered with hiding their hatred, but we don't see as many of them as we do regular folks who want to get a haircut or a shave and don't much care who does it so long as the service is satisfactory.

Edenton is a coastal town, a melting pot, with folks arriving on ships passing through all the time. But even that constant flow of people from so many backgrounds and walks of life can't stanch the racism entirely. This is still the South, and the echoes of slavery remain. Perhaps, if I'm fortunate, I'll live to see a day when tolerance reigns over bigotry.

Returning to my station, I reach into my apron pocket and check the time on my bronze watch. It's a quarter past nine, and business will soon begin to pick up. I take a moment to get my area in order, ensuring that all my clean combs and implements are placed in the glass container of white vinegar and pine oil I keep them in. I've found that the concoction, one of my own creation, clears away the residue of the tonics and potions I use to treat patrons' hair, and leaves the implements clean and fresh-smelling for the next use. I use the same concoction to wipe down my countertop and my barber's chair between clients, so I give everything a quick swipe.

"Morning, Learys!"

I turn toward the sound of the boisterous greeting, delivered in that familiar voice. "Mr. Green. Good to see you."

He takes off his Stetson, holding it to his chest as he nods his head in my direction. "Likewise, little lady." Taking the pen from Octavious, he signs his name to the ledger. "Salutations, young man."

I chuckle. Herschel Green, a transplant from Indian Territory, can always be counted on to bring a little Western charm into our establishment. He owns a blacksmith shop about a block up the road from us, near Broad and Albemarle.

Sweety greets Herschel as he eases into his barber chair. "Morning, my friend. What shall it be today?"

"Just take a little off the top and the sides. Make it look neat." He runs a hand through his sandy-blond hair. "Been looking a little shaggy lately."

I watch them chat while Sweety combs through Herschel's hair.

Rosa Jackson enters then, her hair hidden beneath her favorite wide-brimmed pink hat. She wears a pair of brown leather moccasins, the denim trousers she favors over dresses and skirts, and a pearl-button blouse that matches her hat. Her fair complexion is sun-burnished, a product of her work outdoors. To look at her, no one would know she was the daughter of one of the wealthiest landowners in the county. "Morning, Jo."

The sight of my friend warms my heart. Ever since we bonded over peach cobbler, coffee, and our insatiable love of reading, I see her at least once a week for a chat. "Hello, Rosa. You're looking well."

"As are you, compadre. Looks like I came at the right time." She stops to sign the log, then walks my way. "How is Milly?"

"She's doing well. Grandma complains about her knees now and then, but you know her. She isn't going to let a little pain stop her from going on about her business."

"Certainly not. She's a real pistol, your grandmother."

"I wouldn't have her any other way." I wink.

Rosa eases into the chair, then looks up, her blue eyes locking on me. "You won't believe what that insufferable Eunice Fitz said to me just now."

I sigh, knowing I'll soon find out. Rosa and Eunice have never gotten along. I suppose they're simply too different from one another, and too stubborn to try and make the best of it. "What did she say this time that was so bad?"

Her expression tight, she tilts her chin up and mimics the seamstress. "If you came in and let me make you a dress, you might finally get yourself a husband."

I shake my head. "Eunice means well, but she's often a bit snide in her delivery."

"You give her too much credit, Jo. She was rude to me on purpose," she huffs. "I swear that woman is a thorn in my side."

"Well, let's not dwell on the negative too long, Rosa."

"You're right. Let me stop putting my energy into such nonsense. I meant to ask, how is Jeanette? Haven't seen her out at the farm in a couple of weeks."

I snap my fingers, ready to deliver the news I've been sitting on. "I'm so glad you asked, because I have good news." I beckon her closer.

Her eyes widen. "Really? Do tell."

"Dorsey Stewart has asked for my mother's hand in marriage!" I can feel the grin spreading across my face as I speak.

"My word, that is good news. Do give her my congratulations."

"I will. I'm so pleased she's found love; she deserves it." Mama's life hasn't been an easy one, and to see her so enamored with her sweetheart, and watch him treat her with such care, warms my heart. "All right, we've wagged our tongues enough. Let's have a look at your hair."

Rosa cringes. "Jo, I need your help. I've got a birthday party to attend this evening, and my hair looks like a crow's nest."

I laugh, gently taking her hat off her head. "Come now, Rosa. It can't be all that bad."

She looks at me in the mirror to watch my reaction. I'm met with a tangle of brown curls, which does bear a striking resemblance to the bird dwelling she mentioned. As I see in many of my octoroon clients, her curls are loosely patterned but still prone to fierce tangling. "Oh, goodness."

"Still think it's not so bad?"

I chuckle. "It's . . . well, I can handle it, anyway." I grab my favorite comb for attacking such tangles. The wide-set teeth let me loosen the knots without tugging too hard on the strands. "You haven't been braiding it for sleep at night as I said, have you, Rosa?"

She gives me a sheepish look.

I can only shake my head. "I'll try to restore it. But you'll make both of our lives easier with a simple French braid in the evenings, all right?"

She nods. "Yes, yes. After seeing what I saw in the mirror this morning, I won't neglect that duty again."

It takes me a full hour to go through the process of washing, detangling, and trimming her hair. Rosa favors a shorter cut that just brushes her chin, even though society favors long hair on ladies. Once I've shaped her curls to frame her heart-shaped face, I turn her chair to the mirror so she can see the fruits of my labor. "How's that, Rosa?"

She plays with the curls around her hairline, a broad grin on her face. "Jo, you're a miracle worker."

"Hardly. But I do appreciate the compliment."

She laughs, reaching into the pocket of her denims and handing me a quarter eagle. "Keep the change, dearie."

I tuck the money away in the strongbox I keep beneath my station. "Many thanks. Let me walk you up front."

After I've escorted Rosa to the door, and we say our goodbyes, I return to my station to tidy it. A few minutes later, Herschel is finally done with his haircut, shave, hot-towel treatment, and shoulder massage. He doesn't come in often, but when he does, he enjoys a full groom. He tips his hat to me on his way out, and I wave, watching him leave through the open door.

I sidle over to Sweety and give him a peck on the cheek. His whiskers tickle my lips. "My, my. You'll soon need me to give you a shave, I see."

He rolls his eyes in response to my teasing, but a smile forms at the corners of his lips. "Go on with you, Jo." Before I can move away, though, he hooks his arm around my waist and gives me a kiss full on the lips.

"Ew," Octavious complains.

I shake my head, knowing that when the right young woman comes along, my brother will quickly shed his feigned disgust for all things romantic.

I draw back from Sweety at the sound of heavy footsteps. A man I don't recognize has just entered the shop. He wears a blue work shirt, dun-brown pants, and worn brogans. His dark hair hangs down in oily ribbons, grazing his shoulders. The brim of his beat-up brown hat is pulled low, obscuring his eyes.

He opens his mouth, framed by an overgrown black beard. "Who's in charge here?"

I swallow.

Sweety speaks up. "I'm the proprietor here, sir. I'm Sweety Leary. And you are . . . ?"

The man reaches for the hat, and when he removes it, his piercing blue eyes fall on Sweety's face, then dart to mine, then back. Finally, he speaks. "I'm Charles Wilton Rea. I go by CW, if you please."

Sweety nods. "Pleased to meet you, CW. What brings you into Central Barbershop today?"

A ghost of a smile crosses his face. "I've been traveling, looking at properties all through North and South Carolina. As you can see, I had precious little time for grooming while I was on my sojourn." He scratches his overgrown beard. "Now that the prospecting is done, I need to look presentable again. Shave and a haircut, please."

"Not a problem. Octavious will show you where to mark your name in the logbook, and then you can come on over to my station."

I watch as CW signs the book, then settles himself into Sweety's chair. He glances at me. "You must be the little lady."

"Yes, sir, I'm Sweety's wife, and co—"

"Yes." Sweety cuts me off mid-phrase. "She's my dearest, most indispensable wife."

I narrow my eyes.

Sweety cocks a brow. "Can you see to refilling the tonic bottles, dearest?"

I grit my teeth and say, "Of course, my love." I retreat to the rear of the shop, to the small storage area where we keep our supplies.

In the small, dimly lit space, I close my eyes and take several deep breaths. The smell of our tonics and treatments fills my nostrils as I try to set aside my frustration with Sweety. We've been in business for several weeks now. And in that time, Sweety hasn't referred to me as co-owner, co-proprietor, or anything of the sort, either in private or in front of our customers. It doesn't seem to matter to him that my funds covered the first two months' lease payments, or that I'm the one who spotted the empty storefront to begin with. And whenever I begin to introduce myself as such, he interrupts me and assigns me some menial task to keep me out of his hair for a while.

It's enough that he doesn't want to share credit for this place, and I can almost understand that. Society has deemed men the breadwinners and women the caretakers, and Sweety and I are a part of that society. But to send me off to do chores as if I'm a child? Or the cleaning lady? That just beats the Dutch.

I know all the tonic bottles are full. I filled them myself this morning, and we've had fewer than five customers so far. Sweety knows they're full, too. I'm sure this was just the first task he could think of to keep me occupied with something other than conversing with our newest client. I only came back here to the closet so I could release a bit of tension, cool off some. Grabbing a cloth from the shelf, I return to the main shop, intent on polishing the glass bottles we both know are already filled.

I move from station to station, retrieving and polishing our amber glass bottles of hair tonic, scalp treatment, and facial steam drops. We purchase the hair tonic from a Mr. Dudley in Atlanta, but the scalp treatment and facial drops are all handmade by me, from my own recipes. I know herbs and essential oils like a fox knows his foxhole, thanks to my grandmother Milly's teachings.

While I busy myself, as my husband intended, I steal surreptitious glances at him and Mr. CW Rea. I watch him take his shears to the shaggy ends of his customer's dark hair and open my ears to hear what they're saying to each other.

"I've a vision for this town," CW declares. "It can be so much bigger, so much more modern. Sitting right on the water like it is, there will always be folks coming in from all over the place."

"That's true enough," Sweety replies while lopping off a few more inches of hair. "We do get a lot of travelers, though many are shippers who use the port to take goods inland."

"And I plan to broaden the horizons of this town, to take advantage of all those travelers. I see new horizons of entertainment, right here in Edenton."

I'm not sure what he means by that, and when I glance at Sweety, I can tell he seems similarly confused.

"Just what are you planning for our sleepy little town on the water, CW?" Sweety tilts his head slightly to the left, as he often does when he's contemplating something.

He grins. "All will be revealed soon enough."

I shake my head. I see that CW fancies himself forward-thinking, and there's an air of mystery around him. I hope he'll become a regular client, if for no other reason than to satisfy my curiosity about what he's up to. He's correct in his assessment of Edenton: it's not very large or very exciting. At least not for a man like him. As a woman of color, I have plenty enough excitement just going about my daily business.

After the haircut, Sweety begins to brush thick, frothy shaving cream over CW's beard. With the aid of his favorite straight razor, he clears away the fuzz from CW's face to his specifications. When the job is done, CW looks like a totally different man. I've seen the transformative power of grooming in action many times, but I wasn't prepared for CW Rea's unobscured handsomeness. He's quite the looker beneath all that wool.

Eyeing his fresh haircut and neatly groomed mustache in the mirror, CW smiles. "Excellent. You've restored me, Mr. Leary."

"Sweety. Everyone calls me that, especially my valued clients." He uses a small brush to dust the hair from CW's shoulders. "That'll be one dollar and twenty-five cents."

After CW pays his fee, he leaves, tipping his hat to us.

Once the door has shut and CW passes out of view, Octavious speaks. "Do either of you know what he meant with all that talk of 'new horizons'?"

I smile inwardly at my brother's admission of eavesdropping. My brother and I spent countless hours on the plantation with ears open for the information that would keep us safe. How many nights did we listen late at slightly open doors, just to hear a bit of news about the head of household's mood, just to know to make ourselves scarce the next day? To do so now, in a business I own, with a white developer paying my husband to make him presentable, feels impossibly different. And yet, we find ourselves using the same skills we've always used to survive.

Sweety shrugs. "Who knows? White men are often full of bluster. We'll just have to wait and see if he follows through with his grand plans."

I sidle over to him, my eyes narrowing. I don't want him thinking he has gotten away with his little display. "My love, do you intend to hide my co-ownership of this place from everyone who enters, or just the male patrons?"

He frowns, turning up his nose as if I'm wasting his time with something ridiculous. "For heaven's sake, Jo. Why must you be so prickly about this?"

"I'm not being prickly. I'm simply asking to have my role acknowledged. Is that really such an inconvenience?"

He sighs. "Let's not discuss this now, Jo."

"Yes, we are going to discuss this now, Sweety. Because if I leave it to you, it will never be the right moment to discuss this. Let's discuss how I found this building for lease during one of my searches through the advertisements in the *Fisherman and Farmer*. Or how I paid the down payment on this building. Or how my special tonics, which no one else knows how to make, keep the customers coming back to this shop. Let's discuss any of those things, Sweety."

"We came up with the notion of owning a barbershop together, as a team."

"Yes, we did. So why can't you conceive of letting people know that I'm an integral part of this business?"

His eyebrows draw close together, and his shoulders stiffen. "I'll not keep talking about this, Josephine." And before I can say another word, he's gathered up the supplies he used on CW and retreated to the closet.

I glance at Octavious, and we share a knowing look. He's seen Sweety and me have some version of this conversation many times before, and I suppose he's going to keep seeing it.

I turn my mind away from that bleak thought and return to pondering CW's words about Edenton. In many ways, he's right. The town is growing and is ripe for development. As an investor myself, albeit on a much smaller scale than the man with the lofty vision, I can see opportunities on every block.

I return to my station, picking up the small jar of earth I keep there as both a reminder of my capabilities, and motivation for my future endeavors. The land in Elizabeth City was my first property purchase, and I never intended it to be my last. I'm always looking around for my next opportunity to expand my collection of properties; I see more new construction and property listings every time I open one of the regional newspapers, and I read the auction notices and builders' reports so closely that the names of the auctioneers and contractors now feel like familiar friends. Eastern North Carolina is undergoing a boom of property growth, and when the time is right, I'll be joining it.

Now that Mr. CW Rea has made himself known, I see I'll have a bit more competition than I thought. No matter. He's a white man, and he's all but guaranteed to get whatever he wants. Because I'm a woman of color, the odds aren't in my favor, but knowing that won't stop me from trying.

I set the jar down and tidy my station again. For now, my focus is on my clients. But I know that if I keep my eyes and ears open, I'll soon be able to add another jar of earth to my station.

# 3

## JOSEPHINE

### *November 1873*

I awake on a beautiful autumn day, sitting up and shaking off the cob-webs of sleep. I climb out of our bed, where Sweety is still slumber-ing, and go to the window, opening the shutters. The gold and amber leaves shimmer as the sunlight cuts through them, tempting me to lift the sash. I raise the window just a bit and a crisp, cool breeze skitters across the room.

"Whew." Sweety awakens then, propping himself up in bed. "Shut that window, dearest."

I chuckle but do as he asks. Soon enough, we'll all get our fill of the cool fall air. For today, my mother will be married in the grove just beyond St. Paul's Episcopal Church. We are all members there, but Black members like us aren't allowed to use the sanctuary. It is unjust, and unchristian, so far as I'm concerned, but things are what they are. So my mother and her sweetheart will take their vows outdoors, beneath the sight of God.

As I stand by the window, I can't help feeling reflective of all that has taken place in my life this year. I began it as a bride, shortly thereafter becoming a property owner and a businesswoman. And now, as the year comes to an end, I look forward to taking on another role: mother. While I knew Sweety and I would have children, I didn't expect it to happen so soon after we wed. As Grandma Milly often reminds me, the Lord's timing is perfect, whether or not we understand it.

I feel the child inside me move, and my hands fly to my belly. "Sweety, hurry and come. The baby is kicking."

He jumps to his feet and is by my side in a flash, his hands joining mine on my burgeoning stomach. We wait in silence for a few moments before the movement shakes my abdomen again.

Sweety's grin is bright as the morning sun outside our window. "Hot damn. He's a strong one."

I purse my lips. "Yes, *she* is." My grandmother has told me the babe is a girl, and she's not yet been wrong, so I'll stick with her prediction over his.

"Pshaw. I'm going to get dressed." He stifles a yawn as he lumbers away toward the bathing room.

I know I should stop dawdling myself, because there is much to do to prepare for Mama's ceremony.

The morning flies by in a blur of activity. After we've eaten a simple breakfast of bacon and eggs, Mama comes to my house to prepare, while Sweety and Octavious go to the home of Dorsey Stewart, Mama's intended, to get themselves ready.

I hug my mama tight and ask, "Are you ready for today?"

She smiles. "Child, I'm as ready as I'm going to get. Never thought I'd get married." A wistful look comes over her face, and she looks as if she is remembering something in the distant past. "You know, I once loved a man, when I was fifteen. His name was Jeffrey."

"I remember him," Grandma Milly chimes in. "Tall, strapping thing. Worked the fields on the Williams spread."

Mama nods. "I remember sneaking off to the willow grove behind the quarters to see him. He always talked about freedom, about going up North, maybe to Canada. When he held my hand, my heart would beat so loud I just knew folks could hear it in Virginia." She places her hand over her chest. "One night, he ran. Master went looking for him with a posse, and when they returned, they didn't have him." A watery smile creeps over her face. "I hope he made it. I really do. But after that, I closed my heart off to loving any man. Till Dorsey came and opened me up like the sun does a flower bud."

Grandma Milly wraps her arms around us both. "This is a blessed day, indeed. My daughter's marrying a fine, upstanding man of the race, and my granddaughter will soon birth the very first free Williams woman." She sighs, and her eyes sparkle with unshed tears. "My stars, I'm so pleased."

I feel myself smiling and getting a little weepy too. Since I've been with child, I cry at the slightest thing, but this moment is worthy of my tears. Grandma is right; my baby, the baby that Sweety and I created in love, will be born free. There are some who take that birthright for granted. But for us, for our family line, this child will be an answered prayer, a beacon of hope for a future where all will be free.

We share a silent embrace. My grandmother's hand rests gently on my shoulder, a reassuring reminder of her loving presence. My mother's arms wrap around our waists, her hand resting gently on the side of my belly. No words are needed because, in our hearts, the three of us know the joy of this day, and of those to come.

Mama says, "All right, enough sentiment for now. We need to hurry and get ready."

"Jeanette's right." Grandma Milly wipes her eyes with the back of her hand. "It just won't do to have my daughter be late to her own wedding."

We go upstairs and set about the preparations. The three of us are the bridal party; Grandma Milly will give Mama away, while I will stand up for her as her bridesmaid. The seamstress Eunice Fitz had sewn two beautiful gold satin dresses for Grandma and me. Grandma's is a regal creation with a fashionable button-front design and a high neck, while mine has a round neck and Empire waist, allowing room for my belly.

As lovely as our dresses are, though, Eunice has truly outdone herself with Mama's wedding gown. She's transformed the yards of snow-white satin and hand-spun lace into a resplendent garment, complete with a sweetheart neckline and a long train. She's even fashioned a pair of matching gloves, as well as a lace veil.

Grandma and I dress first, then take our time fussing over Mama, to ensure she is properly gussied up for her big day. Standing before the looking glass in my bedroom, Mama regards her reflection for a long moment.

"My word. To see myself dressed so finely . . ." A tear slides down her cheek.

"Careful of your face paint, Mama." I dab her face lightly with a linen handkerchief. "If you cry it all off now, there won't be time to redo it."

She nods, and I can see her blinking furiously as she tries to keep more traitorous tears from falling.

"It's past noon," Grandma announces. "High time we head over to the church."

We head downstairs, carefully carrying Mama's train, our purses, and Mama's bouquet of yellow roses and lamb's ears. Outside, a fancy carriage, complete with a coachman, waits at the curb.

Grandma balks. "What's this? I was going to drive us over in my wagon."

The coachman, dressed in black trousers and a red jacket, announces, "The carriage is compliments of the Stewart family. A wedding gift for the bride."

"Heavens." Mama is obviously impressed. "What a family I'm marrying into."

We all climb aboard and let ourselves be whisked away to the church.

There, the grove has been set up with a few dozen chairs. The seats are filled with neighbors and friends who've come to witness the happy event, and they're all facing the old wooden gazebo. Some of the Stewart cousins were kind enough to give the gazebo a fresh whitewashing and to festoon it with flowers and crepe paper in celebration of the nuptials. Dorsey is there, along with Dorsey's cousin and best man, Talbert, and the Reverend Samuels, who ministers to the colored members of St. Paul's. All the men are smiling.

We're driven right up to the end of the aisle so that our entrance can be as grand as the setting allows, I suppose. As the coachman helps us out of the carriage, I take in the scene. *What a wonderful day.*

Hubert, a talented young man from our congregation, sits beneath a willow tree, playing his violin. The strains of the melody rise on the cool air, adding another layer of magic to the moment.

Sweety waits for me at the top of the aisle, looking very dapper in his dark suit. He extends his arm and smiles in my direction. I take my small purse and the nosegay of yellow roses and link my arm with my husband's. Then we make our slow march toward the gazebo.

Once we arrive next to Reverend Samuels, my grandma escorts my mother toward Dorsey. Sighs and exclamations accompany my mother along the way, but the grove descends into a reverent silence as the reverend begins the ceremony. As their promises of love are made, I find myself brushing away tears. Goodness, pregnancy seems to have made me quite the crybaby. By the time I hear my mama announced as the new Mrs. Dorsey Stewart, I'm sure I've cried a whole river.

We retire deeper into the grove, where trestle tables have been set up for the post-wedding celebration. One is longer than the others, and practically creaking under the weight of the many delicious dishes the guests have prepared for the festivities. My stomach growls loudly as I head for the food. I'm eating for two now, and after a long day, my baby is demanding satisfaction.

Toasts are made, prayers sent up, and I heap my plate with everything the baby is craving. Roast chicken, mashed potatoes, rice, seasoned greens. . . . Sitting next to Sweety with my fork in hand, I'm in heaven.

Sweety chuckles. "Goodness, Jo."

I toss him a glance. "Go on with you, Sweety. The baby is hungry."

He snorts a laugh. "If you say so, dearest."

Dancing follows the meal, and I have a lovely time being twirled around the grove in Sweety's arms. That is, until my feet begin to swell like cantaloupes. My husband leaves me to rest with Grace and Nelda, two of Dorsey's cousins, while he goes off to socialize with the menfolk. I know I should be socializing too, but I'm off gathering wool as soon as my bottom hits the chair.

"What do you think, Josephine?"

"Hmm? About what?" I look into the face of Grace, the young woman who asked the question.

"Some of the colored members are thinking of leaving St. Paul's. You know, forming our own church, where we can worship without the white folks sneering at us."

"Yes," adds Nelda, another young woman of the Stewart clan. "When I marry, I want to be able to use the sanctuary."

I nod, giving my honest answer. "Considering the way we've been treated here, I can understand why you'd want to break away. And I'd be inclined to join you."

They continue on with their conversation, and I return to my own fantasies. Holding my belly, I think about the future. What will my daughter be like? Will she resemble me or her father more? Will she grow up shy and docile, or fiery and courageous? Where will she choose to bow her head or raise her hands in prayer? I suppose some of that is up to me.

My baby will enter this world free, ushering in a new era for our family. I can't change the hearts of those who will treat her badly or think of her as unworthy because of her skin color, nor can they change the fact that my baby will be just as free as they are from the moment she takes her first breath. In my arms, and in our home, she will find respite from a world that is sometimes cruel and unjust. At home, she will be given time and space to explore, to learn, to rest, and to grow, and I will love and protect her with everything in me.

I sigh. I can't wait to meet her.

As if summoned by my thoughts, Grandma Milly appears. She takes a seat beside me, resting her hand on my belly. "She's going to be something special, Josephine. Beautiful. Strong."

"I hope you're right, Grandma."

She smiles, squeezes my hand. "Of course I'm right, dear. The ancestors speak to me. They've spoken to me always, and they've never once steered me wrong."

Grandma winks at me, rises, and disappears back into the tangle of revelers. At sixty-six, she still possesses the same fire that burns in the hearts of girls forty years her junior. She loves our family fiercely, and never tires of showing it. One day I hope to have grandchildren to spoil with love, as Grandma Milly has pampered me.

Octavious dances his way over, grabbing my hand. "Get up, sister, and dance with me. It is a party, after all."

I laugh, doing my best to shoo him away. "Have pity on my poor pregnant self, Tavious. My feet are troubling me."

He shakes his head. "Come now. Exercise is good for you and the baby."

I know my dear baby brother won't allow me any peace until I comply. So I hoist myself out of the chair and let him tug me out into the soft green grass.

# JOSEPHINE

## *February 1874*

I adjust my position a bit, sitting sideways on the settee so that I can elevate my legs. The late-afternoon sunlight shines through the window, giving me light to read by. My calves ache, and are so swollen that they resemble melons. I groan, wishing I could reach my ankle well enough to massage it. Alas, with my round stomach and tired joints, it simply isn't possible.

Trying to ignore the dull throb in my lower extremities, I return my attention to the book on my lap. It's a copy of Walter Barrett's *Old Merchants of New York City*, and it's all about the many giants of industry who are making astronomical sums of money, all while changing the landscape of American manufacturing. I'm amazed by the descriptions of all the new machinery and equipment coming into use now, things meant to make life simpler and more convenient.

But what has really held my attention in this book is the section on the exploits of Mr. A. T. Stewart. I'm already aware of John Jacob Astor, who owns about 30 percent of the available land on the island of Manhattan; I've studied Astor's transactions in order to emulate his style of property acquisition. A. T. Stewart, however, did not start out as a landlord, but as a store owner. His dry-goods stores supply the city of New York with much-needed staples, but it turns out that he is also the second largest landowner in New York, with his portfolio only exceeded by Mr. Astor's.

Reading through the pages, I take mental note of A. T. Stewart's buying habits, the rationale he used to decide which properties to acquire, and the methods he utilized to leverage his properties for profit. I turn the information over in my mind, searching for ways to apply it to my own situation. My goals aren't so lofty; I'm not looking to conquer the world. But I am intent on building a secure future for my child, and that will require just as much savvy.

I yawn and stretch, then close the book and grab my copy of the *Weekly Era*, a newspaper published in Raleigh. I skim the reports of the latest legislative session, noting all the items being taken up by the state government.

Sweety enters through the front door, taking off his apron and slinging it over his broad shoulder. "Hello, Jo."

"Welcome home, dear."

He walks over to me, leaning down so that I can peck him on the cheek. "What are you reading, dearest?"

"This week's copy of the *Era*. I think you should hear this quote from Vice President Wilson that I just came across."

He parks his hips on the edge of the settee, occupying the small space left by my positioning. "Let me hear it, then."

I read aloud from the folded paper in my hand. "'Speaking at a women's suffrage meeting this week, VP Henry Wilson said, 'Twenty years ago, I came to the conclusion that my wife, my mother, and my sisters were as much entitled to the right of suffrage as myself, and I have not changed my mind.' Quite a statement, don't you think?"

Sweety scratches his chin. "I suppose."

I eye him. "You don't have any opinion on suffrage? I mean, if it's good enough for the vice president, why can't other men get on board?"

He shrugs. "I wouldn't begrudge you or Milly or Jeanette voting, dearest. But not all men share my opinion, because not all women are as shrewd as the three of you."

I can feel the frown creasing my face, but I don't want to argue with him. Suffrage will come eventually, despite the narrow-minded opinions of men, and it will come partly because of their tendency to underestimate our gender.

Feeling the twinge in my ankles again, I tap his shoulder. "Could you please massage my lower legs?"

He nods, drawing my legs across his lap. "It seems like they've swollen up so much more over the last few days."

"They have." I can feel my expression relaxing a bit now, as his touch soothes the pain and his words soothe my spirit. "I didn't know you noticed such things."

"Of course I do." He winks, wearing that half smile he defaults to when he thinks he's being clever. "How could I not notice everything about you, with that radiant glow just rolling off you?"

I shake my head but can't help smiling at him. "Go on with you, Sweety Leary."

We lapse into comfortable silence for a moment and I go back to leafing through the newspaper. "Hmm. Looks like there was a ladies' temperance society meeting this past week in Wilmington. It was very well attended, according to this write-up."

"Heavens, not that again," he grouses. "Men work hard. We ought to be allowed a space to smoke cigars, enjoy a bit of fine whiskey, and speak our minds after a long day." He stops massaging my aching feet and reaches into the back pocket of his denims to produce a small glass bottle. "That reminds me, I purchased this well-aged bourbon from Randall Lipsey just today."

I sigh. "Sweety, exactly how much did that bourbon cost?"

"It wasn't cheap, I can tell you that much."

I balk. "You're not serious."

"You must understand how hard it is to come by a bourbon of this quality." He holds the bottle up and shakes it, the dark liquid swirling around inside. "You get what you pay for, dearest."

"Did he at least give you his 'lily white' discount?" I don't bother to hide my annoyance. Sweety's passing is something I don't approve of, but I've come to accept it—most of the time. If he can use it to benefit our family, so be it. But for this sort of thing, I would rather he didn't.

"You know he did," he snaps. "But it was still a pretty penny."

"This sort of thing is precisely why that temperance meeting had so many attendees, Sweety."

His jaw tightens. "Now, Jo, don't start."

"I've been home resting three weeks now, because the swelling in my legs won't allow me to stand at my barber station." I look at him pointedly. "How many heads a week have you been doing without me there?"

He shrugs. "Thirty, or thereabouts."

"When I'm working, we can easily do double that." I clasp my hands together. "So the shop is bringing in less money, and you think now is the proper time to spend our limited funds on expensive liquor? What of the rent? It's due at the end of the week."

"It's only Tuesday. I'll have the funds in time to make the payment Friday." He stands, turning his back to me. "Stop this nagging, Jo."

"I'm not nagging, Sweety. I'm just trying to make you see that this drinking isn't good for you, or for us as a family."

He's already walking away with his bourbon in hand. "Yes, dearest. Your concerns are noted." His terse tone stings like a cut as he disappears into the dining room.

I close my eyes for a moment and take a few steadying breaths. Putting the newspaper aside, I turn to the pile of baby clothes sitting in the half barrel next to me. My mother laundered them for me, since I couldn't stand over the washtub long enough to handle the task myself.

Lifting the first item from the barrel, a tiny muslin sleeping gown, I immediately feel my mood soften. I lay the garment over the swell of my belly, rubbing it in a circular motion. Upstairs, the crib is in place in the nursery, and a stack of folded diapers await. Grandma Milly even knitted a new afghan for the baby.

I let my head fall back against the armrest as a sudden wave of tiredness overtakes me. Shaking it off as best as I can, I fold the sleeping gown, set it on the table, then reach for the next minuscule garment.

# 4

JOSEPHINE

*April 1874*
*Edenton, North Carolina*

Everything is dark, soothing.

I open my eyes slowly. My head is swimming, and I can barely move at all. Every part of me below the waist is beset with a dull but persistent ache.

Raising my head a bit, I take in my surroundings. I'm in my bed. As consciousness rises, so do the memories of this day. I see the large washtub sitting in the room with me, and I remember.

I was in that tub, surrounded by warm water and my mother's loving embrace.

And I brought forth life.

I listen for the sounds of her, and a smile tilts my lips as her fervent cries reach my ears. She's in the house, somewhere. My sweet babe.

I look to the door, and Grandma Milly enters. "Oh, good. You're awake. Our little one is hungry."

She approaches the bed, and I ease up into a sitting position, resting against the pillows piled behind me. Leaning down, she places this little bronze cherub into my arms, and my very heart melts like a block of ice in the sun.

I feel the tears sliding down my face. "She's so beautiful."

"That she is." My grandmother's smile mirrors my own. "You fainted not long after I caught her. We've been looking after her for a few hours, so you could rest yourself."

"Did you give me something? I feel out of sorts."

"A little willow bark tea, to soothe the pain. You don't remember that?"

I shake my head. My memories are fuzzy at best.

She taps her chin with a fingertip. "Hmm. Maybe I let it steep too long."

"Where's Mama?"

"She'll be up in a minute." Grandma leans in, kisses my forehead. "Go on. Feed the babe."

I haven't the foggiest idea what I'm doing, but my daughter is wailing, and I will figure it out. I run my hands over the dark curls crowning her head as I adjust myself so she can nurse. She fumbles about a bit, then latches on, and her wailing finally ceases.

Mama walks in then, smiling. "How are you feeling, Jo?"

"A bit sore, and fuzzy-headed." I look down at the baby, quietly suckling. "Amazed."

"I'm so proud of you, Jo. So, so proud." Mama walks over and sits at the foot of the bed. "I know the pain firsthand; that's why I suggested the washtub. It was hard, but you soldiered through."

"Where's Sweety? Is he here?"

"He's downstairs, having cigars with the boys." Grandma Milly waves her hand. "You know how menfolk carry on at times like this. He did get to see her, though."

"Why didn't he come to see me?"

"I shooed him away," Mama admits. "He's been drinking with Dorsey all day, and besides, you need your rest. Y'all can talk tomorrow once he's sober and you're rested."

"You know, I did say it was going to be a girl." Grandma Milly gives me that I-told-you-so look she's prone to give.

"And I never doubted you for a minute." I glance down at the baby, who's drifting to sleep now.

Grandma claps her hands together. "I made you some zoomkoom; it will help you get your strength back and build up your milk for the baby. I'll bring you some shortly." She slips from the room.

I sigh. "Mama, is she really going to make me drink that thick millet stuff?"

"You can be sure of it, and I advise you to just do as she says. You don't want to get on your grandmother's bad side." Mama winks at me. "I drank it after birthing you and Octavious. I survived it, and so will you."

I can't hold back my groan. The only thing I have an appetite for right now is sleep.

"She knows the old ways, from home. Her mother passed them down to her, and now she's passing them down to you."

When Mama says "home," I know she doesn't mean the old Williams spread. She means our true home, Africa. Ghana, more specifically. Grandma Milly can trace our people back there, through the stories she heard from her mother, Amina.

"We don't know what village we were taken from. But we know we are Tamale." Mama's eyes go from my face to the baby's. "She is a carrier of a proud heritage, Josephine."

As I gaze at my new daughter, the weight of my mother's words settles over me like a sturdy blanket. My child may never lay eyes on the land where our family originated, but she will know from whence she came.

Grandma returns then, with a tumbler in hand. "Here, drink. When you are strong enough, we will take the baby outside for the naming."

I sip from the tumbler, letting the sweet, thick liquid wash down my throat. "What must we do, again?"

"With the willow bark still in your system, you may not remember anything I say. I'll guide you through it as we go along. So just trust me, all right?"

I nod and take another gulp of the syrupy mix. It takes some time, since it is too thick to drink quickly, but I manage to swallow it all. Giving her back the empty tumbler, I say, "I'm ready."

"Good. We'll return when we're properly attired." Grandma and Mama slip from the room, leaving me alone with my new daughter.

I stare at her, watching her sleep. Unable to resist, I bring her close to my face and inhale, letting the sweet scent of her innocence wash over me. She smells like honey and oranges; for a moment, I wonder if that is just how babies smell. Then I realize my elders have probably already bathed her while I rested. I sigh. They've already shown me so much love and support; it strikes me that while I'm a mother now, I will always be a daughter and granddaughter too. I will always need them, and they will always find new ways to care for me. Something tells me I will need them more than ever now that I'm journeying into motherhood.

Grandma and Mama return, wearing long white robes. Necklaces of wooden beads and pearls hang around their necks, and their heads are wrapped in white cloth. To my bleary eyes, they resemble angels.

The two of them help me out of bed. Mama holds the baby while Grandma wraps my hair, then dresses me in a fresh white gown, along with fresh drawers lined with two cloth diapers to catch the flow following the afterbirth. Mama hangs a necklace around my neck that looks similar to what she and Grandma wear, save for the bead pattern.

"What does this all mean?" My curiosity has gotten the better of me.

"The necklaces celebrate our motherhood," Grandma says. "If you look closely, you'll see the blue beads. I have one, you have one, and your mother has two—these denote the number of children we've had."

"I see." I touch my necklace, running my fingertip over the blue bead centering it.

Next, we put the baby in one of the tiny white muslin gowns my mother has held on to since I was a babe, and the three of us take her outside to the backyard.

Night has fallen, shrouding the town in darkness, but the sky is sprinkled with stars. The moon is new, like the babe in my arms, and I can just make out the shadowy outline of its light.

There, I hold the baby and watch while Mama and Grandma go about their work. Mama digs a shallow hole beneath the shade of an old willow, and Grandma places the placenta inside. As they both whisper words I can't quite make out, Mama covers the placenta, using the shovel to smooth over the mound of dark earth.

"Jo, hold her up, so the ancestors may see her." Grandma's gaze is already raised to the sky.

I lift my slumbering child up to the heavens.

"Give thanks to the ancestors. Call out the name you wish to give her." My grandmother's instructions are clear and strong.

I take a deep breath. "Thanks be to the ancestors for this child. I will call her . . . Clara. As the nurse Clara Barton healed the bodies of many a wounded soldier . . . so shall this child heal the wounded hearts of our family line."

"Jeanette," Grandma whispers my mother's name. "The affirmation."

"Gracious ancestors, we ask your blessings of protection and prosperity over the life of Clara Leary." My mama's voice trembles but doesn't waver. "May her life honor your sacrifices and fulfill your wildest dreams."

"Ase." Mama and Grandma speak in unison.

The act of lifting Clara above my head has tired me, so I let my mother take her. "Please help me back to bed. I'm hanging up my fiddle for the day."

"Come, child. You've earned your rest." Grandma's arm encircles my shoulders, and with her help, I return to the warm embrace of my bed.

With the baby tucked into a wicker basket next to the bed, I settle against the pillows.

The door opens, and Sweety enters, bringing with him the scent of cigar smoke. "How are you feeling, my sweet?"

Stifling a yawn, I answer him honestly. "Tired, but happy."

He smiles, approaching the bed. He places a soft kiss on my forehead, then steps back from the bed and begins to undress. "She's sleeping well, I see."

I nod. "Yes. She's been very settled ever since I fed her."

I watch sleepily as Sweety strips down to his union suit, then slides into bed next to me. Draping his arm around my waist, he says, "Darling, our daughter is the most perfect thing I've ever laid eyes on. I know it isn't enough, but I want to thank you for her."

I feel the smile lifting the corners of my mouth. "You're welcome." I cup his face in my hands. "And if you're very good, I may give you another babe."

His brow hitches.

I jab him playfully with my elbow. "Not for at least a year, now. Let me heal, you bounder."

"I promise to be good, and to be patient as well." He chuckles, and leans in to kiss me.

Our lips meet, and I spend several long moments enjoying his embrace and the feel of his tongue mingling with mine.

He pulls away slowly. "Good night, my love."

"Good night, Sweety."

He lies down on his pillow, and in short order, his deep snores are rattling the silence. I shake my head, hoping he doesn't wake the baby with his racket.

I'm fading, and I know I won't be awake much longer, but I must chronicle what I can of this day. I take my journal from my bedside table and set pen to paper.

*Today, I have brought forth life. Right now, little Clara Leary is asleep next to me. I could not have asked for a more perfect gift from my ancestors. The willow bark is starting to wear off, and my lower half feels like it was run over by a speeding buggy. But when I look at her tiny face, I know it was all worth it.*

*I don't know where the journey of motherhood will take me, nor do I know if I'm fully prepared for the adventure ahead. What I do know is that I will love and guide this child to the very best of my ability. I have Sweety, my family, and the blessings of the ancestors to help me, and with all that, I know I can face whatever life throws at me.*

*Holding my child up to the sky, I felt something I've never felt before. Perhaps maternal pride, perhaps the presence of all the mothers in my family line, perhaps a bit of both. Clara was meant to be mine, to continue our legacy. I am ready.*

# SWEETY

### *April 1874*
### *Edenton, North Carolina*

As I ascend the stairs to the bedroom I share with Jo, Dorsey and Octavious wait in the parlor.

Jeanette meets me in the hallway outside the closed door, a blanket-wrapped bundle in her arms. She raises a finger to her lips. "Jo is fine; she's resting, and Mother is watching over her."

I nod, unable to speak as I stare at the blanket. "Is this . . ."

She wears a knowing smile. "Sweety Leary, meet your daughter."

She tugs an end of the blanket, revealing a small, scrunched-up brown face.

I hold out my arms, and my mother-in-law passes the babe to me. I stand there in awe as I bring her tiny, warm body to my chest. Her eyes are closed, but her little lips are parted, and I can hear the soft sound of her cooing as she sleeps.

I take a deep breath. A feeling rises in my chest, unlike anything I've ever felt before. She weighs less than a sack of sugar but far surpasses it in sweetness. In this moment, I know that should it ever be necessary, I would lay down my very life for this child, this tiny representation of the love I feel for Jo.

Jeanette smiles. "She's a beauty, isn't she?"

I say the only words I can form, the words that rise straight from my heart to my lips. "She's perfect."

My mind wanders back, and I can hardly believe how I passed the time waiting for the arrival of my firstborn.

*Sweety walked into Lipsey's Store and Barroom late in the day, letting the doors swing shut behind him. He nodded to the proprietor, Randall, and moved toward a table in the back. The place, on the corner of King and Broad, was just a little way down the road from the barbershop. It was the only place in town where a man could retreat, have a drink and a cigar, and use the kind of plain talk that would offend the female sensibilities. Here, he could drink his fill, put his elbows on the table, and speak his mind . . . things Sweety rarely got to do around the house or even the barbershop.*

*Seated at the table, he helped himself to the fried peanuts sitting there in a bowl. The salty crunch seemed to help break through his worry. He needed this time, this break. For on this day, he would become a father. Never having had one of his own, he didn't know if he'd be any good at it. But since Jo was already laboring, he didn't have too much of a choice other than to buck up and handle his responsibilities.*

*The doors swung open again, and he saw Dorsey, his father-in-law, followed closely by Jo's little brother, Octavious. They headed right for Sweety's table, taking seats on either side of him.*

*"How're you holding up, Sweety?" Dorsey watched him expectantly.*

*"Pretty good, I suppose." He wasn't sure how he was supposed to feel. This would be his first child, the start of his legacy. "I hope for a strong son, but I don't care about that as much as I care that the babe is healthy." Did all fathers feel this strange mix of joy and fear?*

*"You look a little bedraggled," Octavious insisted, grabbing a few peanuts for himself.*

*Sweety cut him a look. "I know that. Considering what's happening, I think I'm entitled to such."*

*The bar girl came over then, in her flouncy red blouse and dark trousers. The girls at Lipsey's served drinks and smiles, but nothing more. "What will you gentlemen have?"*

*"A round of soda punch, and keep them coming," Sweety said. "Put it on my tab, will ya?"*

*From his post behind the bar, Randall cleared his throat loudly.*

*The bar girl gave Sweety a sidelong glance followed by a curt nod.*

*Sweety knew that meant his tab was getting a little long, but if Randall wasn't going to bring it up, neither would he. Besides, he was good for it, Randall knew that.* I'm an upstanding businessman. I'll pay my tab in no time.

*"Just soda and juice for me," Octavious interjected. "No spirits."*

*Sweety shook his head. To his mind, his brother-in-law was well old enough for a strong drink, but the boy still preferred his refreshment without any teeth.* One of these days, I'd like to see him with a brick in his hat, just to see how well he handles his liquor.

*"Three soda punches, one light on its feet. You got it." She sashayed away to fetch their order, and in no time she returned with three tall, filled glasses. "Enjoy, fellas."*

*Sweety took a long draw, letting the cold splash of liquid slide down his throat. It was made just the way he liked it, tonic, fruit juice, and a healthy portion of vodka. He enjoyed the slight burn of the alcohol as it flooded his system.*

*Dorsey set his glass down, having drunk half the contents. "I don't know that I'll ever have any babies. Not sure fathering is in me. But I've seen my fair share of it, being from such a big family."*

*"I'll take any advice I can get." Sweety took another long drink. He wanted to be a good father, though his own father had never acknowledged him. He felt the need to purge his woes, probably brought on by the spirits in his belly. "My mother was a great beauty, highly sought-after. Men paid a high price for her company, and one of those men sired me." He sighed. "Mother raised me on her own after one of her loyal clients died and left her his estate. So I had no suitable example of a father."*

*"The Stewarts are a close-knit bunch," said Dorsey. "Not only did I see my own father with my brothers and me, but I saw my uncles with their broods, as well."*

*"Then why don't you want any? You scared?" Sweety couldn't help asking.*

*"Not a bit. I wasn't born in the forest to be scared of an owl. I just ain't keen on the idea, is all." Dorsey scratched his chin. "But I did watch what went on around me. Seems to me what fathering requires is a lot of patience, a good deal of discipline, and a dose of fun."*

*Octavious chuckled. "I don't know about the patience or discipline, but Sweety can certainly be fun when he wants."*

*Sweety rolled his eyes.*

*"Oh, come now. You've told enough bad jokes around the barbershop for me to know you're full of beans." Octavious leaned back in his chair.*

*"I can't deny it." He knew he could be a bit of a jokester at times. "But I'm patient. I put up with your foolishness." He reached over and gave Octavious a slug in the shoulder.*

*Octavious stuck out his tongue. "Love you too, brother-in-law."*

*"I wonder how Jo is faring." He gazed out the front window of the bar,*

and while the passersby on the street moved through his field of vision, he didn't really see them. Instead, he saw his wife's sweet face. She'd made his life the best and brightest it had ever been and was now engaged in giving him a gift he could never truly repay.

"She'll be fine. Jeanette and Milly are with her, and when we're needed, they'll send someone around to get us." Dorsey drained his glass. "Just remember, women have been birthing babies since forever."

Sweety recognized the wisdom of Dorsey's words. He'd been kept in the dark about childbirth his whole life, but he'd heard the shrieks coming from a laboring room or two. He couldn't even fathom the level of pain involved. I just hope my Jo can withstand the travails of birth.

"Being serious, though, Sweety," Octavious began, "I don't think you have anything to worry about. I think you'll make a fine father to my little niece."

"Nephew," he tossed back.

Octavious merely shook his head. "Grandma Milly ain't ever been wrong yet, so . . ."

He sighed. "Fine. But you're right. I may not be a Philadelphia lawyer, but I'm smart. I've got my own business, a stable home, and enough sense to teach the little one a thing or two about life. What more do I really need?"

"I'd say you're off to a hell of a start, Sweety." Dorsey raised his hand for another round of drinks. When he caught the girl's attention, he called out, "Another round, and three of your finest cigars. We're celebrating."

Their glasses were refilled, and snipped cigars placed in their hands. Dorsey and Sweety lit up, but Octavious hesitated.

"What are you, a schoolmarm? Light the damn thing and take a drag, boy!" Dorsey struck another match and lit the tip of his cigar.

Octavious brought the thing to his mouth and took a single puff. Seconds later, he began hacking so hard, Sweety feared he might spew his lung out on the table. Octavious, at fifteen years old, would be considered a man by most. Sweety could see he still had some growing to do.

*While Octavious recovered from his coughing fit, Sweety slipped off into his own mind.* I wonder how labor is progressing. Will Milly give Jo something to ease the pain? How long will it be before the baby appears? *He'd heard of childbirth dragging on for hours—days, even. He was on pins and needles as it was, he doubted he could wait that long to see his firstborn.*

"It's not uncommon for men of the race to be fatherless. For those born in bondage, they were often sold away from their parents at a young age."

*Dorsey's words were filled with sage confidence that spoke to the years of living he had over the other two men at the table. He was nearly forty and had obviously seen a thing or two in his time.*

*Sweety cocked his brow.* "Men of the race?"

*Dorsey leaned in.* "Sweety, I know most people think you're white. I've seen how you're treated, and how that contrasts with the way I'm treated. But I know better."

*Sweety swallowed, nodded. His dark hair, hazel eyes, and fair skin had allowed him to pass his entire life. He knew many octoroons who did the same; while Jo was not particularly excited about it, she didn't mention it very often, so he assumed she understood.* "I say, why take on the heaviest burdens of this life, if one can easily avoid them?" *He managed his trepidation about passing by simply not acknowledging it. But every now and then, he ran across someone like Dorsey, someone who was shrewd enough to see the truth of his background.*

"Don't worry. I don't necessarily agree, but I do understand. You'd sooner catch a weasel asleep than you'd catch me revealing your business."

"Thank you." *Sweety held his gaze.* "In any case, you've got the most stable family experience among us. So I'll be leaning on you, Dorsey."

*He slapped his shoulder.* "And I'll be there, Sweety."

*The saloon doors swung open, and young Simon, Sweety's ten-year-old neighbor, called out breathlessly,* "Mr. Leary, Mr. Leary! The baby!"

It's time.

*They rose from the table and walked, shoulder to shoulder, out of the bar.*

Bringing my focus back to the present moment, I sigh, holding my babe close to me. There will be less time now for evenings at Lipsey's, but looking into my child's eyes, I know the trade-off will be worth it.

# 5

JOSEPHINE

*June 1874*
*Edenton, North Carolina*

I stick out my bottom lip, blowing a fallen curl out of my face. My hands are too tied up at the moment, sitting in the old rocker in the nursery rocking Clara. She's just over two months old now, and while she's a very sweet baby, she's a handful. Her appetite keeps me at her beck and call; I feel like I'm nursing at every waking moment. Even now, she's just finished a midmorning meal and is drifting off to sleep. Or so I hope. For now, all I can do is rock, hum, and pray she'll close those little eyes and take a nap.

I'm nodding off myself when I hear someone whispering my name. "Hmm?" I open my eyes and see Grandma standing in the doorway. I rise slowly from the chair, moving in silence as I place the baby in her bassinet. Clara yawns placidly as she settles onto the softness of her bed, and I tiptoe out of the room.

Downstairs in the den, I finally release the breath I've been holding. "If she sleeps at least a half hour, I can finally get some things done."

Grandma laughs. "You act as if you're doing it alone. I've taken care of that last pail of dirty diapers. They're hanging on the line to dry."

I sigh. "Thank you, Gran."

"That's why I'm here, child. I know what you're going through. I'm not so old that I can't remember what it's like taking care of a young babe." She sits down on the settee, among a pile of Clara's clean blankets and gowns.

I join her and start to fold; more hands will make lighter work. "Tell me about it, Gran. What was Mama like as a baby?"

A smile stretches her lips, a twinkle coming to her deep brown eyes. "Jeanette was a wailing child. Lord have mercy. Those first few weeks, I paced the floor in the basement many a night, trying to figure out how to get her to hush up." She chuckles. "I probably slept six hours in her first two months."

"Goodness."

"It was quite a time. I was a mess, running back and forth between her cradle and the kitchen. I was working in the big house, but me having her didn't mean I got a lighter workload." Her gaze shifts, and she seems to be looking off in the distance. "I was so tired. Plumb wore out. On top of that, I was always afraid her hollering would wake the master or the mistress one night. Thankfully, the bricks insulated the basement well enough that they couldn't hear her up on the second floor."

"I can't imagine what that must have been like. Sometimes I worry Clara will disturb the neighbors, but at least I don't have to worry about taking a beating simply because she cries."

Grandma nods solemnly. "Then, when she was about ten weeks, the crying spells just . . . stopped. Don't know why, or what changed, and frankly, I didn't care. I just knew my baby was finally settling down, and I thanked the ancestors for the blessing."

"And what about me? Was I fussy too?"

She shakes her head. "Not nearly as much as Jeanette. But you were very insistent about your feeding."

I feel a measure of relief. "I suppose I'll adjust to this new life. In many ways, I already have." Just weeks ago, putting my daughter into her bassinet to sleep would've taken the better part of my concentration. By now we've found our rhythm; she coos and cries and I nurse and swaddle, in a sort of call-and-response that feels more natural with each passing day.

"Don't fret, dear. You'll find your footing." She pats a pile of freshly folded laundry. "Women have been mothering for ages; we're built for it."

I let my grandmother's calming presence wash over me. I hear the truth of her words, and I know she's right. She's always been there when I needed a kind word or a gem of wisdom. Now, as I try to make sense of motherhood, I need her more than ever. Easing nearer to her, I rest my head on her shoulder. "I'm so glad to have you, Gran. So, so glad."

Her arms encircle me. "And I'm glad I've lived long enough to see you as a mother. Seeing my great-granddaughter born, and knowing she will walk in freedom, is the greatest gift I could ever receive." She gives me a soft peck on the cheek.

I enjoy the warmth of her embrace until Clara's wails pierce the quiet. With a knowing smile, she asks, "Do you want me to fetch her?"

I shake my head as I get up from the settee. "No, Gran. I've got her." I go up the stairs and enter the nursery. Lifting Clara's small form into my arms, I bounce her gently. "There, there, my sweet. Mama's here."

Her plaintive cries soften as she nuzzles her face into my shoulder.

I stand in the window, letting the warm sun hit us, and she lets out a small sigh, her body relaxing noticeably in my arms. I look down at her, and she looks back at me with those large amber eyes shimmering with wetness. At this moment, I am aware of all the magical aspects of this child, my child. The slight weight of her in my arms, the smell of innocence and the olive-and-honey hairdressing my mother uses on her curls, the sounds of her small, cooing breaths. She is an angel, a miracle. I love her so much that my chest aches with the weight of it.

Yet, I feel a certain emptiness, a longing. Caring for Clara demands my attention, my patience, and both my physical and emotional fortitude. Still, something is missing. I don't know what it is, as I rarely have time to contemplate such things. At the day's end, when I lie in bed, exhaustion whisks me off to sleep before I can entertain anything more.

With my daughter in my arms, I return downstairs to the settee.

Grandma smiles up at us. "Look at my sweet girls."

Suddenly, realization hits me. "I miss working, Gran. I miss going into the barbershop, I miss chatting with my clients. Does that make me a bad mother?"

She shakes her head as I pass the baby into her arms. "Of course not. When I was mothering, I didn't have a choice. What the master said was what I did, no matter how I felt about it." She kisses Clara's tiny forehead. "But you? You have the choice, and you can earn the funds you need to support your family, rather than simply working so a white man can reap the benefits of your labor."

I nod. I remember what life was like on the plantation, so it isn't hard for me to relate to what Grandma is saying.

"I envy you, child." Grandma sighs, getting a faraway look in her eyes. "You got your freedom while the flower of youth was still upon you." She pauses. "I'm grateful to be free now, but I often wonder what I would have done with my youth, given the choice and the chance."

"Heavens, I hadn't thought of that." The burden of those years lost to bondage must be a heavy one. "I'm sorry, Grandma."

"Nonsense, dear. It isn't your doing." She returns her gaze to my face. "Go on with what you were saying."

I watch her eyes for a moment, to see if she is all right. Since she seems genuinely interested in hearing what I have to say, I continue. "I want to contribute to the family in that way. I know there's value in my raising Clara—she's our legacy. But I want her, and any other children we might have, to have as easy a life as possible."

"Amen to that, dear." She runs her aged fingers through Clara's dark curls. "You do realize that you can contribute without being on your feet in the barbershop all day, don't you?"

I cross the room and grab the copy of the *Chowan Herald* that Sweety left on the sideboard. "You're right. That reminds me to check the property listings." I return to the settee with the paper and a pencil, and once I'm seated, I begin my search.

"What's become of your land down in Elizabeth City?"

I shrug. "Nothing as of yet. I've had a few offers on it, but no one would give me what I considered a fair price." I'd been somewhat frustrated by the negotiations, and especially disliked the way male potential buyers treated me. "All is well with the talks until the buyer discovers that 'J. Leary' is Josephine, not John or Jacob. If I were a man, I doubt I'd have these difficulties."

"I see."

I spend a few minutes circling properties that pique my interest, but in the back of my mind, the gears are still turning. How can I make the plot on Road Street in Elizabeth City work for me?

I actually don't want to sell the land; I've not owned it very long, to begin with. My purpose in purchasing it was to make it a source of ongoing income, not to gain just a one-time chunk from a sale.

Scratching my chin, I stare out the window for a few moments at the passing traffic on Broad Street. Our leased home is just a few blocks up from the barbershop, close enough for Sweety to walk to work. Watching the passing conveyances, I'm struck with an idea. I clap my hands together. "I've got it."

"Do tell." Grandma leans in, while gently patting Clara's back.

"I could lease the land to one of the nearby businesses, or to the town itself, as parking for buggies and such. Put in a few hitching posts. Then take those funds and put them toward the household budget."

Grandma's expression conveys her approval. "I'm impressed. I think it's a wonderful plan."

I'm already on my feet, pacing. "I'll need to set a monthly rate, then go down to the telegraph office and . . ."

Clara, as if sensing that I might leave the house, starts caterwauling again. I return to my seat and take her from Grandma. Unbuttoning my simple white blouse, I let her latch.

Grandma simply shakes her head. "The babe's timing is something, isn't it? It's a good thing, though. You'll need to do a little planning before you make a mad dash for the telegraph office."

I give her a crooked smile. "I suppose you're right."

"Of course I am. I haven't lived this long by being daft, dear." She stands, giving my cheek the same little pinch she's been giving it since I was a tot. "Take heart, Jo. Everything will settle out in good time." Grandma heads off to the kitchen to start lunch, and I settle back against the cushions. Looking down at the baby happily nursing, I sigh.

My grand business plans will have to wait . . . at least for a little while.

Once Clara has nursed herself to sleep, I hand her over to my grandmother and don a clean blouse and skirt. Slipping my feet into my favorite moccasins, I take my purse and head for the telegraph office. Once there, I place a carefully worded advertisement in the *Chowan Herald*, the *Albemarle Register*, and the *Wilmington Morning Star*.

*To let: Land at Road Street and City Avenue, Elizabeth City. Good space for parking of conveyances and hitching of horses. Price negotiable contact J. N. Leary, Edenton.*

With the receipt and a copy of the announcement in hand, I leave the office and return home. Entering the house, I note how quiet it is. No one is in the parlor, the kitchen, or the sitting room, so I make my way upstairs.

I tiptoe to Clara's nursery, finding the door slightly ajar. Taking a peek inside, I see my grandmother seated in the rocker. She's asleep, and Clara is napping in her arms. One of her colorful hand-made afghans covers her lap, and her soft snores barely break the silence. The sweetness of the scene touches my heart; I can imagine Grandma holding both my mother and me this way when we were babies.

Smiling, I back away and retreat downstairs as quietly as I can. In the sitting room, I go to the two-door cabinet sitting against the wall and open one of the doors. Inside is the strongbox I keep my records in, so I slip the receipt and copy of my advertisement text inside, return the box to its place, and close the cabinet again.

I go to the parlor, sit down on the settee, and try to enjoy this rare moment of quiet. Soon enough, I will have to prepare dinner, iron the aprons we wear at the barbershop, and wash the windows. But for now, I am a woman of leisure. Settling back against the cushion, I sigh.

And before I can take another breath, I hear the baby crying, and my grandmother trying to soothe her.

I wait a few moments to see if Grandma can calm her, but in that time, her wails grow even louder.

"Jo?" my grandmother calls.

I can only chuckle as I climb to my feet and head up the stairs.

## SWEETY

The sun is hanging low in the sky. Glancing to the rear of the shop, I see the day's pile of used towels and capes nearly overflowing the laundry pail. The tonic bottles at my station are nearly empty, and the counter-top and mirror are flecked with the day's trimmings. I drag my comb through a tangle on Mr. Rigsby's head, preparing it for trimming, and draw a deep breath. He's a regular, and my last client of the day before I can finally get home to my wife and babe.

"Sweety, I haven't seen your Jo for three haircuts now." Rigsby scratches his chin. "Does that mean she's come to her senses?"

I know what he means, but I would rather sidestep his meddling. "She's doing fine. She's home, taking care of our bouncing baby girl."

Rigsby grins. "Good, as she should. Is the child well?"

I answer truthfully. "She's amazing." Looking into those little brown eyes is nothing short of a miracle by my estimation.

"Wonderful." He sounds pleased. "Knowing Jo, I thought she'd be back by now, working with the baby tied to her hip or some such nonsense." He chuckles because apparently, he's made a joke.

The humor has missed me. "She knows the baby needs her full attention right now." I don't mention that she plans to return soon; I don't see any need to prolong the conversation. I enjoy Mr. Rigsby's company, and I can say the same for most of my clients. But I'm tired. I want to get home. And the longer he talks, the longer I'm delayed gratification.

"It's a good thing you got her with child, Sweety. A woman like Jo? She'd probably never settle down otherwise."

I take my shears to his shaggy ends but say nothing. I'm simply listening to whatever yarn he's about to spin.

"I had one home just like her. My Mabel was determined to work and drive and do all the things men do. Even took to wearing trousers instead of skirts. She somehow got it in her head that she was my equal, that tending to our home was a waste of her time and talent." He shook his head.

"Hold still, Rigsby. I'm trying to even you out." It won't do to have a client leave here with his head looking like a badly trimmed bush, no matter how tired I may be.

"Sorry 'bout that. Anyway, after about a year of being married to her, I come home one day and find a letter. She'd up and left. Took her trunks and just hit the trail. The letter said I was stifling her, and that even though she loved me, she wouldn't live in a gilded cage." He snorts a laugh. "A gilded cage. Can you believe it? Such nonsense."

"Well, I'll be." I'm almost done with his haircut, so I don't add anything more.

"I gave her everything she needed but she couldn't be satisfied." He sighs. "No matter. I have my Dianne, and she's a proper wife and mother through and through."

My curiosity gets the better of me, and I ask, "Whatever became of Mabel?"

He pops his lips. "She's in Indian Territory, writing for a newspaper." He releases a mirthless chuckle. "That's what she wanted. To be a journalist. So I suppose she's happy out there with those savages."

I can hear the bitter edge in his words.

"Enough about her. My Dianne is a gift. She cooks real good, keeps a tidy home, and rears our two sons with love and discipline." He strokes his beard. "Yep. And never has a cross word for me."

Having had a fair number of conversations with Rigsby, it is impossible to believe that no cross word has ever entered Mrs. Rigsby's mind. I stifle a smirk as I wonder what she must think of her husband's pomp and propriety, and what else she might be keeping to herself. Does Dianne have any dreams outside of being Mrs. Rigsby, or mothering? Something tells me Rigsby never wondered this, and never will.

My Jo didn't need prodding; she told me from the beginning about her ambitions. She has always looked to the stars and seen endless possibilities.

"Women can be so ridiculous," Rigsby quips. "And here you are, entertaining Jo's silly notions that she ought to be at work, when she's got a house to tend to." He laughs, seemingly amused by his own cleverness.

My lips tighten. With Jo being home, I can't afford to lose any more customers, so I simply say, "Well, Rigsby, you're all set. That'll be a dollar fifty."

He recovers from his mirth and regards his reflection in the glass for a moment, giving a nod. "You've restored my good looks once again, Sweety." He reaches into his pocket for the money. He takes it out but doesn't immediately pass it to me. "Can I just say one more thing? I think you need to hear it."

Eyeing my money, still in his fist, I acquiesce. "Go ahead."

"I know your Josephine will probably be champing at the bit to come back to this place. But you really ought to try and keep her home. I mean, your progressive thinking is commendable and all, but she ain't never really gonna be happy until she accepts her place. Tending to the home, raising the children. That's what women are meant to do."

I smile as I add the funds to my strongbox. "I appreciate your wise words. You have a good evening, now."

He stands, puts on his brown bowler, and goes out the door, whistling.

I tilt my head toward Octavious, and he bars the door before falling against it. "What a day. I'm beat."

"Me too. Let's get this place cleaned up so we can go home."

Octavious is already headed for the closet. "You don't have to tell me twice."

I begin sweeping up the floor, while Octavious works on cleaning all the implements we used. He passes me, carrying the bucket of Jo's cleaning-liquid mixture, setting it down on my station. The smell of pine oil fills my nose, and it's as though Jo is in the shop with me again. Every inch of this place holds some reminder of her presence, of her contributions to the shop's daily functioning. Gathering up my combs and shears and such, he stops and looks me in the eye. "You aren't buying that bull puckey Rigsby spouted, are you?"

I squint. "I didn't know you paid much attention to what the customers said."

"I do when they are as loud and wrong as Rigsby was." He drops my straight razor into the bucket of solution. "I just need to know you're not buying into any of his foolishness."

I sigh. "Clients often get chatty in the chair, Octavious. In order to maintain my professionalism, I have to let them talk."

He narrows his eyes. "You're dancing around my question."

I try to be a supportive husband to my Jo, I really do. But sometimes she is simply too much. Why can't she do as most women do, and find her happiness tending home and hearth? How can I indulge my love for her without every hardheaded man in town sitting in my chair telling me how to mind my wife? Mostly I just do what I did with Rigsby, just smile and nod and let them talk. But deep down, I'm unsettled. I sigh. "Octavious, I—"

"No. Listen to me. I come from a family of strong, incredible women. I've watched them move mountains since I was a tot. Jo comes from that, and you'd be a fool if you're set on changing her or taming her."

"I wouldn't even try." I love Jo just as she is. I know most men of today think just like Rigsby does, but I like to think I've evolved beyond that.

"See that you don't." He grabs the handle and walks away with the bucket. "My sister is a force of nature, and I won't stand for anyone trying to bridle her."

Alone at my station, I think about Octavious's words. He's not yet seventeen, but he's a man in my eyes. He's got a good head on his shoulders, my brother-in-law. A hard worker, fastidious, responsible, and observant. I respect the fierce desire he has to protect his sister and the way he venerates his mother and grandmother.

Can a woman like Jo ever be happy with a husband and children? Will I be enough for her? Or will she always be reaching, always seeking her fortune and fulfillment elsewhere?

Shaking my head, I push the thoughts away. Standing here pondering isn't going to get this place clean, and my growling stomach and aching feet need to make it home as soon as possible. I lay my shears and combs on a clean towel to dry overnight and take a final look at the quiet shop, assuring everything is in place for the next morning.

When I arrive home with Octavious, we both stop in our tracks as we approach the house, inhaling the delicious aroma coming from the kitchen window.

"Smells like smothered chicken." Octavious rubs his hands together in anticipation.

We head for the backyard, to visit the pump and cleanse our hands of the day's grime. The women won't allow us near the food until we've washed up.

When we enter the house through the back door, I find Jo at the stove, stirring mashed potatoes. I can smell the garlic and pepper she's added to the pot. Our sleeping daughter is bound to her waist with the sling she fashioned from a long piece of muslin. I can see the sweat on her brow from lingering over the heat. I stop, watching her for a moment, amazed by all the ways she makes my life sweeter.

Noticing my attention, she turns my way. A hint of a smile tilts her lips. "Hello, Sweety."

"Dearest." I lean in, kiss her lips. Then I place a soft kiss on the baby's forehead, careful not to awaken her.

"Sit down. I'll bring you each a plate shortly."

Octavious smiles. "You don't have to tell me twice."

"You're such a dunderhead, Octavious." She chuckles.

On the heels of her words, I ask, "Jo . . . I've been thinking. Do you really want to come back to the barbershop? As far as I can see, you've plenty of work here to keep you busy."

Octavious clears his throat.

I hazard a glance his way and find him giving me a hard stare.

Turning from him, I return my attention to Jo.

She looks my way with narrowed eyes and ceases her stirring. "We've spoken about this. I'm absolutely coming back to the barbershop, just as I intend to keep building my property portfolio." She sets the spoon aside and shifts Clara's position on her hips. "I've worked since I was a tot, and it's only recently that me and mine can benefit from my labor. I'm not afraid of hard work, Archer."

"I know you aren't, dearest." I tread softly. I don't want to upset her, nor do I want my brother-in-law after me. Right now, he looks ready to knock me for a cocked hat.

She extracts a letter from the pocket of her skirt and holds it up. "This came in the post today. According to this document, our house is now owned by Mr. CW Rea." She extends it to me.

I cringe as I take it from her. "So Paul Jackson finally sold." Skimming the page, I read for myself and confirm my wife's words.

"Yes, and to the self-proclaimed prospector himself." She shakes her head. "You're going to need me working, because I don't see Mr. Rea being so understanding as Paul was about us being late on rent."

"I can do this, Jo. I can make a good living for this family, without you." Even as I speak the words, I'm unsure. I'm just one man with two hands. But it's my duty to provide for my family, and I don't want to shirk that duty.

Jo stares at me in stony silence. Her eyes narrow, her lips tighten. To me, she looks like a big pot on a burner, about to boil over and toss its lid. "It always comes to this, doesn't it? You rarely say it outright, but I know how you think of me, Archer."

I shift on my feet. "How's that, Jo?"

"You think of me as too big for my skirts. Too ambitious. Not as docile as you'd like. Too much like a man."

I feel the hair stand on the back of my neck. "Now, dearest, I—"

"You think of me as fearless, I bet." There is fire in her eyes now.

"I know *I* do," Octavious says.

I nod and answer her question truthfully. "Yes. I've never known you to cower before anything or anyone."

"I'm not without fear, Archer." She laces her fingers together and makes a motion of wringing her hands.

"What scares you then, dearest?"

"The only thing that truly frightens me is the idea that I might not take full advantage of the gift of freedom. I refuse to let that happen." She turns, crossing the kitchen to fetch a plate from the cupboard.

Octavious folds his arms over his chest, looking quite pleased with his sister's words.

She's made her feelings known, and now she's giving me her back.

I clear my throat, preparing to speak.

She turns to me with a look so venomous, I snap my mouth shut.

Retreating to the table, I sit down, feeling the relief of finally being off my feet.

But knowing that Jo and I are at odds makes the experience far less satisfying than I'd hoped.

Milly enters the room then and joins us at the dinner table. "Evening, Sweety. Evening, Tavious. How was the shop today?"

"Busy. I'm glad to be home."

"He's right," Octavious adds. "We had about twelve heads today. Good tips, though."

"Good, good." Milly shifts a bit in her seat. "Sounds like Jo's return to work can't come soon enough."

I cringe, knowing she must have overheard some of my conversation with Jo. I've really done myself in, and I only have myself to blame. I can tell I better keep my own counsel for a little while, lest I land myself in even more trouble.

Josephine sets down plates in front of me, her brother, and her grandmother, then goes back to get her own plate. The four of us consume her expertly seasoned chicken, potatoes, and sweet peas in relative silence. My wife eats with the baby still attached to her.

When the meal is finished, I get up and gather the dishes. "I'll take care of this, dearest." Washing up the dishes is the least I can do after agitating my bride. I want her home, but I also want to stay in her good graces.

# 6

## JOSEPHINE

### July 1875

I step out of the house Wednesday morning after breakfast and imme-diately feel the heat. This time of year in the Carolinas, the air is so thick with humidity, it's like a heavy cloak. I try not to let the weight of it slow my footsteps too much. Grandma Milly is watching Clara, and I've taken the morning off from the barbershop.

I've worn a light, summer-weight blouse, a blue skirt, and thin but sturdy moccasins. With my hair pulled back in a chignon and my face devoid of paint, aside from a little lip rouge, I know I appear feminine but still professional. Men may wear whatever they please and still be taken seriously, but here I am after hours of consideration, still knowing I'll have to be twice as prepared to earn a fraction of the respect an average man is granted the moment he walks through the door. I'll not stand to be dismissed by anyone today, not when something I want so much is on the line. I tighten my grip on my handbag and quicken my steps.

I pass by the barbershop, and by Eunice Fitz's dress shop a few doors down. Her door is propped open, and I can hear the faint sounds of her foot pedal striking the wooden floor as she works at her sewing machine. Then there is the singing of metal against metal as I pass Herschel Green's blacksmith and tack shop. A breeze blows off the water, bringing with it temporary relief from the humidity, and the smell of ash and steam rising from Herschel's forge.

As I reach King Street, I glance at the shuttered doors of Lipsey's Store and Barroom and shake my head. I'm no temperance zealot, but I still don't see the need for such a place in town. There are plenty of places like it in the larger cities surrounding Chowan County. Many an evening, I've seen men stumbling out of the place, carousing and carrying on in a way that simply isn't proper; I've smelled the whiskey on my husband's breath. The very existence of such a place reminds me how men are given space to act badly and bring embarrassment to themselves, in a way women are not.

I turn left at the meeting of Broad and King Streets, and a few minutes later, I arrive at the courthouse. The stately building is two stories of whitewashed brick, topped by a hexagonal cupola. A large clock occupies the face of the cupola, and glass-paned windows look out on the street below. Three wide stone steps lead up to the double doors at the entrance; the doors are painted red and surrounded by an ornate stonework framing. According to a small plaque in the foundation, it was erected in the 1760s. It's a very fine building, though as a woman of color, I do my best to stay out of it unless absolutely necessary.

A grouping of chairs has been set up on the lawn in front of the grand old building, all of them facing a simple pine podium. Adjacent to the podium is a small table, bearing a basket filled with white wooden bidders' paddles. A few other people are present, one of them being a stout white man in a brown suit. I see him from the right side as he speaks to another man. His thinning white hair is wild, the wind playing through the tendrils, and he has a serious look in his blue eyes. Though I don't know him personally, I have seen him before, and I believe him to be the auctioneer. When he turns, allowing me to see the wooden gavel in his right hand, my suspicions are confirmed.

I've attended a few auctions over the past few months, simply to see my competition for properties in the area. I wanted to know if any of my neighbors are as interested in real estate as I am, and I've found that quite a few of them are. I won't let that deter me, though.

I've observed, I've studied. I am now reading every article and essay I can find about Mr. Thomas E. Davis, Esquire. He is the third largest landowner in New York, behind Mr. Astor and Mr. A. T. Stewart. Mr. Davis also works as a lawyer, but he seems to do that mostly as companion labor to support his property acquisition. I can see how being able to fully understand the complex language used in contracts, and even being able to draw up one's own agreements, could be useful.

I know where the bidding will likely begin for a property like the one being auctioned today, and I know the pain point at which most of the bidders will drop out. That will leave only the wealthier ones, and if I can call their bluff, the building will be mine.

I nod to the strangers I pass, choose my paddle from the basket, then take a seat in the rear of the grouping. I want a good view of everything going on around me, but I don't want to draw attention to myself.

More folks come, filling the seats around me as the auctioneer makes his way to the podium. In a rustle of perfumed silk, a white woman in a fancy blue traveling costume takes the seat next to me. Immediately, she turns my way, her cornflower-blue eyes sweeping over me.

I swallow a sigh. Apparently, I'm not as inconspicuous as I would have liked to be.

The large, flowered hat she wears atop her long blonde ringlets casts a shadow over her pale, porcelain face. Her thin lips are pursed so tight, they've all but disappeared.

Tired of her rather impolite regard, I offer a false smile. "Good morning, miss."

"It's *Missus*, thank you very much." Her tone is as bitter as lemon rind. "*Missus* Jeffrey Anderson, that is."

I ignore the fact that she hasn't returned my greeting, choosing haughtiness over propriety. No matter. My mother raised me better. "Pleased to meet you, *Missus* Anderson." I use the same emphasis as she did.

"And what did you say your name was?" Her eyes narrow, as if she suspects me of something foul.

"I didn't." I don't intend on revealing anything about myself to this rude woman. What purpose would that serve?

"Hmph." She makes no effort to hide her offense. "I remember a time when your kind would be compelled—"

I cut her off. "That time is long past. So could you kindly stop talking?"

Her eyes grow wide. "The nerve!"

I hold her gaze. "Your sensibilities are very tender, I see. Must be difficult living in today's world."

She stands, angrily brushing down her skirts as she storms away. I watch in bemused silence as she stomps around, asking people to switch seats with her. No one budges, and with no other choice, she returns to her seat. This time, she does not acknowledge my presence, and that suits me just fine.

I turn toward the sound of the gavel striking the podium, to signify the start of the auction. "Hear ye, hear ye. I now declare open bidding on the former Cheshire storehouse, located at numbers 421 through 425 South Broad Street here in Edenton. It's a prime piece of property in a fast-growing area often called Cheapside. English bidding is in play, meaning the highest bidder takes the property. Do I hear an opening bid of two hundred dollars?"

Several paddles fly up. I keep mine down until the smaller bidders are weeded out.

"I have two hundred. Who'll raise me?"

"Two fifty." A man holds his paddle up near the front.

"I have two fifty. Who'll give me two seventy-five?"

Two paddles shoot up, one to my left and one to my right. The woman on my right shouts, "Three hundred!"

The auctioneer runs with it, calling out numbers as the bidding heats up. I note that Missus Anderson, who is shooting daggers at me with her eyes while driving up the bid, finally puts her paddle up and calls out, "Six hundred dollars, sir."

I smile. So she does have manners; she just reserves them for those she considers her betters. It gives me great pleasure to raise my paddle and say, "Six fifty."

She narrows her eyes, raising her paddle again. "Seven hundred."

I tilt my head slightly to the right. "Seven fifty."

"Eight hundred," calls a man near the front.

He seems to be the only other bidder who hasn't dropped out.

"Eight hundred fifty," the Anderson woman shouts.

"Nine hundred." My voice is loud enough to be heard, but not a shout.

The man up front shakes his head, indicating he's out.

She stares at me as if her gaze alone will harm me. "Nine hundred fifty."

It's clear to me now that Mrs. Anderson wants to keep me from getting the property far more than she wants it for her own use, and I have a pretty good idea why.

"Looks like it's down to those two ladies in the back. You got a bid, darlin'?" The auctioneer watches me expectantly.

"I do. One thousand dollars."

A smug look comes over Missus Anderson's face as she searches through her handbag. "Ha. I bid precisely one thousand twenty-seven dollars."

I merely smile. "Excellent. Now I bid one thousand thirty dollars." She deflates like damaged bellows.

"Can you beat that?" The auctioneer's question rings out in the silent grove.

All eyes turn toward the two of us. I'm no longer fading into the crowd, but it's of no consequence. I've achieved what I came for.

Her lips retreat into her drawn-up mouth as she raises her chin, shaking her head.

He bangs the gavel. "Sold, to the little lady in the white blouse for one thousand thirty dollars."

Mrs. Anderson stands up, her free hand curled into a fist. "Why, I'd planned to set up my social club for Confederate widows in that building!"

The auctioneer shrugs. "Sorry, darlin'. You've been outbid." He gestures to me. "Come on up and claim the deed, ma'am."

I smile in her direction. I've encountered her type before, at an auction where I observed but placed no bids. She isn't the only one of her ilk, dead set on keeping the properties in this area in the hands of traitorous Rebs, who've held power in the South for far too long. It pleases me that I have become the bee in her bonnet. "Take heart. I may be of a mind to lease the space to you . . . if the terms are agreeable."

"As if I'd ever pay my money to the likes of you!" The outdone Mrs. Jeffrey Anderson storms away, tossing her paddle into the basket before going to the road and climbing into a waiting carriage. As she drives away, I see her last angry glare.

I don't care. I'm incandescent with excitement as I claim my deed from the auctioneer.

Later, with the paperwork signed and recorded, I go to the barbershop to help Sweety with the afternoon clientele. As I tie on my apron, he asks, "Where have you been all morning?"

I look at him in confusion. "I told you I was going to an auction. Remember?"

Running his comb through Mr. Wiley's dark mop of hair, he shakes his head. "Heavens, Jo. You've been to so many over the last little while, I didn't think anything of it."

I wave him off. "No matter. Anyway, look. I want to show you something." I bring over the deed to the Cheshire storehouse and show it to him.

He sets down the comb and takes up the paper, silently reading. I watch his eyes, and before long, I can feel the tension rolling off him like waves on the ocean.

"What is it?"

He begins reading aloud. " 'That the said first part for and in consideration of the premises . . . does by these present sell, grant, and convey unto the said second party and to her heirs forever as her own separate estate free from the rights or control of her husband a certain storehouse and lot —' " He stops mid-sentence and stares at me. "Josephine, what is this?"

"It's a deed. I bought the old Cheshire place down the road."

He closes his eyes, his fingertips grazing his temple. "I know it's a deed. What is this language that's written in, denying me any rights or access to this property you just bought with *our* money?"

I shake my head. How convenient that it is "our money" when *I* make a purchase. He comes home with as many expensive bottles of liquor as he pleases and expects me to hold my tongue. "With *my* money. It's all the money I saved from barbering and from selling the herbs from my garden to Mr. Hammond at the general store."

"We are joined in marriage, Josephine. What's yours is mine, dearest."

I gesture around us. "Then what's yours—this shop—is mine as well. Yet you can't bring yourself to refer to me as co-owner."

He sighs. "You're being childish. All I'm saying is, it's not proper for you to go around proclaiming the money is yours alone."

I rest my fists on my hips. "And why should you have rights to it? Surely you don't think that just because you're my husband, you're owed such."

Mr. Wiley breaks his silence by way of a long, drawn-out whistle.

Sweety bristles. Foisting the papers back into my hand, he picks up his comb again. "I don't have time for this. I'm with a client."

I've no time or desire to coddle my husband's ego, so I take my documents and fold them, placing them in my purse as I return to my station.

Still, I can't help wondering what's gotten into him. He should be proud of the discipline and drive I've shown, yet he seems to be . . . threatened by it? I don't know.

Doesn't he know by now that I love him, that my success is his success? We're partners in life, not competitors. Is it some flaw of the male ego that makes him constantly seek to undermine me, to rise above me instead of working alongside me?

I push the thoughts away, putting my focus on the work ahead.

# JOSEPHINE

## *May 1876*

"Ice cream, Mama!" Clara's impassioned wail is accompanied by her bouncing up and down, the motion rocking my buggy ever so slightly. She has her small fist curled around one of the ears of the stuffed rabbit my mother sewed for her, the poor thing just flopping in time with her.

We've only just arrived at Jackson Farm, but I made the mistake of mentioning ice cream to Grandma Milly before we left the house, so my child knows why we are here.

"Goodness, baby. In a minute!" I reach for her, lift her into my arms, and carefully step down from the driver's seat. Shifting my rambunctious two-year-old onto my hip, I stroke Sugar's mane briefly before tying her to the hitching post one-handed.

I'm halfway up the front steps to the big blue farmhouse when the screen door swings open and Rosa steps outside. She's wearing a yellow blouse and a pair of denims she's trimmed to knee length, and her trusty straw hat. "Hey, Jo!"

I greet my friend with a hug. "Hey, Rosa. How are things on the farm?"

"Can't complain. We planted a mess of strawberries, and we should have quite a crop over the next few weeks."

"Sounds like I'll be making some more strawberry jam, then." Clara wiggles in my arms, but I know better than to set her down just yet. "We'll be outside today, won't we?"

"We sure will, weather's too nice to be cooped up inside." She tweaks Clara's nose. "Isn't that right, little one?"

Clara giggles with delight, then says, "Ice cream, Miss Rosa?"

I shake my head. "As you can see, she's only got one thing on her mind."

Rosa laughs. "I can understand that. After all, we do make the best ice cream this side of Raleigh." She gestures out to the vast yard behind the house. "Let's get on back there to the table."

I follow my friend around the side of the house. There, beneath the shade of a few tall pines, sit a small trestle table and two benches. The old hand-crank ice cream churn rests atop the table, along with a stack of earthenware bowls and a few metal spoons.

"Take a seat," Rosa invites. After I sit down and park Clara on my lap, she says, "I'll be right back." I watch as she jogs over to the smallest of the farm's three barns and disappears inside.

She reappears with what looks like a small pile of fence posts in her arms.

"What's that?"

"It's an old pen we used for the young sheep. Today, it's a baby jail."

I chuckle as I watch her stake the posts, one by one, in the soft grass near the table. Once it's secured, the contraption resembles a small cage without a top. "That's actually pretty smart, Rosa."

She nods. "Of course it is. I learned it from a lady I know who watches little ones. Anyway, we can put her in there after we've had our ice cream, and that way we can talk without worrying that she'll wander off into the wild blue yonder."

It's difficult for me to articulate how good it feels that my friend came up with this to give me a break from the near-constant worry of motherhood. So I simply say, "Thank you."

"Anything for you, friend." She returns to the table, opening the lid of the churn.

I lean closer. "So what kind did you make today?"

"I call it blueberries and cream. I got some vanilla bean from the Hammonds' store this time, and I think it makes a nice combination with those fresh berries and a pinch of cinnamon." She scoops a small amount of the bright purple treat into a bowl and slides it my way, along with a spoon. "Let's let Clara do the taste test."

"Here you go, sweetie." I hand Clara the spoon and scoot the bowl close to her.

Needing no further prompting, she digs into the ice cream. Moments later, she's smiling, with the melted purple liquid running down the side of her mouth. "Yum."

"High praise indeed." Rosa slides me a filled bowl, then makes one for herself.

I spoon up some of her creation. It's cold, sweet, and bright, filling my mouth with a blast of fruit and cream. "Wow, Rosa. It's really good."

"I think so too," she says, offering her agreement around a mouthful of ice cream. "I'm going to keep experimenting, but this is definitely going into my favorites file."

We enjoy the ice cream in companionable silence for a few moments before Rosa asks, "How's life in town?"

I can't help sighing. "Things are mostly good, but . . . I'm a little out of sorts, honestly."

Her brow furrows. "Why? What's going on?"

Clara has finished her ice cream, so I set her and her toy in the grass, safely inside the confines of the baby jail. "Remember how I had to stay out of work while carrying Clara, and her first four months so I could get her settled and all?"

"Yes, I remember."

"Well, we lost a lot of profit at the barbershop during that time, and it's really done a number on our finances." Out of the corner of my eye, I see Clara's upturned bottom as she leans down to pull several strands of grass out of the soil. "We're still rebuilding our savings."

Rosa frowns. "Goodness, Jo. I'm sorry to hear that."

"It's gotten so bad that Octavious has taken to drinking with Sweety now. For so long, he refused to touch alcohol. But since he's had to take on more work and less pay to keep the shop afloat, he's feeling the strain too." I cringe, thinking of my husband and brother, wasting precious hours and funds in that blasted bar.

She shakes her head, her mouth turned down. "You know I'd be happy to lend you some funds, if you need them. It won't be much, but I'll help however I can."

Her kindness lifts my spirits. "Thank you, Rosa. I won't take your money; we've got to work our own way out of this mess. I may need to start a tab for my eggs and milk, though."

"Not a problem. I know you're good for it." She scrapes the last bit of ice cream from her bowl. "Now let me tell you what's been happening out here. Guess who came knocking a couple of days ago?"

"Who?"

"CW Rea, that's who. My papa has already sold him three houses in town, all the property he owned aside from this farm." She gestures around her with her hand. "Now this man comes here, trying to buy five acres of land from us. Can you believe him?"

"Actually, I can." I feel the knot of tension building in my neck. "He's got quite a collection now. He's bought up the tack shop, two houses, and a bit of land up near Hertford."

"Whoa." Rosa's eyes are as big and round as the dinner plates in my china cabinet. "And how do you know about all this?"

"He's in the shop every week, and he never misses an opportunity to brag." I shake my head. "He has what I want: a robust portfolio with a mixture of property types. But his path to get there, as a white man, has been easy. Mine has been fraught with struggle at every turn."

"He may be a white man, true enough. But you know what, Jo? He's no smarter or better than you." She taps her palm on the table. "You've got what, two properties now?"

I nod. "Yes. My lot in Elizabeth City, and the old Cheshire storehouse."

Tugging a loose curl near her temple, she remarks, "Seems to me, if you want to make a splash, you ought to do something big with the storehouse."

"You're right. I've been thinking about it." I turn toward the sound of Clara's laughter, and laugh myself when I see her trying to feed the blades of grass she's pulled up to her stuffed rabbit. "Money is an issue, though. I can't make any moves until we catch up on our expenses." I fold my arms over my chest. "CW isn't my favorite person by any stretch, but he is a reasonable fellow. He's been very understanding, and willing to work with us while we catch up on our rent."

"Well, that's a mark in his favor, at least." She tucks the curl beneath the brim of her hat.

I nod. "I'm back at my station in the barbershop. The extra funds will help with household expenses, and with my plans on expanding my holdings."

"I can't say I understand your ambitions, though I do respect them. I just want a simple life on this land. Maybe a husband; but I've got enough animals that I don't need any children." She looks over at Clara. "Plus I've got you, isn't that right, little one?"

Clara sticks out her tongue, then bursts into peals of laughter.

Rosa shakes her head. "Isn't she something?"

"Yes, she certainly is." I draw a deep breath. "I've got time to figure out how to use the building while I get my finances together. I just hope I make the right decisions. Big building, big potential for failure."

"Oh, horse puckey. You've got a good head on your shoulders, and if anybody can figure out the grandest way to use that old building, it's you." Rosa grasps my hand. "Believe in yourself, as I do, and you'll be just fine."

I squeeze her hand. "Thank you for being you, Rosa Jackson."

"I think I'd be pretty terrible at being anybody else," she quips with an exaggerated wink.

I laugh, grateful once again to have her as a friend.

# 7

## JOSEPHINE

### *December 1877*

"Clara . . . stop running, dear. Let me clean your face." I've been chasing after my child for the better part of a block, moving as quickly as weather conditions and my attire will allow. While I enjoy her youthful exuberance, now just isn't a convenient moment for it.

With a giggle, she stops, spinning to look my way, and waits while I close the short distance between us. My darling little one is the joy of my life, and I try to remember that in moments like this when she vexes me.

I glance at Sweety, who stands next to me with a mirthful grin, and shake my head. "Your daughter is a handful."

"*Our* daughter," he reminds me, adjusting the lapels of his jet-black suit jacket. "Why is she *my* daughter when she's up to nonsense?"

"Because she obviously gets her nonsense from you," I chide. While my grandmother has dressed her in the most precious little blue gown and matching wool cloak, knit stockings, and tiny brogans, her face is smudged with the crimson remnants of the raspberry preserves she pilfered from the pantry before we left home.

Stooping, I take my handkerchief from my purse, wet it with the tip of my tongue, and clear the stain from her cherubic face. Those large, round eyes of hers arrest me, and I smile. I kiss her cheek, detecting the fragrance of the berries lingering there. "You are too much, child. Hold my hand and stay with me, do you hear?"

"Yes, Mama." She reaches up and I wrap her tiny hand inside the safety of my own, keeping her at my side for the rest of the walk. I keep my pace even and slow, so as not to drag her along faster than her short legs can carry her.

There's a heavy chill in the air. My emerald-green satin gown has a matching overcoat, made of velvet and trimmed in black ruffles. Its high neck and long sleeves protect my skin from the cold. A small green hat, festooned with ivy leaves and red feathers, is more for looks than for warmth. My hair is wrapped in a tight chignon beneath the hat.

The frozen ground crunches beneath our boots as we make our way to the evening's festivities. Our destination is so close, it would have been too much trouble to drive the carriage over.

We're to attend the annual holiday party at the home of Hannibal and Evelina Badham. Hannibal, one of the most prominent architects in the region, has achieved things many Negro men could only dream of, not the least of which is his stately home on East Gale Street. He and his wife are both regular patrons at the barbershop.

I smooth a gloved hand over my skirts once more as Sweety and I walk up the cobbled path to the Badhams' front porch. We're greeted by the houseman, who takes our outerwear and my purse before escorting us into the front parlor.

I can't help wishing Rosa were here, but she despises gowns. I suppose it is just as well, since this crowd is full of business owners and investors; farmers were not invited. Growing my businesses sometimes means walking in two worlds: one filled with propriety and parties, the other with hard work and humility. It is a delicate line to tread.

"Presenting Mr. and Mrs. Sweety Leary and young Miss Clara." With a bow and a flourish, the houseman is gone.

A smattering of applause greets our entrance, and I curtsy, feeling my cheeks warm. I'm not one for such displays, but I know well enough that participation in such social events has numerous financial benefits. I am barely upright again before our gracious hostess appears, a bright smile upon her face. Evelina is resplendent in a custom gown the color of spun gold. Its shoulder-baring sweetheart bodice isn't the best for cold weather, but I can't deny its stylishness. A small headpiece, fashioned of feathers, netting, and a few sprigs of spruce, sits atop her pinned-up curls. "Sweety! Jo! So glad you could join us tonight."

I notice the way Sweety's eyes dip to her cleavage, just for a moment, as he responds, "Thank you for such a warm welcome, Evelina."

With a laugh, Evelina kisses my cheeks before stooping to speak to my daughter. She squats, getting at her eye level. "Clara, look how big you've gotten. You'll soon be working at the shop with Mommy and Daddy, won't you, love?"

Clara giggles and nods. "Hello, Ms. Lina." She lifts the hem of her skirt, making an attempt at a curtsy, but mostly just exposing the bottom of her pantaloons. "You look pretty."

"Thank you, love." Rewarding her cuteness with a small hug while surreptitiously righting her dress, Evelina releases my little one before standing again. "Come, you must say hello to Hannibal. He's around here somewhere."

While we wade through the thick crowd of revelers, I hold tight to Clara's hand, so she won't wander off. I take in the elegant beauty of the Badham home. Brocade wallpaper covers the walls, and many imported rugs protect the polished oak floors. There are rich mahogany furnishings, upholstered in shimmering rose-hued fabrics; vases and china plates on display; gilded mirrors; and crystal chandeliers hanging overhead.

Evelina stops near a young woman holding a blanket-wrapped bundle in her arms. "Come, look at our babe."

I peer at the small brown face, the only thing visible inside the mound of blue fabric, and I can't help smiling. "He's beautiful. What's his name again?"

"Miles. Little Miles Badham." Evelina's eyes sparkle with adoration for her son. "He's a perfect angel, isn't he, Betsy?"

The young woman, likely the family nanny, nods. "Yes, miss. He's no trouble at all."

I can't help thinking how many changes will have to be made once young Miles is old enough to get around on his own. It's a lovely home, just not very practical for small children.

Hannibal, looking stylish in a dark blue cutaway suit, appears behind his wife, placing a hand on her shoulder. "There you are, dearest."

"Oh, heavens. I've been looking for you, Hannibal. You remember the Learys."

"Why, it's been so long since I've been able to get away for a shave and a haircut, it's a wonder I haven't forgotten them," Hannibal teases in his deep, booming voice. "Welcome to my home, you two." He stoops low. "And welcome to you as well, little Miss Clara."

Hiding behind my skirts, Clara offers a soft hello. I can see she's intimidated by his deep voice and tall stature.

We talk a few moments more with the Badhams, before they are off to attend to their other guests, as good hosts do. Sweety and I decide to work the room; after all, most of the prominent Negro citizens of Edenton and the surrounding hamlets are present. We take time to speak with the undertaker and cabinetmaker, Louis Ziegler.

"Haven't seen you in a while, Louis," Sweety says, giving him a friendly slap about the shoulder. "How've you been?"

Louis chuckles. "Can't complain, Sweety. Business is booming, and fortunately, it's on the cabinet-building side of things."

"Thank the heavens," I respond.

"Yes, yes. Lots of new people moving into the county means a lot of work for me. Folks have been coming in left and right to outfit their new homes with my hand-built cabinets." Louis tugs at his suspenders. "They'll get many years of good use from them, to be sure."

"Come now, Louis," I tease. "You don't have to tell us; we know your quality work firsthand."

"Oh, pshaw." Louis looks rather pleased with himself. "You flatter me, Miss Jo."

After speaking with Louis, we make small talk with two of the Badhams' out-of-town guests, a chef, and a florist we've never met before. Then there are our old friends, baker Vernon Fitz, and his wife, dressmaker Eunice Fitz. As we pass by the haberdasher Curtis Brooks, Sweety calls, "Hey, Curtis, I'll be there first of next week for a new hat or two."

"Come on by," Curtis calls back with a wave. "I've got a shipment coming in soon."

While we weave through the house, I even spot a glimpse of our landlord, CW Rea, the "property prospector," holding court in the Badhams' dining room. He stands out as one of the few white men present.

Sweety and I eventually separate in the tangle of people, and after letting Clara play with some of the other young children under the maid's watchful eye, I find my way back to CW. Thankfully, the crowd around him has thinned, and I can approach him easily.

"Good evening, Mrs. Leary." He bows dramatically.

"Nice to see you, CW." I offer a small curtsy. "I'd like to speak with you about the house, if I may."

He chuckles. "Oh, Mrs. Leary. I admire your gumption, but I do hate to talk business at a social gathering, you know."

I nod, keeping my expression neutral to hide my disappointment. "I see. We can always speak another time." CW drains the amber liquid in his glass, gives me a quick nod in farewell, and heads to a tight cluster of men engaged in a lively conversation. Their circle opens to welcome him instantly, and I wonder whether he would entertain *their* business talk. Somehow, I imagine he would.

By the time ten o'clock arrives, I'm exhausted. A whole night of being social, eating and drinking, and looking after Clara in a crowd has worn me down. Besides that, Clara is beginning to fade like a wilting flower, and if her drooping eyes are any indication, she won't be upright much longer. Gathering her into my arms, I take her and search for Sweety.

I find him in the backyard, pitching horseshoes and tall tales with some of the other men. Their laughter floats in the air, echoing off the trees. I carry Clara over to him and tap his shoulder. "Are you about done, my love? We're both exhausted."

He pecks my cheek. "Of course, dear." Bidding a reluctant goodbye to his companions, he takes our sleeping daughter from my arms. Draping her over his shoulder, he extends his free hand to me. I grasp his hand, and after we retrieve our winter gear from the houseman, we make our way home.

A deeper cold has settled, and the half-moon is high in the darkened sky. Over the fading sounds of the party, and Clara's soft, tiny snores, I ask, "What were you men talking about, anyway?"

"Oh, this and that. Man talk."

I tilt my head and purse my lips.

He chuckles. "Is something on your mind, Jo?"

"I'm thinking about purchasing another property, and I wanted to get your opinion on it."

He nods his head. "Yes, yes. If you're thinking we should purchase the barbershop, I'd say you're absolutely right."

I crinkle my face into a frown. Hasn't he thought about this, even once? "No, Sweety. I'm talking about the house."

"Our house?"

I nod. "Yes. We ought to purchase it from CW."

Now Sweety's the one frowning. "I don't know. I think we ought to put our coins into the business."

Convenient he would say that about the business, for which he gets the most glory. "I agree that we should invest in the barbershop, by all means. But why not purchase our home first?"

"The house isn't going anywhere, Jo. Meanwhile, the success of the barbershop is going to depend on what we put into it."

"That's true enough." There's logic to his point, and I won't deny that.

"Then it's settled."

I sigh. "No, it isn't."

He frowns. "Jo, why are you making this such a crusade? Must you contradict me at every turn?"

"You know that isn't what this is about."

"Isn't it?" His tone is accusatory.

I draw a deep breath. "Just listen to what I'm saying. We plan to live there for the foreseeable future, and the funds we pay in rent could be redirected, at least partially, if we purchase it."

Sweety looks thoughtful, scratches his chin. "Is this about CW? I thought you liked him?"

"I do, honey. But this isn't about that. Do you remember what it was like to be enslaved? To have your free will stripped from you? To have a boot on your neck every waking moment. To have your every move determined by the whims of a white man?"

"Of course." His eyes grow dark with unspoken memories. "I'll never forget it."

"Then you should understand why I want us to own our home, Sweety. I vowed, from the day I was freed, never to live at the whim of another white man. If the home is ours, no one can remove us. Do you understand now?"

He is silent for a few long moments as we approach our home. The windows are dark, save for a lantern glowing in my grandmother's bedroom.

We both stand in silence, watching the soft flicker in the upper window as the cold wind swirls around us, bringing with it the sound of the crackling branches, laden with ice.

He clears his throat. "You may be onto something. Maybe we should start saving to purchase the house."

I smile and lean up to kiss him. "Thank you, Sweety. That's all I ask." Hand in hand, we go inside and shed our cloaks. After we carefully tuck Clara into her bed and tiptoe out of her room, Sweety retires.

I stop by my grandmother's room. "Are you waiting up for us?"

In her nightgown and spectacles, she sits by the window in her old rocker. She looks up from the open book in her lap and yawns. "Yes, child. Old habit, I suppose. Been doing it ever since Jeanette was old enough to go out on her own."

I smile, walking over to peck her on the cheek. "Well, we're home now, so you can go on to bed."

"I will, once you tell me what's troubling you."

I'm confused for a moment, then I shake my head. "You've always been able to detect my moods. How do you do that?"

She shrugs her thin shoulders. "Call it a gift. Now, what's the matter?"

I recount my conversation with Sweety. "I love him so much. But so often, he just doesn't seem to see my point of view on things."

Grandma smiles. "That isn't as uncommon between husbands and wives as you might think, Josephine. I've never been married, but I've seen my fair share of marriages play out."

I sigh. "Somehow, knowing that doesn't make me feel any better."

"All you can do is love him, encourage him, and take this journey with him, day by day." She touches my shoulder. "Just promise me this, child. Promise me you'll never let him rule you. We Williams women were not made to be ruled."

"I promise." I give her another kiss on the cheek. "Now, will you go to sleep?"

"Not a bad idea. These old bones could use the rest."

She moves from the rocker to her bed, and I pull the covers up over her. "I love you, Gran."

"I love you too, child. See you in the morning."

I leave her, softly closing the door on my way out. As I make my way to my bedroom, I realize I am, once again, the last person stirring in the house. Covering a yawn, I shake my head. The work of a wife, mother, and magnate-in-the-making is never done.

When all the lanterns in the house are out, and the pump handle high enough to prevent it from freezing, I finally seek the warmth of my bed.

# JOSEPHINE

### *August 1879*

I roll onto my left side in my bed, seeking a comfortable position. Blowing out a breath, I settle into the feather mattress as deeply as my burgeoning belly will allow. My hand rests on the swell and I sigh. Another babe will soon join the family, probably after the New Year. Will this be the strong, handsome son Sweety has longed for? Or will it be another daughter, as curious and lovely as our Clara?

Grandma Milly says she knows the babe's gender, but she's chosen to keep it to herself this time. We will simply have to wait until the child arrives.

I close my eyes against what little sunlight has penetrated the heavy drapes at our window. I know I must get up, for there are important tasks to attend to today. Yet I'm finding it difficult to leave my bed. Between the stomach-roiling sickness and the general exhaustion of carrying the babe, I'm plumb worn-out, even though the day hasn't started yet.

"Good morning, Jo."

I turn toward the sound and see Sweety entering our room, with a tray in hand. He sets the tray on the bed in front of me, and I smile at the sight of the warm oatmeal and dry toast, about the only things I can eat without my stomach rejecting it. A tumbler of cool water accompanies the food. "Thank you, dearest."

"You're welcome. Now eat up. You and the babe need nourishment."

He hooks his hands beneath my arms and helps me into a sitting position.

"I'll be back in a bit to take the tray, all right?"

I nod.

He pecks me on the forehead before leaving the room.

I dig into my breakfast, taking small bites so I don't overwhelm my sensitive system.

After finishing my meal, I reach for the small table at my bedside. There, Sweety has stacked the three newspapers we read. He insists on staying apprised of all the goings-on in the state, and I'm of a similar mind. One of the papers, the *Tarborough Southerner*, mentions a social gathering here in town that I'd forgotten about, and I'm grateful for the reminder. The Chowan County Agricultural and Mechanical Society is hosting its first annual county fair. The festivities will continue for three nights, and upon checking the dates in the piece, I see it started yesterday. I know Clara will enjoy such a gathering, and I make a mental note of it.

After getting up from bed, I dress in a simple blouse and skirt, forgoing the corset. It's been weeks since I could wear one, and I don't miss the god-awful contraption in the least.

I can hear Sweety moving around downstairs. He's taken the day off from the barbershop, in light of the important task we must complete. I'm certain Octavious can handle things in our absence; midweek is usually not very busy.

Once I'm dressed, I head to Clara's room. I find our five-year-old sitting on the bed, still in her thin cotton nightgown. Clutching the little doll Grandma Milly sewed for her, she busies herself fussing over its strands of black yarn hair.

Clara smiles in my direction as I enter. "Mornin', Mama."

I kiss her forehead. "Good morning, sweet. Come now, let's get dressed. Granny Jeanette is expecting you."

She looks confused. "I don't stay home today?"

"No, darling. Grandma Milly needs a day of rest. So it's off to Granny Jeanette for you."

I spend the next few minutes helping my giggling, wiggling child into a simple muslin dress and old brogans, suitable for play. I know she'll be dirt-streaked and sweaty by the time I pick her up, and it will be no loss. I only hope my mother will let her exhaust herself enough to take a nap later.

I meet Sweety at the foot of the stairs. He's donned one of his best suits. The rich sable brown contrasts his blue vest nicely, and his dark curls are combed back to reveal the strong lines of his handsome face. I stroke his jaw and kiss him. "Look at you. As handsome as the day we wed."

He winks. "You flatter me, dearest."

Sweety and I walk Clara to my mother's home, hand in hand.

"Did you see that mention of the latest issue of the *North American Review*, in the *Wilmington Morning Star*?"

He nods. "I did. And I suppose you want to order a copy?"

"Absolutely. Harriet Beecher Stowe has written an impressive paper on the education of freedmen in this issue. I think we might find it illuminating."

He scratches his chin, glances down at Clara. "Yes, I suppose so; we want our children to be well educated."

"I agree."

We arrive at my mother's home, where we find her sitting on the porch in a knotty pine rocker. She waves as we approach, then opens her arms, allowing Clara to barrel into her embrace. We follow her onto the porch, at a much more reasonable speed.

My mother catches Clara and lifts her into her arms. "Goodness, child. So much energy!"

Clara's laughter echoes around the yard. "Let's play, Granny!"

My mother laughs. "My grandchild. She's something else."

I wink. "You're telling me." Clara's exuberance is both endearing and exhausting, but my love for my daughter is as wide and as brilliant as the night sky.

"Morning, Jeanette," Sweety calls. "Dorsey's off to work, I suppose?"

She nods. "Yep. He and his crew are building a fancy home on the outskirts of town. They hope to have it finished before the frost."

"We'll be back for her in a couple of hours, Mother." I give her a peck on the cheek. "Thank you for looking after her."

"It's nothing. Besides, Mama is past seventy. Though she's hard-pressed to admit it, she needs her rest now and again."

I smile, knowing exactly what she means. These days it seems my grandmother is made up of equal parts wisdom and obstinance, though at her age, I suppose she's earned it.

We say our goodbyes and get underway again. One of the things I love about Edenton is the way it's laid out. Most of the things we need are right within walking distance of our house. The carriage in our backyard is only used for longer trips out of town, to pick up food and supplies, or for ferrying my grandmother to her quilting-circle meetings.

We arrive at the office of our landlord, CW Rea, on Water Street. The outside facade is whitewashed brick with black trim, giving an air of elegance. Inside, the chintz settee and carved mahogany table continue the trend. His secretary, a slight woman wearing wire-rimmed spectacles and a dun-brown day dress, directs us to the settee to await CW's summons.

"He certainly wants people to know he's well-off," Sweety remarks under his breath, pointing to the wall facing us. A gold-framed oil painting of fruit on the wall, flanked by two intricate brass sconces, indicates both good taste and wealth.

"Seems that way." We've never been to the office before, because CW was kind enough to bring the rental contract for our house to the barbershop during his regular trim and shave. Today's business, however, seemed to warrant a visit.

"How do you think he'll react?" Sweety asks, scratching his chin.

"I don't know. Hopefully he'll say yes." I can't imagine how disappointed I will be if he isn't amenable to our offer. We worked so hard to get to this point.

Soon, the man himself appears in the corridor near the reception desk. He's wearing a dark suit, the vest festooned with fancy contrast border stitching. His blue eyes twinkle with merriment. "Top of the day to you, Learys. Please come to my office. Let's chat."

The inner office is mostly taken up by a large carved oak desk and a big leather chair. Several smaller works of art dot the walls, and gold brocade drapes are open to reveal the lone window behind the desk.

Once we are seated in the smaller chairs across from CW's big one, he folds his hands together atop the desk's surface. "What brings you in today?"

Sweety clears his throat. "Well, we were . . . thinking maybe, I mean . . . if you'd be amenable—"

I interject. "We'd like to buy the house from you."

CW's eyes widen. "Really? What brought this on?"

I clear my throat.

Sweety looks at me, silent pleading in his eyes because he thinks he knows what I'm about to say.

"To be frank, CW, it's always been my intention to purchase the house. It's simply a good investment for us to own our family home."

Sweety's sigh of relief is audible.

I shake my head. He really thought I would be as plainspoken with CW as I was with him, and I haven't a clue why. I'm a businesswoman, and I know deals are made with a mixture of honesty and flattery. It's in my best interest to know when and how to soften my words and tone, especially when dealing with men. They rarely have any tolerance for women who are obviously smarter than them.

"I see." CW rubs his hands together. "I usually hold on to my properties so I can count on the rental income. But I'm willing to hear your offer."

Sweety speaks up then. "We can offer you three hundred dollars."

CW scoffs, not bothering to hide his amusement. "Heavens. That's an insult for such a fine home."

My husband balks.

I take over the negotiation then, since Sweety doesn't really have the stomach for it. "Four hundred."

CW rolls his eyes.

"Honestly, Josephine. I'm certain you didn't come all the way here to play games."

"I didn't."

"Seven hundred." CW tents his fingers as if he thinks he's gotten the better of me.

"Six hundred, and not a dollar more." I lean forward in my chair and mimic his posture and position.

He stares as me in silence for a long moment.

I don't flinch.

Finally, a smile cracks his lips. "You weren't born in the woods to be scared by an owl, I see."

"Not at all."

He sticks out his hand. "Six hundred it is, then."

We shake hands and just like that, the deal is done. Sweety looks on in amazement as I pull out the bank draft and write it out for the agreed amount. It's fifty dollars less than what we've set aside for the purchase, so I'm satisfied I've made a good deal.

"You know, this infusion of funds is a boon to me, in a way." CW lays a sheaf of paper on the desk and lifts his fountain pen from the well. He chats easily while he writes. "I've a new investment project I'm working on, one that will bring some much-needed culture to Edenton."

Curiosity gets the better of me, so I ask, "What's your project? If you don't mind saying."

"Not at all. It's rather exciting." He pauses in his writing and looks at me with a rapturous expression. "I'm going to open the county's very first opera house, right here in town."

Sweety's brow lifts. "An opera house? Do we even have the population to support a place like that?"

"I believe we do, especially since people will come from miles around to experience my top-notch entertainment." He starts writing again. "Anyway, I don't want to reveal too much."

"I can understand that." I'm pleased when he doesn't say any more and devotes his full focus to completing the contract.

Outside, Sweety holds my hand within his own as we walk toward the waterfront. "Jo, you are quite the pistol. I don't think ol' Mr. Rea was ready for you."

"What man has ever been ready for me?" I wink, laughing at my own cleverness.

We sit down at Smith's Dockside Café for a celebratory lunch. Sitting outdoors near the water's edge, I'm reminded of the meal we had on our honeymoon all those years ago. I'm happy we made our home close to the water, where I can get fresh seafood whenever my heart desires.

"How is that catfish?" Sweety eyes my plate.

"It's good." And it is: crisply fried and accompanied by corn fritters and hearty chunks of fried potato. "You can try a little bit if you like."

I watch as he takes a forkful. "That is good."

"Now in exchange, I'll have a bit of your shrimp." I use my fork to spear one before he can protest, and pop it into my mouth. "Delightful."

His brow furrows as he feigns annoyance.

I merely grin. We have always carried on in this playful way and I hope we always will.

After lunch, we return to my mother's to retrieve Clara. Her day of play with her grandmother has left her just as messy as I predicted. When she hugs my mother tightly at our departure, it warms my heart to see how close they are.

Sweety walks us home and departs for the barbershop. Clara and I work on the laundry, and I toss her mud-streaked dress into the wash-tub with the rest. "Clara, what did you and Granny do today?"

"I helped in the garden, and we made mud pies." Clara's broad grin reveals the fun she's had.

I laugh. "That explains plenty."

While I listen to her chatter on about the finer points of mud-pie making, I smile, thinking of what I've done today. I've ensured that my daughter will always have a home. She won't have to worry over where she'll lay her head at night; no, she can go right on chasing rab-bits, braiding her doll's hair, and making prize-winning mud pies with her grandmother.

It has taken so much work to get here, so much sacrifice to set aside the funds to buy the house.

And knowing I have given my child the freedom to dream makes it all worthwhile.

# 8

## JOSEPHINE

*February 1880*

"You can do this, Jo."

Through the searing pain, I hear my mother's voice, encouraging me to go on. "I can't."

"You have to, dearest. The babe is almost here."

A cool cloth is pressed to my brow, soothing the fire there. But there is no remedy for the hot, slicing pain in my lower half.

Grandma Milly coos in my ear. "Come now, honey. One more big push and it will be over."

Heaven knows I need this to be over. While it is not as intense as my laboring was with Clara, I suspect that is due to knowing what to expect, rather than it being less physically taxing. Whatever the case, I have grown weary of this.

So I gather what little strength I have left, and push. The pain intensifies for a moment before it finally, mercifully subsides. I feel the pressure lifted from me and I weep.

Fierce cries fill the room, along with the joyous exclamations of my mother and grandmother. I weep even more from relief. My child's cries indicate its general health, and for that I am grateful.

I close my eyes against the tears now streaming down my face. I let them come, let them cleanse me of the strong emotions I feel.

I hear the door swing open, and Sweety's booming voice. "I heard crying. Where is the baby?"

"Right here," my mother says. "It's a girl."

I smile. Sweety may have been denied his male heir, but we've been blessed with another daughter. I imagine Clara will be very excited to have a baby sister.

A few moments pass in silence, and I open my eyes, turning my head. I see Sweety holding the baby, with my mother and grandmother looking on. The expression of wonder and love in his eyes as he looks at our newborn child touches my heart.

Soon he walks over with her. "Here, little one. Meet your mama."

Tears spring anew as her tiny, swaddled form is placed in my arms. "Hello, beautiful."

Her large brown eyes gaze at me, and she seems settled immediately. She's not crying or fussing; she's simply observing. "What do you think of her, Grandma?"

Grandma Milly's smile is serene. "This child will grow up to be very special. She'll possess amazing courage and fortitude and will carry this family's name to places we can't even imagine."

My mother nods. "Yes. The ancestors have smiled on this one."

I cuddle her close to me and ease her to my breast to nurse. "I have a name in mind for her. What do you think of Florence?"

Sweety grins. "After my favorite aunt?"

I nod. "Yes. I've always liked the name. Do you approve?"

"You know I do." He leans down, placing a soft kiss on my damp brow. "Thank you, Jo. Thank you for Clara, and for Florence."

"You're welcome." I can hear the tiredness in my own voice. "Enjoy them, because I don't plan to give you any more."

Sweety balks. "Now, dearest, I'm sure you don't mean that."

My mother claps her hands. "It's the pain talking, most likely. I'm going to make her some willow bark tea." She disappears from the room.

I sigh. My mother is partly right, because this pain has taken on a life of its own. However, I meant what I said. I've lived through the horrid ordeal of birth two times, and I have no desire to do it again. Besides, with everything I hope to accomplish, I don't think having more babies is practical.

Alas, I know better than to reiterate what I said to my husband. He will want to debate, and I simply haven't the strength right now.

When I feel sufficiently drained, I switch the babe to the other side.

My mother returns with the cooled tea, and I take it gratefully. The first sip of the bitter brew is like strong liquor, but I swallow it without hesitation. I know the effectiveness of the old remedy. Not only will my pain be dulled, but I'll be asleep in short order.

Grandma Milly speaks. "Come now, everybody. Let's leave them to recuperate—they've whipped their weight in wildcats today." After shooing Sweety out, she and my mother set about scrubbing and sweeping and setting the room right again, before leaving me to my rest.

Alone in the room with my new daughter, I down the rest of the tea and set the cup on the nightstand. Then I scoot myself lower in bed so I can lie down. Florence is done feeding now, and her eyes are already closed. A full belly makes for a sleepy babe, and labor a sleepy mother. Within moments of lying down with Florence in my arms, everything fades to black.

I awaken sometime later to a small voice. "Mommy, are you sleeping?"

A smile tips my lips as I look down at Clara, standing at my bedside. Her hair is in disarray, having come loose from the braids I put in it a few days ago. Her eyes are large as she stares at the babe in my arms.

"I'm awake, sweetheart."

"Can . . . I hold baby sister? Please?"

Just then, the door swings open and a harried-looking Missouri runs in. The only daughter of the Armstrong family from Gates County, she's precisely one year younger than my brother. Dressed in a white blouse and dark skirt, she's breathing like she's been chasing the wind. Her words tumble out in a rush. "Oh, heavens. I'm sorry, Jo. I told Clara you needed your rest but she's so excited about the baby and she got away from me."

I stifle a giggle. She's a bit high-strung, but in an endearing way. "Missouri, I know it hasn't been long since you and Octavious married. But I'd hoped it was long enough for you to know that Clara's never a bother to me."

She blows a wayward curl out of her face. "Yes, I suppose I should have thought of that before I ran up the stairs, then." She heads for the armchair in the far corner of the room, where Sweety often reads his papers, and plops down. "Let me just get my breath."

"Thank you for looking after her, Missouri." Knowing someone had been solely dedicated to watching my elder child while I gave birth had taken quite a burden off my mind.

"You're welcome, sister. One day, it will be my turn to mother, and this way I'll have had some practice." Missouri winks in my direction.

"Mama," Clara's small voice pleads, "can I hold her?"

"Sure, you can. Come up on the bed with me."

I offer my hand as she clambers up onto the feather mattress, settling in against one of the pillows.

"Now, hold your arms out like this," I demonstrate for her, balancing Florence on my chest, "and I'll put her in your lap."

Clara sticks out her arms, and I adjust them so they will cradle the baby. Then, scooting gingerly up in bed, I set the still-sleeping babe in her lap. She looks at the baby, then up at me, eyes filled with wonder. "She's so pretty, Mama."

I'm holding back tears. Seeing the two of them together just warms my heart. "You were just as pretty, Clara." I kiss the curls crowning her head.

For a while, the room is silent as Clara enjoys her new baby sister, I enjoy my two precious daughters, and Missouri recovers from her mad dash up the staircase.

Mama comes into the room, breaking the silence. "I've finished up supper." She looks my way. "Jo, do you feel like eating?"

I shake my head. "Not just yet."

"All right. I'll bring you up a plate after a while."

"What did you make, Granny?" Clara takes her eyes off her sister for the first time.

"I made your favorite. Roast pork and baked apples."

"Yum!" In her excitement, she starts to get up but stops short. "Mama, you can have the baby back now. I'm gonna go eat."

I can't hold back my chuckle as I take the baby. "I've got her, go on downstairs."

Missouri's on her feet now. "Looks like it's off to the races again."

Clara runs off, with Missouri close behind her.

Mama turns to go, but I call out to her. "Mama. Can we talk?"

She stops short. "What is it, Jo?"

"I'm just feeling . . . out of sorts."

She crosses the room while untying her apron strings. Draping the muslin apron over her shoulder, she sits down on the bed with me. "How so?"

My eyes return to the baby. Her small button of a nose twitches with each deep inhale as she sleeps. "Florence is perfect. Just wonderful. And Clara . . . she's a handful but such a sweet child. I love them both so, so much."

"As any good mother should." She touches my thigh reassuringly. "So what's your trouble, then?"

"I just can't see how this is going to work. I have my work at the barbershop, my property ambitions, the cooking and cleaning, and washing, looking after Sweety . . . and now, two little ones." I sigh as the weight of my responsibilities rests on my shoulders like an anvil. "How am I to do it all, Mama?"

Mama chuckles. "Oh, Josephine. Mothers have been figuring that out as they went along since time began."

"I know, but somehow knowing that isn't very much comfort to me now." I stroke the baby's soft curls and wonder what she might be dreaming of. "Moments like this, it just seems so . . . impossible."

She weaves her fingers together, placing her hands in her lap.

I can sense the story coming, and since I'm seeking reassurance only she can provide, I'm ready to listen.

"I can remember what it was like raising you and Octavious while working for those layabout Williamses in the big house." She shook her head. "Getting up before dawn to make the biscuits for breakfast and to set the cauldron on to boil so the mistress could have her hot bath and the master his precious coffee." Her words hold an edge of bitterness. "I can remember how hard it was to leave the two of you there, on that cold, hard basement floor, so I could go do their bidding."

I swallow because my mother's pain is palpable. I feel as though I've breathed it in, and now it sits in my throat like a burr, poking and scratching on its way down. "You must have been so tired."

"Honey, tired isn't the word. Tired doesn't begin to cover the bone-deep weariness I felt every evening. And those nights I had to work late, rubbing the mistress's old rusty feet." She cringes, makes a gagging sound. "The one time I couldn't hold back my disgust, she hit me upside the head with a heavy book. Blacked my eye. I can still remember her grinning at me while I lay there, bloody. She relished hitting me . . . enjoyed it."

I shiver. I remember the mistress and her heavy hand. She'd laid into me many a time, for any little reason, or no reason at all. I sincerely hope she's gotten her comeuppance for her spite and brutality. But when my mother speaks again, I push her out of my mind.

"After all that work, all that abuse, I came to the basement ready to drop. But when you'd run to me, showing me something you'd made, or your brother brought me a frog he'd caught, I'd smile. You two were my light in a dark world, a world where I was no better than a dog. I looked at y'all, my babies, and I saw something pure, something precious, something I'd made. And I knew I could go on."

I smile, feeling the tears gather in my eyes. I pray to one day possess a tenth of her strength. "I feel silly for complaining, after all you've been through, Mama."

She shakes her head. "No, child. Don't feel silly. Our struggles are different, and I thank the ancestors for that. But mothering is still hard. Being a wife is hard. Working and running a household is hard." She puts her arm around my shoulders. "But you're made of sterner stuff than any of it. Take heart. You will find your way, I promise."

My smile deepens. "You've never steered me wrong yet, Mama. So even though I can't see how, I trust you."

"Good." She pecks me on the cheek. "But more important than that, Josephine, trust yourself. You were born with a purpose and a gift, and believe me, you're going to achieve that purpose even with all the demands in your life." She stands. "I'm going to eat. After I'm done, I'll be up with a plate for you, and I'll expect you to eat. That baby's going to need some good-quality milk. Understood?"

I nod. "Yes, ma'am."

She smiles that same comforting smile that's been salving my woes since I was a tot at her knee. Then she departs, leaving me alone with my new baby and my thoughts.

# SWEETY

## *December 1881*

I open the door on the cast-iron stove, checking the fire. It isn't the newest model, and it still uses wood, unlike the fancier ones with piped-in gas. I prod the smoldering pile with the long iron poker, and once I'm satisfied the stove is hot enough to prepare lunch, I shut the door.

Reaching above for the spatula on the shelf, I feel an insistent tugging on the leg of my trousers.

Turning, I look down into the huge brown eyes of my elder daughter. Clara's small lips are tightly pursed. "Papa, I'm hungry."

"I know, sugar. I'm starting to prepare lunch now."

She folds her arms over her little chest and stamps her foot. "But I'm hungry now, Papa!"

Her emphatic tone indicates her belief that I can perform miracles, like snapping my fingers and making a hot plate of food appear in her hands.

"I know, and I'm sorry. But it's going to take some time to get your lunch ready. Please be patient for Papa."

Her face crinkles into a frown, and she marches sullenly out of the room as I return to my meal preparations.

Shaking my head, I turn to the cabinet for the skillet. My plan is to fry up a bit of fish left over from the past weekend's catch; it needs to be cooked before it spoils. Setting the pan down, I add a bit of lard and leave it to melt. Grabbing a small pot, I add some of the water I brought in from the pump this morning, intending to boil some squash from the garden.

I spread the ingredients on the kitchen table while also listening out for the girls. The house is quiet, which I assume to be a good thing. Florrie, who is fighting the aftermath of an earache, is still tucked in her bed upstairs.

I slice the two squashes into thick rings, then set them aside. Opening the paper wrapped around the leftover fish, I take out the fillets and dust them with salt from the ceramic crock and pepper from the mill. I pause, frowning.

*What else does Jo use to season fish? I haven't a clue and didn't think to ask her before she left for the women's convention.*

I shrug, supposing salt and pepper will have to do. Reaching for the flour sack in the lower cabinet, I'm befuddled to find it missing. *I know there was flour here earlier. What could have happened to it?*

As I stand here, puzzling over the missing flour, I hear a cry coming from upstairs. *Heavens.* Florrie must have woken up and doesn't sound too pleased about it, either. Wiping my hands on a tea towel, I head up to check on my baby girl.

Headed across the wooden floors and up the stairs, I find my eye is drawn to a set of small, dusty white footprints. I can see the floors could stand sweeping and mopping, but think nothing else of it as I walk to Florrie's room.

When I arrive in the doorway, I stop in my tracks.

Florrie is still in bed, crying. Clara stands over her, giggling.

They are both covered, head to toe, in flour; the missing flour sack lies crumpled on the floor at Clara's feet.

"Clara!" My tone is sharper than I meant it to be, but my frustration has gotten the better of me. "What possessed you to do such a thing?"

"I was playing, Papa. Florrie and me are ghosts." She looks so innocent; her eyes as large as saucers as she tries to explain her game. "I didn't mean to wake her up, but I wanted to play."

"Ghosts? Honey, this isn't *A Christmas Carol.*" I gesture around the room at the small hills of flour, the white handprints and chalky streaks. "Look at the mess you've made!"

Clara's lip begins to tremble.

I fold beneath the weight of my rising guilt. "Clara, my dear . . ."

Her eyes well with tears, and moments later, her wails are added to her sister's. As I look around the room and think of the effort it would take to clean everything up, I briefly consider crying along with them.

Leaning against the doorframe, I touch my fingertips to my temple. For a long moment, I contemplate the folly of my actions. Recalling my conversation with Jo, I realize I should never have been so flippant with her when she asked if I could handle the girls for three days while she went to her convention.

"It isn't as easy as you might assume, Sweety," she'd admonished. "Yes, the house is tidy, the meal prepared, and the girls happy when you come home. But that takes more effort than you can imagine, and I have Granny to help."

"Come now," I'd said, waving her off. "They'll be no trouble at all. I'm a fully grown man. I manage a business, for heaven's sake. I can handle two small children."

*I can handle two small children.* I repeat the words in my head, but they ring a little hollower now. I'm on my second day, and while I retain some sense of control, I've certainly lost a lot of confidence.

The wails of my children draw me back to the present, and to the work still at hand. I sniff the air and smell something burning. "Oh, no. The lard!"

Picking up my thoroughly breaded children, I tuck one under each arm and dash down the stairs as fast as the added weight will allow. Setting them down in chairs at the kitchen table, I snatch up the tea towel and move the smoking skillet of burned lard off the burner. The water for the squash has just come to a boil, and that is one saving grace.

I pause, taking several deep breaths, ignoring the acrid smell of scorched grease as I attempt to gather myself. What I feel at this moment is similar to the feeling when all the chairs in the barbershop are full and more clients are waiting. That scenario, which happens fairly often, always makes me feel fortunate but overwhelmed.

I steel myself and take a few minutes to set things right. First, I add the squash to the pot and cover it. Next, I send Clara to the line for a clean cloth and drag the remaining water in the half barrel next to the table.

When Clara returns with the cloth, I wet it and begin scrubbing the flour off the girls. Soon the water is murky, but the children are much cleaner. Satisfied, I offer, "My dears, if you can stay seated like good little girls, we shall have some of Granny's apple pie with our lunch."

Clara smiles brightly, and even the still overtired Florrie seems buoyed by the announcement.

I take the barrel outside and dump the cloudy water. Then I pump more water into it to rinse out the residue. Once it is clean, I refill it again with fresh water.

When I return with the fresh water, my girls are still dutifully seated at the table. "Good job, girls." I'm relieved that my offer of sweets proves enough to keep them well-behaved, even if only for a few minutes.

The squash is simmering, so I scrub the skillet and replace the dab of lard. "Well, there's no flour, so we'll just see how it tastes without it, shall we, girls?"

Clara giggles. "It might taste funny, Papa."

I shrug. "It might, but we'll see."

"No eat, Papa." Florrie's small voice is just above a whisper.

I go to her, kissing her brow. She still feels warmer than I would like, and I know the earache is still plaguing her. "You don't have to eat, Florrie. Papa will make you some tea." I've already given her the mix of willow bark, cinnamon, and chamomile that Milly left for her once today, but she is due for it again by now. I add a little honey to soften the taste.

A short time later, I set a plate of crisp catfish fillet, squash, and a sliver of pie in front of Clara, and a mug of warm, not hot, tea in front of Florrie. Sitting down with my own plate, I enjoy a quiet meal with my girls.

"Does it taste all right, Clara?" I've asked her that at every meal since her mother's departure, to mixed reviews.

"It's salty and . . ."

"Not like Mama's?" I finish her sentence, anticipating the ending.

"Yes. But it's still good, Papa."

I chuckle. "Thank you for that generous compliment, Clara." It's the highest mark I've gotten so far. I don't expect my cooking to match my wife's. It has been a long time since my days as a bachelor subsisting on simple suppers and the occasional hot plate from a generous neighbor. Jo's skill level in the kitchen, and in the home in general, far exceeds mine. But that is as it should be.

Once the dishes are in the basin, I take the girls into the sitting room. There, I strip them of the flour-besmirched clothes and place the soiled things in the laundry barrel. Once they're dressed in clean muslin dresses, I lay the still sleepy Florrie on the settee next to me and cover her with one of Milly's afghans.

Clara takes up a spot on the throw rug with her jacks and rubber ball. "Want to play, Papa?"

I smile. "You'll likely beat me, but why not?"

My words turn out to be prophetic, and Clara handily beats me in five rounds of jacks before I slink away in utter defeat.

"You did your best, Papa." She pats my shoulder, and her expression is so earnest, I can't help but laugh.

I tap my chin, thinking of an activity to keep her occupied while I tend to a few things. "Why don't you get your slate and practice your lettering? You'll be starting school again soon, you know."

She looks put out. "Aw, Papa. That's not fun."

"Of course it's fun. Plus, everyone knows that proper ghosts must have fine penmanship." I wink.

She thinks on it for a moment. "I suppose." She jumps up and runs for her slate and chalk.

Once Clara is settled next to her sister and working on her letters,

I haul the laundry to the washroom. Housed in a small shed behind the kitchen, the washroom has all the essentials but little more. There is a large hand-crank wringer-style washer, a pail filled with wooden clothespins, and another pail that holds Jo's homemade washing soda. Her handwritten sign, scrawled in chalk on a plank, lists the ingredients: shredded lye soap, citrus rinds, and sodium bicarbonate.

I load the basin of the washer with water, soap, and the children's dirty clothes from the last thirty-six hours and start the work. Once they are clean, I run them through the wringer, then carry them to the clothesline in the backyard. With all the tiny dresses, socks, and underthings hung, I return to the sitting room.

There, I find Clara passed out, with her slate and chalk still in her lap. The day's mischief has finally caught up to her. She's leaned over on top of her sister, who still hasn't stirred from her own slumber.

I can't suppress my smile at the scene. I'm tired on a level I've never experienced. But this time with my girls is as precious as it is exhausting, so I shall do my best to cherish it.

Leaving my two little mischief makers to their rest, I trudge up the stairs to clear the floors, walls, and bedding of three pounds of spilled flour.

I work as quickly as I can, knowing I only have until one of the girls awakens to finish cleaning. With an old towel dampened with water and a bit of soap, I wash away the evidence of Clara's midday game.

On the landing, I pass a rectangular looking glass Jo hung there. Regarding my reflection, I can see that I look disheveled at best. My clothes are damp from both sweat and the day's cleaning. Washing soda and droplets of lard cling to my trousers and shirt, and somehow, there is even a dusting of flour in my hair. I can only shake my head and keep going.

Parenting is not for the weak and, as far as I can say, is best left to the womenfolk. I simply don't have the desire or the capacity for this work.

That is why I can't abide Josephine's insatiable desire to work, to take on more and more things outside of the household. As she goes about becoming some sort of property baron, who is to deal with the washing and the cooking and the cleaning? It certainly won't be me; if I had any inclinations of that sort before, this ordeal has taught me better. Soon enough, she'll be demanding a maid, and why should I have to pay someone to provide the services that are a wife's God-given duty to perform?

*No, I'm much better suited to the barbershop. And whether Jo knows it or not, she's meant to find her purpose here, in this house.*

# JOSEPHINE

### *December 1881*

"Lord, I'm tired. All this socializing is a bit much for me."

I turn toward my mother's voice and shake my head. We're seated in the ballroom of one of Rocky Mount's finer hotels, listening to yet another speech being given on the stage before us. "Mama, why didn't you go up to the room with Grandma Milly to rest?"

She purses her lips. "I'm tired, but I've still got some fire left in me, child."

"That's good," Missouri interjects. "Because if we're to win our full rights, fire is just what we'll need."

I nod, agreeing with my sister-in-law's astute assessment. This is our third and final day attending the United Negro Women of Carolina convention, and I must admit that the days filled with activity, gatherings, and strategizing are starting to take their toll on me as well. Still, three hundred women of African descent, from all around the state, have united here for a purpose, and we mean to achieve it.

I turn my attention back to the speech at hand. A young student from Oberlin College named Mrs. Anna Haywood Cooper was speaking on the importance of literacy among freedmen and children alike, especially girls. "So often, we girls are denied the chance to learn to read. But those who would deny us literacy deny our people, and our society, the gifts we could bring if we were properly educated. So I urge all of you present to teach your family members to read. Teach them all, but give special attention to your daughters, granddaughters, and nieces. They need you."

I join the rest of the assemblage in applause for Mrs. Cooper as she leaves the podium. "What an impressive young lady. She's going to go on to do amazing things, I'm sure."

"Certainly." My mother scratches her chin. "How many more sessions are left, Jo?"

I shrug. "I haven't a clue. Boy, you really are worn out, aren't you?"

She waves me off. "Just check your convention program and tell me what's left on the schedule, child."

I do as my mother asks. "Let's see. There are two more sessions; the next is one on temperance, and the last one is on suffrage."

Missouri shifts in her chair. "I only hope I'll last through them. This corset is taking on a life of its own."

I giggle, though I'm similarly plagued by the whalebone contraption giving structure to my dove-gray traveling costume. "I think we're all feeling similarly, Missouri. Take heart. In a few hours, we can all toss our corsets into the nearest trash bin."

"Go on with you!" Mother's quiet outrage is plain. "You'll do no such thing; proper ladies don't go prancing around without proper undergarments."

I don't know how much of a "proper lady" I am, but I also know better than to sass my mother, so I reply with the best possible answer I can think of. "Yes, ma'am."

We spend the rest of our short break chatting, until the sound of the bell being rung brings our attention back to the stage.

Mrs. Hester Coleman, chair of the UNWC, stands at the podium.

"Please offer your welcome to our next speaker, Mrs. Thea Franklin, who'll educate us about the importance of temperance for our families and our race."

We applaud as Mrs. Franklin takes the stage. "Thank you, thank you. I'll begin by asking, how many of you have a saloon, barroom, or drinking establishment in your town? Raise your hand, please."

The three of us all raise our hands, as do many of the women in the room.

Mrs. Franklin shakes her head with a *tsk-tsk* sound. "Far too many of you, as far as I'm concerned. Alcohol is poisoning our communities. It takes our men, many of whom are left fraught by the ravages of their former enslavement. It seduces them with the promise of relief from their daily stresses, then entraps them with its addictive qualities."

A murmur goes through the crowd as the women bemoan the truth of her words.

"Alcohol is a vice, and the consumption of it only leads to devilment and malicious mischief. Men curse and slur. They stagger about, brawl in the streets like animals. Then they come home and visit the horror of their behavior on their wives and children."

More murmuring. I can't help but think of the barroom in Edenton, and how much time Sweety and Octavious spend there. They claim they go there to have "man time," to talk about things that are of no interest to us women. But what really goes on there? Do they become so ill-behaved when they imbibe?

"Goodness," Missouri mutters. "I remember having to patch up a knot on Octavious's head once when he took a drunken tumble down the front steps."

My mother's face is grim. "She's making good sense, unfortunately."

"Is that not an insult?" Mrs. Franklin continues, pacing the stage floor. "Is that not an affront to our community? After everything we've gone through to be free, will we now surrender our husbands, our fathers, our uncles, and sons to yet another form of captivity?"

"NO!" three hundred female voices respond.

"Will we sit idly by and let them be enslaved by the whiskey bottle?"

"NO!"

"Will we let them bruise us or our babies when the devil's drink drives them to madness?"

"NO!"

"Then we're in agreement." Mrs. Franklin returns to the podium, raising a sheaf of paper high for everyone to see. "We're all women of good sense and fine reputation. Before you leave today, please come to the registration table and sign your name to this petition, asking the governor to outlaw the sale of alcohol in North Carolina. Some say temperance will be too difficult to achieve. But if we stand together, we can do what's right for our menfolk. For our children. For ourselves."

We join in the boisterous applause as Mrs. Franklin leaves the stage.

"Are we going to sign?" Missouri asks.

"Of course, we are," I reply. "I can think of many more productive things for Sweety to do than while away the hours drinking gin."

"I'm signing. I remember the beatings I took from Williams whenever he'd had too much corn liquor." Mother's tone is solemn, and her eyes seem locked on some distant point. "Wouldn't wish it on nobody."

The next speaker comes on and speaks on the quest for suffrage for women. "My great-grandmother was a dreamer, one who had the gift of second sight. Back in our homeland on the shores of Senegal, she communed with the ancestors and shared their wisdom with our tribe. She died in captivity in Wake County. But before she died, she told me of a day when all people in these United States will be able to cast their ballot, with no regard for race or gender." She pounds the podium for emphasis. "We must press on toward that day, sisters. It is our sacred duty, in honor of the ones who came before us, and the ones who will come after."

I think of Clara and Florrie and of the kind of world they will inherit when they are full-grown. Things as they are now aren't acceptable, not for my daughters. I will do all I can to secure a future for them, one where they are free to thrive and to prosper just as much as their white counterparts.

As the conference ends, at half past noon, we rise and gather our handbags and programs.

"Let's go to the table and sign the petition so we can get on the road before it gets too late." I see the line forming and start walking over to it.

"Right. Buggies are bound to be packed together like sardines on the roads leaving the city before long." Missouri tugs the tail of her corset. "If it's all the same to you, I'll be taking this thing off in the back of the carriage."

I laugh as we come to a stop at the rear of the line.

We're still chatting when we leave the hotel, headed for our carriage parked in the field behind it. Mother and Missouri climb inside, shutting the door behind them. As I approach the post to untie the leads of my two mares, Cinnamon and Sugar, I hear the sound of someone clearing their throat.

I turn toward the sound and see a pair of white ladies standing just beyond the post. One is tall, with brown hair put up in a very severe bun. The other is short and round, her blonde hair dangling in long sausage curls around her face. Both are staring at me.

"Pardon me, is there something you need?"

The short one snaps, "Yes. I need to know what you darkies have been doing in the Cameron Hotel for the last three days."

I blink several times. "A simple convention, that's all." Having untied my horses, I move to climb aboard the seat for the drive home.

"What sort of convention?" Now the taller one is making the demands. "Can't be nothing good, I reckon."

I slide onto the driver's seat, intent on ignoring them. Their fine silk gowns and coiffed hair may appear classy, but their ungraceful talk and utter lack of manners reveal their lack of breeding as well as their bigotry.

"Answer us, you uppity Negress!" The short one's face is red, as if she's taken offense at my silence.

"Jo, don't," I hear my mother say from inside the carriage.

I sigh. I'm too tired to deal with this, and I'm ready to get home to my family. There is much I could say, but what would it benefit me? I'm not going to change their small minds and hate-filled hearts. Besides, I'm in Rocky Mount, a good distance from home. Police in this city are known to be stricter and more brutal. Despite my inner outrage, speaking now could keep me from making it home safely.

So I swallow my words and plaster on a fake smile, saying nothing. I straighten on the seat, tug the reins slightly.

I wiggle my fingers as I get my horses underway with a flick of my wrists. "Good day, ladies." And just like that, I leave them standing there, fairly vibrating with offense as I drive away. Mother sticks her head out of the window in the back. "That's my girl."

While we ride, I let the pastoral scenery of rural North Carolina soothe me, helping me forget the encounter. The clusters of pines stretch toward the sky, their branches bursting with green needles. In some places the trees are so thick, I can see nothing beyond them. The chill in the air rustles my cloak as the wind rushes past me, invigorating me and carrying with it the scent of the trees and damp earth.

We pass many homes along the way, some near the road, and some set back so far in the woods that only the smoke rising from their chimneys indicates their presence. I wave to a man we pass on the road. He's headed in the opposite direction and is hauling a six-foot Leyland cypress in the bed of his buggy. The sight of his cargo reminds me that Christmas is only two weeks away.

Cinnamon and Sugar get us into Edenton as the sun is beginning to set. After leaving Mother at home with Dorsey, and Missouri at the little love nest she shares with my brother on Queen Street, I return home at last. Once the carriage is parked and the horses stabled, I trudge up the steps to the back porch and enter the house through the kitchen.

Sweety is in the parlor. He's sitting on my imported damask chaise, reading his paper by lamplight. The ivory and gold brocade drapes are drawn over the windows, and his boots rest on the coordinating Oriental rug beneath the carved oak coffee table. He sets down his paper as I enter with my bag. "Welcome home, dearest."

I go to him and sit on his lap, placing a soft peck on his lips. "Hello, sweetheart. Did you miss me?"

"Endlessly." He smiles as he weaves his fingers in my hair and brings me forward for a languid, lingering kiss.

When we part, I ask, "How did it go?"

He sighs. "It went. Lots of missteps and blunders, but the house is still standing, so that counts as a victory, right?"

I smile. "I'd say so. Are the girls asleep?"

"Yep, for a half hour now. I let them run around the backyard until they tuckered themselves out, then gave them a bath and put them in their beds."

"I wouldn't mind having you do those last two things for me." I wink.

"I will . . . if you promise never to leave me with the girls again. At least not until they're older and less needy."

I frown. "What?"

He details his adventure keeping them alive these past seventy-two hours much the way a war veteran describes a fierce battle. "It's all too much. I don't know how you and Milly do it, but I've no desire to do it again."

He can't be serious. And if he is, I'm too tired to box his ears right now. "Whatever you say, dear. Anyway, about that bath . . . would you?"

He chuckles. "I suppose I'll put you on some hot water." Nudging me off his lap, he gets up and walks to the kitchen.

"Good. I want to be fresh in the morning when I go to purchase the barbershop."

He stops. "What?"

"I'm buying the shop tomorrow. I told you about it before I left." I watch him, confused at the tightness I see in his face. "Why do you look so put out? Isn't this what you wanted?"

"Yes. I wanted *us* to buy it. Not just you."

I shrug. "I've got a good history with the bank, so it's easier to finance things if I just . . . do it myself."

His lips tighten. "I see. Well, if you want that bathwater, how about you do that yourself, too?" He turns and stomps up the stairs like a petulant child.

Left alone in the dim parlor, I shake my head. Today I've been insulted by a couple of nameless white women, but the truest of insults has come from my own husband. It seems there are cogs in the machinery of the male mind that I'll never be able to make sense of, and I suppose it's best I give up trying.

It pains me to come home to this, after spending the past few days pursuing something that's so important to me, and to society at large. I dream big, and my husband reminds me of how small I am, at least in his eyes.

# 9

## JOSEPHINE

### *May 1882*

I hold tight to Clara's and Florrie's hands as we file silently into our pew toward the center of the St. John the Evangelist Episcopal Church of God. St. Paul's parishioners of color, having organized themselves and raised the necessary funds over the past few years, opened up this church last fall, and our family has been attending services here since that very first September Sunday. Now, I know that when my daughters marry, they may do so inside the building, rather than being relegated to the churchyard, as my mother was when she wed Dorsey.

Sunday school has just ended, and now that the youngsters have been apprised of the story of Shadrach, Meshach, and Abednego, we gather in the sanctuary for service.

It is just the girls and me, as Sweety was more interested in sleep than worship. I wrangled the girls, fed them, and got them dressed, all without any assistance from their father. He practically shooed me out the door as he pulled the covers up over his head. I declare, that man will be my undoing.

We enter the church during the prelude, and I sigh, relieved we aren't late. The familiar serenity of the interior washes over me as we make our way to our seats. The whitewashed walls are punctuated by the tall stained glass windows; I love how the triangular points at the top of each frame seem to reach heavenward. The rich mahogany pews mirror the dark beams and supports surrounding the space. The pine floors gleam beneath our feet, having been lovingly swept and scrubbed by the laity. I took a turn with the cleaning team this week, and I'm pleased to see the fruits of our labor.

As we move into place on our pew, I remind the girls of my expectations. "Remember, dears, we're to be pious and well-mannered. Understood?"

"Yes, Mama," they answer dutifully, in unison.

We participate in the opening hymn as the clergy members process into the sanctuary. I bow to the cross as it passes, the girls mimicking my gesture of respect. Even though I know they are simply doing what I've taught them, I hope in time they will grow to embrace the true meaning of these rituals.

While I know it isn't the faith of my foremothers, I still find comfort in the presence of an almighty creator, whose hand guides the path of our lives with wisdom and love. Deep down, I've always thought that the God we worship is merely a symbol and that all spirituality leans toward this same great spirit, this force of nature. I believe faith matters more than how we refer to this universal master.

My faith has been a safe haven for me ever since I can remember. I guide my daughters in nightly prayers, and in weekly study of the Bible. I pray for a daily dose of patience and strength, to allow me to do the many tasks I face as a wife, a mother, and a businesswoman. When I interact with others, I try to let goodwill and love for humanity guide me. I don't always succeed, but I pray for the grace to do better the next time.

The Acclamation and another song follow, and after the Collect prayer, Rector Billups begins the day's liturgy.

The rest of the service goes by without any trouble from the girls, leaving me free to enjoy my time with my fellow congregants. By the time we greet the rector on the way out of the church, I'm feeling much lighter than I did when I arrived.

I can't help but think of Sweety as I drive the girls to my mother's house for Sunday dinner. I recall his terseness this morning, and the lingering stench of whiskey from last night on his breath. I don't even know if he will crawl out of bed to join us for the meal, but I try not to dwell on it. Sweety is a man, fully capable of making his own decisions. I'm his wife, not his mother, so I refuse to press him on matters of personal choice. He's got to do what he feels is right, and so do I. That's why I made sure our girls attended services this morning while he was cocooned in the quilts.

We arrive shortly at my mother's home on Queen Street. We always drive instead of walking on Sundays now, to lessen the chances of the girls ruining their good dresses. I leave the carriage parked in the yard and take the girls up the steps to the front porch.

The door swings open, and Dorsey greets us with a smile. "Hello, Jo."

"Hi, Dorsey." I give him a brief hug. He's a truly likable fellow, and he loves my mother and treats her well. He makes it clear that he loves my children too; I couldn't ask for a better mate for my mother.

"Come on in. Your mama's still stirring pots." He steps aside.

We enter, and I help the girls take off their shoes and put them in the wicker basket by the front door. "Let's go see what Grandma is doing."

Clara giggles while Florrie rocks from side to side, wringing her hands in that shy way she does.

We tiptoe down the hall and I peep into the kitchen. There, I see my mother, buttering biscuits. I watch her in silence, amazed once again by all she does. She's wearing a dusting of flour and even has some in her hair.

"Hey, Mama." I ease to her side, peck her on the cheek. "How was the early service?"

"Good, yours?"

"Good." I gesture to the girls. "These two behaved like perfect little angels."

She smiles, dusting off her hands. Squatting down, she opens her arms to them. "Come here and give your granny some kisses."

They run to her and are enveloped. I stand back and watch because I never tire of seeing them like this. They love her just as I do, and to see my mother, who worked so hard during the dark days of slavery, living a life of ease and enjoying her grandchildren feels like a miracle to me. And I don't discount the role Dorsey has played in giving her this life, either. He works hard at his trade, and leaves my mother able to pursue whatever brings her joy.

I spend time helping Mama ferry the dishes to the table for our meal. The sound of the front door opening draws my attention, and as I look up, Sweety saunters in.

"Papa!" The girls run to him, nearly barreling him over with enthusiastic hugs and kisses.

"Hello, my sweet ones." He returns their ardor. "All right, now. Go take your places at the table like good girls."

As our daughters go to their seats, Sweety stands to his full height and his eyes meet mine. "Hello, dearest. How was service?"

"I could tell you about it, but you could have seen it for yourself." I regret the words as soon as I say them, but they can't be taken back now.

He draws a deep breath. "I see." Without another word, he takes his usual place at the table, gesturing to the chair next to him.

Clearing my throat, I sit.

He leans close to my ear, speaking so that only I can hear him. "I realize you're miffed that I didn't attend church this morning. But there's no need to spoil Jeanette's good cooking with your sour persimmons."

Keeping my face unreadable and my voice just as low, I retort, "You are right, husband. And if you hold your tongue and tread lightly with me, then dinner won't be spoiled."

His brow arches, as if he's surprised by my words.

I don't care. He's been complaining about every little thing I do, or don't do, around the house for the past few weeks. And after the way he fussed at me this morning when I tried to wake him for service, I'm in no mood.

Soon, we're all digging into Mama's delicious supper. There is a pot roast with chunks of potato, sliced carrot, and pearl onions, along with spicy collard greens and thick biscuits running with fresh butter. For a while, the only sounds in the room are of the silver striking the china.

Sweety's is the first voice to break the near silence. "So, Dorsey. What are you and the boys building now?"

Dorsey takes a sip of his lemonade. "We're building a little cottage for Rosa Jackson, on the edge of her family's land. Coming along nicely, I'd say."

"Really? I didn't know she'd moved out of the main house."

"She hasn't yet. But as I understand it, she's courting somebody, and they might be moving toward marriage."

Sweety's eyes widen. "You don't say! I never thought Rosa would take a husband. She's been wearing trousers ever since I met her."

"Well, you never can tell with folks, I always say."

I'm amused, and a bit perturbed, at their banter. When women talk like this, it's gossip. When men do it, it's a "discussion." Aside from that, Sweety's less-than-subtle dig at my friend Rosa hasn't gone unnoticed, either. Why must he make judgments about her, simply because she chooses comfort over convention?

Florrie flings a piece of potato at Clara. It lands atop her head.

"Ow!" Clara howls as if she's been hit by shrapnel.

I rap my fist sharply on the table. "Girls!"

Clara takes the potato from her hair and places it in her napkin, and they both look contrite as they fall silent.

Dorsey scratches his chin. "In any case, it's gonna be a nice place. Storm shutters, gingerbread trim, fine tin roof."

"Sounds like a fine home." Sweety wipes his mouth, setting the napkin aside. "How much longer before it's finished, you think?"

Dorsey shrugs. "A couple of weeks, I reckon. Then we're on to the next project."

"Yes, yes." Sweety nods. "The work just goes on, doesn't it?"

Mama gets to her feet and begins clearing the table.

I instinctively rise to help her.

As we're clearing the dishes away, Mama asks, "Dorsey, do you want me to pack up some of this roast for your lunch tomorrow?"

He nods. "Yes, please. And put in a couple slices of bread with it."

"I will."

We head to the kitchen, arms laden with the dishes, and set them on the butcher block.

From the other room, I hear Sweety say, "I can't remember the last time Jo packed me a lunch."

"Ain't you both working?" Dorsey asks.

Sweety doesn't answer, choosing to scoff instead. "Still. It's a wife's duty to—"

My mother must see my eyes flashing, because she reaches for me.

But she's too late. I storm back into the dining room. "What's a wife's duty, Sweety? Certainly not to get her husband to church on Sunday, when he'd rather spend the day laying about like a bump on a log."

Dorsey's on his feet in a flash. "Girls, let's go in the backyard and play."

I hold my peace until he and Mama have taken the girls out of earshot. "The nerve of you, speaking about my duties."

"It's true, Jo!" Sweety leans back in his chair. "All you do now is work and look after the girls. When you have a free moment, you've got your nose in the papers, looking at those property listings."

"So you're upset that my entire world does not revolve around you?" I lean my back against the wall. "Isn't that something?"

"That's not fair, Jo. All I want is for you to be more like . . . more like . . . well, more like your mother." He gestures around him. "Look around. Her home is immaculate. Dorsey's business is thriving because he doesn't have to worry about anything. She looks after him so well. What man wouldn't want that for himself?"

I can feel my face getting hot. "You'd praise my mother to insult me? You do realize I'm raising two small children, working at the barbershop, and keeping a home, don't you? Honestly, Archer."

"Oh, you're back to calling me by my given name again?"

"If you're going to carry on this way, you should be happy I call on you at all."

He narrows his eyes.

I fold my arms over my chest. "You may as well fix your face. I'm not going to yield simply because you look at me harshly."

He shakes his head. "What happened to my sweet Jo? Where is the starry-eyed girl I married?"

"There are still stars in my eyes. But you try at every opportunity to extinguish them."

He looks away.

I sigh. "I'm not a girl anymore, Archer. I'm a mother and a businesswoman."

"And wife. You're my wife, Josephine. Or have you forgotten that?"

"No." I've tired of this conversation, and of his refusal to see me for who I am. "I suppose you've forgotten all the plans we made in our youth. Plans to build an empire, alongside building our family."

"I haven't forgotten, I just—"

"You just can't abide building that empire, unless it's all on your terms." I turn away from him. "I'm going outside to play with the girls."

"Jo, wait."

I pause.

He stands, comes to me, and drapes an arm around my waist. "I know I'm an ogre at times. It's simply because I love you, and I . . . just want to be enough for you."

I let him peck me on the cheek. "I know." Touching his jaw, I turn and walk out the back door, knowing that his words are true.

As I breathe in the warm afternoon air, Sweety's words echo in my head. My husband is enough for me, but how could my life revolve solely around him? I think of his sighs as I turn on the lamp in the study after dinner, rather than joining him in bed. His wordless protest when I rise before him, leaving a cold breakfast on the table and a quick peck on his lips as I run out the door. I recall the parties when I'd catch myself chatting about business and look up to see his cheeks flushed, his jaw set, and I'd painstakingly dial down my passion, letting the conversation trickle back to more leisurely topics.

It's like swimming against the tide every day to stop myself from pursuing my business with the full force of my energies, but my husband would rather I not swim against the tide at all. He'd rather see me out of the water entirely, wrangling our children and watching *him* delight in the waves from the shore.

He does love me. But he doesn't love my ambition, and it's an inextricable part of who I am.

# 10

JOSEPHINE

*May 1882*

Ah, Mondays.

Draining the last of my coffee, I set the mug in the sink along with my empty oatmeal bowl. I've lingered long enough over my breakfast, and now I need to be on my way. I'm dressed in a soft pink traveling costume and low-heeled boots, and as I walk past my writing table in the parlor, I grab the small valise in which I store my logbook. Stopping at the foot of the stairs, I call up for my assistant du jour.

"Clara? Are you ready, sweetie?"

"Yes, Mama!" Seconds later, she appears on the landing above me. Dressed in a brown skirt, pink blouse, and boots, she looks almost as ready as me. Almost.

When my gaze sweeps up to her unkempt hair, I sigh. "Clara, bring down the hairbrush from my dresser. And a pink ribbon."

She dashes off to retrieve the items I requested.

Grandma Milly appears next, bouncing Florrie on her hip. My youngest just turned two, but is a bit small for her age, allowing her great-grandmother to carry her about with ease. "I've wrestled this little one's hair into submission, but Clara wanted you to fix hers."

I chuckle. "Are you sure you'll be all right looking after Florrie? We won't be back until well after lunch."

She nods. "Don't worry about us. Florrie and I will be fine, isn't that right, my dear?"

Florrie doesn't answer but tucks her face into her great-grand-mother's shoulder.

Grandma laughs. "That'll do, then."

Florrie is the shyer, more reserved child, and while we encourage her to explore, we never push her to be someone she's not.

Clara comes running down the stairs with the hairbrush and ribbon in hand. I beckon her over to the settee, and she sits on the floor while I brush her hair into a high bun, securing it with the ribbon. "There, that looks much better."

I'm standing near the front door, making my final preparations to depart, when Grandma carries Florrie downstairs with one of her big afghans and a familiar-looking potato sack. She spreads the blanket on the floor in front of the settee, then sits Florrie down, handing over the bag. My delighted younger child immediately dumps out the contents of the sack, a pile of painted wooden blocks spilling out.

Seated on the settee, Grandma remarks, "I'll let her build and play for a while, then we'll use the blocks to practice the alphabet."

I smile as I head out the door with Clara, knowing Florrie and Grandma Milly will have a lovely day together. Once I've hitched Cinnamon to the buggy, we get underway.

As the buggy rollicks along the northwestern road outside of town, Clara asks, "Mama, what are we doing today, again?"

"Today is my maintenance day for my property. We're going to drive to Elizabeth City and talk with Ms. Brown and collect her quarterly payment. After that we'll grab some lunch and head back home."

"I see. This all sounds very businesslike. I suppose that's why Ms. Badham didn't mind me missing a day of school."

I chuckle. "When I spoke with Evelina, we both agreed that it would benefit you to see how I conduct my business. It's a practical life skill that I'm sure you'll put to use someday."

We share a lively discussion of a book we both enjoyed, *The Three Musketeers*, to pass the time. Soon we arrive in Elizabeth City, and I park my buggy in one of only two vacant spots in my lot at the corner of Road and Main Streets. Pleased to see so many of the spaces occupied by all manner of conveyances, I set the hand brake and climb down to hitch Cinnamon to the post. Once that's done, I help Clara down. Holding her hand to keep her near, I lead her inside Brown's Tack and Leather Goods.

The interior of the store is brightly lit, thanks to the four windows surrounding the entry door. The other three walls are lined with saddles, bridles, and tack, as well as belts, vests, and other wearables. The spicy scent of pine oil and the musky aroma of freshly tanned leather follow me as I walk to the counter.

Sheila Brown emerges from the storeroom behind the counter and grins in my direction. She has a short, sturdy build, and a round, friendly face framed by salt-and-pepper curls. She wears her trademark green blouse and black skirt beneath a brown leather apron. "Jo Leary. Good to see you again, lady."

"Hello, Sheila. Good to see you too." I place my hands on Clara's shoulders. "I've brought my oldest with me today. Clara, say hello to Ms. Brown."

"Hello, ma'am." Clara offers a small curtsy.

Sheila's grin broadens. "Hello there, dearie. My, Jo, she's got such lovely manners. Of course, I'd expect no less." She claps her hands together. "Let me get my bank draft. I'm sure you have plenty to do today, and I certainly don't want to hold you up."

I lean against the counter as Sheila slips into the back room again, looking at the new leather purses on display above me. They seem to be of fine quality, and one bag, with a studded sunburst appliquéd to the front, catches my eye.

When Sheila returns and hands over the signed draft, I tuck it into my bag. "Sheila, how much for that sunburst bag up there?"

She looks to where I'm gesturing. "If you're willing to barter, I'll give it to you for half off one month's rent on the lot."

"You're a shrewd woman, Sheila. And you've got a deal."

Soon, I'm leaving with my daughter, carrying the paper-wrapped purse. As we get back in the buggy, Clara asks, "What was that called again? Bargain?"

"Barter," I respond. "It means to trade one valuable thing for another. Not all transactions have to involve the exchange of money."

"Oh." Clara settles into her seat for the ride back to Edenton.

On the way out of Elizabeth City, we stop at a small stand to purchase ham sandwiches, crisp apples, and lemonade. We enjoy our meal in the bed of the buggy before departing for home.

When we arrive, I enter the house to find it strangely quiet. As Clara dashes off to use the washroom, I walk through the house, listening for sounds of Grandma Milly and Florrie.

The tinkling of laughter draws my attention, and I follow it through the parlor, the dining room, the kitchen, and out the back door. There, I see Florrie tearing across the grass, as fast as her little legs will carry her, while her great-grandmother pretends to give chase.

Finally Florrie tumbles, but before she can make a fuss, Grandma feigns falling down next to her. On their backs in the grass, they both giggle, and watching them warms me to the core.

Standing on the back porch, I feel a familiar tug at my skirt. Looking down at Clara, I say, "What is it, dear?"

"Granny Jeanette is here."

"Let her in, and tell her to come to the back."

Soon, the five of us are sitting on the porch. Grandma Milly is in her old rocker, with Florrie in her lap. My mother and I sit on the back steps, with Clara between us.

"So how did it go today?" Mama asks.

I fill her in on the visit to Elizabeth City. "Now that I've taken care of that, I'll go to the bank tomorrow to settle some things there."

Mama nods. "You're doing well with this property business, Jo, and I'm proud of you."

"So am I, granddaughter," Grandma Milly chimes in from behind me.

"But I have to warn you, Jo. Don't forget about your marriage while you're off chasing rainbows." My mother's eyes are filled with concern.

"I promise, I won't, Mama." I wonder what's brought this on. "I'm only doing this so that our family can be secure."

"I know. But men are fragile. They need to feel useful." Mama pats my shoulder.

I nod, waiting for her to tell me where this is coming from.

"I went by the barbershop the other day, dropping off those aprons I washed for you. I just took them around back so I wouldn't disturb anything. While I was in the storeroom, I overheard some of the men laughing at Sweety and teasing him because 'his wife wears the pants.'"

I cringe. "Oh, no." I expect I'll need to do some tall ego-stroking this evening.

"Just let Sweety know he's still your hero. That's all."

I give the only response I can. "I'll do my best, Mama."

Later that night, when Sweety and I are alone, I whisper his name.

"Yes, dearest?"

"You know I love you, don't you?"

He shifts in bed, turning to face me. His wears his exhaustion on his face, but he still manages a small smile for his wife. "Yes. I love you, too."

I open my arms and pull him into my chest. There is nothing more to say; only my actions to speak for me. I would never force him to relive his pain, so I don't bring up what my mother overheard. I simply hold him close to my heart, hoping he will know what he means to me, that he will feel it in my embrace.

A short time later, his rumbling snores fill the room, and I smile.

# JOSEPHINE

I adjust my hat as I enter the office of Miss Charlotte Hammond, inside the First Bank of Edenton. The bank, located on Court Street, is the only financial institution in town, and I'm glad the owner is open-minded. Anyone with the funds can open an account here, and that's as it should be.

Charlotte shuts the door and joins me, sliding into her seat behind the desk. She's wearing her typical banker's uniform of a dark skirt and matching fitted jacket, white blouse with a lace collar, and low-heeled boots. "Good to see you again, Josephine."

"Always a pleasure, Charlotte." I smile in her direction. "I've been meaning to ask you . . . how did you get into banking as a profession? You're the first woman banker I've ever encountered."

She rests her elbows on the desk. "I've always had a head for numbers, ever since I was a child. It drove my father crazy—he always said no man would want me as a wife because I was too smart for my own good." She chuckles.

I shake my head. "Men."

She sighs aloud. "Yes, yes. Anyway, I studied accounting and bookkeeping under my uncle Randolph, who's a banker in Wilmington. He invested in this bank when it was being built, and that's how I got the position."

"I see." It's an interesting story, but the details are familiar to me. "You and I have more in common than I would have thought."

"How so?" She leans forward.

"I'm an unconventional woman as well. My ambition has put me at odds with plenty of people, even my own husband." I didn't mean to say the last few words, but there it is. "We simply have to do what we're meant to do and ignore those who would subdue us."

She gives a firm nod. "I agree." She pulls out a leather book and opens it on the desktop. "I've got your ledger here, so let's get on with it, shall we?" She takes the loose papers from the ledger and spreads them out.

"Yes. Tell me what you found in assessing my books."

Charlotte clasps her hands together, her eyes grazing the pages in front of her. "In terms of assets, you now have four properties in your possession. That includes the lot on Road Street in Elizabeth City, the land and dwelling at 102 North Broad Street, the barbershop located at 317 South Broad Street, and the Cheshire storehouse at 421 through 425 South Broad Street. Any other recent purchases to add?"

I shake my head. "No. I wanted to see where I stood before purchasing anything else."

"Good. It's an impressive list of assets, and I think it's better that you met with me before adding anything else." She flips a few pages in the ledger, then turns the book so I can see it. "This is the combined value of your properties."

I smile at the figure. "Excellent. Can you show me the profits?"

"Certainly." She picks up her quill pen and turns the page again. "Here's an accounting of the monies deposited in your account. These are lease payments for the lot in Elizabeth City." She points to another grouping of numbers. "These are deposits you made from your earnings at the barbershop."

I frown. "The lot isn't bringing in as much as I'd hoped. What can I do about that?"

"I'd recommend you consider raising your lease rates. They're extremely low based on the limited parking in the area, and I think you could easily double your rate without losing your customers."

I nod. "I'll consider that. How about my expenses?"

She turns a few more pages. "Here are your expenses, based on all the receipts and documents you submitted to me. As you can see, there's not much expenditure going into maintenance and repairs."

I hesitate to look at the numbers, but when I do, they aren't as high as I anticipated. "Thank goodness Dorsey does a lot of the work for me at no charge. The benefits of having a carpenter as your father-in-law."

Charlotte nods. "Yes, you've undoubtedly saved a lot of money on repairs. But you still have the partial mortgage you took out on the house." She slides the ledger closer to me. "You're welcome to take a more thorough look at the numbers if you like."

"I will, but first I wanted to get your advice on something."

"Sure."

"What more should I do with the storehouse?"

She leans back, shifting her gaze upward. "That depends. What is your goal for the property? Is it strictly to bring in a profit, or do you wish to do something loftier with it?"

I tap a finger on my chin. "A little of both, I suppose. Profit is always nice because it allows me to give my family a good life. But I'd also like to make a statement with the building."

Charlotte returns her gaze to my face, narrowing her eyes. "Can you be a little more specific?"

"The vision is still forming in my head," I admit. "But I'm thinking of keeping the storehouse as one large building, rather than dividing up the three storefronts."

"Go on."

"I don't know what I'll do with the building yet. The inside will need some repairs before I can move any business into it." I look toward the window as I try to describe my rather amorphous plans. "But the exterior must make a bold statement. A lasting one. I'm going to be spending a lot of time on the exterior design so that it will catch the attention of anyone who passes by."

"All right. Well, in the meantime, I think you should continue leasing the building out for its original purpose: storage. Plenty of business owners around here could use the extra space for inventory, equipment and the like, and I'm sure they'd be willing to pay a good price," Charlotte says.

"That sounds reasonable. I'll look into getting more clients who need storage."

She slides the loose papers my way. "As for your current holdings, my advice is to pay off your mortgage first, then raise your rent on the Elizabeth City lot and keep saving the profits from that and from your barbering work. Use that money to add to your property when the time comes. I've outlined a financial plan for you; you can take it with you for reference."

I nod, taking the papers and returning the ledger. "Thank you for your help, Charlotte."

"Not a problem."

Leaving the bank, I return home. Since I expected to be at the bank for a good while, I've designated today for spring-cleaning. The girls are at my mother's house, because at their age, they are more of a hindrance than a help for such tasks.

In my bedroom, I take off the nice skirt and blouse I wore to the bank, along with my corset. Changing into an old pair of trousers and a shirt that's seen better days, I put on my moccasins.

Sweety enters the bedroom then, dressed similarly. "Are you ready to trade the mattress?"

I nod. Mattress trading is the most arduous task of all, and we prefer to tackle it first, to get it out of the way.

We work together to strip the bed of its sheets and quilts, then drag the mattress to the floor. It isn't that heavy, but care must be exercised to keep from snagging and ripping the cover and releasing a torrent of goose feathers all over the room. Laying the soiled mattress on the floor, we work in tandem, lifting the clean one.

"Back up, Sweety. You're too close."

He moves. "Like this?"

"Yes. Now a bit to the left." He does as I request, and we drop the mattress in its proper place. "Grab those clean sheets over there, dear." I point to the folded pile sitting on the armchair in the corner.

He retrieves them and we remake the bed with fresh linens.

After the floor is swept and mopped, we move on to the room our daughters share.

I brush my palms over my trousers. "Well, we'd better get started." It's time to go about the arduous task of replacing the stuffing in the children's mattresses. Years back, we used hay mattresses for the girls' beds. Once we discovered that Florrie was allergic, we switched to a stuffing made from finely shredded corn husks. The process involves taking the mattresses off the beds, washing the covers, and replacing the filling with the fresh filling material.

"You get that bed, and I'll get this one," Sweety says as he grabs one end of the mattress on Florrie's bed. I grab the one from Claire's bed across the room. That done, we each drag a mattress down the stairs, through the house, and out the back door, careful not to snag them on anything.

We open the cotton covers using the snaps along the sides and dump out the old corn husks. Next, we take the cotton covers to the washroom and load them into the washing machine. I add a healthy amount of my homemade washing soap to the water, and Sweety begins cranking the handle.

"So how was your meeting this morning?" Sweety eyes me expectantly, waiting to hear the details.

"It was fine." The memory of the way he behaved that Sunday at my mother's house when he insinuated that I'm not devoted enough to him or this family is still fresh in my mind.

"Come now, dearest. Surely the details are more exciting than that."

I look away. He doesn't seem to understand that the way he's related to me lately leaves me hesitant to share my activities with him. "They really aren't. We talked a lot about facts and figures, but I certainly wouldn't call it exciting."

Sweety scoffs, slowing his turning of the crank. "Is that really all you're going to say about it?"

"My investments are doing well."

"How well, exactly? I've never seen your books."

"And I've never seen the book you keep of your barber earnings, either. Besides, my banker retains my books. I simply stop by the bank once a week with my savings deposit and my receipts and she keeps track of them for me."

"That seems like a lot of extra trouble when you could just keep your own books."

"Perhaps. But this is a business decision I made, time versus money. She's very efficient, and I'd rather pay her a small amount of coin to free up the time it would take for me to keep my own books." I straighten the scarf that's holding my hair out of my face. "Think of Octavious. You had him work at the counter of the barbershop rather than checking in every client or fielding every question on your own not to save money, but to devote more time to barbering. Correct?"

Sweety abruptly stops cranking. "Your turn, dearest." His tone is less than affectionate.

He moves aside, and I approach the machine. As I run the freshly washed mattress covers through the wringer, he stands at my side, arms folded over his chest, watching me in stony silence. I suppose he thinks this will compel me to give him more information about my financial status. I am unmoved. He's made it clear to me that he doesn't deserve access to my business. Why should I reveal my plans to him, only to have them shot down or criticized?

Once the mattress covers are clean and wrung out, we take them to the clothesline and pin them up to dry.

We bring down a load of the girls' clothing, wash it, and run it through the wringer without another word from Sweety. He's stating his disapproval with his silence. I know it and he knows it. But I refuse to meet his rather immature demands.

Finally, he opens his mouth. "When we first married, I knew you were independent and ambitious. I just never expected those qualities that I found so admirable would relegate me to the outskirts of our marriage."

"Not saying or doing everything you want isn't equivalent to pushing you away. I'm simply acting to protect my dream. You used to be the spark that lit the fires of my imagination." I sigh. "You made me believe I could do anything. But at some point, you changed. Now the dreams that once excited you seem to annoy you, to threaten you somehow."

"If you are to become some sort of land baron, then what do you need me for? It's my duty as husband and father to care for this family, to provide you and our daughters with a comfortable life."

"There is so much more to being a good husband and father. Why would you reduce it to only money?"

"You're a woman, and you simply can't understand my point of view on this." He shakes his head and looks away. "Certain things are simply irrefutable."

"I love you, Archer Leary. I love you as the moon loves the night. And I would hope that after all these years you can see that you mean so much more to me than what you can provide." I ease closer to him, touch his hardened jaw.

"I love you, Jo. Sometimes you are simply too much."

I don't respond with words. Instead, I peck him on the cheek and walk away.

My husband may be overwhelmed by all that I am, but I won't shrink myself. Not for him or anyone else.

I shrank beneath the lash. I shrank beneath the weight of my work, beneath the pressures of a life of enslavement.

The time for shrinking has passed.

Now, I bloom.

# 11

JOSEPHINE

*July 1883*

I slip out of my bedroom, fully dressed, on a warm Wednesday morning. Sweety is long gone, having left before sunrise to accommodate an early client at the barbershop. Now my task is to get out of the house and make it to my meeting.

Easing the door shut, I tiptoe across the landing to the stairs, my moccasins whispering against the wood floors.

I make it halfway down when that one stair creaks beneath my feet.

I close my eyes, pausing mid-step.

The door to the girls' bedroom bursts open.

"Mama, where are you going?" Three-year-old Florrie, still in her nightgown, latches onto my leg.

I sigh. "I have an important meeting today, sweetie. I'll be back before you know it."

"But Mama, I want to go," she whines, her big brown eyes staring up at me.

I feel the twinge of guilt squeeze my heart as I take her into my arms and hoist her onto my hip. "I'm sorry, Florrie, but you're too young to come along. Don't worry, you will have lots of fun with your sister and Grandma Milly."

Clara pokes her head out of the bedroom then. "Mama, when are we going to make kites? You promised we could do it."

I cringe, realizing I'm probably going to be late. "I haven't forgotten, Clara. I'm going to see Eunice today to pick up the fabric remnants we'll use."

"See if she has pink." Clara disappears back into the room.

I make it downstairs, with Florrie on my hip, and find my grandmother sitting in the kitchen, a cup of coffee in hand.

"Morning, Jo." She raises her cup to me. "Here, hand me Florrie and go on. You're going to be late."

"Thank you, Grandma." I sit Florrie on her lap and finally head for the front door.

I drive my buggy up to the front of St. John the Evangelist. I step down from the seat, offering a snuggle and a head stroke to Cinnamon as thanks for getting me here safely. With her tied to the last available hitching post, I make my way inside the church.

As I enter the grand quietude of the sanctuary, I'm aware of the hushed whispers of the women and girls assembled on the pews. It isn't like me to be late to a Ladies' Auxiliary meeting, least of all one where I've been charged with speaking to the group. I draw a deep, centering breath.

I hastily move down the aisle toward the pulpit, with my handbag and notes in hand. I run my hands across the polished knotty pine surface of the podium as I place my things there. "Good morning, ladies. Please excuse my tardiness. My children have been quite rambunctious today."

A few murmurs of agreement rise from the pews, and I feel my mood soften a bit. Many of these women are also mothers; they understand the ups and downs of the job.

"All right, then. Ida, we're ready for you." I scan the group until my eyes land on the kind, familiar face of our recording secretary. As always, Ida Jenkins is sitting next to her twin sister, Isabelle, or Izzy, as she prefers to be called. The two of them are spinsters, well past sixty years of age, and as close as the silk is to the corn. While Ida's denim trousers and men's work shirt are the antitheses of Izzy's lace-trimmed blouse and dark skirt, I've known them long enough to know that either of them would gladly box someone's ears in defense of her sister.

With a smile, Ida rises and goes to the podium as I take a seat on the front pew.

"Good morning, ladies," she begins, her voice echoing through the sanctuary. "This month's meeting of the Edenton Ladies' Auxiliary is now called to order. First, let us discuss old business."

As Ida goes over last month's minutes, my mind wanders to what I will say when I return to the podium. My hands are a bit shaky, and my palms slightly damp. A thrill of energy buzzes within, though, because I've been waiting a long time to speak on this topic and I'm eager to share my perspective.

"That concludes old business, so let's move on to new business." Ida's twinkling eyes fix on me. "I'm excited to hear what our charter member, Mrs. Josephine Leary, has to share with us. But more than that, I'm glad that the youngsters of the Junior Ladies' Auxiliary are present as well. May we all welcome Jo to the podium and glean what we can from her well of knowledge." Ida begins to clap, and the assemblage joins her as I return to the podium.

I draw a deep breath. "Greetings, ladies. I hope you'll find my talk as engaging and helpful as Ida's glowing introduction would suggest." I shuffle my notes, then clasp my hands. Looking out over the group once more, I regard the faces of the Junior Auxiliary members seated on the second pew. Hannah, Alice, Nell, Frances, and Bella are all between thirteen and eighteen years old, the daughters and nieces of the older members. They sit quietly in their uniforms of white blouses and tan skirts, dutifully and expectantly looking to me for guidance. If I reach no one else with my talk today, I must reach these girls.

The older contingent seated in the third and fourth pews includes my good friends Rosa Jackson and Eunice Fitz, Ida and Izzy, church acquaintances Patience and Rachel, and a new member I haven't yet gotten to know well, Concepcion.

In the fifth pew sits a lone figure, the perpetually overdressed Alberta Stone. Her husband, Lee, is a local attorney, as she will tell anyone who will listen, regardless of the current topic of conversation. I've got a theory that her manner of dress is a self-important attempt to convey her status to everyone she encounters. Her deep blue satin traveling costume is more suited to a fancy dinner than to a club meeting. Her matching hat crowns a mass of thick black curls framing a pale, heart-shaped face. Her expression would suggest that she spent the morning sucking lemons, and her brown eyes settle disapprovingly on me. And while I strive to see the good in everyone, I've yet to see any redeeming quality in Alberta other than her sense of style.

"Today, I'd like to speak briefly on the societal roles of the modern woman, and how we might act and speak in ways that will increase our levels of success and satisfaction in life."

Alberta snorts loudly, like a pig eating too quickly at the trough.

She may be well-dressed, but there's no substitute for good upbringing and manners. I ignore her rudeness and continue. "I've narrowed my scope into three concepts, in the hopes of making it more approachable. The first concept I'll advocate is that, as women, we should have our own money and set aside a certain amount in savings."

Rosa nods. "Yes. Having your own funds is the best way to make sure you can get what you need, no matter what."

Alberta scoffs. "You *would* say that, Rosa. You are unconventional in just about every way."

I feel my eyes widen because I know Rosa won't take that slight lying down.

Rosa swivels in her seat. "I'm going to guess Lee handles all your finances?"

"Of course he does. I have no knowledge of our money, and I don't care to." Alberta folds her arms over her chest.

Eunice titters. She and Rosa have never seen eye to eye, and I suppose she's amused by this exchange. Remembering the last time I saw Eunice and Rosa cross verbal swords, I send up a brief prayer that Eunice doesn't insert herself into this conflict.

Rosa's eyes narrow. "You'd best change your ways, Alberta. A woman needs her own money. Especially in the event that she loses her husband, heaven forbid, or finds him otherwise distracted."

I clear my throat to stifle the laugh I desperately want to release. Rumors of Lee Stone's womanizing ways abound all over Chowan County, but that's certainly not what we came here to talk about. "Ladies, let's stay focused, shall we?"

Patience and Concepcion, however, are less discreet with their mirth, and their barely stifled laughs echo from the fourth pew to my podium.

Lips pursed tightly enough to disappear from view, Alberta sinks into sullen silence.

Bella, the youngest of the juniors, raises her hand.

"Yes, Bella?"

"Um, Miss Jo, if I want to save money, where should I keep it? You know, so it will be safe?"

"Good question, dear. For now, I'd suggest a mason jar or other empty container, hidden in a place only you know about." I tap my chin. "However, as you get older, I'd recommend getting a bank account. More and more banks are allowing women their own accounts now. And if you have more questions about that, let me know and I'll get you in touch with my banker."

"Thank you, Miss Jo."

"You're welcome. My second concept is that women own property when possible." I move right into the next point, in hopes of cutting off any further sniping between the ladies. We need to set a good example for the young ones, after all.

Eunice nods. "I agree. Owning my dress shop has saved me quite a bit of money that I would have paid in leasing fees."

"Thank you for that example, Eunice. I purchased my first property on my honeymoon trip and have been seeking to add to my portfolio ever since then." I pause, realizing I should be more specific. "I'm speaking of owning property of our own, separate from our husbands or male relations."

Patience balks. "I don't know, Jo. Is it really our place to do things like that?"

"Your question makes the perfect connection to my third point. Our husbands are our life partners. We love them, respect them, and cherish them." I pause for emphasis. "But we must remember that we aren't their property."

A hush falls over the group. I watch as the women whisper to each other, while the girls look perplexed.

Alice raises her hand. "But Ms. Jo, my mother says husbands have authority over their wives."

I look into the eyes of Alberta's only daughter, and once again ache for her. "Alice, that only goes so far. I spent the first nine years of my life toiling in bondage. I married for love, not to trade one set of shackles for another."

Alice doesn't say anything more, but her expression transforms from confused to thoughtful.

Alberta is on her feet within seconds. "Now just hold on, Josephine. I'll not have you poisoning my daughter's mind with such radical talk. You're setting these children up for a life of sin and regret!"

I frown, knowing she's made far too much of my words. "I've said nothing radical, Alberta." I gesture to the girls. "The young ones need to hear this. They need to know that being a good wife does not equate to lying down at a man's feet and becoming his doormat."

Rosa nods, smiling.

Raising her fist, Alberta shouts, "What are you saying? I'm no doormat to my Lee. But as a well-respected attorney . . ."

I roll my eyes.

". . . he has certain expectations for me, and I strive to meet them." She points at me. "It's what a good wife does, and I won't be chastised for it."

I shake my head. "I'm not chastising anyone; I'm simply making a point. You were a person before you married, and you should still maintain your identity afterward. There's no need to martyr yourself to marriage; you are still your own woman, with your own mind."

"Well, I'll have you know——"

I strike the gavel against the podium, the sharp crack of wood against wood echoing in the sanctuary. "That's enough, Alberta. I'm not going to argue with you."

"That's because you know I'm right," she snaps.

The meeting is now abuzz with whispers and wide eyes. I simply shake my head. "Fine, Alberta. Let me level with you here, because I think you're missing my point."

Rosa Jackson's grin widens.

Alberta swallows.

"Alberta, I want you to think about what I'm saying. What would you do if something were to happen to Lee?"

Her answer is a blank stare.

"If he were to be taken suddenly, would you know where to access the household funds? Do you know whether or not he has a will?"

Alberta shakes her head slowly. "No, Jo. I don't . . . I don't know any of those things."

"You see? That's a problem. When men exercise complete financial control over their wives, it leaves them at a huge disadvantage. And while you should have been more fastidious, societal power dynamics are at play, and the fault lies with Lee." I clasp my hands together. "If he loves you, he should allow you some personal financial security. It's wrong of him to deny you that."

Eunice, Rachel, and Alberta all look as if they've seen a two-headed goat.

I stop myself, already feeling a twinge of guilt for being so bold. Still, the feeling is far outweighed by one of satisfaction. "Alice, forgive me for speaking so plainly about your father."

Alice appears nonplussed. "It's okay. My grandma says the same things about him all the time. Says he needs Jesus."

My brow lifts in surprise at how well she handled an awkward moment. With a grandmother like that, I have hope that Alice will be all right, despite her mother's antiquated thinking.

Alberta appears thoughtful for a moment, and a silence falls over the sanctuary. Her words quiet, she meets my gaze. "I . . . will look into it."

"That's all I ask." I give her a small smile before turning my attention back to the larger group. "That's all I'm asking of any of you. Please seek information about your financial situations, so that you can have security for yourselves and your children. We can't depend on our husbands for everything. It isn't fair to them, or to us." I clap my hands together. "I hope you all have gotten something useful out this."

"I certainly did." Izzy speaks, having observed the entire meeting up until this point in silence.

Seventeen-year-old Nell raises her hand. "I thought it was good, Miss Jo. It gave me lots to think about since I'm going off to university soon."

I smile, feeling accomplished. "That's wonderful to hear, Nell. And I know you'll do well at Saint Augustine's. Have you decided what to study yet?"

Nell nods, proudly stating, "Business."

Patience, Nell's aunt, who raised her niece as her own after losing her sister to the perils of childbirth, dabs at her eyes with a handkerchief. "I just know her mama's up in heaven, burstin' with pride."

"Absolutely." I couldn't be more pleased. Sending a young lady of the community off into the world is never easy, but at least I've helped equip her for what's ahead. There's a satisfaction in that, a feeling I can't get anywhere else.

Yes, one day I'll have to send off my own two daughters into the world beyond the safety of our little hamlet. But before they go, I'll do whatever I must to make sure they're ready.

# JOSEPHINE

### *January 1884*

I turn my key in the lock, and the door to the barbershop unlatches with a loud click. Swinging it open, I gesture to everyone behind me. "Come on in, ladies."

I enter the shop with my daughters and my sister-in-law, Missouri, behind me. It's an overcast Sunday afternoon, and as soon as everyone is inside, I shut the door, blocking the heavy chill hanging in the air.

"Mama, it's cold in here," Clara grouses.

We've all dressed warmly and comfortably in denims, shirts, and our heaviest cloaks, but there is only so much garments can do to stave off the cold on such a dreary day.

"I'll go put a few logs in the stove." Missouri eases past me and goes to the old iron stove, which sits against the wall adjacent to the store-room door. Stooping, she tosses in a few good-size pieces of wood, and works to get the fire going.

"All right, girls. Let's do some of this cleaning while the stove heats up."

Florrie pokes out her lower lip. "Mama, do we have to?"

I laugh. "Yes, that's why we're here. Besides, moving around will help us warm up a bit."

I hand my daughters dustcloths, sending Clara to take care of the counters and mirrors while Florrie dusts my plant stands, the window-sills, and all the other things I can think of that are low enough for her to reach.

Walking over to the reception desk, I keep a watchful eye on the girls while I pull out the strongbox containing the barbershop's funds and logbook.

Missouri calls out to me from the storeroom. "There are a few things we need to replenish back here, Jo."

"Let me bring the logbook, and we can go over them."

For the next half hour, we complete an inventory of the supplies in the storeroom. I tally what we have on hand and mark down all the items we need to reorder. On a separate page, I note which tonics I need to make.

I reconvene with the girls. "Now, Clara, you can do the sweeping, and, Florrie, I need you to sort the combs and shears into the jars for each station."

Florrie tugs on the tail of her shirt. "You want me to . . . count them?"

"Yes. Don't worry, I'll help you, and it will be good practice for you." I stoop down and give her cheek a small squeeze. I often look for opportunities like this, to teach my youngest a practical life skill she will use later. Since she is not yet old enough to enter the Badham School, I know it's important that I use this time to prepare her.

After the cleaning is done, I let the girls play with their rubber balls and jacks in the waiting area, while Missouri and I pore over the books.

Missouri, tapping a pencil against her chin, asks, "What does 'OO' stand for here?"

"Olive oil. I use it as a base in my hair-growth tonic." I point to the line on the page. "I've added fifty cents to the budget for this month so I can replenish my supply."

"Ah, I see." She makes a note in the margins of the page, then sets the pencil down. For a moment she is quiet, and though she is looking at the page, she doesn't seem to be focused on it.

I nudge her gently. "Missouri, what's the matter?"

"Octavious and I are having trouble conceiving."

I offer a solemn nod. "I see."

"Don't tell him I told you," she adds. "He thinks he is at fault, that he isn't virile enough." Her tone is low, and her voice has a slight tremble. "Maybe it's me, I don't know. I only know I want what you have." She gestures to the girls, quietly playing in the front of the shop.

"I can't imagine what you're going through. Most of us take being able to have a family for granted. I know I did." I look at my daughters, the embodiment of my ancestors' dreams of freedom, my legacy. "There is something special about motherhood. It is unique, a blend of happiness and sadness, of exuberance and exhaustion. I can't think of anything else that compares. And trying to balance motherhood with a career?" I wipe imaginary sweat from my brow. "Trust me, it isn't for the faint of heart."

"I know. I've seen you chasing that balance ever since we met." She chuckles. "I'm going to try to relax and put less pressure on myself. It gratifies me to know that, even if I'm not meant to be a mother, I'll always have two of the world's best nieces to keep me busy."

I smile. "Your love for my daughters is a gift. And they love you right back, as do I."

"You are truly the sister of my heart, Jo."

We embrace, and I give her a firm squeeze. "Please know you can talk to me about this anytime, and I'll listen without judgment."

I hear a light tapping that draws my attention toward the door. Through the glass, I see Rosa standing outside, and I head to the front of the shop to let her in.

"Rosa, what are you doing here?" I let my gaze sweep over her, and notice her attire. "Are you wearing a skirt?"

She smiles, doing a full turn to reveal the white lace-collared blouse and matching skirt peeking from beneath her favorite blue wool cloak. "I am. Jameson and I are heading to St. John's to get hitched." She gestures to Jameson Carter, her intended, who is sitting on the seat of a fancy buggy, wearing a dark suit. The black Stetson on his head shades his face, and he touches the brim to acknowledge me.

I wave back as I try to shake off my surprise. "Right now? Goodness, Rosa, why didn't you tell me?"

"I didn't know myself until about an hour ago." She giggles. "It was Jameson's idea. We'll marry today, then have a celebratory dinner later."

I'm still taken aback, but the happiness dancing in my friend's eyes is unmistakable. "Then go on, with my blessing. But I'll expect you to notify me of this upcoming party, Rosa."

"You'll be the first to hear of it." She leans in, gives me a tight hug. "I've got to go. The rector is waiting on us."

I peck her on the cheek, then watch her dash off to the buggy. Jameson helps her up into her seat, and then the two of them drive off.

Shutting the door again, I shake my head in amazement. Soon, my friend will become Mrs. Rosa Carter, and I could not be more pleased. "Missouri, can you believe it?"

"She's always been unconventional," my sister-in-law quips.

By suppertime, we have finished our work. I drive Missouri to the small house she shares with my brother on King Street, then take my daughters home. After a meal of roast pork, mustard greens, and rice, I retire to the settee to read.

Across from me, Sweety settles into his favorite chair, with our daughters at his feet. "Who's ready to continue the story?"

Both Clara and Florrie react enthusiastically, and Sweety opens the copy of Mark Twain's *The Prince and the Pauper* that he's placed on his lap. The rich timbre of his deep voice fills the room as he reads aloud from its pages. Since he managed to find an illustrated edition, he periodically stands the open book up so the girls can see the pictures.

I feel my heart swell as I watch our daughters, their attention rapt, their gazes locked on their father's face. They are hanging on his every word, and it's wonderful to see them this way. It reminds me not only that we've done a good job raising our daughters to love the written word, but also how valuable a role their father plays in their lives. His choice to stay home tonight instead of carousing with his friends at the barroom has made it possible for him to share this precious time with our children.

I set aside my own book, settle next to my daughters on the floor, and let myself join them in the world created by Mr. Twain and brought to life by the man I love.

# 12

JOSEPHINE

*September 1885*

O n a cool September Tuesday, I sit on Florrie's bed, watching her get ready. The day is somewhat dreary, but the sun still peeks through. A soft rain falls outside, the droplets singing against the tin roof above our heads.

Breaking the silence, I ask my younger daughter, "Are you excited about today, honey?"

Florrie shakes her head as she hoists up her skirt. "No, Mama. I don't want to go to school. I want to stay with you."

"Come now, Florrie. My years at the freedmen's school in Williamston were so valuable. I had a lot of fun and met a lot of good friends there."

It's not easy staying upbeat about this, but I know I must set a good example for her. My baby girl is going off to school, and it seems only yesterday I brought her into this world. Where has the time gone? The days have passed in a flurry of activity: diapers and nursing, chasing naked toddlers, cooking and cleaning and washing. Add to that long days of monitoring the real estate reports and trimming ends at the barbershop, and it's a wonder I recall any of it.

I exist in two worlds, barbering to help Sweety keep the shop productive and profitable, and building my portfolio to generate passive income that will serve this family long after we finally retire.

This day is bittersweet for me, even more so than Clara's first day. The difference is that now, I'm fairly certain there won't be any more babies in the house.

"*Why* can't I stay with you, Mama?" Her whining has only intensified over the past few moments.

I inhale deeply before I speak again. "Everything in life has its season, honey. You're a big girl now, and it's time for you to go to school and learn the things you need to know for life." Eyeing the dangling hem of my daughter's blouse, I remind her, "Don't forget to tuck it in, just like I showed you."

Florrie huffs and puffs like an old chimney as she roughly stuffs the end of her blouse into her skirt. The result is a disheveled mess, and I'm certain my child doesn't much care.

I sigh, crooking my index finger. "Come here and let me fix it."

She trudges over to where I'm sitting, her little face marred by her despondent expression. "Mama, why can't *you* be my teacher? Or Granny Jeanette?"

While righting Florrie's clothes, I try to be gentle with her. "Granny Jeanette is working on getting her garden ready for fall harvest so she can sell her vegetables to Mr. Hammond at the general store. And I have to go back to work at the barbershop." In reality, there's more to it than that. I need my days back to assist Sweety at the shop, yes, but also so I can look after my properties.

Traffic being what it is in Elizabeth City, I've switched Sheila Brown to monthly accounting. Beyond that, I'm now spending at least one afternoon each week at the Cheshire storehouse, taking measurements, assessing damages, or showing the building to potential lessees. There is much to do, and very little time to do it in.

Florrie sticks her lower lip out. "I don't want to go, Mama!"

"Now, Florrie, you just tuck that lip right back in. If we were outside, you'd be collecting rain." I draw her into my arms. "I know you're nervous, and that's natural. Everybody feels at least a tiny bit nervous when they are doing something for the first time."

Her big brown eyes damp, she says earnestly, "I don't like it, Mama."

I stroke my hand over her hair, taking the bone comb and tin of hair-dressing from my apron pocket. "You can't say that about something you haven't tried. But either way, you are going to school. It's time, and you'll be fine. Besides, you're lucky. You have a big sister right there to look after you." I gesture for her to sit on the floor, between my knees, so I can style her hair.

Florrie sniffles as she sits. "Will I be in the same room with Clara?"

I rub a bit of the hairdressing through her hair, the scent of oranges floating to my nostrils. Working the comb slowly through her tresses, I answer her question. "I don't know. But you definitely won't be far from her." I give her a little squeeze and a peck on the cheek. "And don't you worry. If you need us, really need us, your daddy and I will be there faster than you can say 'sarsaparilla.'" I pull her hair into a ponytail and tie a short piece of twine around it, wrapping it a few times to keep it secure.

"Shish . . . sis . . . saparilly . . ." Florrie's expression brightens as she makes her attempt at repeating the word. "Shishpariley!"

I can't hold back my giggle. "That's close enough, honey. Feel better now?"

She nods. "A little."

"That's a start. Now, let's get your sister and go downstairs for some breakfast."

Clara emerges from her room, fully dressed in a white blouse, dark skirt, and well-worn boots. The leather belt she uses to carry her books is already in her hand, two volumes dangling at the end.

"You've done well preparing for school, Clara."

She winks. "Of course, Mama. I'm eleven whole years old now, I can take care of myself."

I shake my head as I raise my gaze to her hair. She's managed to collect her wild curls into a high bun, but it's woefully lopsided. "I'm proud of you, dear. But you know I'm going to have to redo your hair, right?"

A sheepish look comes over my elder child's face as she reaches up to touch her hair. "Yes, Mama."

Sweety has gone early to the barbershop to do inventory, so I cook a meal for the three of us: scrambled eggs, grits running with butter, and crisp bacon. After the girls and I have had our fill, and I've corrected Clara's crooked hairstyle, I hurry them outside and load them into the carriage for the short drive to the Evelina Badham School. My intent had been to walk them to school, but the rain changed that plan.

We arrive at the schoolhouse on East Gale Street in short order, and I view the familiar structure with fresh eyes. The Badham School, run by the wife of Edenton's premier carpenter, is easily the best school in the county, accepting students of all races. It's housed inside a white-washed two-story structure resembling a fine home. Two steps ascend to a wide, covered brick porch that leads to the main entrance. The children gather on that porch twice a year, in the fall and the spring, for a class photograph. The front door, painted bright blue and sporting rectangular glass panels on either side, matches the paint on the ornate window frames and shutters. Double chimneys punctuate either side of the hand-shingled roof; I've seen the steam pouring out of them when Evelina runs the stove to keep the students warm on cold days. I've always admired the structure, especially since I'm so well acquainted with Hannibal. I can see his personal touch in every detail of the schoolhouse that he built for his beloved wife.

As I step down from the wagon seat, Evelina appears on the porch. "Y'all come on in out of this rain!"

Once I've gotten Florrie and Clara safely to the ground, the three of us dash inside, leaving Sugar tied to one of the porch posts.

In the front parlor where Evelina keeps her office, I watch as my daughters hang their cloaks on the designated wall-mounted hooks. I'm pleased to see Clara instructing Florrie on what to do, and the sight offers me even more reassurance that my elder child will look after her baby sister in my absence.

Evelina, ever the picture of confidence and subdued style, smiles at Florrie. Dressed in a navy-blue skirt, crisp white blouse, and long navy-blue overcoat with a small, flowered hat, she looks every bit the savvy educator and headmistress I know her to be. She nudges her silver-rimmed spectacles up the bridge of her nose. "My, my. Seems only yesterday she was a babe, and now young Florence is ready to become a Badham scholar."

Florrie's shy smile is her only response.

"Yes, yes," I concur. "They grow up far too quickly."

"Clara, why don't you show your sister to Mrs. Cullen's room, on your way to Miss Pullman's." Evelina gestures toward the door by inclining her head slightly in that direction.

"Yes, Mrs. Badham."

I give the girls a hug and kiss in parting, then watch as Clara leads her sister out of the room.

Once we're alone, Evelina sits behind her desk and gestures to the chair across from her. "Come, sit a moment."

I take the offered seat. "I do hope Florrie will do well. She was a little nervous about coming."

"I wouldn't worry about it, Jo. All the children are like that on their first day." Evelina tents her fingers, elbows resting on top of the polished white oak desk. "Soon enough, your little one will take to school like a duckling takes to water. Just give her time."

I nod. "Logically I know that. But it's so hard to be logical when it comes to your babies sometimes, you know?"

"I certainly do. Listen, Clara is one of my brightest students. And I have found, in all my years of educating our youth, that children from the same household often have similar academic proclivities. If Florrie is anywhere near your elder daughter in intelligence, I'm sure she'll do excellent work here." Evelina smiles, then reaches over the desk to squeeze my hand. "I can't tell you how many of these first-day chats I've had with worried mothers. But she's going to be fine."

I take a deep breath, letting her words settle on my spirit. "Thank you, Evie. I'd better be on my way; I've so much to do today."

"I know you must be very busy; you've missed the last two quilting circles."

"I do have my squares, though. I work on them in the evenings after everyone's asleep." I give her an apologetic look. "I hope to get caught up today so that I don't have to miss the next one."

"It's been years since you've had the day to yourself, Jo. Go on, make the most of it."

With a parting hug, I leave the office. Outside, the rain has stopped, giving way to a sun-dappled yet hazy day. I can still feel the humidity hanging in the air. I untie Sugar and climb aboard the carriage seat. With the vehicle underway, I head to my next stop: the old Cheshire storehouse.

The large building is fashioned of stone and stands two stories high. Occupying space for three storefronts, 421 through 425 South Broad Street is my largest property purchase to date. Standing on the walk in front of it, I gaze up at the roofline. A property of this magnitude deserves to be used for something grand.

Right now, it brings me a decent amount of leasing income, as the Hammond family utilizes the space to store nonperishable inventory for the general store. Standing before it today, I'm reminded again that I want more for this building. I'm simply not sure of what, at least not yet.

I'm a patient woman. I'll wait until my vision is fully solidified in my mind before making any major changes. For now, my main concern is keeping the building in good repair and saving funds toward its future purpose.

I turn, waving to a few passersby as I drive up the block from my storehouse to the barbershop. Once there, I enter through the propped-open door.

Sweety is working on the curly brown mop of a man I don't recognize. "Morning, dearest," he calls out to me while working his shears.

"Good morning."

He asks, "Is Florrie settled at the schoolhouse?"

"As much as can be expected." I walk over and peck him on the cheek before heading past him to my station. "Evie and I both agree she'll be fine, given enough time."

He nods, shifting his focus back to the haircut.

"Where's Octavious?"

"You know your brother. Now that he and Missouri are trying to have a baby, he just pops off at random times of the day to—"

I hold up my hand. "Sweety, don't you dare finish that sentence." Often, when I look at my brother, I still see that chubby-faced, fast-talking little boy who loved to climb trees and make mischief. I know he's grown, but he'll always be that little boy in my heart and mind.

Sweety's client chuckles, as if amused by our exchange. "Get it while you're young, I always say."

I roll my eyes as the two men begin snickering. This is the thing I enjoy least about barbering. Men love their plain talk, and their two favorite places are the saloon and the barbershop. Maybe it's because I'm efficient, maybe it's because I blend in well, but often I think the men forget I'm here and just go on wagging their foul tongues. I've learned to ignore them most of the time.

Thankfully, I get my first client a short time later. It's Rosa, and I'm relieved to see improvement in the condition of her hair. "You've been using the hair oil I gave you, haven't you?"

Rosa nods. "Yes. And I love how shiny and easy to comb it is."

"See? Told you." I look at her face and smile. "Aside from that, you've got the glow of love on you. Seems married life is treating you well."

She blushes, but offers no denial. "Go on with you, Jo."

"Did you make a decision on whether to grow out your hair?"

"I'm still going to keep it short for now." She runs her hands through her curls, which have reached her shoulders. "I don't think I have a proclivity for long hair. Too much trouble for a girl like me."

"I understand. Let me try a layered cut on you this time. I think you'll like the way it turns out."

Rosa sits back in the chair. "Okay, Jo. I trust you, so have at it."

I take my time in layering Rosa's hair, working with her natural part to enhance and frame the soft lines of her face. The shears sing in my hands as snipped strands fall. Finally, I remove the cape, dust her shoulders with my brush, and hand her a looking glass. "What do you think?"

Rosa's eyes widen as she fluffs her hair. "I love it! Jo, you're an artist."

I shake my head, speaking to her in playful tones. "I'm glad you like it. Now show me your gratitude by giving me two dollars." I hold out my hand.

She laughs as she passes me the money.

# JOSEPHINE

## *April 1886*

I open my eyes, squinting a bit against the early-morning light. A moment later, I sit up, blinking a few times so that my eyes can fully adjust. A glance to my left confirms my sense that I'm alone, and I slip from the bed, moving across the room to the window. I open the curtains and tie them back so I can look out on the street below. Much of Edenton still slumbers, as it's just past sunrise. My body clock has snatched extra sleep away from me; after years of getting up early to work or care for family and home, I've lost the ability to sleep in.

I crack the window a bit, letting in some of the fresh spring air as I reflect on this day.

It is Friday, the sixteenth of April. And today, I am thirty years old.

I sigh. Thirty. Three decades of life; thirty revolutions around the sun. It feels wonderful and strange all at once. So many things have happened in my life up to this point, I can only imagine what the next three decades will bring if the Lord blesses me with a long life. My grandmother is just a year short of eighty. Though she doesn't get around as well as she once did, she's certainly still got her wits about her. I see her longevity as a good omen for me.

The pattering of small feet sounds in the hallway, and I turn toward the bedroom door.

It swings open, and Sweety, Florrie, and Clara appear. My husband, grinning broadly, carries a wooden tray.

"Sing, my darlings," Sweety encourages. The three of them then break into "For She's a Jolly Good Fellow."

I feel the smile tugging at my lips as I dutifully return to the bed, reclining like a queen against my pillows as I wait to be served. Sweety places the tray, holding a plate of grits, eggs, bacon, and a slightly misshapen biscuit, along with a steamy mug of coffee, over my lap. The three of them then pile into bed with me.

"My goodness, what a feast." I pick up my fork. "Thank you all for such a lovely breakfast."

"We helped," Florrie sings.

"I'm glad you did. It would have taken your papa all day to make such a meal without your help." I jab him gently in the side with my elbow.

He rolls his eyes but leans to whisper in my ear, "I'll be giving you extra birthday whacks for that later."

I shake my head, gesturing to the children. "Sweety! The girls."

He sobers up, straightens his posture. "There's more," he announces. Going out of the room briefly, he returns and hands me a small bunch of yellow roses and lamb's ears. "Happy birthday, my dearest love."

"Thank you, husband." I accept the blooms, then lean up and place a soft kiss against his lips.

"We've brought you something too, Mama." Clara produces a small satin bag.

Opening it, I find a lovely necklace inside. It is made of braided silver and pearls and has a lovely rosy quartz stone as a centerpiece. "It's beautiful. Wherever did you get something so unique?"

"We made it," Florrie announces proudly. "Ms. Ida helped us with it."

I gasp. I knew of Ida's jewelry-making hobby, but I had no idea she possessed this level of talent. "Ida is quite the silversmith."

"Yeah," Clara interjects. "We got the pearls from Wilmington, and Ms. Ida found the quartz herself, down by the creek."

I drape the necklace over my head, letting the pendant rest in the hollow of my neck. "I'll never take it off."

While I eat my breakfast, Sweety leads the children from the room to ready them for school. The eggs are a bit plain since my husband rarely remembers to season them, but everything is otherwise delicious. There's something to be said about a meal made with love; it enhances the flavor of the food.

Finishing my meal, I go to the wardrobe and pull out my clothes. After a quick trip to the washroom to handle my morning routine, I dress in a dark blue skirt and my favorite soft blue blouse. The throat and sleeves are edged with fine lace, and I wear it only on special occasions. What could be more fitting than to wear it today, on my milestone birthday?

I grab the bag I prepared last evening according to Izzy's instructions. I'm to celebrate at the Jenkins twins' home today, and Izzy asked me to bring a dressing gown, my slippers, and a book. I've chosen my well-loved copy of Alexandre Dumas's *The Black Tulip*. First published nearly a decade before my birth, this tale of political intrigue, forbidden love, and a rare flower has been a favorite of mine since I first read it in my early twenties.

Sweety meets me at the bottom of the stairs. "Off to the Jenkinses' place, then?"

I nod. "Yes, and I'm looking forward to finally discovering what they have in store for me today."

"You mean you don't know?"

"Nope. They didn't tell me a thing, other than what to bring and when to be there." I lean up and kiss him on the cheek. "I'm just going to take Cinnamon, since their house is a bit too far to walk."

"All right. Have a wonderful birthday, dearest."

With a smile, I depart. Outside in the barn, I saddle up and mount Cinnamon, securing my bag to the saddle horn. I urge the palomino forward with my heels. "Giddyap, girl!"

We are off, and I enjoy the familiar scenery flying by, as well as the cool spring breeze whipping my hair around my head. We leave the boundaries of town in short order, and the buildings and noise soon give way to the pines, spruces, and oaks lining the sides of the road, and the relative quiet of the countryside.

Arriving at the Jenkins house, I take in the stately structure. The house, a two-story log cabin–style home, sits a good half mile back from the road in a secluded grove.

Ida greets me as I ride up the gravel path. Standing on the wide front porch, she calls to me, "Take your mount around back to the barn, dear."

"Thanks," I call back, directing Cinnamon around the side of the house. Once she is tucked into an empty stall, with a bit of hay and a water trough to sustain her, I climb the four steps up to the back porch.

Ida lets me in the house. "Come on in. Happy birthday, Jo."

Inside the warmth of their kitchen, I accept her offered hug. "Thank you. Do I get to know what we're doing today now?"

"In a moment, dear." She turns and calls for her sister. "Izzy, she's here."

Izzy floats into the room. "Happy birthday, Josephine! How do you like thirty so far?"

I shrug. "The day has gone well up to now, so I suppose it's fine." I find myself eyeing both twins, wondering what's next.

Ida and Izzy exchange knowing looks.

Izzy declares, "I suppose we can tell you now. Take a seat, child." She gestures to the round oak kitchen table.

I take a seat, while the twins sit on either side of me.

Ida begins, "Today, you've reached thirty years old. You are now at the peak of your womanhood, and we want to spend the day helping you embrace the divine feminine within."

I frown. "I'm not sure what that means."

"I know, child, but trust us. Call it a rite of passage, if you will." Izzy's tone and expression are comforting, reassuring. "You'll leave here tonight more confident and ready to take on whatever life throws at you."

I think about what they're saying, and how much I trust them. Since I came to know them years back, the two of them have been like the aunts I never had, but so desperately wanted. "I'm still not entirely sure what this will entail, but let's do it."

Ida claps her hands together. "Good girl. First thing, change into the dressing gown you brought. Wouldn't want to sully those nice clothes."

They lead me to the parlor and leave me to change. As I don my dressing gown and fold my clothes, placing them in my bag, I can't help wondering what we're about to do. Knowing the Jenkins twins, it could be anything.

A knock sounds at the parlor door. "Are you all changed, dear?"

"Yes."

The door opens and the twins enter. Izzy is first, with Ida close behind, each of them carrying a tin basin. The steam rising from them scents the air with a heady combination of fruity and floral aromas: citrus, hibiscus, rose.

"That smells marvelous, whatever it is." I watch as Izzy sets her basin on the floor and pulls a short stool up to it.

"Just some hot water and herbs, dear." Izzy smiles. "Here, sit, and place your feet in the basin, please."

I do as she's asked, sitting, and sinking my feet slowly into the fragrant warmth of the water.

Ida pulls a taller stool behind me and sets her basin atop it. "All right. I'm going to cleanse your hair and scalp."

"Yes, ma'am."

Ida slides the pins from my hair, releasing its length. I lie back, feeling the heated water drench my curls.

For the next few minutes, I simply enjoy the feeling of Ida scrubbing my hair and scalp with a scented bar of soap, as well as the heat engulfing my tired feet. I don't feel a need to inquire about the purpose of this exercise, because I'm too busy relaxing. I've never been treated with such care, and I won't ruin it with unnecessary questions.

Ida squeezes the water from my hair, then wraps a towel around it while Izzy dries my feet.

"How do you feel, dear?" Izzy asks.

"Relaxed." I smile. "Thank you for that."

"You're welcome. A bit of pampering now and then is good for the soul." Ida takes up her basin. "Next, we'll all have mud masks and some herbal tea."

"Do mud masks work as well as I've heard?" I ask.

Izzy nods. "Absolutely. What do you think keeps Ida and me looking so young?" With a wink, she takes her basin and the two of them disappear from the room again.

They lead me out onto the back porch, where a porch swing and two weathered rockers reside. Izzy and I take seats in the rockers, and Ida disappears into the kitchen, returning with a large bowl.

I stare at the creamy, brownish contents. "And where do you get this mud, exactly?"

Ida chuckles. "Lady up in Bertie County mails me some of the clay she uses for her pottery. I add the water myself. Purest mud you can get." She digs in with one hand. "Go ahead, grab you a glop."

In short order, the three of us are slathering the stuff on our faces and necks. It's cold, thick, and heavy. "I feel like I'm icing my face."

"Once it dries and you wash it off, you'll see why we swear by this stuff." Izzy lays her head back against her rocker.

Ida agrees from her seat on the porch swing. "Yep. Just lay back and let it work, child."

Silence settles over the porch; for a few moments, all I hear is the buzz of the bumblebees and the wind rustling the pines beyond the borders of the yard.

Izzy giggles suddenly, her voice cutting through the quiet. "Ida, do you remember the Baker twins? Every time I get a whiff of pine sap, I think of those days in the grove with them."

Ida laughs heartily, shaking her head. "How could I forget those two dunderheads?"

I'm intrigued as I glance back and forth between them. "All right, somebody tell me the story before I go mad with curiosity."

Izzy begins, "Forty years back, when we were still spring chickens and working the Jenkins land up near Raleigh, the Baker twins were the only other set of twins around."

"Yes, yes," Ida says, looking off into the sky. "Benjamin and Bartholomew. Strong, handsome fellows. Unfortunately, less sense between the two of them than the good Lord gave a goose."

I stifle a snort with my hand. "Go on with you."

"We used to see them every Sunday when we had time off for church. Bart was sweet on Ida, and Ben had his eye on me." Izzy sighs. "If I could have convinced him that he should learn to read, no telling where he'd be now."

"I think our masters would have married us off to them if it hadn't been for our unsuitability. We both came into this world barren, unable to bear children no matter how many times the master tried to breed us." Ida's expression darkens to one of sorrow. "I loved Bart, I truly did. And I think that's precisely why they were sold to Alabama."

"I cared for Ben, but not the same way Ida loved Bart." Izzy goes to her sister's side, resting a comforting hand on Ida's shoulder. "Our mistress despised us since her husband wouldn't quit tipping to our cabin at night, even after it became clear neither of us could carry. She saw Ida and Bart sparking in the woods one day, and after that, she made it her mission to separate them. Wouldn't quit nagging at old man Baker till he sold them."

I feel my heart squeeze in my chest in response to their palpable pain. It hangs between the three of us, thick and heavy like a wool blanket, yet unseen by the eye.

"I'll tell you what I learned from it all, Jo." Ida's voice is shaky as the tears stream down her face. "Your peace and happiness are priceless. All your life as a Negro woman, you'll be expected to work for the good of others. The best thing you can do is give some of that love to yourself first."

"That's why you're here, child," Izzy says. "Our gift to you isn't just the pampering, but the lesson. Love on yourself, Jo. You're no good to anyone if you don't."

# 13

## JOSEPHINE

### *April 1887*

Juggling the heavy tray loaded with food, I walk out of the kitchen onto the back porch. Slowing my advance, I carefully make my way down the two steps until my bare feet touch the soft grass. I walk to the trestle table that Dorsey and Sweety set up in the yard earlier. Setting down the tray filled with bowls of popped corn, Saratoga chips, blister-fried peanuts, and paper-wrapped caramels, I blow out a breath.

The blue sky above holds only a few wispy clouds, and I feel grateful for the blessing of warm, sunny weather today. Clara's thirteenth birthday party will be underway in less than a half hour, and I can't wait to celebrate my daughter's life with family and friends.

The back door swings open again with a loud creak, and I turn to see my mother, grandmother, and sister-in-law, all in a line, carrying more food toward the table.

As Mama sets the covered pan holding her roast chicken down, she asks, "Do you think we have enough food?"

Grandma Milly scoffs as she adds her dishes of famous potato salad and roast turnips. "Yes, Jeanette, dear. I'm certain of it."

"We have enough food for an army here," Missouri remarks as she puts the birthday cake in the center of things. Baked by Eunice's husband, Mr. Fitz, the cake's two tiers are frosted a bright pink and adorned with pink roses from Missouri's garden.

"It's just the family and a few of Clara's school friends." I shake my head at the bounty of food. "I shouldn't have to cook for a week after this shindig."

Missouri laughs.

"Wait. If we're all out here, who's with the girls?" My mother looks back toward the house.

"Sweety and Octavious are in there, aren't they?" I scratch my chin, thinking back to the last time I saw my husband. "I think Sweety's upstairs."

"Octavious is in the parlor, looking for the punch bowl." Mama twists her lips in thought. "Last I saw our birthday princess, she was in her room, brooding."

I shake my head. "That child is moodier than the sea, bless her." Clara's moods as of late have been quite an adventure to navigate. It's all a part of growing up, I suppose. "But where's Florrie?"

Grandma Milly raises her arm, pointing a finger upward. "There she is, the little scamp."

We all look, and as I lift my gaze, I see my younger daughter ensconced high in the branches of our pecan tree, an open book in her lap. I approach the tree and call up to her. "Heavens, Florrie. How did you get up there?"

She laughs. "I climbed, Mommy!"

I look to my own mother, who only shakes her head with a knowing smile. "I see she's got a bit of her uncle Octavious in her."

"Well, if she gets stuck, Uncle Octavious will have to be the one to go get her." I shake my head, looking at my daughter but envisioning my little brother up in those branches.

Soon, Clara's schoolmates arrive, and the party begins in earnest. Clara, wearing a pink gown sewn by her grandmother, looks lovely descending the staircase. I feel the tears rising in my chest, she looks so grown-up. Gone is the tiny tot who clutched my hand so tightly, who hid behind my skirts when meeting a new person.

Clara's gaze meets mine across the lawn, and for a brief moment, a smile flickers across her face. A moment later it is gone, replaced by the tight expression she's been wearing for the past few days.

Sweety, dressed in a crisp blue shirt and pants, extends his arm. "You look lovely, my dove."

Another brief smile tugs at her lips. "Thank you, Papa."

He escorts our daughter outside, and the assembled cheer as he walks her toward the table bearing the food and birthday cake.

We all gather around the table, Sweety and I, Mama, Grandma Milly, Octavious and Missouri, the dirt-streaked but grinning Florrie, and the four young girls from Clara's class, and sing her favorite song, "Oh! Susanna." As the final notes fade in the spring air, she blows out the single candle atop the cake, signaling the beginning of the birthday feast.

We get our food and scatter around the yard to enjoy it. I sit on the porch with Missouri, watching the festivities from the comfort of my favorite rocker. As I scan the gathering, I spot Clara, sitting alone atop a barrel. Her school friends and her younger sister are all seated on a blanket on the ground near her feet, but when I look at my daughter's face, the despondence I see there tugs at my heart. Swallowing a mouthful of my mother's well-seasoned chicken, I sigh. "What's the matter with her? I know young girls her age can be moody, but it's her birthday. Why haven't all these festivities cheered her any?"

Missouri takes a long draw from her tumbler of lemonade, and I catch her wide-eyed expression just before she turns her head away from me.

"Missouri. You know something." I don't ask, I state it as fact.

Missouri sighs. "She asked me not to tell you, Jo."

I feel my chest tighten again. My little girl—who's not so little anymore—had an issue and chose to talk to her aunt instead of me. I don't know what to make of it, but I know it stings a bit. "Missouri, please. I need to know what's wrong with my child."

"Nothing's wrong," she assures. "It's just . . . well, she's started her courses, and she was too nervous to tell you."

My hand flies to my mouth. "Her courses? Already?" I didn't start mine until I was sixteen, so I thought I had more time before my daughter journeyed into womanhood.

Missouri nods solemnly. "Yes. She came to me about it a few days ago. I gave her some cloths to use, and a bit of gingerroot because she said her stomach hurt." She cringed. "I'm sorry, Jo. I should have told you, but she was so adamant that I keep her secret."

I take a deep breath to rein in my emotions, then wave my sister-in-law off. "Missouri, don't apologize. You've proven yourself as a wonderful, trusted advisor to my child. You listened to her, gave her what she needed, and respected her request for privacy. I'd wager you're about the best aunt my children could have."

Missy's eyes sparkle with tears. "Thank you, Jo."

"Thank you for being there for her when she needed you." I think about the day I began my own courses. I spent that day grimacing from the pain of cramps as I worked in the field. Looking back at my elder daughter's face, I see that same pained expression I once had. "That's it; that's what's wrong with her. Cramps."

Missouri sucks in a breath. "Goodness, you're right. She only complained of a stomachache and I didn't think to give her anything for pain."

I set my plate of half-eaten food aside, rise to my feet, and go to the corner of the yard where Clara sits.

She looks up from her lap at my approach. The giggling and chatter of half a dozen young girls ceases as an adult invades their space.

Mindful of the listening ears of her friends, I keep my expression and tone upbeat. "Clara, honey, can you come help me in the kitchen for a moment?"

She offers a silent nod, scooting off the barrel and following me into the house.

Inside the kitchen, I let the door close against the sounds of the revelry outside.

She sits at the table, and I watch her nervously smoothing her dress with her hands.

I take a seat next to her. "Clara, I notice you've seemed unhappy these last few days. Can you tell me what's bothering you, honey?"

She swallows audibly but doesn't volunteer anything.

I touch her shoulder gently. "Clara, you're my firstborn, and I want you to know that I love you with my whole heart. Whatever it is, I'm here for you. You can tell me anything. Anything at all."

She blows out a long, slow breath. "Mama . . . I . . . started my courses."

"I see." I'm pleased that I was able to get her to admit what was going on.

She blinks back tears. "It felt like a tummyache at first, but then I saw the blood and I just . . ."

I gather her into my arms. "There, there honey. It's all right."

She sobs quietly on my shoulder. "Mama, it hurts so much. I just want to have a good birthday, but it hurts so much."

I sit back, using my hand to wipe her tears. "I can help with that. I'll fix you some willow bark and cinnamon tea. It will ease the pain."

"Really?" She looks up at me, the tears standing in her eyes.

Knowing she's been hurting these past few days pains me. I cup her chin and kiss her cheek. "Yes, and I'll make it concentrated so it will work even faster."

While she watches, I set a kettle on the stove to boil. Getting one of my ceramic mugs from the cabinet, I sprinkle a small handful of loose willow bark into a piece of thin muslin and tie it up. Adding a bit of honey to the mug, I then grate a generous amount of cinnamon stick into it. When the water boils, I add the water and the willow bark sachet to the cup.

While it steeps, I add the rest of the hot water to one of Sweety's steel flasks. Wrapping a kitchen towel around the flask and tying the ends together, I hand it to Clara. "Honey, put this against the spot that hurts most."

She takes the offered bundle and places it against her lower abdomen. Immediately, the tightness in her face softens and I hear her sigh. "Mama, why does this feel so nice?"

I smile. "Heat helps to dull the pain. Women have been dealing with our courses for many years, so we've come up with ways to make them a little less unpleasant."

"Oh." She settles back into her chair, closing her eyes.

I see her finally enjoying some relief after a few days of pain, and I can almost feel the burden lifting.

I hand her the mug, half-filled with tea. "Here, honey. Drink it down quickly. I added some honey, but it can only do so much to cut the bitterness."

She opens her eyes, nodding as she accepts the mug. Drinking the warm, dark liquid down in a single gulp, she grimaces. "Tastes like the fireplace smells."

I laugh, returning to my seat. "You're right. Willow bark has never been tasty, but it does the job."

She gets out of her chair and, to my surprise, sits in my lap. I hold her close, nestling my face against the top of her head, feeling the softness of her curls against my cheek. For a while, things are as they once were. I'm holding my child, listening to her tell me about her day; watching the expressions play over her face.

"When did you first get your courses, Mama?"

"Not until I was sixteen." I shake my head at the memory. "I was sweeping up the hair after cutting the heads of Mr. Stutts's three sons. Out of nowhere, a pain hit me that was so bad, I dropped the broom. Went to the outhouse and found the blood staining my underthings." I sigh. "Your grandmother fixed me the same tea I just made for you, gave me a few cloths, and sent me back to finish my work."

"Sounds harsh."

"Trust me. Everything about those days was harsh. But Grandma only sent me back to save me from getting into trouble."

We lapse into silence for a while, and I simply enjoy the feel of her in my arms and against my heart.

Eventually, she stands, and I see her smile for the first time in several days. "I feel much better. Thank you, Mama."

"You're welcome, honey. Promise me you'll never suffer in silence again. Come to me, and I'll do whatever I can to set things right."

"I promise, Mama."

"Good. Now go back out there and enjoy your friends. I'll bring your gifts out shortly."

She turns, the pink fabric swirling and rustling around her as she heads out the door.

I watch her go with a smile on my face. She's growing up, becoming her own young lady. I only hope that today I have shown her that she can always come to me. No matter how old she gets, she will always be my baby, and I'll do anything in my power to help her.

I rise, headed for the parlor to retrieve the crate full of birthday gifts. On the way, I run into Sweety, who already has the crate in hand.

"I thought it would be about time for these, so I went ahead and grabbed them."

I lean up and peck him on the cheek. "You were right. Let's go have some cake and let our Clara open her gifts."

He nods, and we head for the back door together.

There is so much more celebrating left to do, and I want to make the most of it.

# JOSEPHINE

## *October 1887*

I awaken on a crisp autumn morning and turn in bed, stretching. The spot next to me is empty, save for the impression of my husband's body in the bed. Friday being our busiest day of the week at the barbershop, he and Octavious have gone in to open up early. Missouri, who must be the best sister-in-law in all creation, also came earlier to dress the girls and ferry them off to the Badham School.

The clock on the wall reads a quarter past nine. I rarely sleep this late; I must have been more tired than I thought.

Today is my monthly errand day, and thanks to my sweet sister-in-law, Missouri, I have only myself and Grandma Milly to attend to.

As soon as I throw back the covers, I feel the chill in the air; my flannel nightgown does little to fight it off without the aid of the quilts. Wrapping my arms around myself, I go to the fireplace at the foot of our bed and throw a log onto the embers. Once it's lit, I take a moment to warm myself by the soft glow of the fire.

After dressing in a dark skirt, a soft pink blouse, and my leather moccasins, I go to my grandmother's room to check on her. I find her, fully dressed, sitting in the rocker by her window with a book in her lap.

"Good morning, Grandma. What are you reading?" I approach slowly and kiss her wrinkled brow.

She smiles. "Good morning, sugarplum. I'm reading *The Women's War*." She moves her magnifying glass over the page slowly, as if savoring each word.

I nod. "Ah, yes. Sometimes I forget that I inherited my love of Dumas's work from you. Do you need anything before I attend to my errands? Have you eaten?"

"Yes, dear. I made myself a bit of porridge not a half hour ago." She raises her free hand, effectively shooing me off. "Go on, handle your tasks. I'll be fine."

I lean in to kiss her brow again. "I'll see you later on, then."

After a quick breakfast of two thick slices of toast and a cup of coffee, I'm out the door to accomplish the myriad of tasks the day will hold. With Cinnamon pulling my rickety old buggy, I make my first stop at Baker and Sons Coach Makers.

As soon as I pull my conveyance into the gravel lot next to the one-story building on Queen Street, young Chastity Baker steps outside, shaking her head. She's dressed in the same dark blue coveralls worn by her father and two older brothers. The Baker family's trade is in both working on vehicles and selling new ones.

I wave to her as I hitch Cinnamon to a post and walk toward her. "Morning, Chastity."

"Morning, Mrs. Leary." She sucks her bottom lip. "Heavens. This is the third time in as many months that you've brought your buggy over to be worked on. What's the matter with it now?"

I shrug. "Only the good Lord knows. But it squeaks like the dickens when I make a turn, and the hand brake just doesn't set as securely as it ought to."

She whistles. "Sounds like quite a pickle."

I look around and, seeing no one else, I ask, "Where are Robert and your brothers?"

"Gone up to Durham for parts and supplies, and to bring back a couple of new carriages." Chastity grins. "It's a rare day that I get to run things around this place."

I smile. "Well, good on you. You've always worked on my buggy and I trust your skill."

"I appreciate that, ma'am. Let me get my toolbox, and I'll take a look at your buggy." She disappears inside the shop. She returns shortly with the flat, wheeled board she uses to slide beneath vehicles, and the steel box containing her tools.

I watch as she sets down the rolling board and slides beneath my buggy. Leaning against the fence post, I wait and listen to the sounds of metal striking metal as she works on the buggy's under- carriage.

A while later, she slides from beneath it. "Mrs. Leary, the axles on this buggy are badly rusted. Not to mention your brake mechanism is so far gone that the metal's mostly worn away. That's why it's sound- ing and acting like it is."

I roll my eyes. "Land sakes. How much will that cost? And how long to make the repairs."

She stands to her feet, wiping her hands on the old rag hanging from her coverall pocket. "I hope you trust my advice like you trust my skill. Just let this thing go on the scrap heap and get yourself a new buggy, ma'am."

I squint. "You really think that's best?"

"Considering that the cost difference between replacing both axles and your brake mechanism and just buying a new buggy is only about twenty dollars, yes."

I cringe. "Goodness. I certainly hadn't intended on buying a buggy today."

"Tell you what. Why don't you take one of the new models on trial? Drive it around, see how you like it. If it suits you, come back and I'll give you a fair deal on it." She jerks her head toward the lot on the other side of the fence, where the new vehicles are kept. "Let me show you something I think will do nicely."

"All right." I follow her as she uses her key to unlock the gate.

Chastity leads me straight to a smart-looking vehicle sitting near the center of the lot. "This is the one for you, Mrs. Leary. The H. A. Moyer Lawrence Top wagon. Just came out in July. Room for the fam- ily, smooth running, sturdy axles. And we add in a little Baker-family extra this time of year: lined velvet curtains to keep the family warm on those winter drives."

I nod, taking in the stylish lines of the vehicle, as well as the upholstered seats, steel floorboard, and embroidered roof. "It's lovely. You'd let me take this on trial? I've errands today."

She claps her hands together. "What a perfect opportunity to see how she runs."

I think about it for a moment. "Sure, why not? I'll take it out for a test."

"Excellent. I'll get the logbook for you to sign her out, then I'll hitch up your horse to it."

Within the hour, I leave Baker and Sons in the snappy new Moyer wagon. Since it's chilly, Chastity was nice enough to attach the curtains, and I'm grateful to have some respite from the cool breezes flowing off the bay.

My next stop is on Oakum Street at the business of Louis F. Ziegler. Mr. Ziegler is the most skilled woodworker in Edenton, serving as both cabinetmaker and undertaker due to his talent in building both home storage and fine caskets for the deceased.

The bell above the door tinkles, announcing my entrance to the store.

Mr. Ziegler appears behind the counter in short order. Wearing an apron over his striped shirt and dark trousers, he's holding a small block of wood—cedar. I can smell it before I see it. Seeing me, he pushes his gold-rimmed spectacles up his nose and smiles in my direction. "Mrs. Leary! Always a pleasure. That is, unless you're bereaved."

I shake my head. "Thankfully, I'm here for something far more mundane. I need a frame made for this." Reaching into the satchel I've brought along, I pull out the portrait I had taken of Clara, just after her birthday.

He adjusts his spectacles again as he views the photograph. "My word, is this your elder daughter?"

I nod, smiling. "Yes. She's grown so much."

"I agree. Looks like she's becoming a fine young lady." He sets the portrait down and opens his logbook. "I can have it all framed up for you by the end of the day if you want it made from wood I already have in stock."

"Do you have mahogany on hand?"

He stoops, and I can hear him rummaging around on the shelves built into his counter. When he stands again, I see he's traded the block he was holding for a different one. "No, I don't, sorry. But I do have this Williamsburg cherry. Just came in yesterday. Fine stock, hardly any variation."

I take the piece, turning it in my hands, noting the heft, the dark richness of the wood, and the quality of the grain. "It's very nice. Can you glaze it for me?"

"Certainly. It'll be three dollars, four with the glass."

"I'd like to add the glass, please." I hand over the coin for my purchase.

Tucking my money into his strongbox, he makes a note of my order and payment in his logbook. "Thank you, Jo. You can pick it up around three thirty."

"I'll be back then." With a wave, I depart Mr. Ziegler's store and head for the next establishment I need to visit.

I walk the aisles of O. Newman's department store, taking in the merchandise. According to the advertisement in the *Fisherman and Farmer*, Newman's has the largest selection of fine clothing and shoes for the family to be found in Chowan County. The ad also said that Mr. Newman meant "strict business and no humbug" when it came to low prices. With two growing girls at home, I'm certainly in need of well-made wearables, but I'm also mindful of my budget.

I've only been in the store for a few minutes when a man approaches me. Tall and rail-thin, he wears a black cutaway suit that only accentuates his resemblance to a cornstalk. His blond hair is smoothed back with a heavy dose of hair tonic, and his brown eyes dance with merriment. "Welcome to my store, madam. And you are?"

"Josephine Leary. Are you Mr. O. Newman?"

He smiles. "Why yes, but all my best customers call me by my given name, Oswald." He takes my hand in his, bowing over it.

I can't help but be amused by his flamboyance. "Pleased to meet you, Oswald. I'm in need of a few dresses, skirts, and such for my young daughters."

"Right this way, Mrs. Leary." He leads me to a section near the rear of the store. "Here are all our high-quality items for girls. I'm sure you'll find everything your daughters need."

"Thank you." I nod to Mr. Oswald Newman as he sidles away to chat up the other customers, then turn my attention to the neatly folded items on the table before me. I soon see that he was right; his selection of items is quite impressive. The prices are mostly fair as well, though there are a few items that cause me to balk. I return to the front of the store for a basket, load it with clothing items for Clara and Florrie, then locate the women's section and add a few items for myself.

Taking my basket to the counter, I wait my turn in line, then set it on the counter when I'm called upon. The girl rings up my items with a mechanical cash register and quotes me a total. "That will be thirty dollars, ma'am."

Just as I reach into my satchel, Oswald appears behind her. "Did you get everything you needed?"

"Mostly. There was a pair of leather slippers I'd have liked for my Florrie, but the price was too high."

His face creases into a frown. "Nonsense."

"You've met my budget on everything else, but I can get those shoes for seventy-five cents cheaper at Hammond's." I begin counting out my money for the purchase.

"I'll beat Hammond's price by a full dollar. How's that?"

I look up, seeing the fire of competition in his eyes, and smile. "You've just made yourself another sale."

"What size?" he asks eagerly.

I tell him my youngest daughter's size, and he leaves, only to return moments later with the slippers. "Thank you for your business, ma'am."

I exchange the money for the large canvas bag the cashier hands me. As I load the bag into the back of my buggy, I can only smile. I've made out like a bandit on new things for us to wear, and it pleases me to know that I won't have to shop for a wardrobe again for a good while.

# 14

SWEETY

*October 1887*

I stifle a yawn as I walk out of the storeroom in the rear of the barbershop, tonic in hand. It's been a long day, as is typical of a Friday. But with the county fair opening tonight in Elizabeth City, I've cut and styled even more heads than usual. Even Octavious is at a barber station instead of manning the desk at the front.

Returning to my station, I speak to my client. "Sorry about that, Clay. I've got a fresh bottle of tonic now."

Clayton Rigsby looks up from the copy of the *Farmers' Almanac* he'd been reading. "Good. My scalp's been itching something fierce."

"It's common around the change of season. This should take care of it." The tonic, one of Josephine's creations, has eucalyptus oil in it and is sought-after by our clientele for its soothing properties.

Rigsby returns his focus to the almanac as I work the tonic through his hair and scalp, feeling secretly grateful that the farm reports have his attention. He's quite the chatterbox and opinionated on top of that. The longer he reads, the less I will have to hear his mouth.

My reprieve is short-lived, however, because as I begin to comb through his tangles in preparation for the haircut, Clay starts up talking.

"You know, it just boggles me that Jo still comes into the shop now that y'all have two children at home." He shakes his head.

"Clay, we talked about this. Keep shaking your head and you'll end up with a gap."

"Sorry 'bout that, Sweety. How come she's not here today? Has she finally decided to stay home with your daughters?"

I sigh. "She's doing family errands today. Once a month, she takes care of all the little things that keep the household running, so I wouldn't begrudge her the day off." I've yet to find another barber to match her skill or rapport with the customers, so while the husband in me wants her home, the businessman in me wants her back at her station. The waiting area has been full all day, with no sign of slowing down.

"Ah, yes. I believe I saw her earlier, coming out of Ziegler's place." He turns the page in the almanac. "She was driving a mighty fine buggy, too."

I feel confusion folding my face. "What are you talking about? That old thing she drives has seen far better days. It's barely viable to drive anymore."

He scoffs. "I know what Jo's buggy looks like, I'm not daft. But whatever she was driving today, wasn't the same old beater she usually drives. This was a fine vehicle. Even had one of those winter wraps on it." He whistles. "Top of the line."

I can't wrap my head around what my client is saying. But since he often talks out of his rear end, I simply nod and dismiss the whole notion. *Most likely he saw someone who resembles my wife, driving a fine vehicle.* Whatever Rigsby's motive, I have nothing to gain by continuing the conversation. I'm relieved when my chatty client goes back to the almanac, and I welcome his subsequent lapse into silence.

I spend the remainder of the day moving from client to client, with barely a break. As four o'clock rolls around and I turn the sign on the door to closed, I'm exhausted. The joints in my hands are tight from the hours spent gripping combs and working my shears, and my aching feet remind me of their displeasure with me for being on them all day.

Octavious groans as he sinks into the chair at his station. "Whoa. Remind me to take the day off the next time the county fair opens."

I know he's teasing and I tease right back. "I'll do no such thing. I need you on busy days like this."

He chuckles. "I knew you'd say something like that." He climbs to his feet, exhaling. "I'll handle the tonic bottles and the implements if you sweep up."

"Deal." As my brother-in-law disappears into the storeroom, I'm left alone with my old whisk broom and my thoughts. Carefully ridding the floor of dust, hair trimmings, and trash, I dump it all into the trash bin by the door. Then I take a cloth and polish up the chairs until the patched leather shines like new.

Around a quarter till five, a soft knock sounds at the door. Looking through the window, I see Josephine waving at me. I smile. She's come to ferry us home, and I'm grateful not to have to walk on my aching feet.

Octavious and I shrug into our coats and head outside, locking the door behind us.

I stop short when I see my wife at the curb.

There she is, smiling at me from the seat of a fine new carriage. "Climb in, get out of this chilly air."

I blink a few times, assuming that if I do it enough, my vision will correct itself. Several blinks later, though, the sight before me remains the same. *Of all the times for Clayton Rigsby to be talking good sense.* "Jo, whose vehicle is this?"

"It's mine. My old one bit the dust, and I just bought this little beauty today." She runs a hand over the wood grain near the driver's seat. "Come on up."

I can barely contain my ire as I climb onto the seat next to my wife.

Octavious moves the velvet liner and gets in the rear seat. "My, my, sis. This is quite a conveyance."

"Thanks. But you know I'm more about practicality than looks." She pulls away from the curb as she speaks, guiding Cinnamon toward home. "It's got all the features our family needs."

"It certainly does. But besides that, it's a capital buggy. You know, something befitting a business lady like yourself." Octavious is all smiles. "Good choice."

I say nothing, knowing that if I speak now, I will only do so in anger. *How could she do this? What made her think it was all right to make such a large purchase without consulting me?* So I spend the entire ride home listening to Jo and her brother's banter but keeping my own counsel.

At home, we eat a simple meal of roast beef, fried corn, and collards. I stay quiet throughout the meal, ignoring the surreptitious glances Jo tosses my way now and then. Once the girls are in bed and we retire to our room, she grabs my hand.

"Sweety, you've been awfully quiet. What's the matter?"

By this point I can no longer contain my irritation. "How much, Jo?"

She frowns. "How much what?"

"How much did that buggy cost us?"

"It cost *me* seventy-five dollars." She scoffs. "I paid for it with proceeds I saved from leasing my land and the old storehouse."

"Hmph."

She tilts her head. "Is that what you've been pouting about all day? You thought I dipped into the family budget for it?"

I'm now so exasperated, I scarcely know what to do. "Jo, that isn't the issue here. It's the way you do things, the way you casually toss around words about having your own money."

She folds her arms over her chest. "And what's wrong with me having my own money? I should hope you'd take comfort in the fact that there's extra income for the house."

"You don't need to hoard funds, because I take care of this family."

She rolls her eyes. "Setting aside money is not hoarding. I'm simply being prudent."

"I make enough money!" I hear myself shouting but can't seem to stop myself. "If you'd stop trying to be the man in the relationship, both our lives would be easier!"

Jo's eyes narrow, her nostrils flaring.

I swallow.

"Archer Leary, if you think I'm trying to be the man, you're as silly as a goose. I've given you two beautiful daughters, I've cooked and cleaned and made this house a home, I've worked right alongside you at the barbershop. And yet you would reduce what we share to money?" She props her fists on her hips. "I won't stand for this. I've had enough of you sniping at me about my ambition as if I surprised you with it after we married."

I feel the heat warming my face and the tightness gathering in my chest. Guilt and frustration swirl around in my head like fallen leaves in a tornado. "Jo, listen. I didn't mean—"

"I don't want to hear another word." She points to the bedroom door. "Grab a blanket and a pillow and go sleep in the parlor." Her eyes flash with anger, but I notice the tears lingering there as well.

I move a step closer to her.

"Get out!" She shouts as loud as I did moments before. In all our years of marriage, I can't recall her ever raising her voice at me that way.

Wordlessly, I gather a wool blanket and feather pillow.

As soon as I'm out in the hallway, Jo slams the bedroom door.

Shaking my head, I make the slow trudge to the parlor. I lie on the settee, and after a few minutes of tossing and turning, I give up on finding a comfortable position. The sturdy build of the settee makes it great for sitting, but terrible for sleeping. It is no match in comfort to the soft, feather-filled mattress upstairs.

I thought myself a reasonable man. I love my wife for all that she is, including her drive and ambition. Somewhere, there has to be a line. A line that separates me as a man from my wife and her endless need to conquer the world. I'm not sure if she has crossed that line, but she's certainly tested the boundaries at every opportunity.

I honestly don't know what I should do. All I know is that I don't want this; I don't want to be fussing and fighting with her, I don't want to sleep in the parlor. I also want her to make me feel needed, to make me feel she depends on me.

I groan into the silent darkness. Sleep will be an impossibility, that much I know for certain. I stare up toward the ceiling, listening to the faint sounds of my wife moving around our bedroom. It sounds as if she might be pacing the floor, but I have better sense than to go up there and see.

I've put my foot in my mouth again, and because of my blunder, I've been denied the comfort of my bed, and of her warm embrace. I'd just as soon sleep on a pile of rocks as on this stiff thing.

It will surely be a long, restless night.

⋰⊱⋱

By morning, I've had my fill of being on the receiving end of Jo's ire. I rise at dawn, make her coffee with a dash of cinnamon and cream, and carry it upstairs to her.

Sitting up in bed reading, Jo turns at my entrance. Her face is tight at first, but some of the anger drains away when she sees the mug. "You made me coffee?"

I nod. "Yes. And I'll make you breakfast, too. Just as soon as you tell me what you want."

She takes the offered mug with a slow shake of her head. "Sweety, you'd save yourself a lot of trouble if you didn't insist on being a dunderhead."

Sitting down on the edge of the bed, I sigh. "I know. I just . . . let things get to me, then take them out on you. I'm sorry, Jo."

She takes a sip from the coffee mug. "I accept your apology. But you need to understand that I'm not going to change, Sweety. I'm going to keep setting aside money, even though you don't approve."

"I know."

"I've yielded much to you in this marriage, dear. But I'm unyielding on this." Her gaze is fixed, showing her determination. "Let me have this."

I draw a deep breath. "I'll do my best. It's all I can promise."

# JOSEPHINE

### *September 1888*

Standing before the paintings hanging on the barbershop wall, I tap my finger against my chin, debating the best way to take them down without damaging them. It's odd for me to be here on a Sunday when we are closed. But with such lofty work ahead of us, Sweety, Octavious, Missouri, and I have come here, right after church. Before night falls, we aim to rejuvenate this place, inside and out.

I turn to Sweety, who's busy stirring paint to my left. "Dearest, do we really have to change the color of the walls? I like the color we have."

He glances up at me, shaking his head. "This isn't about the wall color. You just don't want to take down those paintings."

I give him my best pouty face, even though I know it's unlikely to sway him. He's right; I don't want to remove the paintings. In a way, they represent the last vestiges of my presence here, since I barber less and less these days.

He sighs. "Go on with you, Jo."

"But, dearest." I stick my lip out farther, fluttering my lashes a bit.

He stops stirring. "Then just what am I to do with all this paint? Mr. Hammond down at the general store isn't just going to take it back."

I don't miss a beat. "Use it on the exterior. It could use a new coat."

He groans but stands and takes the pail of paint outside. Triumphant, I return the ladder to the storeroom. There, I find Missouri, searching through the contents of the shelves.

"What are you looking for?"

"That cleaning solution you make." She continues to slide things around on the shelves.

I stoop to the bottom shelves and grab the jug I keep my cleaner in. "Here it is. I keep it down there to reserve the upper shelves for tonic and salves and the like."

"Makes sense." Missouri takes the jug and adds some to the pail at her feet. "I'm going to the pump out back to get water."

As she slips out the back door, I head to the front to assist my brother with the chairs. We're changing out the current ones, with their worn armrests and patched leather, for newer ones.

Octavious is sliding the chair away from Sweety's station when I approach. "I think this one's the worst-looking of them all."

I nod. "Sweety gets more regular clients than the two of us, and most of the newcomers choose him as well." I look at his chair and shake my head. It's falling apart, quite literally, with the leather cover shedding away from the cotton stuffing inside. It was his frustration with the chair that started my husband thinking about improving things around the shop.

Octavious and I get on either side of the heavy chair and drag it outside to the back. We repeat the motions with the three other chairs, including the alternate chair at the station that's never yet been occupied by a barber. Patrons sit in it at times when the waiting area is full, so even though no barber has used it, it's seen its share of wear and tear.

We head to the front, where Sweety is busy repainting the exterior trim around the windows, and haul in the new chairs. Where the old ones were brown, these are black leather, hopefully less likely to show stains and burns. I've been known to drop a straightening comb or marcel iron from time to time, so the dark color is particularly appealing to me.

It takes us nearly half an hour to get the new chairs in place, and once we've finished, I stop to admire them. "They really are nice."

"And comfortable, too." Octavious is seated in the chair at his station. "We'll probably have more clients falling asleep in the chair now."

I giggle, knowing I've awakened a patron or two after they dozed off during a scalp massage or a hot towel treatment.

He scratches his chin. "You know, this morning, I read in the *Fayetteville Observer* that there's a need for barbers up north."

"Where, exactly?"

"Places like DC, New York, and even Philadelphia. They say many of our race are migrating, looking to escape the oppression in the South." There's a faraway look in his eyes. But nearly as soon as I notice his contemplative state, he hops up from the chair. "I'd better get moving before I fall asleep myself."

Missouri walks by me with a pail and cloth in hand. "All right. I've polished the countertops at all the stations and cleaned all the mirrors. Now I'm going to clean the implements."

"Hold off on that," I remind her, "until Sweety shows you what he's bought. We'll be throwing out a lot of the old shears and things."

She nods, setting the bucket down near the unused station. Wiping her brow with the back of her hand, she leans against the counter. "Do you really think we'll be able to get all these things done in just one afternoon?"

I shrug. "I don't know. I suppose there's always tomorrow if we don't finish, since we're closed on Monday."

"I'd like to get it done today," Sweety interjects as he enters the shop. His denims and his blue work shirt are besmirched with drops and splatters of the white paint he's been using. "Tomorrow the shop was supposed to be left for the paint to dry." He eyes me pointedly.

I smile. "We can still leave it for that, and for airing the place out. It hasn't been aired out in a while."

He shakes his head. "I'm going to seal up this paint and put it away for the next touch-up. When I come back, we can start stocking the stations with the new implements."

I watch him walk to the back, shaking my head. He loves to make these grand plans but seems to tire easily during the execution of them. I find that when I set my mind to achieving my goals, my energy becomes boundless.

He returns with a large case, setting it on his station. "Come on over and take a look." He beckons us over with a crooked finger.

I approach along with Octavious and Missouri, even though I've already seen the tools. Flipping the two metal latches, he opens the case, revealing a velvet-lined interior with twenty or so depressions in it. Each depression holds a tool of the trade: gleaming shears, straight razors, combs.

"Wow. These are some good-quality implements," Octavious comments as he admires the contents of the case.

"They'd better be. I paid double what I paid for my first set." Sweety reaches into the case and tugs a pair of shears free from its depression. "These shears are said to trim the hair so precisely, one can use them while blindfolded."

Missouri snorts a laugh. "Don't hold your breath waiting for a client to let you try that on their head."

A ghost of a smile crosses my husband's face. "Very droll, Missouri. Anyhow, bring all the old tools here so we can sort through them and toss the ones we replaced."

"I've got it." Missouri returns to the storeroom.

We chat easily as we sort.

"Did you hear that Mr. Rea is bringing a new show to his opera house?" Octavious asks.

"No," I remark. "What's the name of it?"

"I can't remember—it's been a few days since I read the announcement in the paper. But I remember that it's supposed to be a comedy about two men competing for a lady's affections."

I chuckle. "Sounds amusing enough. Dearest, do you remember that day we sat in CW's office and listened to him go on about the opera house?"

"Back when it was still just an idea he had?" Sweety shakes his head, looking off into the distance. "Yes, I recall that day. I thought him a bit daft, but considering the success he's had with it, perhaps he was right about the town's need for entertainment venues."

I nod. "We haven't been to a show there yet; perhaps we ought to go to one, if for no other reason than to see what the inside looks like." The opera house, situated on Queen Street between Granville and Broad, has a fancy metal facade and a velvet rope over the door. I've passed it a few times, and I've always wondered if the interior is as elegant as the exterior.

Sweety nods. "I'm amenable. I'm not sure if we'll make it to this show, but we should be able to attend at least one sometime soon."

"Well, this refresh is bound to bring in new patrons," Octavious remarks. "You'll be so flush with cash, you'll be able to take in a show whenever you want."

I place my hand over my chest. "May the Lord hear that petition. We've never had a shortage of patrons, but new ones certainly couldn't hurt." I've come to love this place and the folks who entrust us to keep them looking presentable. I think of my regular clients, like Rosa, Eunice, and the Jenkins twins, who've become great friends to me over the years.

"I think you're right, brother." Sweety sets down a jar of solution on his station, with the new implements soaking inside to sterilize. "That's the whole reason I wanted to do this. I could have just replaced that old chair of mine, but I had bigger plans for this place."

"Now that we've got the implements set up, what's left to do?" Missouri asks.

"Just giving the place a good cleaning. After that, we can all go home."

Octavious claps his hands together. "Let's get to it, then."

For the next hour, we sweep, mop, and scrub the barbershop until it is spotless.

It is just past dusk when Sweety and I finally arrive home. We enter the front door and find the house relatively quiet. My mother's intuition tells me that means the girls are likely up to some mischief.

I go upstairs and peek into Florrie's room first, since she's the most prone to lapses in judgment.

Florrie is lying across the bed with a book and looks up at my entrance. "Hi, Mama. Did you finish your work at the barbershop?"

I nod. "We did. Has Grandma Milly gone on to bed?"

"Yes, ma'am, after she gave us some stew and biscuits for dinner."

I feel a modicum of relief knowing I won't have to cook dinner tonight. "Where's your sister?"

She shrugs. "I don't know. She went downstairs a while ago."

"All right." I leave her to her reading and descend the stairs in search of my elder child.

As I reach the kitchen, I hear Sweety call my name. Entering the room, I see him by the back door. "What is it?"

He merely points.

I look, and see Clara sitting on the ground beneath the old willow. With her is Philip Horne, her classmate. His arm is about her waist, and her head rests on his shoulder.

Sweety's face is creased into a deep frown. "I'm going out there and giving that boy a good what for!"

I grab his hand, staying him before he does something rash. "Why? What will that accomplish?"

"It'll let him know I won't stand by and let him sully my daughter's good name, that's what."

I sigh. "Sweety, listen to yourself. Huffing and puffing like a steam engine over nothing."

He points again. "Our daughter is sitting outside in the dark with that boy. It's isn't 'nothing,' Jo."

"Fine, but it certainly isn't the crime you're making it out to be." I lean against the doorframe, my gaze landing on my child and her friend. "Look at them, Sweety. Back off your bluster and look at them."

He turns his head, regarding them again.

"Tell me what you see."

"My daughter and a boy."

I sigh, experiencing his male tendency to speak of things in relation to himself. "Not *your* daughter. Not *our* daughter. A young woman, Sweety. She's growing up and there's nothing we can do to stop it."

He drops his gaze to his shoes. "I don't want to see her hurt. That's all."

"But you will, dearest. She will get hurt. She will make mistakes and have regrets. But it's all a part of life. We just have to step back and let her experience things for herself."

He looks into my eyes. "I don't want to let her go, Jo."

"I know. Trust me, I'm not excited about it either, but it is what it is." I sigh. "Let me tell you what I see. Two youngsters, enjoying each other's company in companionable silence. There's no crime in that."

He takes a deep breath, exhaling slowly. "I suppose. Since you're so well-informed on these things, I'll let you be the one to send the boy home and have our daughter come inside to prepare for bed." With one last, sad glance out the door, Sweety turns and goes upstairs.

I stay there a few moments longer, watching my child. She smiles up at Philip as he strokes a curl out of her face, and the tender scene melts my heart.

I turn away, intent on making myself a cup of tea. Once I've drunk it, I'll call her inside.

But until then, I will leave her to enjoy her company.

# 15

JOSEPHINE

*August 1890*

Doing my best to keep my emotions in check, I watch the scenery roll by. From my vantage point, next to Sweety on the front seat, I can see the sunlight piercing the pine needles along either side of the road. We have been traveling for an hour now in the warm morning air, and I expect we'll arrive in Raleigh by noon if we keep a good pace.

I turn my head, glancing over my shoulder. "Clara, are you all right back there?"

My elder daughter is leaning sideways with her upper body draped over her valises, her eyes looking into the distance with a wide-eyed stare. She seems unaware that I have spoken to her.

"Clara?"

She startles, finally directing her gaze at me. "Yes, Mama?"

"I asked if you were all right, honey."

She nods her head, straightening her posture a bit. "Yes, ma'am. I'm fine."

I hear her words, but I'm not entirely sure I believe them. I nudge my husband. "Sweety, what do you think?"

"'Bout what, dearest?"

I sigh. He's gotten so focused on driving he hasn't been paying me any mind. I suppose I shouldn't be annoyed; his attention to the road is vital on long drives like this. "I asked Clara if she is all right, and she says yes. Do you believe her?"

He hazards a split-second glance toward the backseat, then shrugs his shoulders. "Hard to tell. Ever since she's entered the teenage years, she's harder to read than a Latin manifesto."

I shake my head. "I don't know, she looks nervous to me."

"Perhaps." Sweety shifts on the driver's seat. "I suppose that would be natural for a young lady about to go off to school, away from her family for the first time."

"You do know that I can hear you, right?" Her words are sharp, terse.

I start to reprimand her but decide against it. My husband is probably right about how she's feeling, but knowing my strong-willed child, she'll be hard-pressed to admit her anxiety.

Adjusting my hat, which has been threatening to fall off my head all morning, I settle in for the rest of the ride. Eunice made the hat for me, and it's fine work, though millinery isn't her specialty. It's fashioned of lavender satin, and shaped like a small boat with pearls dangling in the center of my forehead. I wouldn't typically wear a hat like this, but it isn't every day one drops their firstborn daughter off at college.

It's eleven thirty when we arrive on the campus of Shaw University. Formerly Raleigh Institute and later Shaw Collegiate Institute, the college was incorporated under the current moniker when Clara was only a year old. At the time of its opening in 1865, it was one of the first institutions of its kind in this nation, one meant solely for the education and enrichment of African Americans. I'm proud to have my daughter be a part of the legacy Shaw is creating.

Climbing down from the buggy seat with Sweety's assistance, I brush the road dust from the skirts of my lavender brocade traveling costume and readjust my traitorous hat once more.

"Heavens, you've been fussing over that hat all day," Sweety comments with a chuckle.

I sigh. "I know. I was so arrested by the beauty of Eunice's satin, I wasn't thinking practically when I purchased it. My kingdom for a hatpin." Unfortunately, I've already used the three pins I had on hand in my earlier attempts to secure the hat.

"Take heart, dearest. You're a vision of loveliness, with or without that troublesome hat." Sweety leans down and pecks me on the forehead.

I smile, using my fingertips to adjust the lapels of his dark suit. "You're a sight to behold, yourself."

"Hello?" Clara's tone is exasperated.

We both turn to our daughter. Standing there in the school's uniform of crisp white blouse, navy skirt, and matching sash, she looks more grown-up than I've ever seen her. I realize that sixteen years have flown by in a flash, and now she stands before us, no longer a child but on the cusp of womanhood.

"We've got to get to the orientation, and I don't want to be late." She folds her arms over her chest. "So can you please stop canoodling?"

I feel a pang of guilt. "Come along, honey. Let's get you to the dormitory." I take her hand and let her lead me across the grassy commons.

"I'm right behind you." Sweety picks up both of Clara's small valises and follows us.

We arrive shortly at Estey Hall, the school's female dormitory, and I'm immediately impressed. I've a mental list of properties with excellent facades throughout the coastal regions of the state, and this dormitory still stands out. It's a stately structure, four stories high, fashioned of brick and trimmed in white stone-stucco, I believe. Carved stone steps lead up to a wide, covered front porch furnished with four matching wicker settees. Above the porch, both the second and third level feature covered balconies, all of which are surrounded by whitewashed ornamental iron railings. The decorative frames about the windows on the fourth and attic levels resemble those at the fancy hotels downtown that we passed on the drive.

We walk up the gravel path, past the azalea bushes and the lone, towering birch near the building, and climb the steps to the porch.

The screen door swings open and a smiling woman with a sun-kissed complexion greets us. "Welcome to Shaw, and to Estey Hall. I'm Miss Lemuel."

"Pleased to meet you." Sweety bows over her hand.

"Yes, I am pleased to meet you as well, Miss Lemuel." I offer a handshake of greeting.

Clara lingers behind me in pensive silence, and I'm reminded of the little girl who hid behind my skirts at the Badhams' holiday party all those years ago.

Miss Lemuel glances at our daughter. "I assume this is one of our newest young scholars?"

"Yes." I take my daughter's hand and give it a gentle squeeze of encouragement.

She clears her throat. "Yes, ma'am. I'm Clara Leary, class of ninety-three."

Miss Lemuel's smile becomes even sunnier as she shakes Clara's free hand. "We're very glad to have you with us, Clara." Releasing her, she holds open the screen door. "Please come inside. Orientation will get underway very soon."

Inside, Clara's valises join the pile of belongings in the front parlor, where a petite, fiery-haired woman in a maid's uniform sets about the task of corralling and sorting them. Then we are led into a large room on the first floor, where rows of chairs have been set up to face a central podium. As Miss Lemuel floats away, I notice the design detail from outside continues inside, reflected in the fine candelabras sitting atop carved redwood buffets on either side of the room, the trophies and awards displayed in glass-fronted credenzas, and the polished wood floors. I also notice the tall ceramic vases on either side of the podium, and the crowded bookshelf taking up the entire north wall.

Most of the seats are full, occupied by fresh-faced young women and their family members. All the faces show a range of emotion, from exuberance to subdued curiosity. I make eye contact with a woman I assume to be about my age, seated with a young, caramel-skinned girl who must be about Clara's age. We share a moment and exchange knowing smiles.

We both went through the application process with our daughters, paying the application fee, listening as they read us their essays for the hundredth time before sending them off. The waiting, the self-doubt, and then the jubilation when the acceptance letters finally came.

After a brief search, we locate three seats near the rear of the room.

Miss Lemuel appears at the podium. "Good afternoon, new scholars and family members. Welcome to Shaw University, where you will expand the horizons of your mind. And welcome to Estey Hall, a place you will come to call home as you complete your studies."

Clara shifts in her seat and still looks a bit trepidatious to me. So I catch her hand in mine and smile when I feel her stiff posture begin to relax. The tightly wound ball of tears in my throat unwinds a bit, but I'm able to compose myself before my sadness betrays me. This day is bittersweet, indeed.

"I will serve as your home economics instructor as well as your dormitory mother. I hope you all are as excited as I and the other faculty members are about the journey you've embarked on," Miss Lemuel continues, walking from behind the podium and down the aisle splitting the rows of chairs. "Here, you will learn the mechanics of running a household, but you will also learn fine arts, world religions, and music, both appreciation and composition." She reaches the end of the aisle, turns, and meanders toward the front again. "You will have the same educational opportunities as our male students, to study business, finance, education—whatever suits your talents. Understand that the curriculum is rigorous, the standards are high, and the work is hard. But when you graduate, you'll be prepared to go out into the world as a credit to your families and to your race."

We join in the round of applause that rings through the room.

Miss Lemuel gestures toward the doorway, and three more well-dressed Black women enter the room. Each is dressed similarly to Miss Lemuel, in a crisp white blouse and a garnet skirt. Around each woman's neck is a neatly tied scarf, and no two have the same color.

As they introduce themselves, it becomes clear that the scarves represent their respective subject areas. Miss Taylor, in the gold scarf, teaches art; Miss Hart, in a green scarf, teaches music, and the purple scarf worn by Mrs. Courtland indicates her role as the religious studies instructor. I gather that Miss Lemuel's striped scarf of red and white indicates her dual roles as a home economics instructor and dorm mother.

The day moves into a buffet-style luncheon, served in the well-appointed dining room. As we eat the well-seasoned beef tips, potatoes, and greens, I'm once again impressed. I nudge Sweety with my elbow. "Clara will eat well here, I see."

"I may enroll here myself," Sweety says with a wink around a mouthful of food.

Clara balks. "Papa!"

"Just kidding, child. I'm well past my college years." Sweety laughs, then goes on with his meal. I can only shake my head at the two of them.

As the afternoon wears on, the time comes for us to return home and leave Clara to her studies. Standing at the bottom of the steps outside the dormitory, I pull my child into my arms.

"Heavens, Mama, don't squeeze me flat."

"I love you, Clara. I love you, so, so much." I can feel sadness rising within me because now, I can no longer ignore the fact that we'll be leaving Clara here. The tears well in my eyes, clouding my vision.

"Oh, Mama. I love you too." She steps back a moment, concern on her face as she wipes my tears with her hand. "Don't cry, Mama. I'm excited to begin my studies."

"Your mama will be fine, I'll see to it. It's natural for a parent to feel a little sad at such an occasion." Sweety appears stoic, but I know he feels similarly. "Do your best, Clara."

"I will, Papa." She hugs him around the waist, laying her head against his chest. "I promise I will make you proud."

His lip trembles for a moment. "I know you will, honey. Because you already have." He gives her a brief squeeze, then releases her.

She backs up until she's on the porch again. "I have to go in and meet my roommate and sort my things. I promise to write home before the week is out."

I nod. "I'll hold you to it."

She smiles softly. "Goodbye, Mama. Goodbye, Papa." With a wave, she enters the dormitory and disappears from view.

When she's gone, I'm no longer able to hold back my sobs. Sweety reaches for me, and the comforting strength of his arm around my shoulders sustains me as we return to our vehicle.

As we pull away from the dorm, and then the campus, I dab my eyes with my handkerchief. I don't know that any mother can ever be ready to set her child free into a sometimes uncaring world. I will go through this again when Florrie's time comes. But I know my pain will be nothing compared to the joy I'll feel at the wonders she will go on to accomplish.

With a deep breath, I shuffle off the coil of sadness and set my gaze forward.

# JOSEPHINE

### *April 1891*

"Mama!"

Hearing my elder daughter summoning me, I look up from the ribbon-wrapped corsage I'm creating. "I'll be there in a minute, Clara." Tightening the yellow ribbon around the stems of the white roses and baby's breath, I make a knot to keep the small arrangement together. Tying a bow with the free ends of the ribbon, I hold up my handiwork so I can get a good look at it. Satisfied, I take a long straight pin and go across the landing to my daughters' room.

There, Clara is standing before the long mirror my brother gave her as a birthday present last year. My breath catches in my throat at the sight of her.

She turns her head, looking over her shoulder at me. "Mama . . . what is it? Why are you crying?"

I dash away a traitorous tear. "You just look so lovely and so grown-up." The beautiful yellow satin gown she wears, another of Eunice's creations, has a sweetheart neckline that showcases the regal line of her neck and shoulders. One of Izzy's glass-bead necklaces hangs around her throat, and at the moment, my mother is busy fussing with her hair.

"Come here, Jo." My mother beckons to me, speaking around the hairpins hanging from the corner of her mouth. "Hold this curl in place so I can pin it."

I walk over, leaving the corsage on the bed, to assist my mother. Clara's hair has gotten quite long, and hangs well past the middle of her back when it's loose. For now, we are wrestling the dark waves into an elegant upsweep, a style befitting her regal dress.

Once we finish, I step back and admire the finished look. "Perfect."

"Yes, yes," my mother agrees.

"You look amazing, Clara." I give her bare shoulder a squeeze. "And I wanted to say how proud I am of you for the hard work you did in selling twenty-three tickets to the cotillion."

Her cheeks redden slightly. "Thank you, Mama. When you told me the Ladies' Auxiliary wanted to raise money to get more books for the town library, there was no way I could say no."

"A lot of the credit goes to Rosa; it was her idea to make it a father-daughter dance."

"I know. And the collection is sorely in need of an update, so you're certainly doing good work by participating." My mother smiles in Clara's direction.

"We could have raised even more if Florrie had wanted to do it," Clara remarks.

I shake my head. "You know your sister hates to wear dresses. She'll have a much nicer time spending the night at her friend Bella's house."

"Where is Great-grandma Milly?" Clara asks.

"Right here."

We all turn to see her standing in the doorway.

My mother laughs. "Mother, how long have you been there?"

A serene smile crosses Grandma Milly's face as she makes her way toward Clara. Placing a hand against her cheek, she says softly, "Long enough to see how my little rose has bloomed."

Clara's answering grin is so sweet, I have to turn away for a moment lest another treasonous tear falls down my face.

We spend more time fussing over Clara, adding a bit of paint to her lips, fitting her with Grandma Milly's antique silver earrings, and helping her into her fancy slippers.

"All that's left is the corsage." Clara gestures toward the small sprig of blooms, still lying on the bed.

"That's a job for your father." My mother walks to the door and out onto the landing, and I can see her looking downstairs. "Where is Sweety anyhow?"

I shrug. "He left hours ago. Said he'd be back by six thirty."

Mama pointed to the wall-mounted clock in the hall. "Jo, it's already ten minutes to seven. At this rate, our princess will be late for the ball."

A pounding at the door interrupts our conversation, and we all go, in a line, downstairs to see who's at the door.

"It can't be Sweety; why wouldn't he use his key?"

Grandma opens the door.

My face scrunches in confusion. "Octavious?"

There stands my brother, looking handsome in a fine dark suit. "Hello, sister. I know it's not me you're expecting, but . . ."

"Uncle Octavious, why are you dressed up?" Clara's furrowed brow mirrors the confusion I'm sure we all feel.

"Where is Sweety?" My mother isn't interested in background.

"He's . . . uh . . . well, at Lipsey's, and . . ."

"He's at the bar?" I'm shouting, even though I don't mean to.

"Jo, don't go off the deep end. He's there, and yes he drank, but he's only been held up because he helped Randall break up a fight."

Grandma throws her hands up. "Oh, for heaven's sake. Tonight, of all nights?"

Octavious's expression is grim. "He's got a hell of a black eye, but other than that . . ."

I groan aloud. "You're in a suit. Are you going to take Clara in his place?"

"I'd be happy to, if that's what—"

Sweety charges in then. He's dressed in his suit, but his loosened tie and the missing buttons at his throat combined with the angry purple ring around his left eye make him look disheveled instead of dapper.

Clara wails. "Papa! What's happened to you?"

"Nothing to concern yourself with, sweetheart. I'll be fine." He moves immediately to her side, and before I can protest, takes the pin and corsage from my hand. Affixing it to Clara's dress, he says, "Just let me get this tie done up, and we can go."

Her lip trembles. "Are you sure you're all right, Papa?"

He nods. "Yes. And I'm even better now, seeing how beautiful you look."

Clara offers a watery smile. "Thank you, Papa."

My mother's and grandmother's faces are both taut; Octavious looks as if he'd rather not be present. I don't know what I feel. I'm relieved that my husband is here, and not inebriated, but I'm also angry that he went to the bar in the first place. "You couldn't stay away from that place, Sweety? Not even just for tonight?"

His quiet response touches my core. "I should never have gone there, Jo."

I can feel the contrition rolling off him. I turn to my brother. "Octavious, why don't you escort Clara to the cotillion, to keep her from being very late? We will do what we can to fix Sweety up, then send him along."

Octavious gives a curt nod, then extends his arm toward Clara. "Let's go, then."

Clara loops her arm through her uncle's, and with a final, lingering glance lets him escort her out the door.

My grandmother is already headed for the stairs. "I'll leave this to you two. I'm much too tired." She shuffles slowly up the stairs to her room.

In the kitchen, we take seats around the table. My mother word-lessly applies a cold piece of beef from the icebox to Sweety's eye. "Hold it there for a while, to keep the swelling and bruising down."

"Thank you, Jeanette." He takes hold as she lets go.

"You can thank me by doing right by my girls. All of them." She stalks out.

Sitting next to him, I watch him. He's a pitiful sight with that cut of meat pressed against his face. Despite his lowly state, what I have to say must be said. "How could you, Sweety? You've disappointed Clara so much."

He sighs heavily. "I know. I should have remained at home until it was time for the cotillion."

"I'm glad you know that now." I fold my hands in my lap. "I'm strong, Sweety. I can withstand much. But I won't stand for you to do things that cause harm or embarrassment to our daughters. That's where I draw the line."

With a solemn nod, he promises, "Nothing like this will ever happen again."

"See that it doesn't." I get up and leave him at the table.

As I recline on the settee, thinking over what has happened, a sense of calm comes over me. I've risen above my anger while still setting a very clear boundary with my husband, and I'm proud of myself for that.

What we have isn't perfect; that's the very nature of love. Still, at least for now, I believe what we share is worth preserving.

# 16

JOSEPHINE

*June 1891*

I sit down on the old wooden bench, enjoying the feel of the warm sun on my skin as I take in the sights around me. The churchyard of St. John the Evangelist is bustling with activity, as today's Juneteenth festivities enter their third hour. We are now twenty-six years past that fateful day, when freedom finally became a reality for the enslaved, and the celebration is just as poignant today as it has been in years past. I believe that this day will always hold a special place in the hearts of freedmen, a place that the traditional Independence Day could never hold.

I brush a fallen kernel of popped corn from my cream-colored blouse, grateful the butter hasn't yet stained it. I paired my blouse with a simple black skirt and a wide-brimmed straw sun hat trimmed in black ribbon. It isn't my fanciest outfit, but it fits the day perfectly. We usually dress well but comfortably for this gathering, since there are many physically rigorous games and activities to participate in, for children and adults alike.

I look across the grove and spot my husband and brother, tossing horseshoes into the freshly dug pit. Sweety and Octavious are both in denim trousers; Hammond's General Store recently got a big shipment of them and most of the men in town are wearing them. My brother wears a blue shirt and my hardheaded husband, despite my advice to the contrary, is wearing a white shirt. Before the day is out, I know he'll have soiled it with dirt or food of some kind, but I suppose that's of no concern to him. I'll likely be the one running off to the store to replace it if the stains won't come out.

I had more control over Florrie's attire, so I dressed her in a yellow blouse and black skirt. Looking around now, I spot my eleven-year-old sitting beneath a shady willow, with an open book in her lap. Both of my girls are enthusiastic readers, but Florrie's curiosity seems even more boundless than her sister's. Getting up from my seat on the bench, I walk over to the tree and squat next to my baby girl. "Florrie, what are you reading today?"

Her mass of curls swirls around her face as her head pops up. With one hand holding the book open, she uses the other to search around on the ground for a moment. Finding her bookmark in the grass, she then lays the strip of thick red ribbon over the page before closing the book. Looking up at me, she rattles off a string of nearly unintelligible words.

My brow knits in confusion; I haven't the foggiest idea what my child just said beyond the first word. She tends to talk fast when she's excited about something. I repeat back to her the few words I could comprehend. "Dreaming of what, by who?"

She smiles, speaking slowly this time. "It's called *Dream of the Red Chamber*, by Cao Xueqin, Mama. Mrs. Rigsby, the librarian, recommended it for me when I said I was interested in Eastern culture."

"Eastern culture?" Florrie's varied interests and fertile imagination astound me. The world is so big to her, just as I wanted. Nothing and no one can lay a claim to her, but the world is hers for the taking.

She nods. "Yes. It's set in China during the Qing dynasty period, and it follows the story of the Jia family. They are wealthy nobles, and their spoiled son Baoyu is the main character. He is a philanderer, always dating his female cousins and servants, and—"

"Hold on," I say, stopping her. "You know what a philanderer is?"

"Yes, Mama. Mrs. Rigsby always tells me to consult the dictionary whenever I come to a word I can't define, so I learned it that way."

I cringe but feel proud at the same time. "All right, go on with what you were saying, then."

"Anyway, the story is mainly about how the family is going into a period of decline, and a lot of the bad stuff that happens to them is because of Baoyu's bad and selfish decisions."

"Interesting. And what are you learning from reading this book?"

"Lots of things about etiquette and cultural norms in China, mostly. I hope to travel there one day."

"Would you really travel so far from home?"

"Sure, I would, with the right travel companion." Florrie reopens her book. "Do you mind if I go back to reading now? I've just come to a really interesting part of the story."

"Go ahead, honey." I stand and walk away, leaving Florrie to feed her curiosity. I try not to think about how I would feel if Florrie ever does travel to China. What mother wants her daughter on the other side of the world? I push the thought away, headed for Clara.

My elder daughter, home after a rigorous first year at Shaw University, stands near the back of the church building, holding court at the bottom of the stone steps. I spot her by her height among a tangle of young male admirers, since she towers above a few of them. Her pink blouse and wheat-colored skirt are a bright spot on the dull flagstones.

I think of my youth, and how I was so overwhelmed by the newness of freedom, I hadn't the inclination to spend much time in the company of young men. I sometimes wonder if that played a role in my attraction to Sweety. He heaped attention on me that I'd never been in a position to receive. Whatever the case, I love my husband, though he bedevils me from time to time. Still, something in me envies the freedom my daughters have to choose their own social circles; they were born with this freedom and likely take it for granted.

Approaching slowly so I won't embarrass her, I stick to the edge of the small crowd she's drawn and listen. I can hear the young men bantering back and forth about how beautiful she is. I sigh, hoping men will one day learn to value women's minds as much as they do their looks.

Philip Horne, who's been sweet on my daughter for years now, moves closer to her. He wears a fine brown suit and white shirt, though he's forgone a jacket, likely due to the heat of the day. He seems over-dressed for the occasion, and I can't help wondering if a desire to impress my daughter influenced his choice in attire. Clearing his throat, he asks, "What's it like at university?"

Clara takes a breath before answering. "Hard. It's lots of reading, studying, and thinking deeply about tough subjects. But we also play sports for physical education—softball, mostly."

"Capital." Philip winks at her. "I fancy myself a scholar too. Though I've got my eyes set on studying chemical sciences at Saint Augustine's."

Clara's smile is genuine. "I'm certain you'll do very well, Philip."

He blushes.

I'm so entertained by their exchange I can't help smiling. The two of them are just precious together; were I the meddling type, I'd already be planning their nuptials. But I think it's better to let fate guide hearts together, without the interference of man, including well-meaning mothers.

The crowd thins almost immediately, with four sullen, grumbling boys wandering away so that only Philip remains with my daughter. I ease away as well, not wanting to interrupt her time with her old friend.

Wandering away from Clara and Philip, I head for the horseshoe pit and watch the men try their luck at ringing the post.

I look at my husband. His face is the picture of concentration, and his shirtsleeves are rolled up to his elbows, revealing the café-au-lait skin of his strong forearms. He takes his stance, the denims stretching and puckering around his thighs, reminding me of how long it's been since we had any time alone. My eyes follow his motions as he raises the horseshoe with those long-boned fingers of his, flexes his hand at the wrist, then sends it flying.

Missouri appears behind me, adjusting her flowered hat as she speaks. "Your Sweety is quite good at horseshoes."

I nod as the clang of metal on metal signals yet another ringer for my husband. "He's been throwing shoes since before emancipation."

"It shows."

I turn to Missouri. "I love that navy skirt, dear sister-in-law."

She smooths her hands over it. "Thanks. I found it at Newman's store. He's got quite a selection of colors and fabrics. Has plenty of day dresses, too."

"My only qualm is the white blouse. Don't you know you're likely to sully it during the festivities?" I hear the words escape my mouth before I can stop them.

She laughs. "Oh, go on with you, Jo. Besides, it was my only clean blouse. I'm overdue for some time at the washboard."

I turn toward a rumbling sound, coming from the direction of Queen Street, which runs behind the church. I squint, making out the familiar, terrible sight of the Stars and Bars, the old Confederate battle flag.

A buggy careens toward the grove, with horses' hooves thundering and wheels squeaking as the driver turns off the road. I don't know if he's lost control or if he's doing this on purpose; I just know he's barreling straight for our gathering.

Three white men are aboard the vehicle: a driver, the passenger holding that cursed flag high above his head, and another passenger kneeling in the back.

My eyes dart to Florrie, only to see her scurrying up the willow tree she's been sitting under. *That's my girl.*

"Clara!" I scream for my child, who's chosen this moment to cross the grove with Philip.

Bless him, he grabs her arms and yanks her out of the path of the buggy as it whizzes by, close enough to rustle her skirts with the breeze stirred up by its rapidly spinning wheels.

Folks scramble out of the way as the buggy flies through the center of our churchyard, toppling the tables of food and tearing through our hand-painted Juneteenth banner. Sweety runs to me, and we topple to the ground, his body shielding mine, his arms around me.

"Take this, darkies!" one of the men shouts.

A torrent of foul-smelling red fruit is hurled at us as the buggy whizzes by the horseshoe pit, the wheels kicking up a cloud of dry earth. I cough as some of the dirt gets into my nose and mouth.

The driver turns again, this time heading around the side of the church and onto Church Street, speeding westward up the road.

And just like that, they are gone. The whole ordeal maybe lasted a couple of minutes, but it seemed like an eternity. All that remains are the tracks the buggy wheels made across the grass, the destroyed trestle tables and food, and the piles of stinking red mess.

Sweety gets up, helping me to my feet. "Are you all right, Jo?"

I nod. "I may have swallowed a little dirt, but I'm fine."

Rector Billups, already saddling his horse, calls out. "Brother Leary, will you ride with me after these miscreants?"

"I'll return shortly, my love." Sweety pecks me on the cheek, and after mounting Cinnamon, he's off.

I glance to my left, where Missouri was standing not five minutes ago.

I cover my mouth when I see her. She sits on the ground, sobbing. My brother is with her, his arms around her shoulders. Her formerly pristine white blouse is stained with splotches of scarlet.

I rush to them. "Are you hurt?" I ask.

"It was tomatoes. Rotten tomatoes." Missouri gestures to one of the flattened fruits lying next to her on the ground. "They rode through here like Lucifer's own minions and pelted us with rotten tomatoes." She looks at me, tears shimmering in her eyes. "Why, Jo? Why do they do these things?"

I feel my own tears welling up as I shake my head. My sister-in-law is a sweet, sensitive woman without a hateful bone in her body, and I know she sincerely doesn't understand such actions. I don't have an answer for her now; I can't find the words.

My brother has no such trouble. "I'll tell you why they do it," he begins, flinging bits of tomato flesh off his denims. "They are hateful, ignorant fools, and I've grown sick of their madness."

I turn my gaze to his hard-set face. "So have I, Octavious. But what are we to do about it?"

"I don't know what you will do, but I know what I will do." He helps his wife to her feet, wiping her tears with a gentle hand. "I'll take my sweet wife away from this."

I feel my heart squeeze. "Where will you go? And who will look after you?"

"Sis, I know you still see me as a child. But I'm thirty-two years old. I can figure it out, I can make a good life for my wife and me."

"I'm sorry, brother. I know you're full-grown, and I know you're capable. I'd never want to make you feel as if I didn't believe in you." I wring my hands. "But I can't imagine my life without you nearby. We've been together since childhood."

He draws a deep breath. "I know, Jo. And I would miss you and Mama, and Granny Milly terribly. But I simply can't stay here." He cups Missouri's chin in his hand, kisses her cheeks. "Look at her. I love her more than life itself. Seeing her hurt, seeing her shed tears is physically painful for me, and I won't stand by and keep subjecting her to this misery."

Missouri swallows. "I agree with my husband. You know I love you, Jo. Sweety and the girls and the rest of the family, too. But it's all too much. I'm tired of these entitled white girls trying to touch my hair, and of their mothers pursuing me to be their housemaid. I'm tired of these perverse white men who think it's acceptable to ogle me or touch my bottom when we pass on the sidewalk." She shakes her head. "I want to be a mother, and I can't see raising my child in such a place."

"I agree with my wife. And I'm tired of being followed around every store I visit and of watching ladies clutch their purses at the mere sight of me." Octavious runs a hand over his hair. "I've had enough. As soon as I can arrange it, I'm taking my wife north."

As he guides Missouri away, I sigh, dashing away my own tears. I know my brother is well within his rights to want something better, but I know I will miss him. Still, the decision is his.

I see the logic in his way of thinking. I can imagine a life outside of the South, someplace where there are fewer bitter old relics, still clinging to their broken dream of life before the war. Were it not for the properties I hold here, and my determination to leave this place a little better for my own girls, I might follow my brother north.

I gather myself and go to seek out my daughters.

# SWEETY

## *June 1891*

Mounted on Cinnamon, Jo's sturdy palomino, I follow the rector down Church Street. Following the blades of grass left in the road, along with the clods of dirt and rotten tomatoes, we track the buggy to the edge of town where the road gives way to the grass, and the grass gives way to the murky waters of Pembroke Creek.

Rector Billups shakes his head, turning his mount. "There's nothing here. I suppose they've gone back to whatever hole they crawled out of." His words drip with disgust.

I start to wheel my own horse around, but pause at the glint of something silver in the reeds next to the creek. Dismounting, I step over the buggy wheel tracks and pick up the object. Turning it over in my hand to examine it, I can feel my frown deepen. "This is Herbert Westbrook's flask. The monogram gives him away." I tuck it into my pocket. "I'd bet good coin those were his two idiot brothers with him on that buggy."

"So it was the liquor that drove them to their actions." The rector appears distressed.

"For a man like him, too daft to see beyond his own prejudices, it's more likely just good old-fashioned meanness that drove him to it."

Rector Billups's face registers a rare flash of anger. "Goodness. I can't abide by these men's behavior. It's uncouth and uncalled-for."

"You're right. But what are we going to do now?"

"Alert the sheriff. Justice must be done." The rector slaps the reins, headed back into town.

I trail behind, but at a much slower pace. I see no need to rush; the cretins have already retreated. Knowing them, and knowing how these things usually go, they've probably returned to their old homestead in the far reaches of the county.

Knowing that my family was put in danger by a posse of slack-jawed bumpkins has me seeing red. Apparently, it isn't enough that white men have all the advantages in the world. They also need to terrorize freedmen to make themselves feel good. It's a disgrace.

Back in town, I hitch my horse outside the sheriff's office. Located on the corner of King and Court Streets, opposite the courthouse, it's a one-story brick structure that sits a few feet back from the road.

A tin-roofed, low-slung porch features two oak rockers, positioned on either side of the door. The door and windows have black iron bars over the glass.

I sit down on the edge of the porch and wait. *Odds are fairly good that the rector will be calling on me for help. It's just a matter of time.*

As I lean against the porch post, the sound of elevated voices reaches my ears. I frown. Surely the rector isn't arguing with the lawman . . . is he? I stand, intent on taking a peek inside through the glass panel on the door.

Before I make it there, though, the door swings open and the exasperated-looking clergyman walks out, throwing up his hands. "I can't believe you would doubt the account of a man of the cloth."

Sheriff Ed Wilder strolls out casually behind the rector. He's a big man, just over six feet tall and barrel-chested. The brown Stetson pulled low over his brow obscures his blue eyes, the brim casting a shadow over the silver star pinned to the front of his blue shirt. Fingers hooked in the belt loops of his denims, he says gruffly, "I need more'n one account when you're talking about something so outrageous, Billups. What lawman worth his salt wouldn't want to see some proof after a tall tale like that?"

The rector turns his head toward me. "Ask Brother Leary! He was there and saw the whole mess."

Wilder looks my way. "Leary, you saw this?"

*That's my cue.* I clear my throat. "Yes, sir."

"You mean to tell me that you saw three men on a buggy just tear through the churchyard, unprovoked, throwing rotten produce?" He stares into my eyes. "As an upstanding citizen, you sayin' you witnessed that?"

I nod. It's not lost on me the way Wilder's tone changed when addressing me, versus the sharp way he'd spoken to the rector just moments before. "I agree with you that it's outrageous, Sheriff. But it's also true."

Wilder walks a step closer to me, one dark, bushy brow lifting into an arc.

I can't tell if that expression indicates shock, disbelief, or both. "Listen, Sheriff. We followed those rascals, and I found this in the bushes near Pembroke Creek, where the buggy tracks ended." I pull the monogrammed steel flask from my pocket and pass it to the lawman.

Wilder turns the thing over in his hand. "It's Herb Westbrook's."

"I know. Most of the men in town have seen him with it on one corner or another, drinking the day away." I run my hand over my hair. "I know you're plenty busy here, and you don't have time for chasing windmills. But this really did happen, and I think the easiest way to prove that is for you to ride out to the church with us and see the damage for yourself."

"As I suggested," the rector mumbles.

"Pipe down, Reverend, I'm thinking." Wilder scratches at his chin whiskers. "I'd usually take my deputy with me for something like this, but he's out making his rounds." He appears thoughtful for a few minutes more, then says, "All right, I suppose I better look into this . . . as a favor to you, Leary."

I nod. "I appreciate it, Sheriff." I glance at the rector, who seems to have retreated into silent prayer if the subtle movement of his lips and his lowered eyes are any indication.

The three of us mount up and head back for the church. When we arrive, we find many of the parishioners still there, attempting to clean up the carnage.

My eyes dart around until I locate my family. Jo sits with our children, one arm around each daughter, on the church's back steps. Octavious and Missouri are positioned nearby, though her face, turned into her husband's shoulder, isn't readily visible.

Walking across the churchyard, Sheriff Wilder removes his hat. "What in the dickens?"

"It's just as I told you," Rector Billups says. "See for yourself what these men have done, the disrespect they've shown for the house of God."

I follow the sheriff around the clearing like a shadow, watching as he squats to examine the rutted lines left in the earth by the buggy wheels, and the foul, squashed red lumps lying in the grass.

Standing to his full height again, the sheriff shakes his head grimly. "Those Westbrook boys have gone too far with their damn pranks. Was anybody hurt?"

I shake my head. "By the grace of God, no. We've suffered quite a bit of property damage, though."

"I'll have to make a report about it." Sheriff Wilder removes a small leather-bound book and a pencil from his shirt pocket and jots something down. "I'm making a note of everything you said, Leary."

I ask, "And will you be including the rector's statement, or taking statements from any of the parishioners?"

Wilder's eyes narrow, but only for a moment, before he speaks. "It's best to just take one overall statement. Makes things easier for the investigation. I'm sure you understand my meaning, don't you, Leary?"

Feeling my jaw tighten I give a tight nod.

"Good." He leans in, speaking just above a whisper. "You're an upstanding man, Leary. See that you don't go too far outta your way for these folks."

Holding back the torrent of curses I want to say, I reply, "Duly noted, Sheriff." Passing for white is truly a double-edged sword. Yes, I will get some form of justice for my family and fellow churchgoers. But Sheriff Wilder would continue to fail to see their humanity. Whenever I take advantage of my fair complexion and wavy hair, I get to enjoy a moment of triumph or validation. But it is always fleeting. Always. Because soon after, the blade of truth cuts across my being, and a little more of my soul leaks out through the rift.

Wilder stands there a few minutes more to jot down the rest of his official findings, then shuts the small book and puts it away again. "I'll see what I can do about bringing Herb in."

"What about his brothers?" The tone of the question is terser than I had intended, but I correct it by adding a false smile.

Wilder's eyes flash momentarily, then the smoke clears. "I don't see the point in bringing 'em all in. You know Herb's got custody of the brain in that family, though he rarely makes any good use of it. Those boys are dumber than a barrel of rocks, and they do whatever their elder brother says. If I bring in the ringleader and give him a stern talking-to, I don't foresee them pulling any more of this balderdash."

While the sheriff's answer isn't what I wanted to hear, it does hold some validity. Bo and Melvin Westbrook aren't known for their intelligence; I once witnessed Melvin jump into the path of an oncoming buggy because he was trying to leapfrog over a hitching post. "I suppose you're right. Let me know when you've spoken to him, please."

"Will do." Wilder touches the brim of his hat, mounts his stallion, and is on his way.

I spend the next few hours helping my family and the other church members clean up the mess left in the grove. The two trestle tables that are still usable are returned to storage in the church basement, while the broken remnants of the other two tables are dragged to the rear of the grove to be burned later. Barrels are brought out, and all the destroyed food, the pieces of the torn banner, and the amorphous globs of rotted tomato flesh placed inside. Octavious and I help the rector move those barrels to a spot behind the rectory.

"Well, at least we have good compost for the community garden," the rector comments, wiping his hands on an old cloth. "God's work will continue, no matter the actions of man."

I nod solemnly.

At home that evening, I lie in bed with Jo in my arms.

Her head resting against my chest, she sighs. "While you were gone, Octavious told me he wants to move with Missouri out of the state."

"Really?" That comes as a surprise to me, since I can't recall having heard my brother-in-law speak of such a move.

"Yes. After Missouri had her clothes ruined by those bounders today, he said he's had enough." She sighs again. "Oh, Sweety. What will I do? I've never known a life without my brother by my side, and I've come to love Missouri like a sister, too."

I can feel the wetness of her tears on my skin, and her pain tears at my heart. "There now, dearest. I'll be here for you." It isn't much, but it is all I can offer right now.

Deep down, there is a flicker of joy at feeling that she needs me, truly needs me, for the first time in years. I'll do my best to lessen her struggle, as any good husband would do.

# 17

JOSEPHINE

*March 1892*

I keep my eyes on the road as I drive our old but reliable buggy out to the Jackson spread. Rosa's father, Paul, has been nice enough to lend us the use of his widest pasture today, and I'm grateful for his generosity. For today, my elder daughter is determined that she'll learn to drive.

The pines and spruce lining the road still burst with fragrant needles and hardy cones, in contrast to the nearly bare sycamores and maples speckled between them, which are just now sprouting their first leaves of the spring. It's temperate but not yet warm; my passengers and I have all donned light cloaks over our skirts and blouses. Luckily, we are deep into the wilds of the county, far enough away from town to avoid the chilly breezes flowing off the water.

Clara is seated beside me, her gaze fixed on the passing scenery. She's kept her own counsel the entire ride, and I imagine she's mentally working out all the ways she will complete her mission today.

"Clara, are you all right, honey?"

She nods. "Yes, Mama. I'm fine."

I call back behind me. "And you, sister?"

"Right as rain, Jo." Behind us, Missouri reclines on the rear seat, her hand resting on her burgeoning belly. My sister-in-law is nearly five months along now, and I try not to think about the fact that she will be so far away when the baby comes.

The road narrows as we get closer to our destination, the path becoming a bit more rugged. Most folks coming to the farm approach on horseback or in a smaller conveyance, so I'm mindful of my steering as we progress. Sugar is as docile and well-trained as a horse can be, so she takes to every tug on the line like a dream. It's why I've chosen her to pull the buggy for my daughter's lesson.

When we arrive at the iron gate of Jackson Farm, Rosa is there to greet us. I bring my buggy to a halt as Rosa dismounts her mare and unlatches the big scrollwork gate. After pushing the gates open, she waves us in, and I guide the vehicle inside. Rosa secures the gates again, then rides up, matching pace with me as I drive toward the pasture.

"Morning, Leary family." Rosa touches the brim of her old straw hat.

I glance at my friend, offering a smile. "Morning, Rosa. Pasture's clear for us?"

"Yep. We moved all our stock to the south pasture, so the north one's all yours." Rosa looks at Clara. "Best of luck out there, young-ster. I'm sure you'll take to driving like a duck to water."

Clara's smile is soft. "Thanks, Ms. Rosa."

"Well, Jameson and I have got horses to shoe. See you folks later on." Rosa rides alongside us until we reach diverging paths, then rides off to the left as we take the right.

The tall pines and sycamores that lined our path into the farm now give way to wide-open land. In the distance, I can just make out the jag-ged slats of old man Jackson's hand-hewn fences, which provide both safety for his animals and a marking of the northern border of his land.

I bring the buggy to a halt, set the hand brake, and climb down from the driver's seat, with the lines still in my hand. "Are you ready, Clara?"

"Yes, ma'am." Clara scoots over on the seat so that she is to the right.

"Good, then. The first lesson of driving: never let go of the lines. They're reins when we ride, lines when we drive. You must maintain control of your horse at all times." I pass her the lines. "Steady your grip, hold them between your second and third fingers."

"Like this?" She adjusts her hold.

"Perfect." I release my hold, giving her full control of the lines, then go around and climb aboard the seat to her left.

I notice immediately how stiffly my daughter sits in the driver's seat, so I lay a hand on her shoulder. "Don't worry, Clara. Sugar is as easy a horse as you can hope to drive with. She'll take to your commands without a problem, and she won't yank or dart off."

Her shoulders drop as she relaxes a bit. "That's good to know."

"Do you remember the command to get her started?"

"Yes, Mama."

"Good. Then release the hand brake and give the word." I sit back against my seat, resting my hands in my lap. A soft sound catches my attention, and when I glance behind me, I see that Missouri has fallen asleep. Bless her, carrying a child certainly has taken it out of her; I remember the exhaustion well, even though my younger baby is twelve now.

Clara eases the lever back with her right hand. "Sugar, step up, girl."

Dutifully, Sugar starts to walk, pulling the buggy along at a slow pace.

I watch silently, letting Clara find her footing, literally and figuratively. I watch her press her feet against the runner in front of her, moving it from side to side. I see that the extra line is in her way, so I gather some of the slack up. "Here. Lift up your hip."

She does, and I slide the coiled slack beneath her.

"Old driving trick. That way, you don't get tangled in the excess line."

"I see." She keeps her eyes straight ahead as we head across the pasture. The thin blades of young grass give beneath the wheels as we put distance between our vehicle and the pasture entrance.

"You're doing great, honey. Keep the pressure light. Are you feeling it in your back yet?"

"A bit, but I'm fine."

"Let's try a turn." I point ahead of us. "Make a right turn as soon as you can manage it."

She nods, giving the tiniest of tugs on the lead to alert Sugar to change directions. "Here we go, girl."

"Good, good." The turn starts off well but gets a little shaky.

Missouri awakens. "Good heavens, what's happening?"

I put my hand on Clara's forearm. "Careful, now. The buggy is wider than you think, so you need two things when making a turn: care and control."

She sighs. "Mama, we have plenty of room."

"That's true because we're in a pasture. But you won't be driving on open land like this most of the time. You'll be navigating the roads, and there will be other vehicles, and folks on horseback, and folks on foot to contend with." I give her forearm a squeeze. "Mind your space, dear."

Clara gives another tug, this one a little too strong. Sugar picks up her pace at the tail end of the turn, sending the carriage rocking side to side as it completes the maneuver. The three of us are jostled about in the chaos.

Missouri yelps.

"Bring it to a stop, Clara."

Clara does as I ask, halting Sugar and setting the hand brake.

"Keep your grip on the lines." I climb down and go to check on Missouri. "What's troubling you, sister?"

"The rocking of the coach is . . . too much for my weak stomach." She places her hand over her belly again. "Just set me down under a tree somewhere before you continue your lesson, please."

"I've got you." Getting the blanket I keep rolled up on the floor-board of the rear seat, I help Missouri down. Finding a lone willow tree near the gate where we entered the pasture, I spread out the blanket and help her sit. "Comfortable?"

She nods, then yawns. "I'll be fine. Go on back to my niece."

Returning to the buggy, I climb aboard again only to find Clara's face set into a tight-lipped frown.

"I can't believe I did that. Aunt Missouri shouldn't have been sub-jected to my terrible steering, not while she's with child."

"Now, now, daughter. Your aunt is here by choice because she wanted to support you."

She sighs. "Still. I just . . . wish it was easier."

"Don't be so hard on yourself, child. It's your first time driving."

"I know, I know. I've been riding horses for years now, and I thought driving would be just as easy to pick up." She shakes her head. "Is there any chance I can actually learn to drive in time to drive myself back to campus tomorrow?"

I shrug. "I don't know. I know it isn't likely if we keep sitting here with you feeling sorry for yourself."

Her gaze drops to her feet.

"I'll do my best to help you accomplish your goal, even though I think it's a little on the lofty side." I reach for her, cupping her chin in my hand. Looking into her eyes and seeing her uncertainty and ner-vousness, I can still see the innocence of the babe I once cradled in my arms residing there. She needs my guiding hand now, just as she did then. "I've set aside this whole day to help you. We'll stay as long as you need, or at least as long as your aunt can tolerate."

She chuckles. "So I'm on a time limit, then."

"Perhaps." I give her a peck on the cheek. "Still, I have the utmost faith in you, Clara. If anyone can learn this in only a day, it's you."

Drawing a deep breath, she straightens her posture and directs her gaze ahead. "Let's try again, then."

Soon we're underway, our buggy cutting across the grass at a reasonable pace. Once she seems comfortable keeping the buggy moving forward in a straight line, I direct her to practice stopping and restarting. Next we try trotting, letting Sugar get some energy out by picking up her pace.

Drawing the buggy to a halt again, Clara sets the brake and stretches her arms high above her head, still holding the lines. "How long have we been at this, Mama?"

I check the pocket watch I keep in my skirts. "A little more than an hour."

She blows out a breath.

"Good job keeping hold of the lines. Feeling the muscle tension, I suppose."

She nods. "Yes. My upper back and shoulders are pretty tight."

"Trust me, you will feel it even more intensely tomorrow morning."

She groans. "Goodness, Mama. Why didn't you warn me of this?"

"I did. You simply chose not to hear me." I chuckle. "Ready to give up the notion of learning to drive in a day?"

She nods, flexing her neck side to side. "Yes, Mama. I'm pretty much soured on that idea. I suppose I'll have to practice more when I'm home for summer break."

I nod, smiling at my elder child. "Now that sounds much more reasonable." I reach for the line. "I'll switch with you, and after we collect your aunt, we can head home."

We switch positions and drive up to the tree where Missouri is still reclining.

"You've done well, niece," Missouri says as Clara helps her to her feet. "It took me over a month to get any good at turning, and I can already see improvement in you."

"Thanks, Aunt Missouri." Clara helps her back into the rear seat, boards, and we are on our way.

I stop by the main house to alert Rosa that we've finished, and we find her on the front porch, polishing a saddle. "Y'all through with driving practice?"

"Sure are," Clara calls. "I've had all I can take."

Rosa grins. "Hold on a minute, I'll let you out."

After we've left the farm, I glance at Clara as we travel down the road toward home. "I just want to say, I'm so proud of you, honey. You've done so well in school, making good marks, taking on new challenges. Even today's attempt at learning to drive in a single day only reminds me of how determined you are to conquer the world. I'm honored to call you my daughter."

In my peripheral vision, I can see her gazing at me, a broad smile on her face. "Thank you, Mama. It means . . . a whole lot to me to hear you say that. It's mainly due to you, though."

"Pshaw, now. Give your father some credit," I joke, gently poking her in the side with my elbow.

She giggles. "No, Mama, I mean it. I love Papa, and I know he loves me, though he's not always apt to show it. But you've always been there for me and been vocal about your love."

"Can't help it. Just a sentimental type, I suppose."

Missouri yawns. "Heavens, I'm tired. I may fall asleep on the ride home."

I'm almost certain she will, but I wouldn't begrudge a woman creating life her rest. "Think nothing of it, Missouri. You've earned it."

"It's more than that," Clara continues. "You say I'm determined that I want to conquer the world." She touches my shoulder. "I got that from you. Watching you trade in property, work at the barbershop, manage a household . . . you inspire me to strive for success."

I can feel the tears gathering in my eyes. "I always hoped you girls would see my efforts as inspiration, but worried you might see them as neglect, too."

She shook her head. "No, Mama. Florrie and I knew you would be there when we truly needed you, and that you were just trying to give us a good life."

The sigh of relief that leaves my lips is soul deep. Without knowing it, my child has alleviated years of anxiety surrounding my talents as a mother, with a single comment. "Thank you, Clara. Thank you so much."

"I love you, Mama." She squeezes my shoulder.

With my hands on the lines, I have no choice but to let the tears fall. "I love you, daughter."

We continue the ride in a companionable silence, broken only by my sister-in-law's soft snores.

# JOSEPHINE

### *May 1892*

Standing on the platform at the train station in Raleigh, I struggle to keep my composure. Missouri is by my side, and we watch as our husbands help the porters load suitcases, carpetbags, and other belongings into the baggage car.

My mother, sentimental as she is, said her goodbyes this morning before we left Edenton. She has taken my grandmother, who has grown frail and unwell these past few weeks, and was much too weak to travel to Raleigh, to live with her and Dorsey. We don't know if age is catching up with Grandma Milly, or if sadness about Octavious and Missouri's leaving has laid her low, or both.

My mother has much more free time on her hands than I do, so I put up no resistance to the notion. Besides, I'll be able to see them both anytime, since they live so close by.

I sigh, knowing the same will no longer be true for my brother and sister-in-law.

The wooden plank platform extends along the rear of the large, redbrick train station. Tall steel posts support the tin roof over our head and mark the boundary of the platform where it dips to the ground before giving way to the tracks. It's a warm Sunday afternoon, and the area is alive with activity. Passengers and railroad employees rush back and forth.

The train that will take my brother and his wife to the District of Columbia has just disgorged a load of passengers, who are now crossing the platform with their bags in hand. There are folks lined up at the ticket window, and at the window where a woman sells sandwiches and lemonade to travelers. Others sit on the low wooden benches, awaiting arriving trains, holding conversations, reading newspapers. The air, thick and humid, smells of coal and smoke. I cover my nose with my handkerchief, letting it filter some of the soot as I take a deep breath.

"I can't believe we're finally on our way to Washington." Missouri rubs her large belly in a circular motion. "And just in time, too. This little one won't wait much longer to be born."

I offer a small smile, though inside, my heart is breaking. She's radiant in her sunny yellow traveling costume and matching flowered hat, a broad grin on her face. It would be selfish of me to put a damper on the excitement my sister-in-law is feeling right now. "You have a whole new life ahead of you, and I'm sure it will be wonderful."

She puts an arm around my shoulders and gives me a squeeze. "It's such an odd feeling. Excitement, mixed with sadness."

I nod. "I understand, trust me. Life has placed me in such situations many times, where I felt ready for the future, but couldn't quite let go of the past."

"You've put it into words so succinctly, Jo." Missouri sighs. "I'm going to miss that."

"No, you won't," I insist. "Because I'll be bombarding you with succinctly worded letters at every opportunity. Telegrams, too. You'll hear from me so often, you'll tire of me."

She gives me another squeeze, this one a bit tighter than the first. "That will never happen, Jo."

I put my arm around her waist and just hold her for a few moments. She's become a true sister of my heart over these past several years, giving me an experience I thought I'd never get to have. And as special as our connection is, I know it is the depth of our relationship that's causing me such pain at this moment.

Sweety and Octavious return to us. My husband has chosen a simple tan shirt and denims to wear today, but Octavious's dark suit is more in line with his wife's traveling clothes.

"We've loaded everything," Sweety says, eyeing Missouri.

"Yep. We can board now, sweetheart." Octavious drapes his arm around Missouri's waist.

She smiles at him serenely.

A moment passes in silence, with the four of us looking between each other. I suppose no one wants to begin the goodbye we've all put off for so long.

Taking my hand, Missouri looks into my eyes. "Until we meet again, Jo."

"Safe travels, Missouri." I pull her in for a tight hug, holding her without putting pressure on her belly.

She steps back, and my brother moves closer to me. "You have watched over me since I was no taller than a blade of grass. You have talked me down from many a high tree limb, and I don't know what I will do without you."

I smile through my tears. "You won't have to do without me. I'll be pestering you by letter and visiting as often as I can."

He chuckles, his eyes misty. "I will miss you, sister. Keep yourself well."

"I will. You do the same, brother. Promise to send a telegram so we'll know you arrived safely."

"I promise." He hugs me, whispering, "I love you, Josephine."

"I love you, too." My voice wavers beneath the weight of my tears, and I swallow them. My little brother deserves a chance to build the life he wants for himself and his family; I will not make him feel guilty.

He releases me and returns to his wife's side. As the two of them walk toward the train, Sweety pulls me close, and I let his strength bolster me. Emotion has weakened my knees, but his presence steadies me.

I watch Octavious lead Missouri to the conductor, hand over their tickets, then carefully escort her up the steps and into the train car. The scene reminds me of how well he's cared for her since they married, and how he's become even gentler since she got in a family way. I watch through the windows as they take their seats, offering us a final wave.

We wave back as the train whistle blows, the engine huffing and puffing steam and ash into the air. We stand on the platform as the train departs, picking up speed as it rolls down the track until finally, it's out of sight.

Sweety and I return to our buggy, parked in front of the station, and depart for the campus of Shaw University. Our elder daughter has been released for the summer and is riding home to Edenton with us.

I sit next to my husband, silently watching the scenery roll by as he drives.

"Are you well, dearest? You're awfully quiet."

"I'll be all right," I say in response to his question. "I already miss Octavious and Missouri, but I'm happy we're going to get Clara. It will certainly help to brighten this day; it's been a while since we've seen her."

"Not since her spring break, and that arduous driving lesson, as I recall." Sweety winks.

I know he is trying to lift my mood, and I find that endearing. So I offer him a small smile as a boon for his efforts. "Yes. And now, we have a whole summer's worth of lessons ahead of us."

"'We'?" Sweety feigns surprise. "When did I become a part of this?"

I use my finger to poke him in the side. "You're her father, and you're going to help her learn to drive, you dunderhead."

He laughs, long and heartily. "I'm only joking, dearest. Of course, I'll help. I'll admit, I'm not as patient as you . . ."

"Or as good of a driver," I add teasingly.

He makes a show of cutting his eyes at me. "Balderdash. But as I was saying, I'll do what I can to help our girl learn to drive."

I chuckle. "I know you will. It's either that or spend the hottest part of the year sleeping on the settee."

He puts a hand over his heart. "Alas, your words wound me, my love."

I shake my head at his antics.

We arrive on campus in short order and join the other conveyances parked in the front yard of Estey Hall. We meet Clara, coming down the stairs, dragging her two new large valises behind her. She's looking well, still dressed in her uniform. I can see she's filled out a bit, and I imagine the young men on campus have probably come to call during the semester.

Sweety immediately grabs both bags and hauls them to our buggy. Once we've all boarded again, we get back underway, headed for home.

"So, honey. How did the term go?" I'm eager to hear of my daughter's academic experiences, and I'm sure my husband is as well.

"Wonderfully, Mama. I've made high marks in all my classes . . . though I could have done a bit better in chemistry."

"Oh, yes. I recall seeing your marks in the letter I got from the academic affairs office. Good job, Clara."

"Thanks, Mama."

"Yes, you've done well, daughter," Sweety calls back to her while driving. "And if you don't plan to be a chemist, I wouldn't worry too much about that one class."

"I've been meaning to ask that, Clara. I know you're a liberal arts major, but what do you plan to choose as a career? Have you given it much thought?" I turn my upper body on the seat so I can see her face.

She appears resolved. "Actually, I *have* thought about it. I think I want to be a teacher."

"Really? I'm sure Evelina Badham and Miss Pullman would both be over the moon with excitement to hear this."

She grins. "I think you're right about that. I've spent a lot of time deciding, and since I've done so well with English, history, and especially pedagogy, I think it's a great choice for me. You know, I still remember so many lessons I learned from Miss Pullman and Mrs. Badham. Not just academics, life lessons." She clasps her hands together. "I want to be able to have an impact like that on someone else's life."

"That's wonderful." I look at my child, amazed at how much she's grown up in so many ways. She's articulate, she's self-assured, and she wants to share her gifts with the next generation. "There aren't many professions as noble as education, and I'm behind you all the way, honey."

"Hear, hear," Sweety says. "The children of Edenton will be lucky to have such a fine teacher."

Clara grins. "I'm so pleased to have your support. Both of you."

I smile and turn back around. She'll always have my support, and I'm glad she knows it.

When we arrive home, my mother greets us at the door. "Welcome back. Did Octavious and Missouri get off all right?"

"Yes, they did." I give her a peck on the cheek. "Has Florrie been good?"

"She's been reading most of the day. She was no trouble at all." My mother walks out the door as we come in. "I need to get home and start working on dinner for Dorsey and your grandmother."

"I understand. I'll see you later, Mama."

After she's gone, Sweety helps Clara move her things upstairs to her room, while I seek out Florrie. I find my younger daughter in the parlor, huddled beneath my writing table, reading by lamplight. "Florrie, what are you doing down there?"

"Reading. This is the quietest spot in the house." She looks up at me, her brown eyes wide. "Clara's back?"

I nod. "She's in her room. Go on and see her, I'm sure she's missed you."

Florrie closes her book, tucking it under her arm as she heads upstairs.

I make us a simple supper of ham, corn bread, and green beans. When the meal is complete, Clara and I take the dishes into the kitchen to wash them. As we work, we hear the sounds of raised voices coming from outside.

Clara frowns. "Mama, what is that?"

"I don't know." I listen for a few moments before I notice the rhythmic nature of the sound. "I think it's . . . someone singing?"

We set aside the dishes and follow the sound outside, and around the front of the house.

There, in the yard, four young men are gathered. In the front of the group is a familiar face, that of young Philip Horne.

As we climb onto the porch, I realize what they're doing, and smile. "Clara, they're serenading you."

Clara, who still harbors a bit of shyness, blushes. "Oh, good heavens."

I listen in, picking up the words until I recognize the song. I suppress the urge to sing along, knowing that will only increase my child's embarrassment.

*Oh, promise me that someday you and I*
*Will take our love together to some sky*
*Where we can be alone and faith renew*
*And find the hollows where those flowers grew*
*Those first sweet violets of early spring*
*Which come in whispers, thrill us both, and sing*
*Of love unspeakable that is to be;*
*Oh, promise me! Oh, promise me!*

By now, Clara's cheeks are as red as apples.

"I think Philip is sweet on you." I wink.

"Mama!" Clara waves me off.

I back away. "All right, all right. I'll let you handle it." I go inside the house, leaving my daughter to her admirers.

Sweety is sitting in the front room, looking out the window when I enter. "They're putting on quite a show out there, aren't they?"

"They certainly are. I think she's either going to have to let Philip court her, or give him the mitten already." I ease next to him on the sofa. "That poor boy has been after her for years now."

He chuckles. "True enough. He's got determination, I'll give him that." He turns from the window and gives me a kiss on the cheek.

"I'm refreshed by your reaction, honey. You weren't always so keen on young men being around the girls."

He shrugs his shoulders. "I know, but no amount of bluster from me will keep them from growing up. Best I let them have their independence now, so they won't resent me later."

"That's very wise."

A few beats pass before he speaks again. "Here, I've got a surprise for you."

My curiosity piqued, I ask, "Oh, do you?"

"Yes. It's no serenade, I'm afraid. But I did think we could both use a nice outing." Reaching into the pocket of his denims, he pulls out two long slips of paper and hands them to me.

I read them aloud. "Tickets . . . to see a play at Rea's Opera House."

He nods. "Yes. It's called *The Moonshiner*. I'm not terribly sure what it's about, but based on what I've read in the papers, it's got good reviews."

I clutch the tickets to my chest. "Goodness, Sweety. I thought you'd forgotten your promise to take me to a show."

"Forget a promise to you? Never." He leans in and kisses me on the lips.

I kiss him right back. He's given me something to look forward to, and I can hardly contain my excitement.

# 18

JOSEPHINE

*February 1893*

"Hold on, Florrie. Don't put in too much salt." I grab my daughter's hand before she can toss in a third scoop.

She appears sheepish as she withdraws the still-full scoop. "Sorry, Mama." She steps back from the pot of greens bubbling on the stove.

I smile. "Don't worry about it, honey. You're learning."

It's a wintry Thursday evening, one of those nights where the chill hangs in the air and you can see your breath when you walk outside. She's helping me make dinner for the three of us, and as such, the process is taking longer than if I had cooked myself.

My kitchen layout is my saving grace. The wooden shelves I had my brother install over the stove hold crocks of spices, lard, and my cooking utensils. My pots reside in a low cabinet that sits between the stove and the icebox. Beneath the window that faces the backyard and sits next to the back door, I have a table with two side-by-side basins I use for washing and rinsing dishes. The table has a checkered burlap cloth over it, which hides the barrel of water I keep beneath it so that

I'm not always running out to the pump. The rest of the space is occupied by the table I use for food preparation, with enough space to walk around it.

I take my pocket watch from my apron and glance at it. It's nearly seven. Where is Sweety?

Florrie returns to the table, where a pot of boiled potatoes await mashing. "What are we going to put in here besides butter?"

"You can put that scoop of salt in." I stop pondering what my husband might be up to and bring my focus back to the task at hand. "Then we'll add a little cream, butter, some roasted garlic, and black pepper."

She adds the salt and places the scoop back in the salt crock. "Is that what you normally put in? Because your mashed potatoes are always really good."

I smile at her compliment. "Glad to hear it. Go in the icebox and get the butter and cream for me, please."

"Yes, ma'am." She goes to do as I asked.

I get my best wooden spoon from the drawer and begin the process of breaking up the potatoes.

Florrie returns with the small ceramic pitcher of cream and the covered dish of butter. Holding the pitcher, she asks, "How much, Mama?"

"Just a splash."

Under my watchful eye, she adds a healthy pour to the pot. "Is that enough?"

"Perfect. Now add a big pat of butter and you can put them both back."

She adds the butter while I continue mashing. I toss in a few cloves of garlic from my jar of roasted garlic and olive oil and mash them in. Passing the spoon to her, I say, "Now try mashing for me while I add some pepper."

She eagerly takes the spoon and goes to work pulverizing the remaining lumps in the potatoes. I grab the peppermill from the center of the table and grind in a healthy portion. "There."

"Mama, do you know how to cook any foods from other cultures?"

I frown, unsure what she means. "Can you be more specific?"

"It's just that I read about food from all over the world. Dishes from China and Italy sound the tastiest. Do you think I could learn to cook some of those things?"

I chuckle, once again pleased by her boundless curiosity about the world outside of our sleepy little town. She's almost thirteen now, and before I know it, she'll be off to college, too. I can't help sighing as I look at her, in her blue skirt and yellow blouse, her long waves of dark hair tied back from her face with a yellow ribbon. The older she gets, the more she resembles her father. "I suppose, but you and I will have to learn them together. And while we're at it, we'll see if we can learn some dishes from our ancestral home, too."

"Sounds like fun." Florrie gestures to the pot. "Are the greens ready yet?"

"Fiddlesticks!" I run to the stove and grab the lid just as it's about to boil over. "Yes, honey. I'd say they're done."

We spend some time seasoning the greens; then I pull the roast chicken out of the oven. I watch Florrie baste it, and then I get out my big knife to slice it up.

Sweety still hasn't appeared, and I won't let my child go hungry, so we eat. After finishing our meal, we return to the kitchen to wash up our plates.

I hear the front door open, and we both look in that direction. A few moments later, Sweety comes into view, rounding the corner from the sitting room into the dining room. He carries his balled-up apron in his right hand. His dark slacks and blue shirt look disheveled, and his gait is just a bit off. Another quick glance at my watch tells me the time: a quarter till eight, well past the time my husband would normally have been home.

"Hi, honey." I keep my tone light as he enters the room, mindful of our daughter's presence. "Last-minute customers at the barbershop?" I already know that isn't the case; I want to see how he will answer.

He staggers toward me. "No. Just . . . went out after work. That's all."

"Hi, Papa!" Florrie moves toward him.

I put my arm out to stop her advance. The wobble in his walk and the way he's slurring his words tell me all I need to know. "Florrie, go upstairs for a bit, please."

She hesitates, her eyes darting back and forth between us.

Astute as she is, I know she's already picked up on the tension. Still, there's no reason she should have to see things unfold. "I'll be up after you shortly, honey." I give her a look that lets her know I don't have time to debate the matter.

"Yes, ma'am." She skirts around her father and runs through the parlor and up the stairs.

I turn to my obviously inebriated husband. "Archer, you're late."

He laughs. "Oh, so now it's Archer again? You must really be sore with me."

"It's bad enough to come home so late, but to come drunk, too?"

"I may have had one too many, but there's no brick in my hat yet."

I shake my head. "I'm going to make you some coffee so you can sober up; then you can eat supper."

"There you go, giving orders." He raises his arm, stabbing the air with his finger. "You really . . . think you wear the pants in this house, dont'cha?"

"You're talking nonsense." I pull out his chair at the kitchen table and gesture to it. "Now just sit down here, and I'll make the coffee."

He stumbles over and collapses into the chair, tossing his crumpled apron onto the table. "I'm not talking nonsense. You've always been like this."

"Like what?" I fill the kettle with water from the barrel in the corner of the kitchen, adding the coffee grounds before setting it on the fire.

"Bossy. All the men in town are laughing at me 'cause they think you run me."

"I highly doubt *all* the men in town can agree on anything."

He scowls. "Your mouth is too smart, Josephine. My reputation as a man is in shambles."

I stir the coffee with a long-handled steel spoon. "Really. And what do you think, Archer? Do you think I run you? Because for your life, yours is the only opinion that matters."

He climbs to his feet again. "Enough! Enough of your back talk and your highfalutin attitude."

He's angry now, I can feel the charge of it rolling off his skin. I turn off the kettle and back away from him, putting some space between us. "Archer, settle yourself."

"I won't! I'm tired of taking orders from you." His right arm twitches. "You need to learn your place!"

Eyes full of fury, he raises his hand. Time seems to slow as I realize what he plans to do. Reaching behind me into the basin, I grab the handle of my cast-iron skillet, hoisting it into the air. As he swings, I swing. The back of his hand meets the skillet instead of its intended target—my face.

"Shit!" He curses, drawing back his hand, shaking it, then examining his knuckles.

Hot tears of outrage spring to my eyes as I hold the skillet aloft. "Archer Leary! You must have taken leave of your senses."

"Goddammit, Josephine! My knuckles are split!"

Only then do I notice the blood trickling down his hand. That only increases my ire. "Good, it's what you deserve for raising your hand to me. I suppose you wish you'd split your hand against my face instead!"

He cringes, and the fire in his eyes begins to fade. "Jo . . . wait. I didn't mean . . ."

"Eat your words, Archer." I stride past him, still gripping my skillet. "I don't want to hear it."

He tries to follow.

I wheel around in a flash. "One more step in my direction and I swear you will feel this iron." My words are softly spoken and deadly serious.

He stops, backs up a step. "What are you doing?"

I turn and head for the stairs. "I'm taking my daughter and getting the hell out of here." I hear the contempt dripping from my words and the harshness of my language. I don't care.

I march up the stairs and fling open Florrie's door. "Honey, get your valise and toss in what you need for a week."

She's curled up in her bed, on top of the covers. When she stands, I can see the tears streaming down her face. "Why are you and Papa fighting?"

"You heard all that, didn't you?"

She nods solemnly.

I don't know what to say to her, so I tell her the truth. "Adult relationships can be complex, so it's difficult to explain. But right now, we need to leave."

She brushes away a tear with the back of her hand. "Mama . . . did Papa . . . hit you?"

My heart squeezes in my chest, and I'm overwhelmed with guilt and sadness that my child has been exposed to such a mess. I shake my head. "No, he didn't. But he tried, so we need to leave."

"Where are we going, Mama?"

Her eyes are wide as she poses the question: to me, she looks afraid. I don't know if I can ever forgive Sweety for making our daughter feel this way. "To visit with your grandmother for a bit. Hurry and get your things, now."

"Yes, ma'am." She takes a moment to compose herself, then gets the valise from beneath her bed and starts packing.

I stalk to my room, get my own carpetbag, and throw in my essentials. Skirts and blouses, underthings, a nightgown. I take comb and brush from my dressing table, and notice my journal on the table's edge.

I haven't written in it as often as I would have liked over the past few years, and for a moment, I'm struck by how different my life is now from the way I'd imagined it would be. Running an empire and a household while raising a family has left me so little time to commit my thoughts to the page. I wipe a layer of dust from it before adding it to my things.

Once Florrie is ready, the two of us don our heaviest cloaks and gloves and head downstairs. In the parlor, I take all my business receipts and records, adding them to the items in my bag, and we head for the door.

Sweety sits on the settee, watching us. His shoulders are slumped, his expression drawn. "Jo, let's talk about this."

"There's nothing to say." I set the skillet on the console table near the door. "Except this. Sheriff Wilder will be hearing from me. And if you follow us, the law will be the least of your worries."

He stares at me, openmouthed.

I don't wait for a response. Guiding Florrie by the hand, I open the front door.

A blast of cold air and snow greet us, but I'm undeterred. I will get my child away from this man, no matter what it takes. "Come, Florrie."

Outside, the snow swirls around us, carried by the frigid air. Only the moon and the gas lamps lining the street light our way. Being so close to the water during cold winters like this one means having to deal with sudden heavy snow. The covering on the ground is light, telling me the snow is just getting started. "We need to hurry before the roads are covered."

We hike around the house, our boots crunching on the frozen grass, and enter the barn. There, we hitch up my horses to my buggy, toss in our belongings, and climb in. We work together to draw the velvet curtain around us, giving us some respite from the icy winds and the falling snow. With the lines in my hand, I snap the whip over Cinnamon and Sugar, and we're off.

I hear Sweety calling my name, but I don't look back. Instead, I urge my horses on all the more.

Traveling down the snow-dusted road, I can feel my heart pounding in my chest. Beneath the layers of anger and indignation that made me stand up to Sweety, and have carried me and my child out of our home, lie the simmering coals of fear, of pain. Sweety may not have hit me, but he frightened me. And even worse, he dissolved the image of him that I always held dear, the image of a man who would never sink to physical violence against a woman.

I have a key to my mother's barn, so when we arrive, we tuck the horses into two empty stalls inside. By the time we knock at my mother's front door, I'm chilled to the bone. My hands are shaking as I fiddle with the keys, trying to find the one that fits her lock. I drop my key ring, and it clatters to the porch floor.

"What's all this commotion out here?" Dorsey, in his union suit, comes out on the porch. "Good heavens, what's happened?"

When I open my mouth to answer him, a sob escapes instead. No matter how I try, I just can't form the words. Tears stream from my eyes like water flowing from a broken pump.

Florrie's arm goes around me immediately. "Papa . . . raised his hand to her."

"Dorsey, what's going on?" My mother appears at Dorsey's side, dressed in her robe and nightgown. She peers around him, and gasps when she sees me. "What's the matter?"

"Sweety's lost his marbles," Dorsey states grimly.

She then grabs my hand. "Come in here, both of you." She draws us into the warmth of her home, shutting the door against the snow and cold.

I walk up to the doors of the law offices of Pruden and Vann, each step a burden. I'm crumbling beneath the weight of my heaviest cloak, my dark blue traveling dress, and layers of undergarments beneath, and the grave nature of my visit to the one-story building, about a block down from the courthouse. Today, I am doing something I never thought I would: seeking advice on dissolving my marriage to Sweety.

It's cold but dry today, and I'm grateful for the sunshine despite my cloudy mood. I grasp the door handle and enter the building, immediately feeling the warmth of the interior. Turning my head, I see the big fireplace, flames crackling within.

The reception area is elegant yet simple, with brocade wallpaper and fine cherry furnishings. I walk up to the desk, where a diminutive redhead sits, typing away on a typewriter. She looks up as I approach. "How can I help you, miss?"

"I have a nine o'clock appointment with Mr. Pruden."

"What's your name?" She moves away from the typewriter and opens a leather-bound book on the desk.

"Josephine Williams Leary." I rarely have the occasion of stating my whole name, and it seems a bit strange to do so.

Running her index finger along the handwritten lines on the page, she taps my name. "Ah, yes. I'll let Mr. Pruden know you're here."

I wait while she leaves the desk, disappearing into a corridor to the right. While she's gone, I note the fine, gold-framed oil landscapes on the walls and the potted ficus situated in the waiting area. I'm reminded of that day I visited CW Rea's office, only that day, Sweety was my escort rather than the topic of discussion.

The young redhead returns for me and leads me down the corridor and through an open door into a well-appointed inner office. "I'll take your cloak, ma'am."

I shrug out of it and hand it over to her. As she leaves, pulling the door shut behind her, William Pruden rises from behind the huge, hand-carved cherry desk. He's of average height and build, dressed in a fine black suit, a gray vest, and a black-and-gray-striped tie. His brown hair is a little thin at the top; I can see where he's tried to conceal that by combing most of it to one side. His face is clean-shaven, save for a thin mustache. His blue eyes are watchful, yet open and approachable.

"Good morning, Mrs. Leary. William Pruden, Esquire. I'm pleased to meet you."

"Pleased to meet you as well, though I wish the circumstances were more pleasant." I walk toward the chair he gestures to, on the opposite side of his desk, and sit. A visual sweep of the room reveals the items on his wall: a framed image of a woman I assume to be his wife, his undergraduate degree from the University of Virginia at Richmond, his law certificate from Richmond Hill School, his certificate of admission to the bar association. One item gives me pause, and as my eyes rest on it, I ask, "You served in the Confederate army?"

He turns his head, looking at the commendation I'm referring to. "Yes, I did. Made it to second lieutenant."

I watch him in silence, wondering if he thinks I'm impressed by the rank he earned in an army full of slavers and misogynists. "I'm sure you understand my inquiry. Before I reveal anything to you about my personal situation, I need to know: Did you volunteer, or were you drafted?"

"I volunteered."

"Well, pardon my bluntness, but I'll need your assurance that those Confederate ideals don't influence your life and work now."

He shakes his head. "Your concern is noted, but if I harbored any such ideals, I wouldn't have allowed you in my office."

"That's valid, I suppose." A man of his standing probably has no shortage of clients, yet he has chosen to hear me out. That is a mark in his favor, and if I remain vigilant during our interactions, we should work together just fine.

"For what it's worth, I enlisted to earn money for school more than anything else. But I represent all clients in my practice regardless of their race or political leanings, as long as their needs fall within my scope of practice." He rests his elbows on the desk and tents his fingers. "So, tell me, what brings you to my office today?"

"You handle divorce, correct?" I take off my gloves, tucking them into my handbag, and set it on my lap.

"Yes, ma'am. Can you tell me more about your situation?" He opens a book on his desk, then picks up a fountain pen from a copper inkwell.

I clear my throat. "Two nights ago, my husband of twenty years attempted to assault me."

"Attempted assault?" His eyes are wide. "Well, that's certainly serious enough to warrant a visit here."

I remove the folded papers from my handbag and hand them over to him. "It warranted a visit to Sheriff Wilder first. Here's the report he drew up."

He takes the papers, then removes a magnifying glass from his desk. I watch in silence as he reads over the report. His expression goes from one of surprise to disapproval, then back to the neutral expression that greeted me when I walked in. "This information is very disheartening to read, Mrs. Leary."

"Imagine how I felt experiencing it," I remark as the pain of the incident resurfaces once again. "I've spent the past forty-eight hours trying to forget about it and trying to remember why I fell in love with my husband in the first place. But I simply can't forget this. There's just no resemblance between the man I married and the beast who raised his hand to me that night."

"I see." He sets the papers down on his desk. "Is there anything else you want to tell me? You know, information that wasn't included in the report?"

I shrug. "I'm not sure what else would be helpful."

"I'd like to hear about your marriage in general. Would you say it's a happy union?"

"For the most part," I answer. "I do most of the domestic labor and child-rearing, and I work in the barbershop with my husband. Aside from that, I own six properties in Chowan and Pasquotank Counties."

"You own them together with your husband, yes?" He watches me intently.

I shake my head. "No. I own them solely."

He jots something in the book. "I see. And how does Mr. Leary feel about that?"

I feel my grip tightening on the strap of my handbag. "I'd say it's been a bit of a sticking point between us. When we were first married, he seemed to applaud my ambition. But as years have gone by, he's pointed out on several occasions that it makes him feel like I don't need him."

He nods, continuing to write in the book. "Has he ever made you feel physically unsafe before this incident?"

"No, but I wasn't prepared for the escalation. One minute we were arguing, and the next, I had to shield myself with the iron skillet."

He shakes his head solemnly. "I don't condone this type of behavior from men, no matter their disagreement with their spouses or sweethearts." He closes his book and sets the pen down. "Honestly, Mrs. Leary, I think you have strong grounds here for a divorce proceeding. The police report would be the most damning piece of supporting evidence you could produce, and with that, a judge is likely to grant you both the divorce and some form of monetary support."

I wave that off. "I'm not looking for money, I can take care of my daughter and myself. What I want is to feel safe and comfortable in my home again." I sigh. "I haven't even been back there since this all happened."

"So you and your daughter . . ."

"Have been staying with my mother, father-in-law, and grandmother." I shake my head. "I miss my bed, but I don't feel safe going there with Sweety skulking about. I haven't heard from him, and I have no way of knowing what state of mind he's in." It pains me to speak of my husband this way, to feel the way I do. But it's the truth. "I don't want to be around him right now. He's put me in a position I never wanted to be in. I own our home, and yet I don't want to return."

Mr. Pruden taps his finger against his chin, appearing thoughtful. "Since you still have a minor child, it's actually Sweety who should have vacated the family home."

I shrug. "Maybe so, but I was so out of sorts that night, I wasn't thinking about that. I just wanted to get Florrie and get away from him."

"That's understandable. We sometimes do illogical things when under duress." He pushes his chair back and stands. "However, now that you're removed from the situation, I think it would behoove you to return home and ask your husband to leave."

I recoil. "How would I do that? With the sheriff in tow?"

"You could. But I think you'd probably do just as well if you return home with another male escort, someone both you and your husband know." He paces back and forth behind the desk. "From what you've told me, your husband is a man consumed with his personal image. Would you say that's true?"

I nod. "Absolutely." To my mind, it's his juvenile need to be praised and revered by his peers that has caused him to act the way he has.

"Then consider this. How likely is your husband to behave in a foolish and uncouth manner in front of people he knows, possibly even looks up to?"

I pause, thinking on Mr. Pruden's words. He brings up something I haven't thought of: using Sweety's own obsession with his reputation against him, and honestly, it makes good sense. "I think I see the value of your suggestion."

"Do you know someone who fits the description, who could accompany you and your daughter to the house?"

"Yes, I do." I have two people in mind, whom I'm fairly certain would accommodate my request.

"Then that's your next move, I'd say." He comes around to my side of the desk and extends his arm to help me up from my seat. "You can return to the office if anything else occurs, and if not, call on me once you've made your final decision on whether you want to proceed with the divorce."

I stand, still gripping the purse. "Thank you, Mr. Pruden."

"Think nothing of it."

Once I've gotten my gloves and cloak back on, I slip out of the office and back onto the street. I have a stop to make before I return to my mother's home, and I hope things go as I expect.

The following morning, I arrive at my home, clutching my keys in my hand. With me are my father-in-law and our longtime friend the architect Hannibal Badham. With the two big men behind us, I slip my key into the lock and let myself in.

Sweety is asleep on the settee when we enter. Why he chose to sleep on that lumpy thing, I can't imagine. Perhaps he passed out there.

As I wait at the base of the staircase, Dorsey strides over to my sleeping husband and shakes his shoulders. "Wake up, you bounder."

Sweety awakens with a start and sits bolt upright. "What's the meaning of this?"

Hannibal appears next to Dorsey. "Why, it's an eviction, old friend."

His face crumpling into a frown, Sweety says, "What are you about, Hannibal?"

Dorsey chimes in. "You raised your hand to my daughter-in-law. Seems to me you've gone quite mad."

"I'd been drinking. I didn't have my right mind and—"

Hannibal shouts, "Stifle! I'll hear none of it. What matters now is that Jo has asked us to see you out of here, and that's what we intend to do."

Sweety peers around Hannibal's large frame and his eyes meet mine. "Is this true, Josephine? You . . . want me to leave?"

I nod. "Yes."

Dorsey gets hold of Sweety's arm. "You heard her. Now get up and get moving, before we toss you out like refuse."

Sweety shakes Dorsey's hand off. "That won't be necessary. Let me get my things together, and I'll leave on my own." He climbs to his feet just as Hannibal sits down.

"Good, then. I'm sure you won't mind me resting here while you gather your belongings. After that, I'll drive you wherever you want to go." Hannibal crosses his legs and leans back into the cushion.

I step aside, gently tugging Florrie along with me as Sweety trudges past us and up the stairs. Florrie and I move farther into the room. She sits in the side chair, and I stand by the settee. I listen to his movements as he shuffles around upstairs, and a few minutes later, he descends the stairs, carrying two old carpetbags.

Sweety tries to walk up to me, but Dorsey inserts himself between us. "I wouldn't do that if I were you. I hear she's pretty handy with a skillet."

My husband grimaces as if physically hurt. "I'm going to fix this, Jo. I'm gonna do right by you both."

My face is tight. "That may be so, but don't darken this door until I ask you back."

His eyes are wide for a moment; then his face takes on the look of resignation, and with a curt nod, he turns away from us.

Hannibal is on his feet again. "Let's get going to wherever you plan on staying while you consider the error of your ways."

Going to my daughter's side and resting my hand on her shoulder, I watch as Dorsey and Hannibal escort Sweety out the door, with Dorsey closing it behind them.

# 19

JOSEPHINE

*May 1893*

Rosa and I take a seat at the last open table on the sidewalk outside Café Parisienne. Setting my purse near my feet, I inhale deeply. "Whatever's being baked in there smells amazing."

"It sure does," Rosa replies. "I hear they make the best croissants in the state."

"Very impressive for our little town, heh?" The café is owned by Vernon Fitz, the baker husband of our seamstress, Eunice. "I can't believe this place has been open a whole month already."

Vernon approaches the table then, wearing a bright smile beneath his thick mustache. "Morning, ladies. What can I get you?"

"Two café au laits, and two croissants, please."

"I'll have it out to you shortly." He disappears inside.

I sit back in my chair, taking in the warmth of the day and the pleasant breeze rolling off Little Creek and, beyond it, Swan Bay. The café's location isn't far off from the barbershop, near Broad and Queen. "So how are you and Jameson doing, Rosa?"

She grins. "We're doing wonderfully. We spend our days together, working the land. In the evenings, we often go up to Papa's house and have supper with him. He's getting on in age now, so we feed him well."

I frown. "I thought you hated cooking?"

"I do, but lucky for me, Jameson loves it." Rosa winks. "It's a charmed life; I've my husband, my father, and the animals, so you'll hear no complaints from me."

I nod. "It does sound pretty peaceful." Especially in contrast to what's going on between Sweety and me.

She asks gently, "Has he come home yet, Jo?"

I open my mouth to answer, but snap it shut as Vernon arrives with our order. When he's gone again, I take a sip of my coffee. I savor the creamy sweetness and the richness of the brew for a moment before continuing. "No, he hasn't. He's been staying at the Bayview Boardinghouse ever since he left home."

She shakes her head. "Oh, no. I'm so sorry."

I can only sigh in response. "I don't even go into the shop anymore. I spend all my days managing my properties, looking after Florrie, gardening, and reading. Sweety sends me flowers about once a week, but the only time I see him is on the occasional Sunday when he shows up at church."

"What about Florrie? Has he been spending time with her?"

I nod. "Yes. She meets with him regularly. They've been to the library, up to campus to see Clara, and to the creek to fish."

"At least he's still fathering."

"True enough. I just wish we could come to some sort of agreement about our marriage going forward."

"Do you want him to come back?"

I answer honestly. "I don't know."

We sink into a companionable silence, and I tear off a piece of the flaky croissant. The buttery pastry dissolves in my mouth almost immediately, and I groan. "This is delicious."

"Glad to hear it," a familiar female voice replies.

We both look up to see Eunice approaching our table.

"We managed to snag a pastry chef who was born and raised in Nice," Eunice remarks. "You wouldn't believe the amount of butter we go through in a week."

"Having tasted the croissants, I actually would believe it," Rosa quips. I smile at my two friends, who've finally found their own companionable rhythm after too many years of unnecessary friction.

Eunice chuckles, but her humor quickly fades. "Jo, I don't wish to be the bearer of bad news, truly I don't. But I've . . . seen something rather upsetting, and I feel you should know about it."

I lean forward in my chair, resting my forearms on the scrollwork surface of our wrought-iron table.

"I saw Sweety . . . indisposed . . . with another woman."

My breath rushes from my mouth, as if the air has been knocked out of me. "What?"

"It happened last evening, near the boardinghouse." She leans in and lowers her voice. "I couldn't see the woman's face, because I saw her from behind as she embraced your Sweety. I can tell you that she had red hair and was wearing a pink dress." She shakes her head. "Low quality by the look of it, cheap taffeta masquerading as silk. Had a tatted lace border and a few gathers at the rear."

I'm not surprised that Eunice can tell me more about the dress than about the woman wearing it. "You're absolutely certain it was Sweety?"

"Yes. He made eye contact with me and immediately looked away. Next thing you know, he and the woman ran off down the alley."

As she stands upright again, both Rosa and I are wide-eyed.

"Again, I'm sorry to have to tell you such distressing news. But I knew it wouldn't be right to keep it from you." Eunice clasps her hands together. "And since I probably soured your stomach, no charge for your order."

"Thank you, Eunice."

With a solemn nod, she goes back inside the café.

I'm left sitting across from my best friend, stunned. My heart is pounding in my ears, and I can feel the heat in my cheeks.

Rosa says softly, "Are you all right, Jo?"

I can only shake my head. "No. But I will be."

"Are you certain?"

I nod. "I don't have a choice. Florrie needs me, so no matter what, I'll have to gather myself. Somehow."

Rosa reaches for my hand, giving it a gentle squeeze. "You're amazing, Jo."

"I don't want to be. Not like this." I let my head drop forward. "I don't know if this marriage is worth fighting for anymore, Rosa. I just don't know."

"Well, take your time in deciding. And whatever you do, know that I'm here for you."

I offer a small smile. Her friendship has been a balm to me many times over the years, and now, I need her support more than ever.

# JOSEPHINE

### *July 1893*

I straighten the veil on my hat, wishing I could check my appearance once more, as I sit in a chair at Chowan Library. The one-story brick building sits on a grassy lot on Water Street, and I can see the southern terminus of Granville Street through the open window above my seat. A breeze off the water flows in, cooling the interior and bringing with it the cacophony from outside. The sounds fracture the usual quiet of the space: the pounding of horses' hooves, the squeaking of carriage wheels, and the street vendors' cries as they hawk their merchandise. Then bells ring and a steam whistle blows, the noise rising over everything else to signal the departure of a large ship from port.

I've worn my best summer-weight blouse and skirt, both in a soft shade of beige, along with a fashionable brocade corset at my waist. The high neck of the blouse pinches a bit, and I relieve some of the tightness by running my index finger between the collar and my throat. It's not the most comfortable ensemble, but my attire assures that I will be taken seriously. Today's meeting may be tense, but that's no reason I should go in looking anything less than stylish.

Patience, the librarian and fellow member of St. John's Ladies' Auxiliary, walks over to where I sit. Carrying a small stack of books, she pushes a stray hair back from her face. "How're you holding up, Josephine?"

I sigh. "As well as can be expected, I suppose." I gesture to the window. "Please tell me the reference room will be quieter than this."

She chuckles. "Yes, it will be, it's farther back from the road. Sorry about the noise, but if I don't open the windows in here now and again, it gets unbearably hot pretty fast. Not to mention, too much humidity can damage the books."

"Ah, these broiling Carolina summers." I let my head drop back against the top of the chair. "Makes one long for cooler climes, doesn't it?"

"It certainly does." Patience walks past me and places one of the books she's carrying into an empty slot on a shelf just to my right. "The room's unlocked, so when everyone's here, you can just go on back."

"Thank you." I sit up straight again. "And if we need your assistant librarian's services, we'll call for you."

"Fair enough. Now let me get these books put away." She drifts off to the far side of the room, leaving me to my own thoughts.

The door swings open, and my lawyer, Mr. Pruden, enters. His brown suitcase matches the color of his fine suit almost exactly. "Good afternoon, Mrs. Leary."

"Good to see you again, Mr. Pruden." I stand as he approaches me. "Patience has already opened the room for us."

"Excellent. Let's go back there and get seated, then." He checks his pocket watch. "I expect Mr. Leary and Mr. Bond will be along shortly."

We walk around the rows of bookcases until we reach the door to the reference room, which is already propped open. I can smell the cedar planks as soon as we enter, and I recall from a previous conversation with Patience that cedar is thought to help preserve the books by repelling insects that might feast on the pages.

Inside, three of the walls are occupied by built-in bookshelves, starting at waist height and going up to the ceiling. In the center of the room, a sleek rectangular table often used by patrons making their notes from the reference materials housed here has three chairs on each of its long sides.

Pruden sets his briefcase down on the table, then slides two of the chairs away from the table into a corner of the room. He positions the remaining chairs so that two are on each side of the table, facing each other. "There, that should be about right."

The two of us take our seats on the side facing the door, and moments later, Sweety enters with his lawyer, Mr. Bond. My husband is well-dressed in a blue suit and carries his matching fedora in hand. However, his handsome face is marred by a dour expression. His legal representative, a short man with black hair, brown eyes, a full beard, and a ruddy complexion, wears a black suit, a brown vest, and a black tie. If the thin line of perspiration around the lawyer's hairline is any indication, that suit is just as hot as it looks.

The two lawyers exchange polite, professional greetings as we sit across from each other.

Sweety looks into my eyes briefly. "Hello, Josephine."

"Archer." I offer a nod but keep my face expressionless.

Bond places a leather portfolio on the table and opens it. "Let's get down to business, shall we? Mr. Pruden, my client would like to mediate and come to some sort of agreement to prevent the dissolution of this marriage."

Pruden looks to me, and after I give him a tight nod, says, "Go ahead, Bond, we're listening."

Bond shuffles through some papers in front of him. "We'd like to talk about the incident that occurred between Mr. and Mrs. Leary back in February of this year."

Pruden leans forward. "So you're referring to your client's attempted assault on my client, is that correct?"

Bond releases a sigh. "Surely you don't plan on carrying on this entire meeting with that antagonistic tone, Mr. Pruden."

"Your client's behavior that night was abhorrent. Pointing that out does not make me antagonistic. It makes me factual."

Bond's eyes narrow. "Mr. Pruden, I don't think—"

"Wait a minute," Sweety interjects. "Can we just stop this legal banter and speak to each other?" He looks at me pointedly.

After a moment's silence, I respond. "I'm willing to hear what you have to say, Archer."

Drawing a deep breath, Sweety begins. "I miss you. I miss my daughter. And I'm tired of staying in that cramped little room at the boardinghouse." He pauses. "But none of that matters as much as this: I'm sorry, Josephine. I'm so, so sorry. You were right when you said I'd lost my good sense. I never should have raised my hand to you, and I promise you, I never will again."

I feel my lips tighten. "I appreciate your apology, Archer. But what proof do I have that it is sincere?"

"I expected you to say that." Sweety gives a dry chuckle. "I can show you that I've changed. I've quit drinking. If you need confirmation, you may ask Randall Lipsey or any man I've drunk with in the past how long it's been since I've been in a barroom."

I don't know what to make of that. I never expected Sweety would abandon his beloved whiskey; I've tried to get him to stop drinking for years, to no avail. I fold my arms over my chest. "Go on."

"Aside from that, if you are gracious enough to let me come back home, I've arranged for us to attend a few counseling sessions with Rector Billups. I've much to learn, and much to atone for." He appears truly remorseful.

My eyes widen. "You spoke to the rector?" Though he accompanied the children and me to that fateful Juneteenth celebration two years ago, I assumed the times I had seen him in church over the past few months were more for show than out of sincerity. My heart softens.

He nods. "Yes. Not only will we seek his counsel, but I'll be present at Sunday services with you and Florrie as well."

I sit back in my chair. "You've offered a lot in terms of recompense, Archer. But there is something you must answer to as well."

"What is it, Jo?"

I breathe deeply, settling my spirit as best I can. "Is there a possibility that you might have fathered a child while we were apart?"

My husband bristles visibly. "What?"

"You heard me. Eunice says she saw you sparking with a redheaded woman in a pink dress in the alley behind the boardinghouse."

Holding up a piece of paper from his briefcase, Pruden adds, "Mrs. Fitz was kind enough to provide us a written statement, which I'm sure would go far in our favor . . . should this mediation prove unsuccessful, that is."

Sweety's expression changes to something unfamiliar and unreadable. "That Eunice Fitz has a mouth the size of the whole state of North Carolina."

"Then you don't deny being seen at the intersection of Hicks and Oakum Streets, participating in activities that dishonored your marriage vows?" Pruden's question is pointed.

"I'm . . . ashamed of my actions. I was lonely, but I admit that was due to my own terrible behavior." His gaze is fixed on the tabletop.

I shake my head. He can't even look me in the eye as he admits his infidelity. I feel the fires of anger rising inside me.

Drinking is one thing, but defiling our marriage bed? My trust in him was not well placed, and I won't make that mistake again.

"Jo, I couldn't go through with it." For less than a moment, his eyes dart up from the wood grain, and my breath catches as I see the depth of his sadness. "I never shared a bed with that woman, I swear it. I simply couldn't bring myself to betray you that way."

I swallow, feeling some of my anger fade. "I think you have said enough, Archer. Now I will speak my piece. I will admit Florrie and I miss having you home. But I refused to invite you back until I could gain some clarity on your state of mind, and your intentions going forward. I would not endanger myself or our child simply for the sake of comfort."

"I understand." His gaze is directed at the table.

"You have no idea what I have suffered. There have been many long, lonely nights in our bed, but it gets worse. I've had to be both parents to our Florrie, had to try to explain your absence." I tilt my head slightly. "If you are to come back home, understand that the penance you pay will be high. I still love you, and likely always will. But you will work every day to earn my trust."

"Whatever it takes, Jo." His voice wavers. "I'll do anything."

I push past the pain of his betrayal and speak from a place of strength. "I may be willing to reconcile with you, Archer. But I can't fool myself into ignoring what has happened between us. I think I'll be taking some legal precautions. I need to protect myself going forward, and I won't be dissuaded from that." I gesture to my lawyer.

"Here's what we propose," Pruden begins. "We're prepared to quash all divorce proceedings in exchange for an agreement that bars Mr. Leary from ever seeking any access to properties owned by Mrs. Leary, now and in the future."

Sweety pounds his fist on the table. "This again? Why must you always shut me out of this side of your life, Josephine?"

I don't waver. "Whatever may or may not have happened behind closed doors, you made no denial of your uncouth behavior during our separation, and to be perfectly honest, I'm of no mind to hear that tale. But what I won't do is have my children's future jeopardized by your selfish actions. Every bit of property I've acquired, I did so with an intention of leaving something for Clara and Florrie, and for my future grandchildren." I lean in. "Stop studying the tabletop and look at me, Archer Leary."

He slowly raises his head until his eyes meet mine.

"Whatever you did with that woman can't be undone. But you can be damn sure that I won't have any outside children you may have fathered interfering with my daughters' inheritance."

His eyes go wide.

"Excuse my frank talk, but sometimes strong words are necessary to get one's point across." I straighten in my chair. "Those are my terms."

I sit in silence, watching as my husband confers with Bond in hushed tones.

After a few moments, Bond speaks. "My client is willing to cede all of Mrs. Leary's properties to her . . . with one exception. The barbershop at 317 South Broad Street. If Mrs. Leary is willing to deed the barbershop to Mr. Leary, he will relinquish any current or future claims to everything else."

Pruden looks my way. "What do you think of that, Mrs. Leary."

After a moment's consideration, I nod. "What are the limits of this deed?"

Bond answers, "The deed will extend to cover Mr. Leary's lifetime. Should he pass away before you, the barbershop becomes yours again."

"And if I expire before him?" I want to know the parameters, from every possible angle, even the event of my own demise. I've lived long enough to discard the youthful notions of immortality.

"Then the barbershop would rejoin your estate and be deeded to your daughters, Clara and Florence."

Since leaving everything to my girls was my hope all along, I nod. "I can agree to this arrangement."

"Very good." Bond pulls out a fountain pen and a blank sheet of writing paper. "I can draw up the agreement right now, while we are all here to have input. When I've finished, we can call on Patience to witness both your signatures."

Pruden nods. "With this document, we'll set aside any current divorce proceedings, and we will only revisit them at the request of either of you." He looks between Archer and me. "I do hope you can mend things without further legal involvement."

So the document is drawn up and after Martin, the assistant librarian, witnesses the signing and adds his seal, Pruden and Bond depart together to take the contract to the Register of Deeds.

"Your face gives you away, dearest." His voice cuts through my thoughts. "What is troubling you now?"

I look up to see him standing beside my chair. I must really have been gathering wool, because I didn't notice him getting up from his seat. "It has been quite a day, Sweety. I am merely piecing together all that I've just experienced."

He smiles. "You've called me by my nickname. There is hope for me yet, thanks be to the heavens."

I shake my head. Gazing up into his dark eyes, I see the merriment and the mischief there that remind me of the young man who first stole my breath. In many ways, I suppose he will always have my heart. I can only hope that moving forward, he will treat me with the care and respect I deserve. "You have two strikes against you, Sweety Leary. You would be wise to love me as fiercely and faithfully as you can. I won't be so merciful if you err again."

He stoops low, bringing his face close to mine. "If I ever lose sight of the gift of your love again, you have my permission to flay me."

"Can I have that in writing?" I can't resist teasing him; he's earned it.

He doesn't miss a beat. "Certainly. If we catch up to Bond and Pruden, we can have them add it to the contract." He gives me an exaggerated wink.

I laugh, for the first time in a long time. My heart flutters in my chest, and as I lean up for his kiss, I know he has succeeded in melting my icy ire. When our lips finally part, I take his hand. "Let's go home."

# 20

### JOSEPHINE

*September 20, 1893*

Resting against my bed pillows, I yawn as I turn another page in my copy of *The Three Musketeers*. Sweety is already slumbering next to me, and Florrie has long since gone to bed. A sword fight is underway, but it can't hold my attention, at least not against the rising tide of exhaustion. I feel the book slipping from my hands, but I can't do anything to stop it.

In the hazy realm of my dreams, I'm standing on an arid plain beneath a wide, cloudless blue sky. Tall grasses and reeds sway in the wind, and the sun warms my face. In the distance, I see a female figure approaching me. At first, she is merely a faceless silhouette, but the closer she gets, the clearer her features become. She is statuesque and regal, her dark skin rich like coffee. Her body is draped in a flowing patterned garment that resembles a robe, and her head is wrapped in a scarf of the same beautiful fabric. She looks familiar and unfamiliar at the same time; her features tug at the strings of my memory but connect to nothing.

"Who are you?" I ask.

She smiles. "I am Amina."

*My great-grandmother?* "Am I . . . home?"

She nods, her expression serene. "For now."

I gesture around me. "Is this what our tribal lands in Ghana look like?"

"Yes. But this is not Ghana." She touches my shoulder. "This is home. A different place altogether."

Her words confuse me, but somehow comfort me at the same time. "Great-grandmother, I don't understand."

"In time, you will, child." Her free hand moves to caress my cheek for a moment before falling away. "You will face pain, and you will know joy. When the time is right, you will join us here, and all will be made clear." She takes her hand from my shoulder, slowly moving it until she points in the distance.

I follow the movement, and I'm alarmed to see a raging fire consuming the grasses. It is still far away, but I know it will not be long before it reaches us. "What's happening?"

"Now is the time to awaken." Her tone is still as calm as before.

"We must do something!"

"Awaken, child!" She grasps my shoulders and shakes me.

My eyes pop open, and my ears are filled with the sounds of my own heavy breath. I glance around, seeing only the inky darkness of the night around me, and try to calm my breathing.

As I take a deep breath, an odor permeates my senses. It's heavy and acrid as if something is . . . *burning*.

I throw off the covers and jostle my husband. "Sweety!"

He sits up with a start. "Jo, what is it?"

"Do you smell that?"

He sniffs the air. "Smoke!"

We are both out of bed in a flash. I quickly shrug into my robe and jam my feet into the pair of old moccasins I keep next to the bed.

Sweety has thrown on his trousers over his union suit but forgone a shirt. "I'll see if it's coming from anywhere in the house." Hopping along as he puts on his boots, he dashes out the bedroom door.

I go to the window, peering out. From this angle, I can't see anything but the treetops in my neighbors' yards, and the moonlit sky above.

Sweety pokes his head in the door. "Jo, it's the lower end of Broad Street!"

My heart drops. "Let's go!" As we dash past Florrie's room, she opens the door and sleepily asks, "What's going on?"

"Wait here!" I call back to her without stopping. "We'll be back!"

I run out the door, and across the yard, looking down the road toward the water. The plumes of black smoke rising to the sky bring tears to my eyes, but I don't stop running.

Down the darkened street I go, as fast as my feet will carry me. I lose sight of Sweety as I pass Vernon Fitz's bakery, then the general store. I pass the barbershop, Eunice Fitz's dress shop, the scenery blurring from a combination of speed and my tears.

My leg muscles scream from the exertion, but I keep going.

From the dress shop, I can see the towering flames, reaching heavenward. And by the time I reach the corner of Magnolia and Broad, I stop.

I can't go any farther.

A crowd is gathered at the intersection. All around the area, people are running, pointing, shouting for the bucket brigade.

The blaze has engulfed everything in sight beyond King Street. The flames are so tall, I can no longer see the water beyond. The thick black smoke burns my eyes.

The Market House is nothing but a burning shell. Lipsey's Store and Barroom, a blackened husk.

I turn to my left, slowly.

And I drop to my knees.

My building is burning, disintegrating before my very eyes. Chunks of wood fall from the remains of the upper floors, burning to cinder before they can reach the ground. The sound is awful, the crackling and growling and hissing of the blaze as it consumes my investment. All three storefronts are engulfed, along with the rest of the block. Whatever my clients had stored inside is gone.

I hear an anguished cry coming from my own lips as I kneel there, on the walk in front of my friend's dress shop.

I never got to fully transform that building, never got to put my mark on it.

And now it's gone.

Sweety appears at my side. "Josephine! Josephine! We need to back away so the bucket brigade can come in!"

I can't stand. My legs are too weak, and so, too, is my will.

All I can do is wail.

So he picks me up, lifts me into his arms, and carries me away.

Over his shoulder, I watch as two wagons full of volunteers whiz by. They begin tossing bucket after bucket of water at the inferno, only to have the water hiss and evaporate into mist.

Another wail escapes me, and my body shakes with sobs.

"It will be all right, Jo," I hear my husband say softly into my ear. "I'll get you home."

Another sob rattles my frame; then everything fades to blackness.

I awaken just after dawn, sprawled across the settee in my parlor. Sitting up, I rub my bleary eyes, then immediately wince at the built-up tension in my back and shoulders. An immense ache has taken hold in my thighs, a punishment for my mad dash down the road last night.

I look around for Sweety and find him asleep in the armchair next to me, his neck crooked at some odd angle. His snores rattle the room like a rusty saw cutting through a log.

The crackling of the skillet and the savory aroma of bacon wafts to my nostrils. I turn toward the kitchen to see Florrie standing in the doorway. "Mama, I made breakfast."

My child has brought me a smile, even through the immense physical and emotional pain I feel. "I'll have just a nibble. I don't have much of an appetite."

She nods. "Would you like some lemonade or water?"

"Water, please. And a cup of willow bark tea." I try not to drink it during the day, but if I don't, I won't be able to walk. I have to go see about my building, even if there is nothing left but a plot of land and a pile of ash.

I rest my head against the back of the settee, simply trying to breathe in the new reality I face.

My daughter returns shortly with a tumbler of cool water, the steaming tea, and a tin plate holding a slice of bacon and a small portion of eggs. She hands it to me with a fork. "Here you are, Mama."

I take the offerings gratefully. "Bless you, my child." I sip the tea, then wash the bitter liquid down with a gulp of water. "Wake your father and see if he wants to eat."

Florrie gently shakes Sweety's shoulders. "Papa, wake up."

He awakens with a grunt. "What . . . what time is it?"

I look at the old clock in the corner. "A quarter past seven."

"Papa, would you like bacon and eggs? I cooked." Florrie watches him expectantly.

He smiles. "Yes, please. Thank you, dear."

She returns with plates for her father and herself, and the three of us eat in silence.

By the time I'm finished with my meal and my tea, I can feel the effects of the willow bark beginning to take hold. "Sweety, we must go back and see if anything can be salvaged."

"I know." He stands. "Florrie, can you wash up these dishes, please?"

"Oh, Papa, must I? I want to go down and see what's become of Cheapside, too." Florrie folds her arms over her chest.

He frowns. "There's no sense in you meddling in the affairs of adults. Now get to these dishes, child."

I think Sweety is being too brusque; after all, my properties will someday belong to the girls. So I assure her softly, "I'll explain it all later, dearest. Now please do as your father asked."

Florrie trots off to the kitchen with the armload of dishes, and Sweety and I make our way upstairs to change. Once we're dressed, we set out down the street, albeit at a much slower pace this time.

By the light of day, the scene at Cheapside is even more tragic. The bucket brigade must have succeeded in putting the flames out overnight, and now, all that remains of the entire block from the east side of King Street all the way to Water Street are smoldering piles of debris.

I go to where the old Cheshire storehouse, my storehouse, once stood. I get as close as I dare to the heap of charred planks, and I feel the tears spring anew to my eyes. "I can't see anything recognizable in this heap, can you, Sweety?"

He shakes his head grimly. "No, dearest."

I turn toward the sound of approaching footsteps, crunching through the broken glass and fallen debris, and see Sheriff Wilder standing nearby, his Stetson in his hands. "I'm mighty sorry about your building, Mrs. Leary."

"I appreciate that, though I'm not the only one around here who's lost property." All around me are the ashen remains of people's dreams, their livelihoods.

Sweety asks, "Ed, do you know how this fire got started?"

He gives us a solemn nod. "A few men from the bucket brigade took to digging around this morning at daybreak, searching for a cause." He raises his arm and points to the blackened spot where Lipsey's Store and Barroom stood, just yesterday. "Gas lamp blew up in Lipsey's place. They think it was one of them lamps he kept sitting on the bar counter. Once the heat got high enough to burn through his whiskey barrels, well . . . whole place went up like a candle."

"Good heavens," Sweety mutters.

I can only shake my head. "That devil's drink almost stole my marriage. Now it's stolen away my biggest investment."

The sheriff puts his hat back on. "That's one thing about alcohol that folks tend to forget, you know. It's a carrier for fire. See how the road drops off here just a bit, as you go down toward the Market House?" He gestures toward the water with a jerk of his head.

I nod. "Yeah. It's not too steep, but it's definitely a hill."

"Well, picture that bourbon and whiskey and whatever else was on the shelf at Lipsey's, just running down the road there, acting like a fuse for them flames." He shakes his head. "These old wooden buildings never stood a chance."

"Where is Randall, anyway?" Sweety asks. "He know about all this?"

"Sure, he does. I drove out to his place this morning to get him. When I brought him up here to see it, he passed out. I put him in my wagon and took him down to the clinic. Doc Trent is looking him over."

I sigh. "When Doc Trent finishes with him, I might need looking over myself." The past twelve hours have been hellish, and my body and mind are struggling beneath the weight of all that's happened.

I stoop low to the ground, wave my hand over a pile of ashes. No heat rises from them, so I scoop up some of them in my hand. Forming an O with my mouth, I blow, watching the dark flecks float away on the breeze. Fate has done the same to me, taking my plans and blowing them away as if they were nothing.

I stand and look at my husband. "What am I going to do, Sweety?"

His furrowed brow and drawn lips tell me that he's at just as much of a loss as I am. Instead of answering me, he merely shakes his head.

I stay there for a long time, looking at the ruins of my building, and of Cheapside. Eunice Fitz, whose dress shop has also been utterly destroyed, cries as she clutches to her chest the twisted metal sign that used to hang over her door. And what of the Market House, which has stood on the same spot since before the turn of the century, only to be sacrificed to the alcohol-fueled flames? An irreplaceable icon of the town's history, gone in an instant.

I feel the tears rising in my throat, but I push them down. We've all lost something precious. Randall Lipsey, the other proprietors on this block, and me. But my tears won't turn back the hands of time, won't undo the horror of last night.

I take a deep breath, set my shoulders back, and begin walking toward home, with my husband following close behind. Sheriff Wilder tips his hat to me as I pass him.

There is a path forward through this, and even though I can't see it right now, that doesn't mean I'll give up the fight.

I've taken a major loss, and recovery may not be quick, or easy, or even probable.

But I will not stop.

# JOSEPHINE

*September 1893*
*Washington, DC*

Sitting on the veranda of my brother's home, I sip from the mug of tea in my hand and take in the scenery. The wrought-iron table has a slick glass top and four iron chairs sitting around it.

The small, two-story dwelling is situated just on the other side of the Potomac from the city proper. He shares the home with Missouri, and my one-year-old niece, Vivian. Peering off into the distance, I can see the sun shimmering on the water, and the towering dome of the Capitol Building beyond it.

Missouri, who is sitting with me with the sleeping Vivian in her lap, asks, "You're awfully quiet, Jo. What's on your mind?"

I release a pent-up sigh. "I'm still thinking on what I will do with my lot in Cheapside."

She nods her understanding. "You've been here for a week, and that is all you've talked about."

I cringe. "I know. I'm sorry. Is there something else you wish me to discuss?"

"I'd like to know that my nieces and all the family back home in Edenton are doing all right." She chuckles. "If that's not too much trouble."

I shake my head, knowing she's right. "Let's see. Sweety is doing well and spending more and more time at the barbershop since he never hired a replacement for Octavious. Clara has taken a teaching job in Littleton, and is doing well as of her last correspondence. Florrie has finished her courses at the Badham School and is looking to start foreign language studies at Bennett College next fall."

Missouri nods, smiling. "Wonderful. And how are Jeanette, Dorsey, and your grandmother Milly getting on?"

"Mama and Dorsey are good. She's still gardening, he's still building houses. I don't suppose he'll ever retire; he loves it too much. And Grandma, well, she doesn't get around as well as she once did, but she's still got her wits about her. I go over there once a week to play chess with her."

"And how does that go?"

"She beats the pants off me most of the time, but the conversation is so good, I keep crawling back for another clobbering."

Missouri laughs out loud.

Vivian stirs, awakened by her mother's mirth. She starts to fuss, but her wails are soon silenced as Missouri adjusts her shirt and lets the babe latch on to nurse. "All right, all right. Now that I've heard about that, let's work on your problem."

Octavious walks out of the house then, a tumbler of lemonade in hand, and takes a seat in the empty chair next to his wife. "Yes, let's talk about this Cheapside conundrum. It won't do to have you wandering around my home with such a long face, sister."

I turn in my chair, looking back and forth between the faces of my brother and my sister-in-law, whom I love to the ends of the earth. "I must decide whether to sell the lot or to rebuild. And I must make my decision before I return home to Edenton. I just can't bear to anguish over it any longer."

Missouri, rocking the baby side to side, nods. "I can see how hard this must have been on you. You simply haven't been yourself. I've missed you so, and I hoped your first visit to our home would be a happier one."

"So did I," Octavious adds. "I also hoped you'd bring the family with you, rather than taking the train all this way by yourself."

"I know, I know. Sweety can't get away from the shop for any length of time until he hires on another barber or two, and Florrie has gone to Littleton to visit with Clara." I rub my hands together. "I promise I'll bring them the next time I visit."

"Deal." Octavious points to my journal. "Could you tear a sheet of paper out of your book for me, please? And hand me that pencil."

Not exactly sure what he's about, I do as he asks, ripping the last sheet from the book, and handing over my pencil along with it.

He lays the paper on the table, and draws a line down the center, creating two columns. At the top of one column, he writes the word *SELL* in large letters, then underlines it. He writes the word *REBUILD* at the top of the other column and underlines that as well. "Now, my method isn't exactly scientific, but it does depend on logic."

"All right," I say. "Do you think I haven't been thinking logically up until now?"

He shakes his head. "No, you haven't. You can't, because your emotions are so tied into this. I can tell by the way you've been carrying on."

"How's that?" He's right, but I'm curious to know how he's drawn his conclusion.

"Pacing the floor, talking to yourself. Picking at your food." He shakes his head. "Your whole mind is occupied with your property and what to do next. But in order to make the best decision, you have to look at this situation logically." He taps the pencil on the paper. "We're going to weigh the benefits of selling against the benefits of rebuilding, and that's how we'll decide."

I blink several times, amazed. Gone is the goofy little boy I grew up with, who preferred climbing trees and catching frogs to cracking open a book. "Heavens, Octavious. You're making good sense."

"Of course I am, and don't look so surprised about it!" He chuckles. "Come now, let's start with our list. Tell me one good thing that will happen if you sell that old lot."

I think about it for a moment. "Well, I'd get an infusion of cash from the sale."

"All right, cash is always good." He jots down the word *cash*. "Name something else."

We go on this way until we have four reasons I should sell: money, freedom from maintaining the property, giving someone else a chance to build there, and the ability to move on to something else.

Octavious finishes jotting that down. "Now we move on to reasons to rebuild. Go on, rattle them off and I'll take them down."

I tap my chin, considering the reasoning. "I'd get a fresh start, I'd keep my property portfolio intact, I'd infuse money into the local economy by hiring carpenters and craftsmen. . . ."

"Dadgum, Jo, slow down! I can only write so fast."

I giggle, wait for him to catch up, then start listing again. "The new building would be my own design, not just something I bought. I could increase the overall value of my holdings, I'd be participating in the revitalization of an important historic district, and I—"

Missouri holds up her hand. "Jo, stop."

I look at her, puzzled. "What is it?"

"Do you hear yourself? Do you hear the way you sound, dashing off all the reasons to rebuild?"

That gives me pause. "I . . . suppose I hadn't thought about that. How many reasons do I have now, Octavious?"

"Four to sell, and six to rebuild." He winks. "The numbers don't lie, sister dear."

I exhale, feeling as though it's the first time I've done so since the night of the fire. "There's one more reason, and I think it might be the best reason of all."

"What's that?" Missouri asks.

"Clara and Florrie." I feel my heart clench in my chest as I think of my babies, my beautiful girls. "This is my chance to teach them a life lesson by example. To show them that when life destroys our dreams, we can begin anew, better than before."

Missouri wipes away a tear. "Well, Jo, I believe you've made your decision."

I clasp my hands together, my lips tilting into a smile. "Yes. And it's all thanks to my favorite dunderhead."

Octavious grins. "Anytime, Jo. Anytime."

"I've one more favor to ask. Send a telegram to Hannibal Badham for me and ask him to recommend the best ironwork builder he knows."

Octavious is on his feet in a flash. "Certainly. I'll take a hack to the telegraph office now."

I find another blank page in my journal and begin to write. My thoughts are racing so fast, I can scarcely keep up with them. My pencil flies across the page.

*Specifications for a store, of three rooms, to be built on South end of Broad St, in Edenton, NC, for Mrs. J. N. Leary. The stones to be of brick walls on South side, and on the East, to join the brick*

*wall of John L. Rogerson's wood partitions. To have an ornamental
iron front . . .*

I continue pouring my ideas onto the page, working in fits and starts
as the details come to me. I am still writing when Octavious returns
with a response from Hannibal. He hands over the slip to me, and I read
it aloud. "'For finest ironwork building, seek Mesker Bros, Evansville
Indiana.'" Tucking the slip into my journal, I write out the last few
words and finally set my pencil down.

Inside the house that evening, I sit by a lamp in the parlor, reading
through what I've written. My specifications are strict, but if Mesker
Brothers has won Hannibal's praise, I'm certain they can meet them.
My eyes land on my ironwork plans, and I smile.

*The iron front to be furnished and put up as per plan submitted; the
Pediment to have* J. N. LEARY *put on it . . .*

Up until now, the design of all the properties I've owned has been
predetermined by whoever built them. But this time, that person is me.
I'm going to decide how my building looks, and for what purposes it
will be used. And whatever that turns out to be, my name will be there
along the roofline, for all to see.

Within two days, I return home to Edenton, my spirit light and my
determination renewed. Sweety, driving me home from the train station, asks, "What's gotten into you?"

"Divine inspiration," I answer with a smile.

He grins. "Excellent. It's good to have you back, dearest. In more
ways than one."

I snuggle up next to him for the rest of the ride.

Once we're in town, I send a telegram to Mesker Brothers, requesting their most recent catalog.

"It may take a week or so to come in," the clerk tells me.

"That's fine," I respond as I sail out of the office. My next stop is Herschel Green's blacksmith shop. He stops swinging his hammer as I enter. "What can I do for you, Miss Jo?"

"I'll need all the men you can muster, to help me clean up the site of the old Cheshire storehouse."

He wipes his hands on the hem of his apron. "Fair enough. When do you need 'em?"

"Can you gather them within a week or so?"

He nods. "Should be able to do that."

I offer a smile. "Good. I'll call on you in a few days to see how you're progressing."

I climb back aboard the buggy seat.

Sweety asks, "Can I finally take you home now?"

I shake my head. "One more stop. The courthouse."

"Good heavens," he grouses, but he delivers me there anyway.

Inside, I enter the registrar's office, where I complete the necessary paperwork to get a building permit. Afterward, we drive down Court Street and turn onto Broad, toward home. I can see the remnants of Cheapside in the distance, and for the first time, the sight inspires a smile instead of tears.

At home, Florrie greets me with a smile. "Welcome home, Mama! How was Washington?"

I laugh. "I'm afraid I didn't see very much of it this time, honey. But I did enjoy spending time with your aunt and uncle, and your new little cousin, Vivian."

Her eyes sparkle. "Oh, Mama, I wish I had gone with you. I was bored to tears at Clara's house; all she does is read those dull Shakespeare plays, and prattle on about this fellow she's sweet on." She clasps her hands together. "Do you think we'll get a chance to go up there and see baby Vivian before she gets too much bigger?"

I grin. Florrie is as enamored with babies these days as I was at her age. "I'm not sure, but we'll try. If nothing else, I'll try to convince Octavious to bring the family here for a visit."

"Good." Satisfied, she runs off to the kitchen, calling out, "I'm making beef stew for dinner."

She does more and more of the cooking now, having taken an interest in it in recent months. Having exhausted the selection of Eastern literature our small-town library has to offer, she's recently switched to reading cookbooks, and loves to experiment with the new recipes she's discovering. With everything that's occurred, I'm grateful for the help.

That night, at the dinner table, I tell my daughter my plans. "Your father has already gotten an earful of this from me on the drive home, but I've decided to rebuild on the lot in Cheapside."

"That's wonderful, Mama. How did you finally come to a decision?"

"Your uncle was a great help to me. Turns out he has a surefire decision-making system."

Florrie looks thoughtful. "Hmm. Maybe he can help me decide which language I'll study at college."

I shrug. "I don't see why not. When you see him next, ask for his advice. I'm sure he'll be happy to help."

We eat our meal, and while I savor the flavorful stew and the company of my family, my heart is full.

Where I was lost, I now have direction. I have my brother, and my ancestors, to thank for that.

And now that I have my heading, there will be no stopping me.

# EPILOGUE

## JOSEPHINE

*March 1894*
*Edenton, North Carolina*

S tanding on the walk before my new building, I gaze up at it in amazement. I've been smiling all day, so much so that my cheeks hurt, but I'm unable to stop.

The sun is shining, though the wind is cold. I'm so warm with the glow of excitement, I barely feel the chill.

I'm wearing a gray satin gown and tweed overcoat, both of which I had Eunice design for me, just for this occasion. Sweety stands next to me in a coal-black suit, a crisp white shirt, and a red tie. My daughters are here as well. Clara and Florrie both wear pink gowns, though Clara's is a darker shade.

My mother and father-in-law are here. My grandmother is here as well, leaning against a carved mahogany cane, but grinning like an excited schoolgirl. Missouri and Octavious are here, and I watch as Florrie picks up little Vivian, smiling at her young cousin. It occurs to me that Vivian is the youngest member of my family here; if she remembers this day, she may carry the story of it well into the coming century.

I adjust my hat as my good friend Hannibal Badham hands me the pruning shears.

Taking them, I joke, "You couldn't find any scissors?"

"Not big enough for this ribbon!" He gestures to the long length of bright red ribbon wrapped around the front of my building and tied in a festive bow right over the center door.

With the shears in hand, I turn and look upon the faces of the crowd gathered there. There are so many of them, they spill off the walk and into the street. I see so many of the folks I care about, neighbors and friends. The Jenkins twins; the Ladies' Auxiliary. Eunice and Rosa, who are still enjoying their newfound closeness. Even the illustrious CW Rea is among the assemblage.

I take a deep breath. "May I have everyone's attention, please?"

Chatter dims, then ceases, as all eyes turn to me expectantly.

"I want to thank all of you for coming here today, to witness something that, to my mind, is nothing short of a miracle." I pause, tamping down the emotion rising in my throat. "Today is magical. Today, I see my wildest dreams made real before my very eyes. When I arrived here that fateful night and saw the old storehouse in ruins, I was broken. I thought I'd never be able to recover. But with the help of those I love"—I look pointedly at my brother, who gives me a thumbs-up from his spot behind Grandma Milly—"I was able to see a path forward. These last six months have been the busiest of my life. But when I look at what came of it, it was all worth it." I turn back toward the building and raise the shears, opening the blades. "Here's to new beginnings!" With a forceful squeeze, I bring the blades together again, slicing through the ribbon.

The red fabric falls away, and a loud cheer goes through the crowd. I feel the warm tears coursing down my face. I turn to face the people gathered before me and speak in a loud voice, to assure I will be heard.

"Welcome to the J. N. Leary Building. I am so pleased to share this day with my first two tenants. Unit 421 will be the home of the *Chowan*

*Herald*, and unit 425 will be occupied by the newly formed Cheapside Historic Preservation Society." I gesture to the newspaper editor and the society president, who are standing among the crowd.

Sweety appears next to me and places his hand atop mine as I reach for the doorknob. "Ready to see the inside, dearest?"

I smile up at him. "Absolutely."

A historical marker on the sidewalk in front of the J. N. Leary
Building, detailing Mrs. Leary's life and accomplishments.
*Used with permission of the Edenton Historical Commission*

The J. N. Leary Building, as it appeared in January 2020.
Author Kianna Alexander stands in front of the building,
wearing a long, black coat.
*Charles Boyette, Historic Interpreter, Historic Edenton State Historic Site*

A portrait of Josephine Napoleon Leary,
taken when she was around thirty years old.
*Josephine Napoleon Leary Papers, David M. Rubenstein*
*Rare Book & Manuscript Library, Duke University*

An example of Josephine's handwriting,
including her signature, on a deed to a transaction with CW Rea.
*Josephine Napoleon Leary Papers, David M. Rubenstein*
*Rare Book & Manuscript Library, Duke University*

The price list at Central Barbershop during the early 1930s.
By this time, Josephine's grandson Percy Reeves,
along with a close friend, were the proprietors.
*Josephine Napoleon Leary Papers, David M. Rubenstein*
*Rare Book & Manuscript Library, Duke University*

The J. N. Leary Building, as it appeared in the late twentieth century.
*North Carolina State Historic Preservation Office*

# ACKNOWLEDGMENTS

I extend my deepest gratitude to these great minds and helpful souls, without whom my work to honor Mrs. Leary would have been much more difficult.

Alexis Tobias, historic interpreter, Historic Edenton State Historic Site

Lynn C. Gilliard, Chowan County Register of Deeds

Julie Sharp, director of GIS Land Records, Chowan County Register of Deeds Office

Betty D. Venters, assistant, Chowan County Register of Deeds Office

Jennifer Finley, Shepard-Pruden Memorial Library

Charles Boyette, historic interpreter, Historic Edenton State Historic Site

Staff at the David M. Rubenstein Rare Book & Manuscript Library, Duke University

Dr. Karen L. Zipf, professor of history and women's and gender studies, East Carolina University

Sana Moulder, library associate, North Carolina Local and State History Room, Cumberland County Public Library and Information Center

T. E. Wilson, research assistant

Special thanks are extended to Dorothy Spruill Redford, historian and past director of Somerset Place Historic Site, Creswell, North Carolina. Her presentation, *The Life and Legacy of Josephine Napoleon Leary 1856–1923*, and the accompanying booklet provided a solid basis to guide my research and is the most thorough historical record of Mrs. Leary's life to date.

# BIBLIOGRAPHY

Adatara, Peter, et al. "Cultural Beliefs and Practices of Women Influencing Home Births in Rural Northern Ghana." *International Journal of Women's Health* 11 (June 2019): 353–61. https://doi.org/10.2147/IJWH.S190402.

All About Equine. "Breeds of Horses." Accessed October 23, 2020. https://turing.manhattan.edu/~ocoppola01/breeds.html.

Bishir, Catherine W. "Badham Family (fl. 1850s–1930s)." In *North Carolina Architects & Builders: A Biographical Dictionary*, 2009. Copyright and Digital Scholarship Center, North Carolina State University Libraries. https://ncarchitects.lib.ncsu.edu/people/P000187.

Britannica.com. S.v. "Dream of the Red Chamber." Last modified February 26, 2018. https://www.britannica.com/topic/Dream-of-the-Red-Chamber.

Bryjka, Darius. "Discoveries in the Old North State." *Mesker Brothers* (blog), September 25, 2017. https://meskerbrothers.wordpress.com/2017/09/25/discoveries-in-the-old-north-state/.

Cox, Karen L. *Dixie's Daughters: The United Daughters of the Confederacy and the Preservation of Confederate Culture*. Gainesville: University Press of Florida, 2003.

David M. Rubenstein Rare Book & Manuscript Library. "Josephine Napoleon Leary Papers, 1875–1991" (Biographical/Historical Information, 1893–1988). Duke University Libraries Archives & Manuscripts Collection Guides. Accessed February 12, 2020. https://library.duke.edu/rubenstein/findingaids/learyjosephine/#aspace_a74ebdacfa261b0bc27c0870ecd80fe2.

De Koven, Reginald. "Oh Promise Me" (1889). Genius.com. Accessed December 7, 2020. https://genius.com/Reginald-de-koven-oh-promise-me-lyrics.

"The Edenton Fire." *Weekly Economist* (Elizabeth City, NC). September 29, 1893.

Edenton Historical Commission. "Museum Trail – 1894 – Josephine Leary Building." Accessed January 27, 2020. http://ehcnc.org/historic-places/museum-trail/museum-trail-1894-josephine-leary-building/.

Encyclopedia.com. S.v. "Auctions." Last modified June 11, 2018. https://www.encyclopedia.com/social-sciences-and-law/economics-business-and-labor/economics-terms-and-concepts/auctions.

*Fisherman and Farmer* (Edenton, NC). Social report on Clara Leary. June 5, 1891.

*Fisherman and Farmer* (Edenton, NC). Social report on the serenading of Clara Leary. June 10, 1892.

*Fisherman and Farmer* (Edenton, NC). Social report on Josephine Leary's return from visiting family in Washington. June 15, 1892.

*Fisherman and Farmer* (Edenton, NC). Social report on the debut of *The Moonshiner* at the opera house, under the management of CW Rea. December 2, 1892.

*Fisherman and Farmer* (Edenton, NC). Social report on Clara Leary. June 30, 1893.

*Fisherman and Farmer* (Edenton, NC). Social report on lawsuit involving the Learys. October 13, 1893.

*Fisherman and Farmer* (Edenton, NC). Social report on Josephine Leary's plans for rebuilding. June 29, 1894.

Flickr. "N.68.10.44. Estey Hall, Shaw University, Raleigh, NC, c. 1873." State Archives of North Carolina. May 31, 2007. https://www.flickr.com/photos/north-carolina-state-archives/2431088849/.

Geo. L. Mesker & Co. *Architectural Iron Works* (1892). Evansville, IN: Evansville Vanderburgh Public Library, 2009. Accessed January 27, 2020. https://digital.evpl.org/digital/collection/evaebooks/id/71.

Glymph, Thavolia. *Out of the House of Bondage: The Transformation of the Plantation Household*. Cambridge: Cambridge University Press, 2008.

"John Jacob Astor." *Harper's Magazine* 30 (1865), 309. https://books.google.com/books?id=tX8CAAAAIAAJ&pg=PA309#v=onepage&q&f=false.

Johnson, Julia Myfanwy. "How to Drive a Horse Drawn Carriage." Our Everyday Life. Last modified September 28, 2017. https://oureverydaylife.com/how-to-drive-a-horse-drawn-carriage-12130371.html.

Josephine Napoleon Leary Papers. David M. Rubenstein Rare Book & Manuscript Library, Duke University.

LibGuides. "Nineteenth Century Periodicals: Home." James A. Cannavino Library, Marist College. Accessed November 11, 2020. https://libguides.marist.edu/19thcentperiodicals.

McCutcheon, Marc. *The Writer's Guide to Everyday Life in the 1800s*. Cincinnati, OH: Writer's Digest Books, 1993.

Metropolitan Museum of Art Libraries Digital Collections. "Women 1875–1876, Plate 080." Costume Institute Fashion Plates. Accessed September 9, 2020. https://libmma.contentdm.oclc.org/digital/collection/p15324coll12/id/7298/rec/9.

Mr. Appliance. "What Is an Icebox? A History Lesson." July 23, 2019. https://www.mrappliance.com/blog/2019/july/what-is-an-icebox-a-history-lesson/.